the
curious
case of
maggie
macbeth

stacey murray
the
curious
case of
maggie
macbeth

Red Door

Published by RedDoor
www.reddoorpress.co.uk

ISBN 978-1-913062-09-5

A CIP catalogue record for this book is available from the
British Library

Cover design: Anna Morrison

Typesetting: Tutis Innovative E-Solutions Pte. Ltd

Printed and bound in Denmark by Nørhaven

For Jim

Part 1

Cath

It was the first hot day of the summer and the church bell was striking five past five – it had been slow for as long as anyone in Archdale could remember.

The half-dozen tables of Cath's Community Café were all set up for the following morning, lilac-spotted napkins matching the lilac-spotted tablecloths that covered each one.

Cath dried her hands, took off her apron and shook her sleek, blonde hair out of its ponytail. She was looking forward to going home and doing nothing very much; a bit of pottering in the garden, then curling up in the conservatory with her book, savouring the last of the sun's rays. After all the drama of the last few months it was time to stop and take a breath – to try and look after *herself* for a change.

She pulled the café's windows and blinds shut, pausing to fix a string of her homemade bunting that had been twisted by the breeze. All she had left to do was switch off the radio and turn the sign on the door from 'OPEN' to 'CLOSED'.

The lazy clop of a horse on the cobbles outside made her smile, but there was another sound too. Raised voices in the street? Surely not.

Suddenly the room went dark: there was a six-foot figure standing in the doorway, rapping on the frosted glass. 'Cath! Cath! Are you in there?'

Only a few words, but she would've recognised those Glaswegian vowels anywhere.

She lunged to open the door and Maggie barged inside. She was clutching a traffic cone to her chest and dragging a wheelie case behind her with her free hand.

Cath shrank backwards out of the way. 'Maggie! What are you doing?'

'I've confiscated it,' said Maggie, matter-of-factly.

'Eh…? No. Actually, what I meant was… what are you doing *here*?'

'I got the taxi to take me up to the house,' Maggie replied. 'But you weren't there – obviously. Some old guy was passing by… he told me you'd be down here.' And she put the traffic cone down, her dark brown bob swinging around her chin, unchanged since university days. The black suit she was wearing looked incongruous against the pastel backdrop of the café. And was that a hint of a shoulder pad?

'It's actually illegal,' Maggie announced.

'What is?' asked Cath, faintly dizzy.

'Putting traffic cones out in the road like that. *Wilful obstruction of a public highway*. Section 137 of the Highways Act. It's OK, though. I've put him straight.'

'Sorry, put who straight?'

'That guy outside. The one in the pinny.'

Cath peered out through the blinds into the street. 'It's not a pinny, it's an apron. And *that guy* happens to be Les, the butcher from across the road. He often puts his cone out there. If he's expecting a delivery or something.'

'Yeah well, fair enough,' said Maggie, 'but it meant my taxi couldn't pull up outside.'

Cath rubbed at the sides of her forehead. 'OK,' she said, as patiently as she could manage. 'Let's start again. What brings you to Archdale?'

'I've left home,' said Maggie. And she flashed that grin, revealing teeth made perfectly even by the grinding she did when she was thinking – which was most of the time.

'How do you mean *left home*?'

'I told you I was coming,' said Maggie, ignoring her question. 'Didn't you get my email?'

'Email?'

'To ask if I could come and stay for a couple of days. I need a bit of peace and quiet and good country air – to help me get my head together.'

Cath racked her brain. Things *had* been a bit of a blur lately, but surely she would've remembered this?

'I assumed it would be OK,' Maggie was saying. 'What with you being on your own now and everything.'

Cath felt herself flush. 'I'm not *on my own*,' she protested. 'I've still got Lauren at home. And anyway, why aren't you in Hong Kong?'

'It's a long story – and I'm parched,' said Maggie. 'Is that pub on the corner any good? The Farmer's Arms?'

'It's the only one in the village,' said Cath. 'It's five miles to a better one.'

Maggie sniffed the air like an animal. 'How do you stick it, living in a place like this? There's sod-all here and the smell is stomach-churning.'

'Welcome to the Peak District,' said Cath. 'That'll be the muck-spreading. You don't tend to notice it after a while… Wait! Hold on a minute!' But Maggie had grabbed the handle of her wheelie case again and was heading back out of the door.

Cath sighed, slung her handbag over her shoulder and locked up behind them, taking care to place the traffic cone back on its spot outside.

'I could murder a Pinot Grigio,' said Maggie striding out as Cath's shorter legs struggled to catch up with her. 'Speaking of which, when I got off the train at Buxton, some guy was murdering Lionel Richie in the middle of the station. They really need to abolish those public pianos, you know. Public nuisance, more like.'

Cath's heart was racing, and not just from the effort of trying to keep up. The two of them had always kept in touch over the years – kept each other up-to-date with the latest developments and stuff – but she hadn't actually seen Maggie in, what, nearly a decade? Not since she'd moved to Hong Kong. Not since *the funeral*.

Why had she suddenly turned up now?

The Farmer's Arms

Maggie parked up her wheelie case and flopped down on to the faded chintz chair in The Farmer's Arms. It felt like weeks, not hours, since she'd been charging along the platform at Glasgow Central, forcing her way through the train doors with seconds to spare. The carriage had been crowded and sweaty, but by far the worst thing was having to suffer that ear-splitting announcement on constant repeat all the way down here: '*Ladies and gentlemen, we regret to inform you that, due to a reduction in staffing levels on this route, we will not be in a position to open the buffet car at any point today*.' Ugh.

It was only the thought of a crisp, cold glass of wine at the other end that had kept her sane – which she'd pictured herself sipping on the leafy terrace of a charming, walled beer garden.

But the reality hadn't quite lived up to the fantasy. The weathered old picnic tables dotted around the car park outside this place hadn't looked too inviting and so, instead, she was sitting here in the corner of the dingy pub, watching Cath weave towards her with their drinks on a tray: a glass of white wine that didn't look very chilled at all, and a shallow cup with a teabag on a string that had turned the water the colour of urine.

'What's *that*?' asked Maggie, pointing at the cup.

'Fennel and nettle,' said Cath, settling down in her chair. 'It's an infusion.'

But Maggie had stopped listening and was looking around, scanning the empty room. Even the skinny young barman with the gelled hair had disappeared now, having found something better to do.

Maggie grasped the stem of her wine glass which still worryingly warm from the dishwasher. 'I was hoping for condensation,' she frowned, holding it up to the light. 'Oh well. Never mind. Cheers!' And she bashed her glass against Cath's cup, spilling half the tea in the process. 'Sorry. Sorry…'

'It's OK,' grinned Cath, reaching in her bag for a tissue. 'It tastes pretty foul anyway.'

Maggie took a swig of her wine and the sharp sourness made her shiver. 'This isn't much better, to be honest. I'll go and get us something decent to drink,' she said, setting off in search of the barman.

Finding no trace of him, she knocked on the bar and, when that didn't work, resorted to a loud whistle. 'Christ. The service in here is dire,' she muttered. 'No wonder there's no bloody customers.'

'Is that right?' yawned a voice from somewhere in the back. Then a short, squat bloke emerged, dressed head-to-toe in tweed like Toad of Toad Hall. 'I'll have you know we're Archdale's premier drinking and dining establishment,' he informed her, in a distinct Antipodean drawl. 'The Farmer's Arms Public House, Restaurant and Tearooms.'

'Sorry, mate. Did I wake you?' Maggie asked.

But her sarcasm went ignored as he came up and rested his meaty arm on the beer pump. 'Hiya, Cathy,' he called over to Cath, who was pretending to be engrossed in her phone. He nodded towards Maggie. 'Is this a friend of yours?'

Cath looked up and forced a smile. 'Yep, this is my old pal Maggie. She's come to visit for a couple of days. Maggie, meet Australian Pete. He's my competition – owner of the only other tearoom in town.'

Maggie looked at him like he was no competition at all. 'It's not exactly tea I'm after, Pete,' she said. 'I was hoping for something stronger.'

'You Scots are all the same, hey?' he chuckled. 'You all like a drink.'

'Well...' said Maggie. 'From what I've seen over the years, you Aussies are no slouches in that department either. Now then,' she carried on, 'would it be possible to have a look at the wine list?'

Australian Pete just laughed at this, which wasn't a good sign. '*Wine list?*' he repeated. 'Yeah, right. You can have the red, the white or the rosé – that's the list. The ladies normally have the white, but it tastes like vinegar, so I'd defo recommend the rosé. Yeah?'

'Has it been in the fridge?' she asked.

'Yeah.'

'Fine. We'll have it.'

'OK,' said Australian Pete. 'Two glasses of Muddy Duck rosé coming up! I'll bring them over.'

'OK. Cheers,' she said, and went and sat back down opposite Cath, who clasped her hands together and leaned in. Maggie recognised the expression on Cath's face straightaway: the look of a woman keen to put her own troubles to one side and listen to someone else's woes for a change.

'So, then,' said Cath. 'What's this *long story* you've got to tell me?'

Maggie opened her mouth and closed it again, as Australian Pete arrived at the table with their drinks.

'C'mon,' teased Cath, after he'd gone. 'It must be very juicy if it's dragged you back here from your fancy lawyer job with that oil company.'

'Well, that's just it,' said Maggie darkly. 'I've been forced out.'

'Really?' said Cath. 'Gosh.'

'*Gosh*?' said Maggie. 'Is that it…?'

Cath shifted in her seat. 'Er, well, I suppose you're just the latest casualty of the fall in global oil prices,' she said, like she was parroting a headline she'd seen on the cover of a Sunday supplement before tossing it straight in the recycling.

'Not exactly,' said Maggie. 'More a victim of my sleazy boss's rampant libido. We were away at a conference in Dubai. He tried it on with me.'

'He never!'

'He did. In the hotel bar.'

'Ew!' said Cath, horrified. 'What did you do?'

'I told him where to go, of course. Apart from anything else, do you know the penalties for public cavorting in the United Arab Emirates?' Maggie swallowed her wine dramatically. 'And so – long story short – he replaced me with someone younger. Someone more… *compliant*.'

'Tosser!' said Cath, taking a gulp of her own wine in sympathy. 'And so did you report him? Complain to HR or something?'

'No point,' said Maggie. 'South-East Asia isn't exactly known for its record on employee rights. I got no pay-off, no nothing. And so that was the end of my work visa and – next thing I know – I'm back in Glasgow staying with Joyce…'

'*Joyce*?'

'Yup.'

'As in… your mother, Joyce?'

'I know, I know. I didn't think it through.'

'How long did you last?' ventured Cath.

'Two days.'

'Ah.' Cath tilted her head in sympathy. 'As long as that?'

'Ugh.' Maggie shuddered at the memory. 'She just kept asking me all these questions. Like it was my fault or something. Anyway, I ended up losing it and storming out.'

'Oh dear.' Cath clocked Maggie's empty glass and rose to her feet. 'I think we're going to need a bottle this time.'

'It's vile stuff,' said Maggie. 'But OK, if you insist.' And while Cath was up at the bar, she settled back into her seat and cast her eye around the pub again.

A few more customers had turned up by now: a few saddos, Maggie thought, out drinking by themselves on a Tuesday evening. And a couple of lads, friends of the young barman, were larking around by the corner of the bar. They seemed to be dressed for a night out – in smart shirts, jeans and trainers – but they couldn't have been going clubbing or anything, as it was miles to the nearest metropolis. Supping electric blue liquid out of dainty bottles, they stood out against all the dusty horse brasses and the nautical ornaments that adorned the place – ships' wheels, anchors and compasses. This was ironic, as the map on the wall showed they were about as far from the sea as it was possible to get: in the landlocked county of Derbyshire, in the dead centre of the country. Emphasis on 'dead'.

Maggie prided herself on knowing a lot about a lot of things, but she realised she knew very little about the Peak District and even less about Derbyshire. No, that was a lie. She knew it had a cricket team. And she knew it had 'dales', whatever they were. This village was even *called* 'Archdale'. Yes, everyone had heard of the Derbyshire Dales – but after that she drew a blank.

She'd only been here once before, a flying visit back in the late nineties, not long after Cath had got married and moved up from London. But it had been the middle of winter and, after visiting Chatsworth House like every other tourist, they'd spent the rest of the weekend holed up in front of Cath's open fire. Maybe the summer was more exciting?

'Here we are,' said Cath, back from the bar, slipping into her seat.

Cath had never exactly been fat, but she'd slimmed right down for her wedding to Simon and had been pretty svelte ever since. Now though, it looked to Maggie like she was a bit *too* thin. Probably the stress of splitting up with him, even though he was no great loss.

'So, what's the latest with you and love-rat Simon?' she asked, as Cath refilled their glasses.

Cath put down the bottle and massaged the empty space on her ring finger. 'I'm not in a good place, actually.'

'Literally,' said Maggie, watching Australian Pete on his perch behind the bar, clearly straining to hear Cath's every word.

'She's thrown him out, you know,' Cath was saying now. 'The *other woman*.'

'Already?' Maggie laughed. 'God. He's done well to get thrown out by two different women in the space of six months.' She paused. 'Still, Simon always was an over-achiever...'

Cath stayed stony-faced. 'I didn't technically throw him out,' she said quietly. 'It was his choice to leave.'

'Knobhead.'

'Yep,' nodded Cath. 'It wouldn't have been so bad, but she's fifty-three! He's worked with her for years.'

Maggie shook her head. 'Being traded in for an older model... That's harsh.'

'Thanks for that,' said Cath, wounded. 'Don't rub it in.'

'Sorry,' said Maggie. 'Where is he now, then?'

'Renting a flat in Leeds. Just around the corner from his office.'

'Loser.'

'So,' said Cath, changing the subject. 'What's next for you, Maggie? If I know you, you'll have something up your sleeve.'

'Well,' said Maggie, straightening up. 'I suppose with my CV I could really go anywhere. In the words of the song, I could even "Go West".'

'What? Manchester?' asked Cath.

'New York, I was thinking.'

'Of course.'

'Yeah,' said Maggie. 'But it's a tricky time, the summer. Not many of the big companies are hiring.'

Cath was nodding sagely at her, even though it was a very long time since she'd had to take her chances in the job market.

'It could take a couple of months to find something,' Maggie continued.

'Yeah. I suppose it could,' said Cath.

'So, in the meantime… I was wondering…'

'Ye-es?'

'…if I could move in with you?'

The Arrival of the Queen of Sheba

The following morning, Maggie had been up for ages, waiting for Cath to surface. She'd showered in the plush upstairs bathroom before heading in search of coffee, down to the kitchen that was like something out of a magazine: light and airy, with a cream-coloured Aga, a round rustic-style table, and most of John Lewis's utensil department hanging from the ceiling beams. What a contrast to the cosy little cottage she remembered from the last time!

Yes, Cath had definitely done well for herself, marrying Simon. Financially, if nothing else. This house was massive, with six bedrooms (mostly empty now that her three oldest children had flown the nest) and a conservatory that was bigger than Maggie's mother's council flat in Glasgow. The location was a bit out on a limb, mind you – stuck half way up a hill, with fields on all sides – but the gardens were stunning. Stunning and yet welcoming at the same time.

But then Cath had always had a knack for that sort of thing. When Maggie first met her – freshers' week 1990, in the halls of residence at UCL – she'd even managed to make her tiny box room feel homely and comfortable. Maggie had spent all her time in there, away from her own sparse 'cell', which only had a Morrissey poster and an early-period IKEA rug for decoration. For an only child like Maggie, it was like having a ready-made sister, one that she actually liked. Cath could even drive and, what's more, had her own car – unheard of in those days, especially in London.

14

The following year, when they moved out of halls into a flat together, she'd discovered that Cath was a great cook as well. Instead of 'eating your tea', she called it 'having supper', and would serve up exotic delights night after night: coq au vin, beef bourguignon, dauphinoise potatoes. Maggie knew French, of course – she'd got an A in it at school, as she had in all her subjects – but this was her first taste of French cooking. She'd never actually been to France at that point – had never been anywhere, really – but Cath's parents had a holiday home in Brittany, within striking distance of their main home in rural Dorset. Some summers they didn't even bother going there though, and Cath, her parents and her younger sister would fly long-haul instead, to Thailand or sometimes Australia, even the big red bit in the middle, not just the coastal towns you saw on *Neighbours* or *Home and Away*. Yes, before she'd even started her degree in modern languages, Cath was already a citizen of the world. Which made it all the more surprising that she'd ended up in a no-mark backwater like Archdale…

The journey here in the taxi yesterday had taken for ever. Leaving the station and the shops of small-town Buxton behind, Maggie had felt like she was crossing an invisible border, from civilisation into a strange new land, descending into a vast, grassy cauldron of hills and dips, with more shades of green than she even knew existed.

People said that about Vietnam, that it had more shades of green than anywhere else on the planet, and she'd certainly visited it enough times on business trips and holidays in recent years. But the Peak District was more foreign to her somehow. Yesterday, passing signposts for places like Cutthroat Bridge and Slippery Stones, she'd felt like Martin Sheen in *Apocalypse Now*, heading up the Mekong river for his final face-off with Marlon Brando.

This morning, though, even with a vicious hangover, she felt a lot more at ease. Despite the dodgy pub and the equally dodgy landlord, last night had been a lot of fun – just like old times – and it was really decent of Cath to agree to let her stay for a bit.

Maggie stood by the kitchen window a while, watching the morning haze settle in the bowl of the valley. Her eyes were drawn to the clear blue sky above, where the jet streams from two aircraft had crossed to form a rough saltire, like a Scottish flag. It's a sign, she thought. *Things are looking up.*

She was wondering where the planes were coming from, and where they were going, when the kitchen door creaked open and Cath dragged herself over the threshold, groaning. Her smooth blonde hair had reverted to its natural frizzy state overnight and her eyes were like two pin-holes in her head.

'That's a beautiful tree out there,' said Maggie, coming back down to earth.

Cath squinted out of the window, doing her best to avoid the light. 'Oh. The hawthorn?' she said, her voice still husky from the Muddy Duck.

'So that's a hawthorn, is it?' said Maggie thoughtfully. 'Nature's not my strong point, as you know. Want some coffee, by the way? There's some in the pot.'

Cath nodded very slowly.

'Last night was fun,' said Maggie. 'It got off to quite an unpromising start, I must admit, but things picked up after the first bottle.'

'It was a giggle, wasn't it?' said Cath, attempting a grin. 'Even if I *am* now paying the price. Big time.'

'Tell me about it!' said Maggie. 'My head's splitting.'

'Oh, well,' said Cath, sitting down at the table. 'It's got to be done every once in a while. I've not laughed that hard in ages.

Although I'm worried that we drove that hiker bloke away with all our cackling…'

'Hmm, yes.' Maggie chuckled at the memory. 'He didn't look too impressed, did he?'

'He's not from round here,' said Cath. 'Thank God.'

Maggie took a gulp of her coffee and sat down opposite her. 'That creepy Australian Pete's got the hots for you, I reckon.'

'Oh God. Don't!' said Cath, pressing her eyeballs with the heels of her hands. 'That's the last thing I need right now. And don't say anything in front of Lauren, will you? She'll be back from her boyfriend's house any minute.'

'Lauren's got a *boyfriend*?'

'Yep. Dan. He's a nice lad,' said Cath. 'And just remember, Maggie, she's at an impressionable age, so don't go putting any daft ideas in her head.'

'*Me?*' said Maggie, pretending to be annoyed, but she was cheered by the thought of seeing Lauren again. She'd been a very likeable child, even as a baby she'd had something about her, not like most other babies who were pretty limited. And now she had a boyfriend. Maggie felt old.

'And anyway,' said Cath. 'Australian Pete's alright really. Just a bit nosey… And I'm not sure we'd have made it back here from the pub under our own steam if he hadn't given us a lift. It's nearly two miles.'

'He gave us a lift?!' asked Maggie, cringing. 'Oh God, I've no recollection of that at all. Bit worrying…'

'Yeah. So just remember that before you slag him off again.'

'Fair enough,' said Maggie. 'Listen. I was thinking. I could come down and help you in the café today. I'm sure you could use another pair of hands?'

'Ah, well.' Cath hesitated. 'It's actually my day off.'

'Even better,' said Maggie. 'We could do something. Go to Buxton maybe? It looked very nice from what I saw of it yesterday. Or even Sheffield? It's not that far, is it? I've been googling it this morning. We could go to the galleries at the Winter Gardens. Have a long lunch at one of the places on Ecclesall Road. What do you think?'

'Afraid I can't, sorry,' said Cath. 'It's Wednesday. I've got my mindfulness class on Wednesdays.' She stood up, gingerly. 'In fact, I'm running late.'

'*Mindfulness?*' scoffed Maggie, folding her arms.

'I wouldn't expect you to understand,' said Cath, plonking a box of expensive muesli down on the table in front of her.

Maggie looked at it. '*Duchy Originals*? Isn't that Prince Charles's stuff?' She pushed the box away from her. 'How could you eat that after what he did to Diana?'

'Oh, come on,' said Cath. 'It was well over twenty years ago, for goodness' sake. If William and Harry can get over it, so can you.'

Maggie furrowed her brow. 'That makes it over twenty years since we *last* lived together,' she said, thinking back to the flat they'd shared in Clapham as twenty-somethings.

Cath smiled at her. 'We're not exactly living together *now*.'

'Which reminds me,' said Maggie. 'One thing I wanted to say. I'd like to pay you some rent while I'm here. It's only fair.'

'No way,' said Cath. 'I'm not taking any money off you. You're a mate. And anyway, it's just a stop-gap until you find a new job.'

The back door swung open making them jump and Lauren appeared, dragging behind her a fuzzy, ginger mongrel whose tail was beating against the dresser, shaking the crockery. Maggie was pleased to see that Lauren still had the same gorgeous red curls she'd had as a little girl, even though she was now a head taller than her mother.

'Why's there a traffic cone on top of the fountain, Mum?' Lauren asked, shutting the door behind her.

'Oh, that was Maggie,' said Cath. 'D'you remember Maggie…?'

Lauren spun round to take a look at her. 'Oh hiya,' she said. 'I think I *sort of* remember you…' She pushed her hair back behind her ears. 'Listen. Can I use you two as models?'

'A model? Me?' said Maggie, sitting up in her chair.

'We're doing stage make-up in drama class at the moment,' Lauren clarified.

'Ahhh,' said Maggie. 'I always could imagine myself as an actress. Treading the boards and stuff.'

'It's scars and tumours. Gaping wounds. General decay, that sort of thing,' said Lauren. 'I need someone to practise on for the school show.'

'Oh,' said Maggie, deflating. 'What's the show?'

'*Grease*,' said Lauren.

'*Grease*?'

'Yeah, *Grease*. With a zombie twist.'

'Christ on a bike!' said Maggie, and Lauren giggled.

'Maggie's come to stay for a little while,' Cath explained.

'Cool.' Lauren nodded. 'I'm *not* staying, by the way. Dan's waiting for me in the car. I'm going to do my maths homework at his place.' She grabbed a pile of books from the kitchen table and pushed them down into her bag. 'See you later,' she said, heading back out the door, pulling the mutt behind her.

'What are you going to do with yourself, Maggie?' asked Cath, after Lauren had gone.

'Well, first, I'm going to make some more coffee,' said Maggie, grabbing hold of the pot.

'And then what? How will you fill your days while you're here? I don't suppose job applications will take up *all* of your time?'

'Well,' said Maggie. 'I've been thinking for a while now… It might be time for me to, y'know, give something back.'

'Eh?' said Cath.

'To use my skills and experience to, y'know, help those less fortunate than myself.'

'Really?' Cath nodded her head. 'Very admirable. Who did you have in mind?'

'You,' said Maggie. 'Well, not *you* exactly, but the local community. Around here. Like I said, I could get involved with the café. It's a wee bit of a dump, isn't it? I could help you turn it around. Into a thriving business.' But she could see that Cath was upset and immediately regretted her frankness.

'That's a bit unfair,' said Cath. 'It's a not-for-profit thing. Just a little place for people to get together during the day. I only take a small wage and any surplus is donated back to the village. For the upkeep of the war memorial, the Christmas lights, that kind of thing.'

'Even so,' said Maggie, gently. 'I still think we can do better. Show Australian Pete that we're a force to be reckoned with.'

'*We?*'

'So I'll head down there this morning. See what improvements I can make.'

'Oh God,' said Cath, too groggy to argue. 'Don't upset Neil, will you?'

'Neil?' echoed Maggie. 'Who's Neil?'

'A volunteer who helps me out sometimes. He's working down there this morning. He's a bit, y'know… A bit of a stickler.'

'Don't worry. Leave it to me,' said Maggie, as a BMW convertible screeched up the driveway and came to a halt outside the kitchen window, sending loose chippings flying everywhere.

A tall, slim woman in yoga pants got out of the car and pushed her sunglasses on to the top of her long, glossy hair with one finger. Maggie could hear her nasal voice before she was even through the door.

'Oh, Catherine, darling, it's a gorgeous morning. We're *sooo* lucky to live in such a beautiful part of the world.'

'So true!' replied Cath, springing up to kiss her on both cheeks, and Maggie noticed that the woman had a tattoo of a dolphin on her midriff. At least, Maggie assumed it was a dolphin: she was so thin it could easily have been a sea sprat.

The woman was peering into Cath's face now, examining her. 'You look dreadful, Catherine. Sort of yellow. Are you dehydrated or something? Have you been drinking enough?'

Maggie stifled a laugh.

'We had a couple of, er, glasses of wine last night,' confessed Cath. 'Down at The Farmer's Arms.'

The woman's lips tightened. 'Ugh. I can't touch the wine in there. It literally brings me out in hives. But, as you know, I'm not much of a drinker in any case.'

'Me neither,' said Cath. 'Not these days. Last night was very much an aberration.'

And as the woman smiled her approval, Cath went on to make the introductions: 'Tiggy, this is Maggie. Maggie, meet Tiggy, my mindfulness instructor and now, my friend.'

'Ah,' said Tiggy, looking Maggie up and down. '*The Scottish Widow*? We meet at last. Catherine has told me *sooo* much about you.'

That's funny, she's told me nothing about you, thought Maggie, glaring at Cath.

'Tiggy used to be in that band,' explained Cath. 'The Yips. Remember? They had that big hit song when we were at uni – "Scum Republic". Merlin Crocker was the lead singer…'

'How could I ever forget?' said Maggie. *Merlin Crocker-shit*, she used to call him back in the day. She'd never been a big fan of his – nor his band – and was even less of one now. 'What instrument did you play, Tiggy?' she asked, feeling obliged to make conversation for Cath's sake.

Tiggy cleared her throat. 'I was on tambourine. And backing vocals, of course.'

'Of course,' said Maggie. 'Well, don't let me keep you two ladies from your *mindfulness* class, now. It's exactly what the world needs after all,' she mumbled under her breath. 'More people sitting around doing nothing.'

Cath shot Maggie a look as she ushered Tiggy out of the door.

As it clicked shut after them, Maggie was at the window again, watching them laugh their way down the drive with the roof down.

'*The Scottish Widow?*' Was that what Cath called her behind her back? How could she make fun of her to this Tiggy woman like that? It had been nine years and four months since Andy had died and, yes, she knew she should really be getting over it by now but no, it still hurt like hell.

And, seriously, what sort of a name was 'Tiggy' anyway?

Lost in Translation

The walk down into Archdale – to the café – was taking a lot longer than Maggie had expected and her black court shoes were rubbing at her heels. She'd thought about borrowing a pair of Cath's trainers but Cath was only a size six and anyway, they would have looked daft with her black suit – like something from the eighties.

It had been positively balmy when she'd left the house, but a lively wind had now sprung up from nowhere, turning her bare legs to goosebumps. More worryingly, it had brought with it a mean-looking rain cloud and she hadn't thought to bring an umbrella.

You really need a car to live round here, she thought, unlike the big cities she'd lived in before – Glasgow, London, Hong Kong – where public transport had been plenty good enough for her needs. Still, on the plus side she could make efficient use of her time here at Cath's by learning to drive, and she made a mental note to apply for her provisional licence and book some lessons. She'd need to learn fast, though, as this was a walk she didn't fancy doing every day – especially the trek home, back up the hill.

Reaching the outskirts of the village, she could see the church spire up ahead and Cath's Community Café nestling in its shadow. A short, immaculate man in round glasses was standing in front of the door, fishing some keys out of his pocket, and she marched up to him with her hand outstretched.

'You must be Neil,' she said, warmly.

'The very same,' said Neil, offering his own hand and clicking his heels.

She guessed that he had some sort of military background and, even though she wasn't great with ages, she would have put him at around sixty. 'Very pleased to meet you, Neil. I'm Maggie. An old friend of Cath's from way back. I'm sure she's probably mentioned me before…?'

From the blank expression on his face, it was clear that she hadn't.

'Anyway. I've come to help you out this morning,' Maggie continued, undeterred.

'But… Cath hasn't said anything about this,' he protested, narrowing his eyes.

Maggie moved towards the door of the café, but he was obstructing her with his body.

'It's OK,' said Maggie. 'You can take it from me that Cath has authorised me to—'

'I'm ever so sorry, but you can't be too careful '…these days,' interrupted Neil, standing his ground, pulling his phone out of his inside pocket. 'I'll just have to ring Cath to check your credentials. Now, do you have any ID on you?'

'ID?' Maggie felt her chest go red and the heat spread to her neck. 'Look, Neil. I can see where you're coming from. Security is of paramount importance – in any business – but I don't think we really need to disturb Cath, do you?'

Neil stood firm, as she tried a different tack. 'Come on. I'm freezing my arse off out here in this wind. Can't we just go inside?' And she wondered whether he had ever seen any active service as he looked quite terrified.

'I'm very sorry,' he insisted, avoiding her gaze. 'But it's a risk I'm not prepared to take.'

'A *risk*?' she spluttered. 'Are you for real? D'you think there's anything in there worth stealing? Or are you worried that I'm a terrorist? Part of some sort of jihadi cell, intent on infiltrating Archdale?'

'Well…' he said, thinking about it. 'Not exactly. But you *are* quite forceful.'

A posse of grumbling pensioners had gathered to watch the spectacle, keen for Neil to open up so they could get their morning cuppa.

'What's the hold-up, Neil?' asked a tiny woman with white cotton bud hair, who was waving her walking stick to attract his attention.

He explained his predicament to her, addressing her formally as 'Mrs Winterson', but the old woman was unimpressed. 'Neil,' the woman said, her voice surprisingly firm. 'In Cath's absence, and as the most senior member of staff here, maybe you could exercise your discretion and just let this lady in to help you? I think I speak for all of us here when I say that I'm gasping for a brew.'

The other pensioners mumbled and nodded, prompting Neil to puff out his chest and turn his key in the lock.

Maggie pushed inside first, catching the unmistakeable tang of damp in her nose. Flicking on the lights, her first impressions from yesterday were confirmed: the décor was tired and old-fashioned, not helped by the lilac spotty colour scheme that sprouted across the room like a virus in a test tube.

While Neil was bent down behind the counter switching on the little radio, Maggie took her chance to whip all the cloths from the tables and pull down the faded bunting from around the window. 'That looks better already,' she said, standing back, hands on hips. 'More minimalist. Less twee.' She thought about opening the window to let some fresh air circulate, but decided not to for the time being: Mrs Winterson had taken a seat at the big table next to it and she didn't want the old lady to freeze in the draught.

The radio was hiss-hissing away now: adverts for a skip hire company, a mobile library service and the local Scout jamboree. *What radio station was this, for goodness' sake?* She turned the dial searching for Radio 4 – even Radio 2 would be better – but was forced to give up when Neil informed her they were in a signal black spot so local radio was all they could get. Maggie couldn't believe it: it had actually been easier to get BBC radio on the other side of the planet…

'Right, Neil,' she sighed, pulling on an apron. 'Let's get to work and give these good people a quality catering experience.'

'Right you are,' said Neil, who soon had the ancient coffee machine chugging into life while Maggie took the orders for coffees and teas.

The next time Maggie looked at her watch it was nearly lunch-time, the morning had flown by, all the tables were occupied, and Neil's attitude to her was thawing nicely. Her mind had even turned to dreaming up plans for a loyalty card system for their clients – one that would keep them coming back to Cath's Community Café, out of Australian Pete's tearooms.

The bing-bong noise of the door opening announced that they had some new customers – a group of Chinese teenagers. Wiping her hands on her apron, Maggie went over to welcome them, grateful for the opportunity to use some of the lingo she'd picked up during her time in Hong Kong.

'*Jo san*,' she beamed, trying to shake hands with each of them, pleased that she knew how to say 'Good morning'.

The teenagers looked at each other uncertainly as Maggie showed off a few of her other well-worn phrases. '*I am a Scottish person,*' she told them in Chinese. '*I am forty-five years old.*'

One of the group, a girl in a cool hat and glasses, seemed to be plucking up the courage to reply to her.

Maggie smiled encouragingly and continued: '*I am a lawyer. In Hong Kong.*'

But they just looked confused – which she could understand as she must look to them very much like a waitress in a café in the Peak District. Then the girl spoke up.

'We are from Beijing in the People's Republic of China. We attend Sheffield University,' she said, politely and carefully. 'People from Beijing… they are speaking Mandarin. Hong Kong people are speaking Cantonese. So it is quite hard for us to understand you.'

Maggie felt her cheeks fire up. Bit of a schoolgirl error really, they obviously didn't have a clue what she was on about. And she didn't know any Mandarin other than how to say, 'Thank you'. *How embarrassing*! Especially as Neil and all the other customers had heard every word.

Maggie forced these thoughts to the back of her mind and counted the number of students. There were eight of them in total – perfect! – they could all squeeze in around the big table in the window, apart from the fact that Mrs Winterson was still hogging it, nursing the same cup of Earl Grey she'd ordered when she first came in. She'd have to try and get rid of her.

Maggie went over and placed a hand on the old woman's shoulder. 'Can I get you anything else, madam?' she asked, hoping she would take the hint.

'No thank you,' said Mrs Winterson. 'I'm fine.'

Maggie sighed inwardly. 'Well, look. Maybe I could just move you to that little corner table that's just become free? I'm afraid I need to clear this one. I need it for this group of people here...'

'But this is *my* table,' said Mrs Winterson. 'The window table. I sit here every day.'

'Sure,' said Maggie. 'But you've been here nearly two hours and—'

'I didn't know there was a time limit on tables,' said Mrs Winterson, sharply. 'Or I'd have gone round the corner to Australian Pete's. You don't get this sort of carry on at The Farmer's.'

Maggie tried to clear away the empty cup at least, but Mrs Winterson had pushed it to the furthest corner of the table away from her. Maggie extended her reach, but the old lady had grabbed the cup again and was refusing to hand it over.

'*Just let it go*,' Maggie told herself, under her breath. This was getting ridiculous now. She needed to defuse the situation, smooth the whole thing over.

'No, I will *not* let it go!' shrieked Mrs Winterson, getting the wrong end of the stick. 'Neil was quite right to refuse you entry this morning. You *horrible* woman!'

The bing-bong noise signalled the arrival of yet more customers and Maggie swung round, wondering how on earth she was going to fit them in too.

Standing there in the doorway were Cath and Tiggy, back from their class. Cath was doing that rubbing her temples thing she sometimes did, a sure sign she wasn't happy, while Tiggy was biting the inside of her cheek as if trying not to laugh.

'Maggie,' said Cath, tightly. 'What's going on?'

Maggie sprung back from the table, hands in the air. 'It's nothing. Just a little... misunderstanding.'

Neil was clucking around Mrs Winterson to make sure she was OK, and Cath had got involved now, trying to appease her, but the old lady waved them both away with her stick. Rising to her feet, she deposited her cup pointedly on the counter and shuffled out without saying a word.

Maggie turned to the Chinese students and beckoned them to take a seat at the empty table.

'No thank you,' said their spokeswoman, backing away in the direction of the door. 'We only came in to ask if we could please use your toilet.'

As the rest of the students trooped outside after her, followed by the other pensioners, Maggie turned to Cath. 'I really didn't mean to upset the old dear,' she said. 'I just didn't want to lose eight paying punters, that's all… I'll apologise to her tomorrow. She said she comes here every day, right?'

Cath said nothing.

'Anyway, how was the mindfulness class?' continued Maggie. 'Feeling the benefits?'

'Maggie,' said Cath. 'Thanks very much for your help today. But I don't think we'll be needing you tomorrow. Neil and I can manage the running of this place between us.'

Brief Encounter

When Maggie opened her eyes, it took a few heart-stopping seconds to work out where she was, to remember she was in the single bed in Cath's spare room in Archdale. Twenty-two days she'd been here now – not that she was counting or anything – and it had been the same story every morning.

A quick glance at her phone told her it was half past ten. *Half ten!* She couldn't believe it; half the day gone already. She shouldn't really have started drinking in front of the telly last night, but Cath had been out at a neighbourhood watch meeting all evening and she'd been bored senseless.

The promising sight of six new emails cut through the brain fog, forcing her up out of her pit. Keen to see what was waiting for her, she raced downstairs in her T-shirt and pants to read them on her laptop – her lack of a dressing gown wouldn't be a problem as Cath would be down at the café by now and Lauren was staying over at Dan's again.

Since she'd been in Archdale, she'd freshened up her CV and applied for the one or two legal jobs in the oil industry that had recently come up. And she'd reached out (terrible phrase!) to a few of her industry contacts – at home and abroad – to see if there were any suitable openings. Mainly abroad, it had to be said. She'd much prefer to go and take up another post overseas – Asia again, if at all possible. It would just be easier. She definitely couldn't face the thought of going back to London. Back to the memories. Of Andy. And all the rest of it…

Before she even reached for the coffee pot, she pulled up a seat at the table and grabbed the mouse. *Hallelujah*! For once, the fickle broadband was working.

She clicked on the new messages and her stomach sank: just a load of spam and the usual boring newsletters from The Law Society. Apart from that there was nothing. *Nada*. Not even any office gossip from her old colleagues.

It was still early days, mind you – too early to expect results. It had barely been three weeks after all, albeit the longest three weeks of her life. In the great scheme of things it was nothing. The blink of an eye.

She ventured to the front door to see if there was anything interesting in the post – although why would there be? No one knew she was here. Not even her mother, Joyce.

This morning there were only a few brown envelopes addressed to Cath and a copy of the local newspaper, *The Peak Gleaner*. She scanned the headline on the front page – SCOUT JUMBLE SALE RAISES £56 FOR VILLAGE DEFIBRILLATOR – and rolled her eyes. Riveting stuff!

A low growl on the stairs made her look round. There was the dog, Jazz, regarding her warily from her favourite spot halfway up. She was a funny-looking thing – skinny with long ears that made her look more like a hare than a dog. Maggie had established that Jazz too was a recent immigrant into Archdale: Lauren had apparently persuaded Cath to adopt her from a charity that rescued doomed strays from the slums of Romania. As an act of solidarity, Maggie had tried to make friends with the hound but, despite her efforts, Jazz still treated her like an intruder.

She traipsed back into the kitchen for an overdue coffee to find that they'd run out of the fresh stuff and, since Cath didn't believe in instant, she resigned herself to going without. She felt a rush of longing for city life, where you could just nip round to the corner shop in case of emergencies like this. But the nearest shop was miles away and she was completely reliant on Cath.

That had been the worst thing about the whole debacle with Mrs Winterson that first day, which she'd replayed over and over in her mind ever since. The incident itself had been bad enough, but afterwards had been worse. Instead of just being able to disappear until the dust settled, she'd had to suffer the indignity of accepting a lift from Tiggy – of being driven back up to Cath's house in silence, squashed into the back of the convertible, with her knees up around her ears. *'The black-burning shame of it!'* as Joyce would have said.

Maggie thought about ringing Joyce. It was high time the two of them made up. Life was too short for this sort of feuding, she knew that. The problem was, they were too similar: they either agreed whole-heartedly on something or else they'd get dug in at opposite ends of an argument and refuse to budge. But she also knew that, if she did call her, Joyce would be straight on her case again, asking whether she'd managed to find herself a job yet. This would surely be followed by a lecture on seizing the day – *'You're a lang time deid'* she would say in her broad accent – and Maggie wasn't quite ready for that. Not yet. She picked up her phone again to find that she was off the hook in any case; she didn't even have a signal at the moment.

Maggie was still sitting there, staring at the useless phone, when Cath's car pulled up outside the back door.

'Hiya,' said Cath, breezing into the kitchen. Then she stopped, looked at Maggie and laughed. 'Were you planning on getting dressed today by any chance?'

Maggie pulled her T-shirt down over her knees. 'Uh. Yes. It's just... I've been really busy this morning.'

'Really?' said Cath. 'What've you been up to?'

'Thinking, mainly.'

'Your problem is you think too much,' said Cath, kindly. 'Always have done. It's not good for a person. That's what Tiggy says.'

'Tiggy doesn't strike me as the type who's burdened by too much thinking.'

'Oh, don't be horrible,' said Cath. 'Anyway. I've been thinking too. Maybe you need a hobby?'

'A *hobby*?' Maggie recoiled, like it was a dirty word. 'You know me. I've never had time for hobbies. Always been too busy with work.'

'Well, maybe you could take one up?'

Maggie raised a hand in protest. 'If you're about to suggest golf, then I'd like to suggest you don't bother.'

Cath hesitated. 'Why don't you give mindfulness a go? Have a lesson with Tiggy? You might like it.'

Maggie pulled a face. 'I'd rather cough up both lungs, to be honest. And anyway, the thought of just sitting there *being mindful*...? I feel like I've spent long enough sitting around on my arse. I need to find something to *do*.'

'OK. OK,' said Cath. 'I won't mention it again.'

'How's the café?' Maggie asked, changing the subject.

'Calm,' said Cath. 'Very calm. We've finally managed to persuade Mrs Winterson to come back...'

Maggie huffed. 'Thanks for bringing that up again.'

'Sorry,' said Cath. 'Listen. I was going to suggest we go out for something to eat tonight.'

'Great!' said Maggie, perking up. 'Sounds good.'

'But I've just remembered, it's parents' evening at Lauren's school and so…'

'Never mind,' said Maggie. 'I'll find something in the fridge.'

'Sorry,' said Cath again. Then she brightened. 'But, on a more exciting note, it's the Archdale charity quiz next Friday night. At The Farmer's Arms.'

'Excellent,' said Maggie, flatly. 'I can't wait.'

'Why do you always have to be so sarky?' moaned Cath. 'It's a really fun evening. The whole village comes along to support it. And Tiggy's husband – Phil – he always acts as the quizmaster. He's a really good bloke. You'll like him.'

'You reckon?' said Maggie.

'Yes. I've already put your name down for my team. You'll come in very handy. Seeing as how you know *everything*.'

'Cheeky cow!' Maggie laughed, rocking back on her chair. 'Actually, I've been meaning to ask you, I need to get some driving lessons booked. Do you know any instructors around here?'

'You could try Val,' offered Cath.

'Who's Val when she's at home?'

'Wait a sec,' said Cath, opening a drawer and rummaging around in it. She found what she was looking for – a shocking-pink business card – and handed it to Maggie.

Maggie squinted at the name on it: 'Valerie Bloom, Driving Instructor', the two Ls were in the form of red L-plates. 'Cheers,' said Maggie. 'Is she any good?'

'She's teaching Lauren at the moment. If she can cope with that, she *must* be pretty good,' said Cath. 'But look, I'm afraid I've got to dash off again. I only came back to pick up that lemon drizzle cake I made – I forgot it this morning…' She fetched it from the fridge and headed for the door. 'I'll see you later this evening, probably back around ten or so?' She stopped. 'And could I ask, would you mind moving your laptop and stuff off the kitchen table when you're finished with it? It's just that it's a little bit *in the way.* Thanks.'

'Sure. No problem,' Maggie called after her. 'Oh, and by the way, can you bring back some coffee?' But Cath was already half way down the driveway.

Alone again in the silence, Maggie had the now familiar sense of being watched. She turned round to see Jazz again, staring at her intently from her basket in the corner.

'Come on, girl,' she said. 'Let's go out for a walk. We could both do with the fresh air, eh?'

Jazz jumped up at her, tail thrashing away.

'I'll take that as a yes,' said Maggie, looking out the window at the sombre sky, trying to work out what to wear. Not that she had much choice. The only casual clothes she'd brought with her were a couple of pairs of jeans and a selection of stripy T-shirts, all the same style but in different colours. Jeans would be fine, but a T-shirt wouldn't be nearly warm enough; she hadn't quite acclimatised to the UK after the heat of Hong Kong – even though it was actually the middle of July and, technically, supposed to be summer. She didn't have the right footwear either.

She solved the first problem by rummaging in Cath's walk-in wardrobe, past the rows of greys and beiges in soft, natural fabrics, eventually unearthing an old, bobbly fleece that had been shoved to the back.

The footwear issue proved more challenging, but she soon found a pair of Simon's old walking boots in the hall cupboard (the 'cloakroom' as Cath called it). She tried them on and they fit perfectly, although they made her feet look massive. Her feet *were* massive, though. What was it Joyce always used to say – that she had '*a good grip of God's earth*'. Maggie smiled to herself. These would do nicely.

* * *

The boots weren't such a good idea after all. The fields around Cath's house were a bit boggy to say the least and the moisture had seeped into her toes from the outset: Simon had obviously left the boots behind for a reason. And for such a skinny little thing, Jazz was surprisingly strong; whenever she caught sight or scent of a bird or a squirrel, she would dart after it, pulling Maggie even further into the mud until she decided to let her off the lead for a bit.

Maggie had always imagined the countryside to be fairly quiet, with only the occasional tweet of birdsong or whatever. She certainly hadn't expected it to be as noisy as this – the moany echoes of the cows in the nearby barns, the tree branches creaking like coffin hinges in the breeze, not to mention the roar of the TransPennine Express as it hurtled cross-country to somewhere more exciting. Somewhere that had bars and shops and people and, well, life.

She remembered a time, long before her move to Hong Kong, when she herself had used to criss-cross the UK by train, visiting clients and attending conferences and such like. She would stare out the window of her first-class compartment at the sad individuals walking their dogs in the lonely fields below – and feel sorry for them as, unlike her, they didn't have important meetings to go to. Yes, once upon a time, she had been a 'Train Woman' in a business suit – and now she was just a 'Field Woman'. *In a bloody fleece, for God's sake*! Only temporarily, though. It wouldn't be long before she'd be back on the train. More likely a plane…

What was it that Tiggy had said? How lucky they were to live in 'such a beautiful part of the world'. And Cath obviously thought so too. But Maggie couldn't see it, she literally couldn't see it, as she was scared to lift her eyes from the ground in front of her in case she stood in one of the myriad sheep poos that littered the grass.

There was little point looking up in any case, just to see the series of peaks and trees that surrounded and enclosed her like the bars of a green prison. If it was green, it was because it seemed to rain at some point every day and, if it was a prison, then she was definitely in solitary confinement. It struck her that, on the few occasions when she'd actually left the house, she hadn't encountered another human soul.

The wind in the trees seemed to be telling her to *Shhhhh* now… to shut up… to hush her human thinking… *What kind of trees were they anyway?* Bloody big ones. *Oaks, maybe?* She hadn't a clue. That was the weird thing: she knew that *quercus* was Latin for oak tree, but she couldn't have identified one if her life depended on it… *Shhhhh* they said again, whatever they were… *Shhhhh… Shhhhhh…*

'That dog should be on a lead,' said a deep, Derbyshire voice out of nowhere, and Maggie stopped dead. Turning round, it was a moment before she spotted him in his dark waistcoat and shirt, crouched down by the rotten timber fence, hammer in hand.

'She's not doing any harm,' Maggie protested. 'She's nowhere near the sheep…'

'Makes no difference,' he replied.

'I think it makes *all* the difference.'

'Bloody townies,' he muttered, straightening up and pressing his back like an old man, even though he couldn't have been any older than she was. He was actually quite attractive, with a slight look of Bono, only taller and without the ridiculous sunglasses.

'See!' said Maggie, pointing at Jazz, who was busy rolling in some droppings. 'She's not even *looking* at the sheep. I'm training her to—'

'Look. I'm sorry, it's not a dog exercise area,' he interrupted. 'It's my livelihood. I lose one of these lambs, I've lost thirty quid.'

'Thirty pounds?' said Maggie. 'Is that all?'

'I suppose that's small change to you?'

'No. Sorry. I just meant… Is that all you get for a lamb? It's not very much.'

'Compared to what you pay in Waitrose? No. No, it isn't.'

'I don't pay anything actually,' said Maggie.

'You a shoplifter?' he asked.

'Vegetarian.'

'Even worse!' he laughed, and his green eyes lit up.

'I'm only joking.' Maggie laughed too. 'And I'm not a townie either, by the way,' she lied, tugging awkwardly at the sleeves of the fleece.

'Ah… OK.'

'Not at the moment,' she said. 'I'm bunking up at Higher House over there. With Cath Bridges.'

His eyebrows shot up.

'Not like *that*,' said Maggie. 'Not that there's anything *wrong* with that, of course,' she rambled, tying herself in knots. 'I'm just an old friend of hers. We were at university together.'

'Ah,' he said. 'Well I hope you like it here. It's a lovely part of the world…'

'Hmm,' said Maggie, looking down at her muddy feet. 'So everyone keeps telling me.'

'Er… well then.' He nodded back towards his fence. 'I suppose I'd better be getting on…'

'Here,' said Maggie, keen to keep him talking a bit longer. 'Is it true that when the sheep are lying down, that means it's going to rain?'

He looked straight at her and a grin spread over his face. 'I think you might be getting mixed up with cows,' he said. 'And, in both cases, no. It just means they're tired.'

'Ah. OK. Thanks,' she said, as he turned back to his task, still smiling to himself.

Maggie stood and watched him for a moment. He seemed to have forgotten all about the dog and the lead. As had she.

A Cry for Help

Maggie stared out the window of Cath's car at the endless dry stone walls disappearing to the distance. The evening was cool and clear and they were on their way to The Farmer's for the charity quiz, which Maggie had found herself looking forward to after all. For one thing, it was a welcome distraction from the radio silence on the job-hunting front. And also she was pretty good at quizzes, even if she said so herself. Eighties pop music was her specialist subject (thanks to her lonely youth spent listening to the radio), but she could handle herself across a broad range of serious topics too – politics, history, geography, you name it.

She glanced across at Cath behind the steering wheel. How many times had they been in this situation over the years: Cath confidently negotiating the open road, while Maggie kept up a continuous commentary in her ear about this, that and the other, until she'd talked herself out and they'd carry on in companionable silence? The only thing that had changed was the car. At uni it had been a Mini Metro and now it was a people carrier – albeit with very few people to fill it these days. Richard, Cath's eldest, was away in Philadelphia studying for a master's degree, on the fast track to a job with a big pharmaceutical company over there. And David and Alison, the twins, had both moved to London for university – although, thankfully for them, not the same one. Cath had told Maggie, wistfully, that they didn't make the trip home to Archdale very often; London was only two hundred miles away but it might as well have been another planet.

As Cath signalled to turn right down a long, winding lane, Maggie realised they were heading in the opposite direction from the pub. 'What are you doing, Cath?' she blurted out. 'It's that way!'

'Oh,' said Cath. 'Didn't I tell you? We're picking up Neil and Tiggy on the way.'

Maggie groaned like she'd been shot. She'd known that those two were going to be the other team members of their team, but she wasn't ready to face them just yet – especially Tiggy, whom she hadn't actually seen since the day of Café-Gate.

'I said I'd give them a lift,' said Cath. 'No point in us taking three cars. Plus, it'll be good for team morale to arrive there together – all four of us.'

'What about Tiggy's husband?' asked Maggie. 'I thought you said he was the quizmaster?'

'Phil? He's already down there,' replied Cath. 'He's helping Australian Pete set up.'

Maggie pondered their quiz tactics as the car threaded its way along the rough single track. 'Who's going to be our team captain?' she asked, after a moment.

'*Team captain?*' repeated Cath. 'I hadn't even thought about that. Do we need one?'

'Come on,' said Maggie. She shook her head in disbelief. 'This is basic stuff. You need to have a team captain in case the four of us are deadlocked on an answer. Two versus two. The captain would then have the casting vote.'

'You might be over-thinking this,' said Cath, nonplussed. 'It's just a bit of fun to raise some cash for local charities.'

'*Au contraire,*' said Maggie. 'I've seen friends fall out over this sort of thing.'

'Fine!' said Cath, exasperated. 'You'd better be the captain, then. As you seem to know so much about it.'

'OK by me,' said Maggie, settling back into her seat. She was feeling a bit grungy and was beginning to regret not washing her hair. Not as much as she regretted her outfit, though. She'd come downstairs earlier, all ready to leave, but Cath had screwed up her face and suggested that she wear something other than jeans and a stripy top for a change. Maggie couldn't really see the point – it was only The Farmer's Arms after all and besides, she didn't really have any other options – but Cath had insisted that she borrow something of hers. Running out of time, she'd settled on a tunic-style dress in muted mustard tones – and Cath had said she looked lovely – but Maggie knew she was just being kind. It did nothing for her pale, Celtic complexion, which had remained wilfully untouched by the best part of ten years in the tropics. Plus the empire waist band was cutting into her ribs something rotten.

'Wait until you see Tiggy's place,' said Cath, breathlessly. 'It's a gorgeous converted mill that's just so, well, *modern*. Underfloor heating, state-of-the-art sound system throughout and a wine fridge that keeps your Sancerre at exactly nine degrees.'

'Wow,' said Maggie. 'Nine degrees, eh?'

'Not that Tiggy drinks much. The odd spritzer now and again. She's just so…'

'*Mindful*?' said Maggie.

'Yes, exactly. Mindful about what she drinks. Definitely.'

Maggie yawned. She'd always hated people who could 'do' moderation, especially since she still had a pain behind her eyes from last night when she'd downed a bottle and a half of wine at home on her own – a pain which two paracetamol and two ibuprofen hadn't put a dent in. She slid her hands under her thighs, palms to the leather seat, her knuckles pressed into her legs.

'Tiggy's so fortunate,' sighed Cath. 'She's got everything going for her. Lovely home, perfect family, a rich husband with a place in Barbados...'

'Her own tambourine...' Maggie added, sarcastically. 'Come off it, Cath. You're not doing too badly yourself. Simon sees you alright for cash, doesn't he?'

'Not anymore,' said Cath. 'His business is struggling a bit, to be honest.'

'I didn't think accountants struggled,' said Maggie.

'Neither did I!' said Cath, tartly, as she turned into Tiggy's drive and parked up. 'C'mon,' she said, flinging open her door. 'Let's go in and say hello.'

Maggie checked herself in the mirror and got out of the car, but Tiggy had already wafted out into the courtyard to greet them.

'Hello again, Maggie,' she smirked. 'I like your dress...'

* * *

The Farmer's Arms was thrumming with anticipation as the quiz teams and their supporters filed into the main function room. The site of a thousand country weddings was now the arena for the last kind of conflict acceptable in the civilised world of the middle classes: trial by trivia.

Australian Pete was in his element, sporting a yellow cravat for the occasion, although the effect was more Rupert Bear than English country gent. He stepped up to the pre-historic microphone that had, no doubt, had to endure many a crummy best man speech in its time, and loosened it from its stand. A howl of feedback caused the entire room to wince, as he introduced the quizmaster for the evening, Phil Blanchard.

The crowd gave Phil a warm round of applause as he sauntered up to the front, radiating confidence and expensive citrus cologne, and there was even some whooping from Tiggy who was relishing her role as the supportive wife. Phil was pretty good-looking, Maggie had to admit. He still had a full thatch of silver hair and seemed to be one of the few men who could pull off a goatee without looking like a sex pest. His fitted white shirt set off his caramel tan to its best advantage, completing the look.

Phil tapped the microphone, which was now behaving itself for him in a way that it hadn't for poor old Pete. Beaming out at the room, he gave a nice speech on the importance of supporting the local organisations represented by the different quiz teams. And as the audience lapped up his easy charm, Maggie found herself wondering what on earth he was doing being married to Tiggy.

There would be ten teams competing for the big prize, Phil announced, although the prize wasn't actually that big at all, just half a frozen lamb courtesy of Les the butcher. Not that it really mattered, of course, because the main thing was that all the charities would benefit equally from the proceeds of the evening.

As Phil read out the names of the teams, Maggie noted that they fell into the usual predictable categories, namely: the laboured pun ('Otterly Marvellous', in aid of the local otter sanctuary); the really dull ('The Archdale Archers', for the village archery club); and the actually-quite-clever (like 'Agatha Quiz-Team', playing for the mobile library service).

Their own team name fell into the really dull category – 'Cath's Community Café Quizzers' – but she'd decided against saying anything. She'd just sit there quietly, sipping her double vodka and tonic, a much safer bet than Australian Pete's terrible wine.

Soon, Phil called the room to order. There was a general putting down of pints, a picking up of pens, and then they were off.

The first-round questions were rather pedestrian, Maggie thought, scribbling down the answers: easy ones about the royal family, European capital cities and Oscar-winning films. Neil was particularly strong on 'ranks of the British armed forces', having risen to the heights of sergeant major in his younger day (which explained a lot). Even Tiggy got a few right – a load of crap about celebrities mainly – but they all counted.

Before long, Phil was announcing the half-time interval, a chance for everyone to get stuck into the sandwiches and sausage rolls laid on for free by Australian Pete.

Maggie offered to go and get some drinks for the team – and then regretted it as the queue was three-deep at the bar. She was standing there, trying to remember the round (a pint of bitter for Neil, mineral water for Cath and Tiggy, another vodka and tonic for herself), when she felt a tap on her shoulder.

She swung round to see a tall, ruddy-faced bloke that she didn't recognise.

'I've heard you're a lawyer,' he said in a low voice, coming straight to the point.

'Guilty as charged,' she laughed, nervously, wondering where this was going. Lawyers could be pretty unpopular, to say the least. Most people had their own personal tale of woe – of how some solicitor had buggered up the conveyancing on their house – and Maggie had heard her fair share of them.

'My mate could do with some legal advice,' the guy went on, looking around to check that no one was listening.

'Oh God,' sighed Maggie. 'Don't tell me. Drink driving, is it? I'm not surprised. That kind of thing must be rife around here. There's zero public transport and you can't get a taxi for love nor—'

'It's not drink driving,' said the man. 'Rob wouldn't do that.'

'Sorry, mate, you've lost me,' said Maggie, irritated. 'Who's Rob?' Just because everyone knew everyone else around here, it didn't mean that *she* knew them as well. And besides, the quiz would be starting up again in a minute and she hadn't ordered the drinks yet.

'He's over there,' said the man, nodding towards his friend perched on a lone stool at the other end of the bar, well away from the quiz and the crackle of the PA system.

Even though she couldn't quite see his face, Maggie recognised the waistcoat, the shirt and the tanned forearms as belonging to the fit farmer from the other day.

'Let me guess,' she said. 'Is he getting divorced?'

'*Rob*?' The man grinned suddenly. 'Nah... He's not even married.'

'What's the problem, then?' she asked, curious now.

'Well.' He lowered his voice again. 'His farm's been struggling for a while. He took out a loan, secured on the land. But he can't keep up the repayments and now they're hounding him...'

Maggie frowned, not sure what to say.

'I was wondering if you could maybe take a look at the papers for him,' he continued. 'See if there's any way he can get out of it? He can't really afford legal fees and that.'

Maggie snuck a look back over at Rob, sitting on his own, staring at his pint, then she turned back to his mate. 'I'm sorry,' she said. 'What's your name, by the way?'

'It's Jim.'

'Look. I'm sorry, Jim, I can't help you. I don't do that sort of thing.' She couldn't resist a boast. 'I work abroad, you see, specialising in big-ticket international stuff – oil and gas contracts, working with governments – and I'll be off again soon. I won't be here for much longer.'

'Oh. OK. Not to worry, love. It was worth a try,' said Jim. 'You won't say anything, will you? He doesn't want everyone knowing his business.'

'Sure. No worries,' said Maggie, watching him head back over to Rob.

It had been quite cheeky of him to put her on the spot like that, but she still felt bad for some reason. Even though what she'd said had been perfectly true – that it *wasn't* her area of expertise and that she *was* only slumming it in Archdale till normal service resumed.

Another screech of feedback signalled that Australian Pete was back on the mic and she hastily got on with ordering the drinks, before the next round of questions got going.

The Village Idiot

Deep into the second half, three of the quiz teams were almost neck and neck. Cath's Community Café Quizzers were just in the lead, but were struggling to shake off Agatha Quiz-Team from the mobile library – no surprise to Maggie as she knew that the bookworms were certain to be knowledgeable. Not far behind them was another team with the god-awful name Run for your Lifeboats, which Maggie couldn't understand, as she couldn't see the relevance of the RNLI this far inland.

Phil announced that the next round would be the individual round in which just the team captains would have to answer one question each. Conferring with other team members was strictly forbidden and the theme for the questions would be: The Natural World.

Maggie tutted her irritation. The otters lot would bloody love this, it would be right up their creek. And, sure enough, the captain of Otterly Marvellous dispatched his question with ease and was high-fived by his team all round. The captain of Run for your Lifeboats quickly followed suit and the head of Agatha Quiz-Team soon did the same.

Next up, it was Maggie and a whoosh of adrenaline surged through her as Phil got ready to read out her question.

'Right, then!' he declared. 'Cath's Community Café Quizzers!' He lowered his voice to a comedy whisper, 'As you know, this is my wife's team, so I have to be scrupulously fair.'

The crowd laughed and whooped, which was annoying to Maggie, breaking her concentration. '*Get on with it, mate,*' she muttered under her breath.

'The question is…' said Phil, dragging it out. 'Which bird of prey can be of the Montague, the Hen or the Long-Winged variety?'

Bollocks, thought Maggie. *Bloody birds. I know nothing about birds. I'd struggle to identify a sparrow.* Heart pounding, ears buzzing, she saw that Cath and the rest of her team had relaxed back into their seats. In an awful instant, she could tell that all three of them knew the answer. Around the room, the other teams were all whispering and nudging each other. It was clear they all knew it too.

'I'm afraid I'm going to have to push you for an answer,' said Phil, gently, but it was no use. She was searching the files in her brain, but couldn't find any matches. *Bird of prey, bird of prey…* There was only one bird of prey that popped in to her head. She had to go for it. Had to say *something…*

'I really don't know… Falcon?' she offered, in a reedy voice.

The shocked intake of breath from the room was palpable, worse than if she had cursed the queen.

'I'm very sorry,' said Phil. 'The correct answer is actually…' and he pointed the microphone at the audience, like an ageing rock star at a music festival.

'*Harrier!*' they shouted back as one, and Maggie could see that even a gleeful Mrs Winterson had joined in from her seat at the back of the room.

'Harrier?' Maggie was hissing at Cath. '*Harrier?*'

'Harriers are big news round here at the moment,' Cath whispered back. 'Especially hen harriers. They're endangered. They've just started nesting in this area again after a long spell.'

'I've never even heard of a bloody harrier,' said Maggie. 'Apart from the planes…'

'Ah, yes,' said Neil. 'Of course, the "harrier jump jet" is actually named after the bird. And a very useful military aircraft it is too. Very nimble. Capable of vertical take-off and landing.'

Maggie shook her head and shrugged. 'OK. OK. There's no need to go on about it.'

'I'm surprised at you, Maggie,' drawled Tiggy, amused. 'Catherine had assured me that you knew *everything*.'

Really? Cath had been badmouthing her to Tiggy? But Maggie wouldn't – she couldn't afford to – rise to the bait. *She needed to focus.* Phil was announcing the updated scores and, despite her wipe-out in the last round, their team was still first, equal with Agatha Quiz-Team.

The scores stayed that way right until the final round – Myths and Legends – and Maggie was delighted. She knew loads of stuff about Roman, Greek, even Norse, gods and their mythology. *This would be a cinch.*

And it was. None of her other team members got a look in, as she scribbled down all the answers on the sheet.

Soon it was the last question of the night. 'And finally,' said Phil, with something approaching relief in his voice. 'Question sixty: What kind of animal do you turn into if you suffer from lycanthropy?'

Easy! Maggie had written down the answer before Phil could even repeat the question and was showing it to the rest of her team: *Wolf!*

She turned the piece of paper over to shield it from prying eyes and sat back in her seat, but Neil was tugging at her sleeve. 'I think the answer's actually *werewolf*,' he whispered.

'No it's not,' said Maggie. 'It's *wolf*… You *are* a werewolf. But you actually *turn into* a wolf.'

Neil peered at her over his glasses. 'I think you're wrong there,' he insisted. 'I think we should write down werewolf. It's obvious that's what the question's getting at.'

'But it's not technically correct,' said Maggie. 'And I don't really want to lose a crucial point over something like this.'

'I agree with Neil,' said Tiggy. 'I think it's werewolf.'

'Rubbish!' said Maggie. 'You're wrong. Both of you.'

Cath let out a big sigh. 'Look. Can we just leave it as Maggie's written it?' she pleaded. 'I can't be bothered with all this bickering. This is supposed to be fun.'

'I'm not *bickering*,' huffed Maggie, but she took the hint and went over to hand their completed answer sheet to Australian Pete, who was acting as the scorer. Phil announced another break for drinks at the bar, while the final scores were totted up, but it wasn't long before the teams were heading back to their seats, keen to see who had taken the spoils.

Maggie leaned forward in her seat as, in time-honoured tradition, Phil read out the results in reverse order. A hush descended on the room as he reached the top three.

'In a very creditable third place, one rung higher than last year, we have… Run for your Lifeboats! And, I hasten to add, the good news is that Jim from Archdale Garage has donated five litres of screenwash as the third prize.'

'Woo-ooh!' The crowd clapped and whistled as the blushing team members came up to the front and took a bow. But as they headed back to their seats, their captain holding the screenwash aloft, silence fell again.

Phil continued, 'And now, in the runner-up position, we have… Cath's Community Café Quizzers. And I'm pleased to be able to say that Australian Pete has donated two bottles of Muddy Duck for second place. Although I have it on good authority that it tastes worse than the screenwash!'

The whole place was laughing and cheering as they rose to accept their prize – even Tiggy was punching the air – but Maggie was bracing herself to speak. 'Excuse me, Phil,' she piped up, over the hubbub. 'Can I just ask…? How many questions did we get wrong in that last round?'

'Wait a sec.' Phil went over to check with Australian Pete. 'Just the one,' he confirmed. 'The werewolf one.'

'But the correct answer was wolf,' she said.

'Actually, it was werewolf,' said Phil, all apologetic.

'No. But… The question was, what animal do you *turn into*?' She paused. 'And you actually *turn into* a wolf! You see my point?'

'Just leave it, Maggie,' said Cath, trying to drag her away from Phil.

'But it's the principle of the thing,' said Maggie, standing her ground.

'Look. I'm really sorry,' said Phil. 'As I said at the start, we can only accept the answer as it appears on the scorer's card.'

'Even if it's wrong?' said Maggie. 'I think that's a bit unfair, don't you?'

By this point, the excitement in the room had drained away and people were looking at their watches, but she wasn't ready to back down. Eventually, Australian Pete pulled at Phil's elbow, trying to tell him something and, a minute later, Phil was back on the microphone again.

'Ladies and gentlemen. Your attention please. I'm told that, due to one of the questions not being very clear, we're going to accept one of the answers given by Cath's Community Café Quizzers that was previously rejected.'

Maggie nodded her head self-righteously, but the crowd seemed to have lost interest by now, as Pete watched half his customers drifting towards the door.

'So, therefore, we have a tie for first place,' Phil continued, manfully. 'Between Agatha Quiz-Team and Cath's Community Café Quizzers. Lord knows how they're going to divide up the frozen lamb between them.' But his attempt at humour fell flat this time and he handed the mic back to Australian Pete.

Someone turned the lights up as Maggie and the rest of her team trooped back to their seats.

'Happy now?' seethed Cath, under her breath. 'The atmosphere's gone really weird. But, of course, the main thing is that *you* were right and justice was done.'

As they sat back down in silence, Phil came over to their table. 'Can I buy everyone a drink?' he offered, trying to be cheerful. 'What would you all like?'

'Thanks, but I'm fine,' said Maggie. Her mouth was dry as anything, but she didn't want another drink. Maybe the double vodkas had been part of the problem in the first place. Maybe she'd been too aggressive, too domineering. All she really wanted was to leave. Immediately. If not sooner.

'I think I'm going to call it a night,' she said, getting up and heading for the door.

It was only when she was outside in the dark, starless car park that she remembered she had no earthly means of getting home.

Betrayal

They were well into September now, Lauren was back at school, and the summer – such as it was – was definitely over.

Pressing her phone hard to her ear, Maggie was struggling to hear anything over the din of the rain lashing against the conservatory glass. She was trying to call her mother – on her landline, as Joyce didn't believe in mobile phones – but it was just ringing out, with no opportunity to leave a message. Fair enough: it was nearly one o'clock and she was probably out at her lunch club – or maybe the bingo.

A wave of relief washed over her, as she wasn't relishing the prospect of a grilling about her lack of progress with the job search.

She'd actually bitten the bullet and forced herself to apply for some jobs in London after all. Ahhh, London. It was... *complicated.* There were the heady memories of the early nineties: of university, flat-sharing with Cath, starting work, the Cool Britannia years when the capital city had felt like the centre of the universe. And then meeting Andy right on the cusp of the millennium, a few weeks into the mythical year 2000 that Pulp had immortalised in song. It had felt like fate: launching into a new century with her soulmate. *And too good to last, naturally.* She'd had a year or two of being warmed from the inside by simple happiness. Until their happiness was shattered. After that, the two of them had done everything they could to try and get it back. But they couldn't manage it. And then Andy had died. The biggest shock of all. Just like that.

Bad memories or not, if some suitable opportunity came up in the capital, she'd just have to grab it and get on with it. But so far it hadn't and she was starting to feel paranoid. She'd mentally prepared herself for all the rejection emails – had known they'd be par for the course – but she hadn't expected just to be ignored.

Yes, the oil price was still in the doldrums and the market wasn't exactly buoyant, but she had a CV as long as your arm – over twenty years' experience in this country and overseas. You'd think any of the big corporations would be glad to have her on board.

Maybe that was the problem. The more experienced the employee, the higher the salary they could command. Perhaps they feared she'd be too expensive.

Then a spikier little voice spoke up inside her. Maybe it was her age that was working against her. She'd be forty-six next month… What if they just didn't want to hire a soon-to-be menopausal woman?

She was trying hard to push that thought back down where it came from when she heard a dull thud, followed by the scratch of Jazz's paws on the wooden floor, scampering through from the front door. She was carrying *The Peak Gleaner* in her mouth, which she dropped at Maggie's feet.

The front-page headline had excelled itself this time: LEAVES START TO TURN BROWN. *Really?* Was this what passed for news around here? Anyone could see that just by looking out the window.

This always used to be her favourite time of the year – ever since she was a wee girl, when Joyce was getting her ready for school, the only kid in class with a blazer. From the very start, Joyce had drummed into her the importance of studying hard and passing her exams: this was the portal that would lead to the sunny uplands of a place called 'university', where Joyce herself would love to have gone if she'd only had the chance.

Even after school – and uni – became a distant memory, the crispness of the new season always brought with it that start-of-term feeling, the thrill of new lessons just waiting to be learned, the sense of possibility. *Until now.*

Absent-mindedly, she went to the bread bin. She'd just have some toast for lunch. Even though she'd already had toast for breakfast.

She felt nostalgic for the little rituals of the workplace: nipping out of the office for a sandwich, carrying it back in a brown paper bag, munching it hastily at her desk, washing it down with an over-priced coffee in a paper cup…

Then she stopped herself. She needed to get back to the present. To today. *What should she do with herself?*

She considered catching a bus to Sheffield, but quickly ruled it out; that wouldn't be much fun on her own, with no real reason for going into town and no one to meet up with when she got there. Not to mention that the bus stop was miles away and it was still proper pissing it down.

She thought about venturing down into the village in any case. She'd been borrowing an old cagoule of Lauren's – a purple one, as she couldn't abide the dull, murky colours of most outdoor clothing – and she still had Simon's old walking boots, so she could tramp down there without getting *too* soaked if she stuck to the paths and avoided the puddles. But again, what would she do when she got there?

She headed for the lounge instead and cleared a space on the sofa. Cath had been tidying up again and you could hardly see the thing for scatter cushions. Cath had excellent taste, but she tended to overdo it on the 'three Cs' – cushions, candles and coasters. And it was just the same with photographs. Every inch of wall space in every room was covered in bright-eyed photos of the fruits of Cath's labours over the last twenty-odd years: photos of her kids at every age and stage of their lives so far. Or photos of her younger sister, Pippa, and Pippa's kids. It was a bit over the top, to be honest. The house would look fifty per cent better with ten per cent less clutter, Maggie reckoned.

She lay down on the cool, brown leather of the couch and pulled Cath's tartan blanket up over her head. Sorry – her tartan 'throw'. Cath had already told her off for calling it a blanket.

And when Jazz snuck up beside her and nestled in the crook of her knees, she was very glad of the warmth.

* * *

Maggie woke with a start at the sound of the back door slamming shut. It was almost dark outside and she was stiff from snoozing on the sofa.

'Anybody there?' called Cath, as she flipped on the lights. 'Oh, hiya,' she said, when she saw Maggie.

Maggie noticed a fleeting expression pass across Cath's face. Disappointment? Or something else?

'I thought you might be out,' said Cath.

'*Hoped*, you mean?' said Maggie, massaging a new knot in her neck.

'Oh, don't,' said Cath, wearily. 'It's been a long day. I haven't stopped since lunch-time.'

'Lucky you,' said Maggie. 'I'm bored out of my skull.'

'D'you seriously expect me to have any sympathy?' said Cath. 'So, what goodies have you rustled up for our dinner, then? With all this time on your hands.'

'Don't be like that,' whined Maggie. 'I can barely boil an egg, as you well know.'

'I *do* know. You haven't cooked a thing since you've been here,' said Cath. 'You could always learn. It's not rocket science. It's just chopping stuff and measuring stuff out and following a recipe.'

'I know,' said Maggie, stroking Jazz's belly.

'How have you managed to survive all these years?' Cath wasn't letting it lie.

'I dunno,' said Maggie, defensively. 'Soup, sandwiches at my desk, takeaways, dinner with clients… Tell you what, I'll make a deconstructed cottage pie for us tomorrow night. I can manage that.'

'Deconstructed cottage pie?' asked Cath. 'What's that when it's at home?'

'Otherwise known as mince and tatties,' said Maggie, but Cath didn't laugh at her joke.

'You won't be able to make it without any mince,' said Cath. 'There's none in the freezer and the Ocado delivery's not coming till Monday.'

'Well, you could get some tomorrow,' said Maggie. 'From Les the butcher.'

'Why me?' Cath asked, put out. 'Why don't *you* go and get some? You've got the time.'

'I'm avoiding him.'

Cath raised an eyebrow. 'Avoiding him?'

'Yeah. I feel a bit awkward. After that business with the traffic cone.'

'Oh, come on, Maggie. That was months ago.'

'Months? I feel like I've been here for *years*,' groaned Maggie.

'No one's forcing you to stay…'

'I know, I know. Sorry. I'll go down to the butcher's tomorrow and buy a few things.'

'Great. Thanks.'

'I could make some spag bol as well and we could freeze it,' said Maggie. 'And I promise to start pulling my weight a bit more on the cooking side of things. And with the chores and stuff. It's just… It's quite hard to motivate yourself… when you've got no structure to your day.'

'I know,' said Cath. 'It can't be easy for you. Talking of which, any news on the job front?'

'Not a sausage,' said Maggie. 'But I've got an idea,' she said, sitting up straight.

'Oh yeah?' said Cath, picking up an empty mug from the coffee table.

'It's my birthday at the start of next month.'

'Sixth of October. How could I forget?'

'And I was thinking… We could go away for a girls' weekend. Hit the fleshpots of Dublin. See if it's still standing after the last time we were there?'

'Ah, yes. My hen night…' Cath smiled at the memory.

'Well?' said Maggie, hugging a cushion excitedly. 'What do you say?'

'October the sixth?' Cath carefully pushed her hair behind her ears. She seemed less keen all of a sudden.

'Yeah,' said Maggie. 'We could fly over there on Friday the fifth, come back on the Monday.'

'Erm, I don't think that's going to work.'

'Why not? You can get someone to cover for you at the café? Lauren, maybe? Or Tiggy?'

'I can't,' said Cath, avoiding eye contact. 'I'm already going away that weekend. For the whole week, actually.'

'Are you?' said Maggie, curious. 'Where you off to?'

'I'm going on a wellness retreat. To a little village in southern Crete.' She paused. 'With Tiggy.'

'Oh,' said Maggie. 'You didn't say anything.'

'We only booked it a couple of weeks ago. It was quite, er, spur-of-the-moment.'

'A couple of weeks ago?'

'Sorry for not mentioning it.' Cath was flustered now. 'I assumed you wouldn't be interested. I know all that new age stuff isn't really your thing.'

'No. No, it's not,' admitted Maggie. 'Crete's nice, though. And it'll still be nice and warm.'

'Have you been?'

'Yeah. Don't you remember? Me and Andy went there for our honeymoon. To Sissi. In the north east of the island.' She had a sudden stab of memory – of how, every morning, the sun had crept up behind the hills, bleaching the sea silver. 'Gorgeous, it was…'

'And anyway,' said Cath, hurriedly. 'It'll be good for you to have some time and space on your own. With me out of your hair.'

'Yes… I suppose it will,' said Maggie, although she couldn't help feeling that more time alone might be the last thing she needed.

Cath chewed her lip for a moment. 'Listen. Could I ask you… Would you mind keeping an eye on Lauren for me while I'm away? She's dead sensible and she can look after herself, but it would be hugely reassuring to know that you were around too.'

'Sure,' said Maggie. 'It'll be good practice for her.'

'Practice?'

'Yeah,' said Maggie. 'For when she goes away to uni next year.'

'Oh. Yes. I suppose it will. Thanks.'

'No worries,' said Maggie, trying her best to sound noble. 'You and Tiggy can go off and enjoy yourselves. We'll be just fine.'

Happy Birthday to Me

It wasn't like Maggie saw much of Cath these days anyway – she was always haring around all over the place doing something or other – but Maggie had been dreading her going away on this trip to Crete.

And when Tiggy had come to pick Cath up to go to the airport this morning, waving the two of them off had been difficult. Maggie knew she was being petty, and there was no way she would have admitted it out loud, but she couldn't help feeling a bit, well, betrayed by Cath. True, she wouldn't have wanted to go on some daft *wellness* retreat and, no, she certainly wouldn't have wanted to spend a week with Tiggy. *God, no!* But it would have been nice to have been asked, even if just for the pleasure of refusing. Actually, she wasn't even sure that she *would* have refused. It would've been nice just to have a holiday. A holiday from what, though? She hadn't actually worked since June. But she would still have benefitted from a clean break – after losing her job and all the drama that had surrounded it.

Still, on the plus side, she was looking forward to spending some more time with Lauren and getting to know her a bit better: she'd usually left for school in the mornings before Maggie had even got up, and still seemed to be spending most of her evenings and weekends over at Dan's place.

What Maggie wasn't looking forward to was spending this evening all on her own: not only was it Saturday night, it was also her birthday. *What a loser.*

She wondered what time it would be in Crete now. It was two hours ahead of the UK, so it would be just after seven o'clock. Cath and Tiggy would be swanning around their fishing village – eating fresh feta salad and quaffing the local wines in the early evening sun – while here she was, schlepping up a sodden footpath in the rain. Rain that was running down the front of her hood into her eyes now, blinding her. She wiped it away and saw the open gates of Cath's drive up ahead, steeled herself for one last push up to the house.

She'd taken Jazz out for a walk on their usual circuit up through Rob's fields, about three miles in total. She'd hoped she might cross paths with him and stop for a bit of a chat. But, once again, they hadn't seen hide nor hair of him. Hadn't seen anyone, in fact. And then they'd been ambushed by a sudden downpour. To use one of Joyce's favourite words, the two of them were completely '*drookit*'.

Once inside the house, Maggie peeled off her cagoule and her jeans and hung them over the polished wood of the banister. Then she went to find a towel for Jazz – not before the daft dog had given herself a good shake, spraying the wallpaper with thick, dark spots. All that stuff about nature being 'red in tooth and claw'? What a load of bollocks that was. Nature was actually a greeny-brown sludge: a crappy combination of wet mud and sheep shit.

The rumbling of the boiler told her that the heating had come on, but the place would take a long time to heat up. Comfortable as it was, the house was also very draughty – one of the downsides of sash windows and polished floorboards – and she dreaded to think how high the bills must be. When Cath came back, she'd have to broach the subject of contributing something towards the household expenses; it wasn't fair on Cath to have to pay for everything.

Maggie headed back into the kitchen where it was warmer, and she wondered if it would be so wrong to thaw out her bum by sitting on the Aga?

And then a thought struck her. She checked in the fridge, Cath's cupboards and even the pantry to find her worst fears were confirmed: there was no wine left in the house.

She wasn't sure how this had happened, but it felt like a catastrophe. It was bad enough having to sit at home by yourself on your birthday, but to do it without a drop to drink would be sad beyond belief.

There was only one thing for it. She'd have to force herself to go out again and buy some booze. She'd have to go down to the pub.

* * *

The walk down into the village – long enough in the daytime – felt twice as long this evening. It was still a few weeks till the clocks went back, but the nights were drawing in at an alarming rate and it seemed to have got very dark very quickly. She'd brought a torch from Cath's to guide her – along with Jazz for moral support – but the watery beam of light was hardly making a dent in the pitch-black and only made her surroundings look even more creepy.

Her feet were sinking into the spongy path, every snapping twig made her jump and she had to keep telling herself to breathe. Every few paces, Jazz would stiffen and the lead would go taut, followed by an eerie rustling in the fallen leaves – nocturnal creatures making their escape.

Above her head, the wind rasped through the half-bare branches, but she noticed more the sounds that *weren't* there – the ones she always used to moan about. The cracks and bangs of fireworks which, in the city, would start up weeks before Bonfire Night and keep going long after it was over. Or the wailing of the police and ambulance sirens that used to keep her awake at night, but which were strangely reassuring, reminding you that help was out there, somewhere, if you needed it.

She was talking to herself for comfort – a running commentary on their slow progress down the valley – but her heart stopped when a big grey thing with a huge backside emerged from somewhere into the torch beam, lumbering from side to side across their path. *Jesus,* she thought. *What the hell was that?* But even Jazz didn't seem keen to investigate.

Keep going, keep going, she told herself, planting one foot in front of the other, focusing straight ahead, as another line of sweat rolled down her back.

A few minutes more and she finally swapped the squelching mud for the solid tarmac of the road into the village. *Such a relief.* And then there was the cheering sight of The Farmer's Arms glowing orange in the distance, followed by the ripe smell of roaring-fire-and-wet-dog as she pushed inside the door.

Digging in the pocket of her cagoule, she found a fiver and went straight to the bar. Australian Pete looked up from his paper and seemed pleased to see her, probably because there was no other customer in sight: everyone else in the village had clearly had the good sense to stay home and watch *Strictly Come Dancing.*

Thirsty from the walk, Maggie ordered a pint of lager shandy and, while Pete's back was turned, she wondered if she'd be expected to take a stool and make stilted conversation with him or whether she could just go and sit at one of the tables?

She decided to be sociable and take a stool, just as Rob the farmer emerged from the bathroom at the other end of the room and ambled up to her.

'You're sitting in my spot,' he complained, gruffly.

'Am I? My apologies,' said Maggie and jumped down, in no mood to argue for once. She'd move to the table by the fire.

'Sorry. I'm only kidding,' Rob called after her. 'The place is empty. It was just a joke.'

'Ah… OK,' she called back, feeling foolish now.

He came over to her table with his pint and bent down to stroke Jazz. 'Mind if I join you?' he asked.

'Sure,' said Maggie, fixing her fringe. 'No problem.'

'Is everything OK?' he said, sitting down next to her. 'It's just, you seem a little bit… on edge.'

'Oh, I'm fine, I'm fine,' she said. 'Just a bit… freaked out.'

'Freaked out?'

'Yeah. I've just walked down the hill into Archdale.'

'You *walked* down here?' He sounded concerned for her.

'Yeah, with a useless torch that's running out of battery, and then this massive creature just ran out in front of us and—'

'A *massive creature*?' he asked, eyes twinkling with amusement.

'Yep,' she insisted. 'Well it had a massive arse at any rate. It was swinging from side to side. Like this.' She stood up and did an impression of it. 'Bloody terrifying it was…'

Rob starting laughing. 'I take it you've never seen a badger before, then?'

'*A badger*? Really? Is *that* what it was? I thought badgers were cute little black and white things. Slightly bigger than, I dunno, a big rat…'

He laughed again. 'Can I get you a whisky or something? I think you might be in shock.'

'Haha,' she picked up a beer mat and flicked it at him. 'No thanks. I'm the only Scottish person in the history of the world who can't bear the stuff.'

'Something else, then?'

'OK. I'll have another shandy. Seeing as it's my birthday.'

'Is it? Seriously?' said Rob.

'Don't ask me how old I am…'

'OK. Well, happy birthday!' said Rob, getting up and heading to the bar.

Maggie took the opportunity to remove her damp cagoule – and realised, to her horror, that she was wearing the same unflattering fleece as the first time they'd met.

'How are things with the farm?' she asked, when he'd sat back down next to her with their drinks and a bag of pork scratchings for Jazz. 'Still getting a hard time from the wankers at that loan company?'

'Yup,' said Rob, frowning into his pint of bitter. He looked up suddenly. 'Hang on. How do you know about that?'

'Your mate told me. Jim. The, er, last time I was in here.' She thought it best to avoid mentioning the quiz.

'Jim? Did he now?' Rob shook his head. 'I think I might need to have a word…'

'Oh, please don't be annoyed with him,' said Maggie. 'He was only trying to help you. He'd heard I was a lawyer. He thought I might be able to do something.'

'Look. I'm sorry. I didn't ask him to…'

'Don't worry. I can see that. And anyway, it was no problem. I told him I wouldn't be any use to you anyway. I'm not that kind of lawyer.'

'What kind of lawyer *are* you, then?' he asked, taking a sip of his pint.

'An unemployed one,' she replied. 'For now.' She tossed a pork scratching in Jazz's direction. 'I'm looking for a new job. In the oil and gas sector.'

'Ah,' said Rob. 'Well. I hope something comes up soon.'

'Me too. I'm going stir-crazy at the moment. And Cath's patience is starting to wear a bit thin…'

'Cath's your mate, isn't she? You're staying up at Higher House, right?'

'Yep,' said Maggie, pleased that he'd remembered from the last time. 'I don't suppose you have the time to go stir-crazy,' she said, pinching a pork scratching for herself. 'In your line of work.'

'You'd be surprised,' Rob sighed, running his hand through his hair. 'Farming wouldn't necessarily have been my choice, but here I am…'

'Really? What would you have done instead?'

'Now you're asking.' He looked up at the ceiling. 'I think I'd like to have gone to university and done a history degree. I'm interested in the Civil War, that sort of period.'

'The Civil War? Fascinating, isn't it? How its effects are still felt in the US to this day.'

'Er, no. I meant the *English* Civil War,' he clarified. 'Cromwell and that. Cavaliers and Roundheads.'

'Oh,' she froze for comic effect and pretended to edge away from him. 'You're not into dressing up and re-enacting battles or anything like that, are you?'

'Nah,' laughed Rob. 'What do you take me for?' He took another swig of his pint. 'I think I'd like to have been a teacher – in a parallel universe. But my future was already mapped out for me.'

Maggie felt a pang of something – regret – on behalf of this guy she hardly knew.

'Or I'd have liked to do what Jim does,' he went on. 'He doesn't just run the garage in the village – he's also a part-time fireman.'

'Is he?'

'Yeah. There are no full-time firemen out here in the sticks. It's not busy enough. They're all part-timers.'

'So why don't you, then? Become a fireman, I mean?'

'I can't, really. The fire station's over in Backdale, too far away from the farm. I wouldn't be able to get there in time for the shouts.'

'Still,' said Maggie. 'I imagine farming must be hard enough work on its own.'

'I don't mind hard work. But, yes, it's hard to make a living. And my parents are depending on me.' He paused. 'I'm an only child, y'see.'

'I feel your pain,' said Maggie. 'So am I.'

'Really?' he said, and clinked his glass against hers.

'So what's the story, then?' she asked, clinking him back. 'With this loan company?'

Rob's shoulders sank down a couple of inches, as he spread his knees and stared down at the floor. 'I applied for the money online. It was dead easy… Too easy…'

'What's the name of the company?' she probed.

'AP Finance it's called.'

'I've never heard of them,' she said, shaking her head. 'How much did you borrow?'

'A hundred and twenty thousand. I took it out back in February to pay for some urgent repairs.'

'Interest rate?'

'Forty-two per cent.'

'You what?!' Maggie whistled.

'I only saw it as a bridging loan, really. Just for twelve months. They said they'd find me a new mortgage at the end of it on easier terms. But I can't even afford the interest payments. I'm worried I'm going to lose it altogether.'

'Couldn't you contact them and come to some sort of arrangement?' Maggie suggested. 'Reschedule the payments? Most reputable lenders will agree to that sort of thing.'

'I've tried, but I can't get hold of them. They've got a phone number on their website, but they never respond.'

'How did you arrange it all, then? Did you have a lawyer acting for you at the time?'

'Nah. The forms I filled in had a box on them – a warning to take legal advice – but I couldn't afford to.'

Maggie sighed a big sigh. 'You know, I wish I could help you out but, as I said to Jim, it's not really my area of expertise.'

'No worries,' said Rob. 'I wouldn't even expect it.'

'And anyway,' she continued, aware how feeble this would sound. 'To repossess it, they'd need to get a court order from the High Court. So, if you wanted to challenge it, you'd need a barrister. Whereas I'm a solicitor. I wouldn't be able to appear for you in court or anything.'

'*Repossess it?*' repeated Rob, the words sinking in.

'But, of course, you don't want to get to that stage,' said Maggie, quickly. 'As I said, your best bet is to try and get in touch with them again. Try and sort something out.' But she barely believed it herself: from what he had already said, this company didn't exactly fill her with confidence.

Rob drained his pint and looked at his watch. 'Unfortunately, I'm driving so I'd better not have any more to drink.' He paused for a moment. 'Can I offer you a lift home, by the way? In case the *big bad badger's* lying in wait?'

Maggie flushed at his teasing. 'That'd be great. Thanks.'

'Well, now,' said Rob. 'I know where you live. But I don't actually know what your name is.'

'It's Maggie,' she smiled, sticking her hand out to shake his. 'Maggie Macbeth.'

'Pleased to meet you again, Maggie,' he said, grasping it with his sinewy one. 'I'm Rob... Rob Elliott.'

'Actually, Rob, would you mind waiting there one moment?' she asked, passing him Jazz's lead to hold, and heading back up to the bar. Having endured the ordeal of walking down here in the dark, there was no way she was going back up to the house without wine. Even sub-standard wine.

Australian Pete came over to serve her. 'Did I hear you say you were looking for a job?' he asked, lowering his voice. 'It's just... I'm looking to take on a part-time barmaid. It's only minimum wage, mind you, but it's better than nothing.'

Insomnia

Not wishing to be a burden, Maggie told Rob it was fine just to drop her off at the bottom of Cath's driveway. Rather sweetly, he'd refused: he'd insisted on driving her right up to the door – and waiting until she was safely inside – before driving off.

Only she didn't *feel* very safe.

She'd lived on her own for years – ever since Andy had died – and had had to get used to it. This was different, though. The walk down to Archdale in the dark had showed her how vulnerable she was, out here, in the middle of nowhere – a sitting target for any passing psycho. And Jazz was very sweet and all that, but she was no guard dog.

Maggie dragged the heavy bolt across the top of the back door and glanced at the kitchen clock. Only nine-thirty. The earliest she'd ever come home from the pub in her life.

She took the bottle of wine out of the bag Pete had given her, but she'd already decided not to open it. She'd just go straight to bed – after checking that all the doors and windows were locked. Then she'd make a cup of tea to take upstairs. One of Cath's fruity ones. Something with no caffeine in it.

She was standing by the kettle, waiting for it to boil, when a face in a black beanie hat appeared in the window. She gave a yelp and her stomach turned over, until she recognised it.

'Lauren! For God's sake!'

'Sorry,' sniggered Lauren, as Maggie unbolted the door again to let her in. 'I didn't mean to scare you.'

'*Scare me?* You nearly gave me a bloody heart attack. I wasn't expecting you back till tomorrow.'

Lauren shrugged. 'I was at a party, but I asked Dan to bring me home… He dropped me off down at the gate.'

She bobbed down to give Jazz a hug and Maggie's anxiety dissolved to relief that she wouldn't have to spend the night in the house on her own. 'Would you like a hot drink?' she asked. 'The kettle's just boiled.'

'No thanks,' said Lauren. 'I'm fine.' Although something about the way she buried her nose in the dog's neck told Maggie she was anything but.

Maggie handed her a glass of water anyway and was surprised when Lauren pulled out a chair and sat herself down at the table: normally she'd have been straight upstairs and listening to that dreary Ed Sheeran by now. Or maybe Adele.

Maggie was out of her depth now. She wanted to interrogate her – find out what was wrong – but something told her this would be a mistake. Instead, she sat down as well and waited for her to say something.

Lauren picked up Maggie's one birthday card from the table in front of her, the one Cath had given her before she left. 'Is it your birthday, Maggie? You never said. I'd have got you a card or something.'

'Don't worry.' Maggie smiled. 'I'm not big on birthdays.'

Lauren rolled her eyes. 'I wish I could say the same for Freya.'

'Who?'

'My best mate,' said Lauren. 'The one having the party. At least, I *thought* she was my mate.'

'Have you two had a row?' asked Maggie. 'Me and your mum… We used to argue all the time at uni.'

'Really?' said Lauren. 'I can't imagine Mum arguing with anyone. She never even argues with Dad. Just keeps up these long, passive-aggressive silences. Even though he's a cheating twat.'

'Lauren!' Maggie chided her. 'You shouldn't—'

'*What*?' said Lauren, indignantly. 'I've heard you say much worse!'

'Fair enough,' said Maggie. 'And he may indeed be a cheating twat, but he's still your dad.'

'Hmm,' said Lauren, unimpressed. 'So, what did you and Mum used to argue about, then? Boys?'

'God, no!' said Maggie. 'It was mainly just… margarine. Stuff like that.'

'*Margarine*?' echoed Lauren. 'Mum used to eat *margarine*?'

'Not if I forgot to buy it,' said Maggie. 'And I usually *did* forget. Same as I usually forgot to clean the bathroom. *Plus ça change…*'

Lauren smiled, but the smile soon faded. 'This is a bit more serious than margarine, Maggie.'

The expression on her face was so earnest that Maggie had to swallow a laugh. She could well remember how life-and-death everything had seemed as a teenager and how none of it was any laughing matter. 'So,' Maggie said, after a moment. 'You've had a big row with this Freya at her birthday party – and that's why you're sitting home at this time on a Saturday night talking to me. Right?'

'It's not just that,' said Lauren, stroking Jazz's head. 'She's giving me a load of grief at school as well.'

Maggie hesitated rather than diving straight in. 'Sometimes these things happen,' she said, kindly. 'It usually blows over in a couple of days.'

'I dunno,' said Lauren with a big sigh. 'It's been a few weeks. I'm getting that I don't really want to go to school anymore…'

'Right, that's it!' said Maggie, out of her seat and pacing now. 'You shouldn't have to feel like this, you know. Your studies are the most important thing. Do you want me to go up there and have a word with the headmistress?'

'Head*master*,' Lauren corrected her. 'He's quite scary, actually.'

'I don't care if he's Donald bloody Trump, I'll go over there and give him—'

'No, Maggie,' said Lauren, horrified. 'It's bad enough as it is. I don't want to make things even worse.'

Maggie sat back down. She looked Lauren in the eye. 'Listen, love. You need to do something about this… Maybe you should start by telling your mum? It's usually best to talk about these things.'

'*Mum*?! No way!' Lauren gave a hollow laugh. 'Mum's the very last person I can tell.'

'Look,' said Maggie. 'I get it. Your mum's had a rough time of it lately and you don't want to worry her, but—'

'No. It's not just that,' said Lauren, standing up and grabbing her glass of water. 'Thanks a lot for the chat. I'm just *sooo* tired now. I need my bed. See you in the morning.'

'See you in the morning,' said Maggie, looking down at Jazz, curled up by her feet on the terracotta tiles. *Friends, eh?* She was beginning to understand why dogs were so popular.

* * *

Maggie lay there in the spare room, wide awake in the darkness. The dog wasn't strictly allowed on the beds, but she'd decided to relax the rule in Cath's absence and use Jazz as a hot water bottle to keep from shivering.

Ed Sheeran was creeping out from under Lauren's door now and, my God, the ballads were bad enough but this was off the charts – some cod-Irish rubbish about a 'Galway Girl' he'd copped off with.

Still, it could've been a lot worse. It could've been James Blunt's latest offering, which seemed to be Cath's soundtrack of choice these days when she was feeling pissed off. Why couldn't she like sad music that was half-decent – Leonard Cohen, Joni Mitchell, something like that? She'd always had dodgy taste in music, mind you, even at uni when the most cutting edge CD she owned had been Cat Stevens's Greatest Hits.

Maggie turned over on to her stomach and pulled her pillow over her head, tucking it tight around her ears. Eventually, the 'music' stopped, but she was still no closer to dropping off. If anything, she was more awake than when she'd started, her mind spinning off in circles, bringing a cold sweat. It was going over and over loads of old stuff that had happened in the past… ancient history… long-forgotten incidents and arguments, mistakes, embarrassments from years ago. Long-forgotten until now, that is. Why did the brain do this – offering up unpleasant thoughts like a cat presenting its owner with a dead rat? What purpose could it possibly serve?

She thought about reading her book for a bit – Kafka's *Metamorphosis* – but it wasn't really grabbing her. And the subject matter – a bloke who turns into a giant insect – wasn't exactly conducive to a good night's sleep.

She knew she should avoid checking the time – that it would only put more pressure on her – but she couldn't resist.

She grabbed her phone from the bedside table.

Half past three! The long, dark night of the soul…

Lying here was doing her no good. She'd get up and make another cup of Cath's tea. Maybe she'd try the camomile this time: she'd read that was meant to be relaxing.

Pulling on the fleece-of-doom over her T-shirt, she padded downstairs to the kitchen. Her laptop, she noticed, was still winking and blinking away on the table. She knew that she should leave well alone – that blue light from a screen was another enemy of a good night's sleep – but she couldn't stop herself from sitting down and firing up Google. There was something she had to do…

Maggie typed the name of Rob's loan company – AP Finance Ltd – into the box and hit 'search'. There wasn't much information about the company itself – hardly surprising as it seemed to be registered in the Regis Islands, a well-known tax haven. 'AP Finance' was only its trading name – its full name was Antigone Property Finance Limited. *Antigone?* That rang a bell – it was someone from the Greek myths, wasn't it? She looked it up on Wikipedia and found her answer: 'In Greek mythology, Antigone (pronounced Ann-tig-oh-nee) was the daughter of King Oedipus and his own mother.' *Oh. Yeuch,* she thought, slightly nauseous. What a weird name for a finance company…

She went back to her original search. Only one director of the company was listed – a 'Mr D Nobbs'. And the only address given was a PO Box number on one of the islands. It didn't amount to much at all. Not that this was unusual: this was exactly the sort of thing she used to come across in her work all the time – overseas companies being used for their secrecy, to get around the tax laws and all the rest of it.

She expected the rest of the search results to be a duplication of what she'd just read, but had a quick look at them anyway. She was intrigued to discover that they were all, well, complaints basically. People complaining about AP Finance.

She scrolled down through pages and pages of this stuff, until her eyes started to throb. *Well, well, well.* It seemed that this company had been pretty busy over the last few years: busy stitching up struggling farmers all over the country, from the Highlands of Scotland right down as far as Devon. Tying them into extortionate loan arrangements and then turfing them out and selling their land when they couldn't make the repayments.

What a bunch of bastards.

Biting Point

She was supposed to be reviewing the draft contract for the construction of the gas pipeline in Hanoi, but the sun was bouncing off her computer screen, making it impossible.

She got up to adjust the blinds, glad of the noisy air-con that was pumping cool blasts into her office at regular intervals. It had already been eighty-four degrees when she'd left her apartment at eight o'clock this morning: God alone knew what the outside temperature would be by now. And the heat wasn't even the main problem – that was the ninety per cent relative humidity that made your shirt stick to your skin within seconds of leaving the house.

She lingered by the window for a while, round like a porthole on a ship. From this spot on the twenty-eighth floor of Jardine Tower – the shiny skyscraper where she spent most of her waking hours – you could watch the comings and goings of Hong Kong harbour down below. It was hypnotic after a while; the old-fashioned wooden pleasure junks, the tiny fishing boats and the iconic green-and-white Star Ferries criss-crossing the churning waters between here and Kowloon with their human cargo of commuters, shoppers and tourists. She always had a chuckle to herself when she remembered that 'Hong Kong' actually meant 'fragrant harbour' – usually when she stepped outside the building on a broiling day like this, straight into the dried-fish-and-diesel air that got stuck in your nose.

Among the ex-pat bankers, businessmen and lawyers of her social set, it was *de rigueur* to proclaim loudly their distaste for the stink of the city that was providing them with a very lucrative living. But, for Maggie, it was her favourite smell in the world. It represented industry, commerce, hard work – the sheer energy of the place.

Hong Kong was a city of survivors. Many of its people had come here to escape Mao's revolution in China; some of them had even swum here. Literally.

Whenever she touched down at Chek Lap Kok Airport after a short break or a business trip, she felt like she was home. In her more morbid moments, she mused that, when the time came, she'd like her ashes to be scattered in the harbour. It wasn't like she could make the water any filthier than it already was…!

Beep, beep. Beep, beep. The shrill screech of the phone echoed around her office, dragging her back to her desk. She peered at the caller display and slumped down into her chair. It was Dalton. Her boss. Bollocks, she thought. His office was only down the corridor – he could just have walked round to speak to her. Why did he always have to ring her – have to 'summon' her like this? Did she have to pick it up? Things had been so awkward between them since the 'incident' in Dubai.

Beep, beep. Beep, beep. He knew she was there. She had no choice but to answer it…

'Hi-ya!' said a cheery northern voice down the line. 'It's Val here. Val Bloom. Is that Maggie?'

'Val?' said Maggie, coming back to consciousness with a jolt.

'Yes. Driving-instructor-Val! Just checking we're still on for this morning? I don't normally work Sundays, you see.'

'Oh, hi Val,' said Maggie, sitting bolt upright in her single bed. She'd booked the bloody lesson so long ago, she'd forgotten all about it. 'Yes. Still on. Yes. Of course.'

'OK, then. I'll see you in half an hour,' said Val and hung up.

First sign of madness, shivered Maggie, shaking her head. *Can't tell where dreams end and reality begins...*

Then she threw back the duvet and streaked across the landing to the shower.

* * *

Maggie hadn't opened her mouth since the lesson had begun. She hadn't had a chance. From the minute Val had arrived at Cath's in her pink Nissan Micra, she'd been wittering on. And on. She was very sorry that Maggie had had to wait such a long time for her first lesson, but then she always had such a long waiting list of new clients, and she didn't normally work on Sundays, but she'd gone to a lot of trouble to fit her in, even if it *did* mean that she was missing *The Archers* omnibus. This non-stop patter – and Val's sugary sweet perfume – were filling the tiny car, hurting Maggie's head.

And the lesson hadn't got off to the best of starts. Maggie had bust a gut to be ready on time, but then Val had ended up being ten minutes late and if there was one thing Maggie couldn't stand, it was people being late. And then it had been a bit awkward when she'd come out of the house and tried to get into the car on the driver's side – and Val had had to tell her that she wouldn't be taking the wheel straightaway. Val would actually be driving her to 'a quiet spot on the outskirts of the village', even though it was hard to believe that a quieter spot actually existed.

As they drove along the valley bottom to the place in question, Val's incessant stream of babble showed no signs of letting up, as Maggie cast a furtive glance across at her. She guessed that she was probably around mid-to-late fifties, although her stiff, mousey hairstyle made her look much older. She was one of those women who was as wide as she was tall but, in fairness, she did have quite a pleasant, smiley face.

And as Val piously demonstrated the correct placement of hands on the steering wheel – with her pudgy hands in the quarter-to-three position – Maggie got a good look at her full-on manicure. Her nails had been stencilled with little pink and gold flowers, with tiny crystals in the middle that caught the low October sun dipping in through the windscreen. *How ridiculous!* Why would a grown woman want to decorate the ends of their fingers like that? Maggie couldn't fathom it.

She looked at her watch: by the time they reached this mythical 'quiet spot', the one-hour allocated for the lesson would be over. Maggie was about to point this out when Val swung the car into an old, unmarked lay-by.

They got out of the vehicle to swap seats and, watching Val waddle around to the passenger side, Maggie reflected that driving seemed to come more naturally to her than walking.

'Right, then,' Val announced, securing her seatbelt in exaggerated fashion. 'To move the car forwards… If you could just depress the accelerator with your right foot, while at the same time lifting your left foot off the clutch… Feeling for the biting point…'

'One question before I start,' said Maggie, raising her hand.

'No problem,' said Val. 'I always encourage my clients to ask any questions they've got. Fire away.'

'OK,' said Maggie. 'What's the clutch?'

'I told you,' said Val. 'It's that pedal, there. The one on the left.'

'No. I mean. What *is* it? What does it actually *do*?'

Val narrowed her eyes. 'Come again?'

'What actually *is* a clutch?' asked Maggie. The question was simple enough. 'I need to understand what it is, how it works, so I can understand what I'm doing when I press it.'

Val's mouth flapped open and closed again.

'Surely you've been asked that before?' said Maggie.

'No.' Val shook her head. 'No one's actually asked me that in ten years.'

'Seriously?'

'Seriously,' repeated Val. 'I tell you what. Why don't you just try doing what I say? Move your feet on the pedals until you reach the biting point and then we'll move off nice and smooth.'

'OK,' said Maggie, doubtfully. 'Here goes.' She pressed down with her right foot, but it was far too hard and the engine started revving wildly.

Val had clearly been here before. Unfazed, she explained in staccato terms for a third time what Maggie needed to do and the car miraculously started moving. A frisson of excitement spread through Maggie, which turned to fear when told she was going to have to use the clutch again to change gear.

Grinding her teeth as she gained speed along the quiet country lane, her next worry was how she was going to get the thing to stop, but Val seemed to read her mind. She instructed her to pull in and apply the brake and, as they came to a sharp halt, she placed a manicured hand on Maggie's arm. 'I'm afraid we're going to have to leave it there for today. Time's up.'

Maggie breathed out. 'Oh,' she said, half-disappointed, half-relieved.

'I suggest you book in for a two-hour lesson next week,' said Val. 'Although, actually, I've just remembered, I can't do next week, I've got a couple of clients doing their test and they'll want some extra lessons beforehand.' She leaned flat across Maggie's thighs, groping for her diary in the pocket of the driver's door. 'So could you do the week after?' she asked, sitting up again and rifling through the pages. 'Sunday again?'

'Yep,' said Maggie. 'I've got nothing on.' And they got out and swapped seats again, before setting off again in the direction of Cath's.

Val seemed to have talked herself out by now and Maggie was grateful for the peace and quiet. She stared out the window to where the rocky edges of the peaks met the bruised sky above. 'How long does it normally take people to pass their test?' she wondered aloud.

'Well,' said Val, choosing her words carefully. 'It varies. Three months, sometimes six…'

'As long as that?' spluttered Maggie. 'Bloody hell. I thought it would only take a few weeks.'

'Of course,' said Val, staring straight ahead. 'For some clients, it can take much longer…'

'Hmm,' said Maggie, yawning. Her crappy night's sleep had caught up with her now and she was keen to get back to the couch.

Val reached the gates of Higher House, turned right up the driveway and came to a stop outside the back door. 'So,' she said, as the engine turned over. 'I'll see you again two weeks today.'

'Fine,' said Maggie.

'And, as I say… I don't normally work Sundays, but I'm happy to go the extra mile to fit you in.'

Maggie, irritated by her martyr act, swung round to face her. 'Can I ask? What's the big deal about working on a Sunday? Are you religious or something? I used to have to work on Sundays all the time. Saturdays too, for that matter.'

If Val had sensed her annoyance, she was showing no sign of it. 'Oh,' she replied. 'Did you work in catering or something?'

Maggie took a deep breath. 'Not exactly,' she said. 'I'm an international business lawyer.'

'Really?' said Val, looking her up and down.

'Yes. Really,' said Maggie, and got out of the car. Once inside the kitchen, she looked down at her scruffy attire. No wonder the woman had been sceptical – she looked like a bag lady.

Maggie sighed and dumped her handbag on the table next to a bunch of twigs. Although, on closer inspection, it was a bunch of twigs that had been crafted into a heart shape and tied at the base with a shiny, blue ribbon. It was sitting on top of a homemade card, which she opened. *Happy Birthday, Maggie!* it said. *This is to brighten up your room a bit. And also to say thanks for the chat. P.S. I've gone back over to Dan's place for a few days. P.P.S. Are you OK to look after Jazz…? Lauren xxx*

Awww, Maggie smiled to herself. That was sweet of her. And the decoration looked great actually, really professional: Lauren had obviously inherited Cath's creative genes.

She put down the card and went to rummage in the fridge for something to eat. And tried to forget she'd be on her own tonight – and most of the week, by the look of things – until Cath came back from Greece.

The Wanderers Return

Maggie spent most of the next five days in her usual spot – dozing on the couch under the tartan throw, Jazz curled up beside her – and today was no different. It was only three in the afternoon, but the sky was glowering and a repeat of *Midsomer Murders* was burbling away on the telly in the corner of the lounge. Was this a glimpse of things to come – a preview of her future life as an old age pensioner?

Not necessarily. Her mother, Joyce, was well into her seventies and wasn't the sort to be sitting around watching TV all afternoon. She was more likely to be out doing something at one of her groups. At last count, she was in a reading group, a writing group and another mysterious group called 'Staying Alive', whose tentacles extended into all sorts of things – from aromatherapy to Zumba. Joyce had a better social life than *she* did.

Which reminded her: she should really try calling her again because the longer she left it, the more awkward it was becoming. She'd half-thought that Joyce might have phoned her on her birthday, but hadn't exactly been surprised when no call came: she'd always been as stubborn as hell and was never going to blink first in their Mexican stand-off. No. It would be up to Maggie to swallow what was left of her pride and make the first move.

Midsomer Murders had just cut to an advert for funeral insurance when she felt Jazz stiffen, followed by the deep rumble of a car pulling up outside. *Hurrah!* Her stomach lifted. She'd been so looking forward to Cath coming home it was actually embarrassing, although she hadn't expected her back quite so early – the roads from Manchester Airport must have been pretty quiet.

She leapt to her feet to go and put the kettle on, but threw herself back down on the couch when she heard Tiggy's whiny tones and realised that she was coming into the house with her. *Really?* They'd been together the whole week, for God's sake. Why couldn't she just drop Cath off, say cheerio and then piss off?

Maggie lay there pulling at her fringe, regretting having attempted to trim it herself, as Cath came into the room with Tiggy close behind.

Cath wrinkled up her nose. 'It smells a bit stale in here,' she said. 'It needs some air.' And she threw the window open, despite the chill outside.

'How was the holiday?' asked Maggie from her berth on the couch.

'It was fabulous,' said Tiggy, butting in before Cath had a chance to answer. 'Although it wasn't really a holiday, was it, Catherine? It was quite hard work at times.'

'It was indeed,' said Cath, in a strained tone of voice Maggie hadn't heard before.

'But our hotel was incredible,' Tiggy continued.

'You don't look like you've got much colour, the pair of you,' said Maggie.

'Ah, well. I like to keep out of the sun,' said Tiggy. 'And we had all our meditation sessions inside a huge yurt. It was an amazing space, wasn't it, Catherine?'

'It really was,' agreed Cath.

'And the food was glorious,' continued Tiggy. 'All authentic local produce, all cooked up for us by a chap called Jeff.'

'*Jeff*?' said Maggie. 'Jeff-the-chef? Sounds *very* authentic... Anyway, what were the people like? Did you meet anyone nice?'

'Oh, yah,' said Tiggy. 'It was like we'd really found our *tribe* – if that makes sense?'

'Not really,' sniggered Maggie, avoiding Cath's glare. 'I was really wondering whether Catherine, er, Cath had maybe found a new man?'

'Very funny,' said Cath, straightening up the cushions on the armchairs and folding up *The Peak Gleaner*. 'And anyway. If anyone should be looking for a new man, it's you.'

'That's the *last* thing I'm looking for, I can assure you,' said Maggie, pulling the throw up around her neck.

'So,' said Cath. 'What've *you* been up to this week?' She paused. 'You look sort of different.'

'Is it the hair?' asked Maggie, tugging at her fringe again. 'I cut it myself.'

'I don't think so,' said Cath. 'You look, I dunno… thinner in the face. Have you been eating properly… without me here to cook for you?'

'Well,' said Maggie. 'There's no point just cooking for one, is there?'

'What about Lauren?' asked Cath. 'Where is she?'

'She'll be back at six-ish. After netball. She's mostly been at Dan's since you went away.'

'Really? I thought I asked you to keep an eye on her! Everything's OK, I assume?'

'Er, yes, I think so,' said Maggie, vaguely. Now wasn't the time to go into it – the situation between Lauren and Freya.

'Ah, Lauren,' said Tiggy. 'Such a lovely girl. When her looks catch up with her personality, she'll be just perfect.'

Cath's face fell and Maggie couldn't help herself. 'What d'you mean?' she challenged Tiggy. 'She's a lovely looking girl.'

'Of course she is!' said Tiggy, all indignant. 'It was just a joke.'

'Was it really?' said Maggie. 'Maybe it's best if you don't attempt any more jokes in that case… I'm not sure comedy's your thing.'

'Would you like a cup of tea before you head off, Tiggy?' said Cath, trying to smooth the waters, leaving Maggie in awe at her restraint.

'Thanks, but I won't,' said Tiggy. 'I'm keen to get back and see Phil. I've missed him *so* much. It's been awful spending the week without him.'

'Oh,' said Cath, punctured again. 'Sorry about that.'

'Don't be,' said Tiggy as she kissed Cath on both cheeks and sashayed back out to the car.

When she'd gone, the remaining life seemed to drain out of Cath. She kicked off her shoes and flopped down into one of the armchairs.

'Congratulations,' said Maggie, dryly. 'I really take my hat off to you.'

'Congratulations for what?'

'For putting up with *her* for a week. She's got a voice like a rattlesnake. Every sentence she utters tails off into a sort of bored croak. Does she do that on purpose, do you think? Is it supposed to sound cool or something?'

'She's not that bad,' said Cath, wearily. 'Once you get to know her…'

Maggie shivered and it wasn't just the draught from the window. 'Let's hope that day never comes, eh?'

'Oh, don't,' said Cath. 'She's not the sort you want to get on the wrong side of.'

'Hmm. I get it,' said Maggie. 'You wouldn't want to be upsetting the Queen Bee now, would you?'

'So,' said Cath, ignoring her. 'What *have* you been up to this week? You didn't answer my question.'

'Not a lot,' Maggie confessed. 'While you've been gallivanting around the Med, the furthest I've been is out to the recycling bins. There are so many different coloured bins out there, I don't know how you keep up. They're starting to colonise the garden.'

'You must've done more than that,' said Cath, stifling a yawn. 'What about your driving lessons? When are you starting with Val?'

'I've already started,' said Maggie, breezily. 'Had my first one last weekend.'

'Great,' said Cath. 'How'd it go?'

'Fine,' said Maggie. 'It went fine.' There was no point in saying otherwise. Cath, like everybody else around here, had been driving since she was seventeen. She wouldn't be remotely interested in her trials and tribulations behind the wheel.

'Good stuff,' said Cath. 'And what about the job hunt? Anything to report?'

'Not really,' said Maggie, burrowing deeper into the couch. 'Unless you count being offered a job as a barmaid by Australian Pete…'

'No way?' said Cath, trying not to laugh.

'I've been trying to blank it out of my mind,' said Maggie. 'I'm not that desperate…'

'When was this?'

'Oh, last Saturday. In the pub. On my birthday.'

Cath shot her a sideways glance. 'I'm sorry you had to spend your birthday on your own.'

'I didn't actually. In the end.'

'OK. I'm sorry you had to spend it in the pub with Australian Pete.'

'It wasn't that bad.' Maggie smiled. 'I got talking to Rob the farmer.'

'Oh, yeah?' Cath settled back and closed her eyes. 'What's the latest? Has he still got money worries?'

Maggie looked at her. 'How do you know about that? He's been trying to keep it quiet.'

'Hmm,' said Cath. 'Half the village knows.'

'Really?' Maggie let out a sigh. 'Well, things haven't got any better for him. There's no way he can make the repayments. They're charging him forty-two per cent interest!'

'*How much?*' said Cath, opening her eyes again. 'That's awful. There should be a law against that sort of thing.'

'I know,' said Maggie, shaking her head. 'It's mad that there isn't.'

'Couldn't you help him out?' asked Cath. 'Have a look at the documentation. See if there are any loopholes or whatever?'

'Nah,' said Maggie. 'I'd rather keep out of it, to be honest. I've googled the loan company and they're a right set of shysters. They've done it loads of times – taking farmers to court, selling their land out from under them…'

'Really?'

'Really. And if they take Rob to court – which they probably will – he'll need to find himself a specialist in that kind of thing. A barrister – or a solicitor who's qualified to appear in the High Court. Which I'm not. My job was drafting international contracts and agreements, negotiating terms and conditions, things like that.'

Maggie was on a roll now. 'It's funny, you know, but I've never actually appeared in court.' She laughed, grimly. 'Well, only as the accused. Remember that time at uni when I got dumped by that goth bloke and went out and drowned my sorrows? Remember how it ended? Drunk and disorderly. "Assaulting" a police officer.

Even though I'd only shoved him away from me.' She cringed at the memory. 'I was bloody terrified. Terrified that a criminal record would stop me qualifying as a lawyer. And even more terrified that Joyce would find out…'

She looked across for Cath's reaction, but a gentle snore told her she'd dropped off to sleep. Probably for the best.

Maggie thought about Rob again. He seemed like a nice guy – a real sweetheart. Couldn't she do what Cath suggested? Offer to have a look at the loan agreement, etc?

Normally – not so long ago – she wouldn't have hesitated to try and help out.

But no. She didn't have the stomach to get involved in it. Just getting out of bed in the morning was hard enough these days.

The Towering Inferno

Maggie stared straight ahead, stomach churning, knuckles white on the steering wheel. Here she was… actually driving… on a road.

Nothing about this felt natural, though. Nothing at all. From the stuttering rhythm of the windscreen wipers; to the weird, enforced intimacy of being stuck in a confined space with a stranger; to the terrifying knowledge you were in sole charge of two tonnes of lethal weapon… That one mistake could kill you and those around you. *After what had happened to Andy, she knew that better than anyone.* Not that she was in sole charge of the Micra, of course: Val's tiny feet on the dual controls made sure of that.

The national speed limit might have been sixty miles an hour on these quiet, rural roads, but Maggie hadn't got anywhere near that yet – apart from when she was approaching junctions, when she'd be scolded for going too fast. Val needed to make up her mind, really.

This was her third lesson now and Val was still doing her head in. Her favourite topic of conversation was still how damn 'busy' she was – which rankled with Maggie, as it made her own life feel even more empty. And then, instead of keeping her directions clear and simple (*'Turn right at the next junction'*), Val insisted on navigating by reference to local landmarks that Maggie had never heard of (*'Carry on straight ahead past the Sir William pub, then turn left at the old quarry'*). What?! Where the fucking hell was *that*…?

Sometimes Val was encouraging ('*Don't worry, we'll soon get you sorted*'), other times patronising ('*It just takes some people longer than others to get the hang of it*'), but most of the time she just looked thoroughly demoralised by Maggie's efforts – and who could blame her.

Forty-six was quite old to be learning to drive – positively geriatric – and cars had always been quite alien to Maggie. They'd never had a car when she was growing up – when she would spend her Sundays looking down from her tower block, watching the other kids in the street washing their dad's pride and joy with sponges and soapy water. Not that she'd ever had a dad either, come to think if it. Not a proper one…

'Woah!' Val shrieked, slamming on her brakes, throwing Maggie forward, making her gasp. 'Watch out for the woolly lady!'

'The *what*?' said Maggie. And then she saw it: a sodden ewe that had wandered out into the road in front of them.

They sat there for a minute or so until the animal wandered off again, its grubby fleece merging into the dismal grey of the afternoon.

'Sorry,' said Maggie, taking a deep breath, composing herself. 'I was miles away…'

'Not to worry,' said Val, and Maggie thought she could detect a note of pity in her voice. 'I think we'll begin with the emergency stop next time. That's part of the driving test, in any case.'

Driving test? thought Maggie. She couldn't even imagine it. Why was she finding driving so difficult? She'd done loads of difficult things in her life – too many to count. Despite her fractured childhood, she'd been the first person in her family to go to university; she'd got a job in the City of London at one of the best law firms in the square mile; she'd travelled the world, turning her hand to all sorts of projects – negotiating with boardrooms of Arab sheikhs who'd start by refusing to speak to a woman, but who'd always be won over by her competence and professionalism.

None of these skills were helping her in the here and now, though. And she hadn't even had to do any of the difficult things yet. Like driving in town, parallel parking and – perish the thought – roundabouts.

At Val's signal, she turned the key in the ignition again and they drove in silence back to Higher House, where they juddered up the driveway to the back door. Stepping out of the car, Maggie was surprised to see Lauren standing there, her scarf pulled up over her nose, ready to take her place in the driver's seat.

'I didn't know you had a lesson today,' said Maggie, but Lauren only mumbled something incomprehensible in reply, before she and Val drove off.

A wave of wood smoke swirled past Maggie on the wind, catching the back of her throat. It was coming from the front garden and Maggie followed it round there, to find Cath stabbing at a raging bonfire with a huge stick. Silhouetted in orange against the November twilight, her hair billowing up around her head, she looked positively deranged. And Jazz was nowhere to be seen – presumably in hiding, terrified by the conflagration.

'Hiya,' shouted Maggie, over the crackling of the blaze, which was kicking out a fierce heat.

Cath spun round, like a witch disturbed mid-ritual. Her eyes were streaming from the smoke and she was breathing heavily.

'You OK?' asked Maggie, concerned.

'Fine,' said Cath, pushing her hair out of her eyes. 'Totally fine.'

'You sure about that?'

Cath picked up a rotten old plank and heaved it into the flames. 'It's Simon,' she said, watching it burn.

'What's he done now?' asked Maggie.

'I've just seen him on Facebook,' growled Cath. 'He's golfing.'

'Hanging offence,' said Maggie, under her breath.

'In the fucking Algarve.'

'I see,' said Maggie, unsure of the correct response to this. 'Shall I go and make us a cuppa?'

* * *

The two of them sat there on the garden bench nearest the bonfire. It was starting to die away now and they warmed their hands on their steaming mugs.

'He's a git,' said Cath. 'He promised Lauren that she could go on the school skiing trip in February. Now he's claiming he's skint and he can't afford it—'

'But he can afford to go on a golf holiday.' Maggie finished Cath's sentence for her.

'Exactly. And when I rang him about it, he brought up the fact that I'd just been away to Crete!'

'Fair point?' suggested Maggie.

'Yeah, but that wasn't really a holiday at all. I was supposed to be recuperating... from the emotional stress he's heaped on me.'

'Well, it just goes to prove what I always say...'

'What's that?' asked Cath, squinting at her through the last of the smoke.

'That no good ever comes of Facebook.'

'Bit cynical,' said Cath with a sigh.

'Well, it's true,' said Maggie. 'It's full of all these sickly couples posting about how *loved up* they are and, then the next thing, before you know it, they're getting divorced.'

Cath gave a hollow laugh. 'Like me and Simon, you mean?'

'Not *just* you.'

Cath swilled her tea around her mug. 'Oh, I don't know… It's a good source of gossip. I found out today that Bella Cox just had another baby.'

'You're kidding me?' said Maggie. 'At *her* age?'

'I know! And have you seen what Sean Savage is up to?'

'No.'

'*Trekking to Antarctica in the footsteps of Ernest Shackleton.*' Cath handed Maggie her phone to show her the photos. 'C'mon,' she said. 'I'm waiting…'

'Waiting for what?' said Maggie.

'One of your sarky one-liners, of course.'

Maggie pulled a face and gave the phone back. *Fucking Facebook!* She hadn't even looked at it for months, let alone posted anything. Who wanted to see all those people with full lives, all playing happy families? And what would she have posted anyway? That she was unemployed and kipping in her old pal's box room in the middle of bloody nowhere?

Cath put the phone down. 'So,' she said. 'How did it go with Val today?'

'I dunno,' said Maggie, reluctant to tell her the truth. 'She's a bit… nervous. I'm not sure she's really cut out to be a driving instructor.'

'Really?' said Cath. 'She's been doing it a long time. Over ten years, I think.'

'Yeah. So she keeps saying.'

'Maybe it would help if you got a better night's sleep?' said Cath, delicately. 'I'm not convinced that crashing out on the sofa the night before a lesson is the best preparation.'

'Ah, yes. I forgot to say… Sorry about that.'

'Two bottles of wine *is* quite a lot, for a Wednesday night.'

Maggie said nothing. She knew deep down that Cath was right. It wasn't just nerves that had made her hands shake on the steering wheel earlier.

Maggie looked up at the sky. It was properly dark now: apart from the embers of the fire, the only light was coming from Cath's phone, which was flashing the arrival of a new message.

'It's Lauren!' said Cath, leaping up and punching the air. 'She's just passed her driving test!'

'Great stuff,' said Maggie, trying her best to sound pleased.

'The little bugger didn't even tell me she was sitting it…'

'Probably didn't want to worry you.'

'Oh, bollocks!' said Cath, sitting back down.

'What?'

'Wait till Simon hears he's going to have to fork out for a car as well.'

Best Laid Plans

Maggie stood there shivering. A single figure at a bus stop on a hair-pin bend. A mere speck on the landscape. She was doing her best to ignore the sheer drop, trying not to think about the worrying gaps in the dry stone wall or to imagine the fate of the unwary souls who had taken the bend too fast. *Now she was here, this didn't seem such a good idea after all.*

Cath had offered to take her out one day to Sheffield: for a spot of lunch in the city centre, followed by a quick circuit of the department stores. The idea was for Maggie to buy some new clothes and some walking boots of her own, as Simon's were basically falling apart now. She'd never been that keen on shopping – especially for something as tedious as walking boots – but she'd forced herself to show willing and say yes. And she could've done with picking up a few 'necessities' from Boots: she'd run out of paracetamol for one thing, courtesy of all the red wine headaches she'd been suffering lately, which had forced her to pilfer Cath's.

They'd planned to go this afternoon as Cath had no other obligations and Neil was free to look after the café, but Cath had had to cry off at the last minute: she'd had to go and meet with her solicitor in Bakewell – to sign some forms to kick off the divorce from Simon. Things were obviously getting serious on that front, but Maggie hadn't wanted to pry.

And she hadn't been altogether upset about Cath backing out of the shopping trip – in fact, she'd been grateful for a reason not to go – but Cath had felt awful about it and had insisted on driving her into town so she could at least go shopping on her own.

Maggie still had *some* pride, however, and – at her ripe old age – couldn't face being dropped off like that – like she was being given a lift by her mum. 'I don't want to be any trouble,' she'd said. 'Just take me to the bus stop.'

Cath had frowned. 'Are you sure?' she'd asked. 'It's right up at the Surprise View. Nearly eight miles away. I might as well take you all the way into town.'

'No. It's fine,' Maggie had insisted. 'I'll get the bus.'

And so now here she was. Waiting at said bus stop. Which was literally just a pole in the ground, with no shelter or anything, and no fellow travellers for moral support.

Conscientious as ever, Cath had dropped her off ten minutes before the bus was due – '*Just to be sure!*' – which Maggie was regretting now. The thing was already five minutes late and the Surprise View was an exposed spot at the best of times – even more so at this time of year, in the gloomy guts of November. And today it was properly drizzly and '*dreich*': a good old Scots word meaning 'dreary, bleak' – another of Joyce's favourites.

It was a bit strange because the forecast for Sheffield was 'bright and sunny'. But since she'd been here, she'd learned this wasn't unusual and that this place had its own micro-climate: it didn't take much for the murk to get trapped in the depression of the valley, even when it was perfectly fine on 'the tops', as the locals called the moorland up above.

The wind was whipping down through the gaps in the hills as if to prove a point, forensically removing the last few leaves from the trees, sucking them down towards the valley bottom like a whirlpool. Unable to feel her face now, she jumped up and down on the spot like she'd done when she was a child in the playground, trying to keep warm.

A thought struck her, one she'd never had before in all her years working in office blocks in big cities – the thought that autumn wasn't just the one season, it was two. There was the first autumn of fresh exercise books and heather and mellow fruitfulness, when every leaf was a flower and all that… That season was long gone. They were well into the second phase now, when every wet leaf was a potential banana skin. The season of decay and mould and remembrance. But she couldn't afford to go down the remembrance road now. If she started with all that, she'd never stop.

She glanced again at her watch. The bus was twenty minutes late now. She'd give it another ten. Or maybe it wasn't coming at all? Maybe it had broken down. If so, she'd have to ditch her plans. And then what? These rural buses were a disgrace.

Or maybe everything was fine and she'd just read the bus times a bit wrong. She'd been starting to make a lot of small daft mistakes lately, mistakes she'd never, ever have made before. She'd just check the timetable again… Feeling clammy despite the cold, she fumbled in her bag for her phone.

No signal! *Quelle fucking surprise.* Which meant she wouldn't be able to call a taxi either. She stood and looked around her. There was a phone box up there in the distance, further up the road – and there were bound to be some taxi numbers stuck up inside it.

Maggie slogged up the hill for what felt like ages – lungs bursting – up towards the tops, towards the phone box. But there was no phone in it. Only a sodding defibrillator. How ironic because, right now, her heart felt like it needed one. She bent over, hands on her thighs, feeling like she would puke. What was she going to do now?

'Ring Cath' was the obvious answer – she might even be finished with her meeting by now. *But she'd need a signal for that.*

Should she keep heading up the hill towards the tops, towards the moors, would she at least have a *chance* of getting a signal up there? Or should she head downhill back into the valley? Less hope of a signal, maybe, but at least she'd be headed vaguely towards home and could just keep plodding in that direction if she had to?

Downhill, she decided. *Definitely.* Finding herself up on the moors, alone in the dark, would be her worst nightmare. And downhill would be a lot less knackering.

In theory.

She'd been going for ages now, but she still couldn't get through to Cath on the phone – only her bloody voicemail over and over again. And her legs felt leaden, like her racing heart was depriving them of energy, like they were about to seize up at any moment.

It was dark by the time Cath eventually came and found her – sweaty and distressed by the side of the road, still two miles from home, feeling utterly useless.

Winter is Here

The rain was rattling the windows of the spare room and Maggie couldn't bring herself to lift her head from the pillow. The midday pips rang out in the emptiness of the house: Cath must have forgotten to switch the radio off downstairs when she'd left this morning.

It wouldn't make any difference to anyone if she didn't get out of bed today – not even to Jazz, who was burrowed under the duvet next to her, showing zero interest in going outdoors for her morning ablutions.

Maggie turned on to her side and stared at the framed photo on the bedside table. It had been taken on her wedding day outside the registry office in Kensington. Joyce and Andy grinning at the camera for all they were worth. And she, herself, in the middle of them in a Stella McCartney trouser suit that had cost a small fortune.

Andy's death had been so sudden, such a terrible shock. She'd been expecting him home from his six-week stint at that hospital in Uganda, looking forward to a few weeks of dull domesticity with nothing much planned. She hadn't been expecting the phone call from Nihal, his colleague and best mate. It hadn't been a tropical illness or an act of terrorism or anything dramatic like that. He'd just been on his way to the local market, when he'd been knocked off his scooter by a speeding driver. Just a simple road accident that could have happened anywhere.

And then there had just been the white noise in her head, her brain like a numbed tooth after the dentist. For days on end. Followed by the practicalities and the paperwork involved in the death of a loved one overseas. A next-of-kin.

In the short term, it was the practicalities that had stopped her from going under. The admin. Something she was good at. Boxes to tick off. Something to focus on. Organising the funeral.

And after that, it was her work that had saved her. Sure, moving to Hong Kong to work as a lawyer for an oil company wasn't as noble a calling as Andy's, but it had been the fresh start she'd needed. No constant reminders of her previous life. Just a job to be done, where people were relying on her. No. Losing her much-loved husband at the age of thirty-six hadn't been part of the plan, but her career had been the silver thread that had pulled her through. Just as it had pulled her through the other loss before that – the one she forced herself not to think about.

Her career had been the one true constant in her life. *And now she didn't even have that.* The hunt for a new job was leading nowhere and Cath had even stopped asking her about it.

She'd got her hopes up a couple of weeks ago when a recruitment consultant had contacted her about an opening – a job in the legal team of a global energy company, based at their head office in London. They'd been impressed by her CV and she'd made it on to the longlist, but they decided to go for one of the other candidates as the post was apparently better suited to 'someone at the start of their career'. Maggie knew exactly what that meant: 'someone younger'. She hadn't even been offered an interview.

Every snub made her feel like a non-person. Like she didn't exist. Like she was outside of the human race, looking in. Without the daily routine of going to work – without the myriad little motivations that kept her going during the day, she'd basically imploded within a few short months.

Life didn't have anything to show her anymore. It was time to give way to the new generation in any case – to the likes of Lauren – who had boyfriends and driving licences and their whole lives ahead of them.

On and on went her thoughts, out of control, darting round in jagged circles from one thing to another. Was that the real reason she was so shit at driving: was she subconsciously petrified that what had happened to Andy was going to happen to her as well?

Her eyes were on the wedding photo again. Joyce in a powder blue pastel suit, tall like Maggie, interrogating the camera like Jessica Fletcher in *Murder She Wrote*. And Andy with his collar-length fair hair, brown moleskin suit and dark-framed glasses. Bless him – he was a hipster before hipsters were even a thing.

Joyce had been typically sceptical when she'd told her she was marrying some English guy she'd only known a few months – even if he *was* a qualified doctor. But she'd soon been won over by Andy, signalling her approval with a simple, '*Aye. He's nice.*' It was all the approval Maggie had needed – and all she would have got.

Like most Glaswegians, Joyce wasn't given to gushy praise. She'd always been a tough nut to crack, but then she'd *had* to be tough – deserted by her drunken, deadbeat husband, raising Maggie as a single mother.

Maggie was stung by this thought: that she'd risen above this dodgy start in life, only to end up on the scrapheap, with nothing on the horizon. Just a job offer from Australian Pete. Pulling pints for minimum wage.

She reached across and put the photo away in the drawer. It only reminded her of the day she'd had to clear it from her desk in Hong Kong, along with her other belongings, into the cardboard box they'd handed her. Just after the call from Dalton, her boss, with his smarmy voice down the line: '*Could you wander round to my office when you've got a moment?*' And then going down the corridor to find him waiting for her, his bullfrog face telling her to come in and sit down. And then emerging minutes later – face burning, heart thumping – without a job.

How many times had she relived this encounter in her mind? Too many to count. And all the reliving in the world wouldn't change a thing.

Even in her sleep, it was the same nightmare every night. The one where she goes into the office, but she's forgotten that she doesn't work there anymore, and her old colleagues can't even *see* her, let alone speak to her. You didn't need to be a genius to work out the meaning of *that* particular dream.

Boring herself now, she yawned and rolled over on to her other side. That was the weird thing. Not so long ago, she'd been living on the other side of the world, grafting sixteen hour days and thinking nothing of it – weekends too, depending how urgent the deadline. Now it was completely different. The less she did, the later she got up – the more tired she felt.

She'd been lying here all morning doing nothing. Nothing at all. But 'rested' was the last thing she felt.

All she wanted to do was go to sleep again.

Friday Feeling

The human brain was a strange old thing, Maggie mused, as she sat in the kitchen watching the washing machine go round. Another week had passed in a drowsy blur, it was somehow Friday morning and, even though the world of work was slipping further into the realm of distant memory – even though, for her, every day of the week was now exactly the same – some tiny part of her still looked forward to the weekend.

Years of working hard and playing hard – going out for team drinks at the end of the week to a *chi-chi* bar in some up-and-coming part of town – had hard-wired the 'Friday feeling' into her psyche. Fridays still felt and smelt different. Even if, these days, she mostly spent them sitting on her own in front of the TV.

Cath seemed to be out a lot at the moment and, even when she was at home, she seemed quite distracted, like her thoughts were elsewhere. The old days when the two of them had been a double-act were long gone, that was for sure: Maggie would still make the effort to chat, but the conversational passes that the old Cath would have caught and returned now sailed past into oblivion.

Maggie put this to the back of her mind, though. Today the Friday frisson was justified. The rain – which had been biblical lately – had actually stayed away the last few days and the early December sun was doing its best to see off the morning's frost. And as she'd dashed out of the door to the café this morning, Cath had suggested that the two of them go out for dinner tonight.

Maggie had jumped at the chance to leave the valley behind for a few hours – to go somewhere a bit fancy. And after everything Cath had done for her, it would be a good opportunity to show her appreciation – to treat her to a nice meal. But Cath hadn't seemed keen and suggested just going down to The Farmer's for a bite to eat instead. Maggie had felt a pang of disappointment at this, but she couldn't really complain. Cath would be the one doing the driving, after all.

And also, Cath had seemed a bit distant again this morning. Like she had something on her mind. Something she wanted to talk about tonight? Probably Simon again. What on earth had he done now? Being a wanker about the divorce no doubt.

Maggie glared at the washing machine, willing it to spin faster. She'd been living out of that wheelie case for months now – had washed the living daylights out of her clothes God knows how many times. If she hung her wet stuff over the various grumbling radiators, it would all be dry by this evening, which was good. Even though they were only going to the 'restaurant' at The Farmers Arms, she still wanted to wear something reasonably smart. And she would still insist on paying. She wouldn't take no for an answer this time.

* * *

'*Bon appétit*, ladies,' said Australian Pete, depositing their starters in front of them and disappearing back where he'd come from.

No wonder he was on the lookout for new staff, thought Maggie, as he seemed to do everything around here. That skinny young barman who sometimes helped out was nowhere to be seen and she wondered who did the cooking of the meals. Did Pete have to do that as well?

106

Not that these starters would have required much in the way of cooking – prawn cocktail for Maggie, served in a sundae glass, and pâté with melba toast for Cath. The menu was a good match for the whole demeanour of the place, Maggie reflected. Very much stuck in the seventies. Although this *did* have its advantages. At least there was no danger of being served your dinner on a plank of wood, a slab of slate or even in a dog bowl, like in those trendy, pop-up eateries that – according to *The Guardian* – were spreading across the country like a rash.

The prawn cocktail wasn't half bad, actually, and there was plenty of it. You certainly couldn't accuse Pete of being stingy with his portion sizes. But Cath didn't seem too keen on her own choice, just sitting there picking at the salad garnish with her fork.

Maggie smoothed her serviette over her jeans and rolled back the cuffs of her white shirt, feeling more like herself than she had in ages. 'So,' she said, leaning forward and lowering her voice. 'Tell me. What's he done now?'

'Who?' said Cath, nibbling off a corner of melba toast, doing her best not to drop any crumbs.

'Simon, of course!' Maggie smirked. 'Who else?'

'Oh,' said Cath, not meeting her eye. 'He hasn't done anything. Not since the last time, anyway. I'm trying not to think about him.'

'Quite right too,' said Maggie, digging deep into the sundae glass with her spoon.

'I've been thinking about Christmas actually,' said Cath, slowly and deliberately, taking a sip of her water. 'It's looking like I'm going to have a bit of a full house.'

'Visitors?' asked Maggie, looking up.

'Yeah,' said Cath. 'Richard's flying over from Philadelphia.'

'Aw. That's nice.'

'With his new American girlfriend in tow. Katy, she's called.'

'Really?' said Maggie, wide-eyed. 'It must be serious?'

Cath nodded. 'It seems so. And the twins are coming up from London – which I wasn't expecting as they'd been talking about going off to some castle in Ireland with their mates. And then I'll have my parents as well, for their annual visit.'

'Gosh.' Maggie whistled. 'You're gonna need a bigger turkey.'

'Yup,' said Cath. She took a deep breath. 'Simon's even thinking of coming over to join us for a couple of days.'

'Wow,' said Maggie, taken aback. 'The spectre at the feast.'

'Yeah. So, er, it'll be a bit of a tight squeeze,' Cath continued, pointedly.

Maggie could see where this was heading and was relieved to be able to impart a bit of news of her own. 'Well, you won't need to worry about me adding to your burden,' she said, scraping up the last of the pink cocktail sauce. 'I'm planning on going back to Glasgow.'

'Are you?' said Cath, her face breaking into a smile for the first time. 'That's great news. It really is. So you've made things up with Joyce?'

'Hmm. I wouldn't go that far,' said Maggie.

'But you're on speaking terms again?'

'Sort of,' said Maggie. 'I took the plunge and called her this afternoon. And she was actually at home for once.'

'How was it?'

'If I had to sum it up in one word, I'd say… a bit *terse*.'

'That's three words,' grinned Cath. 'That's good though. Life's too short not to talk to people.'

'Yeah, well. I always think it's the opposite way around,' said Maggie. 'Life's too short to spend it talking to people you can't get on with.'

'But she's your mother!'

'I know. I know,' said Maggie, softening. 'I'm really glad we've spoken. And I'm looking forward to seeing her – I really am. I just needed some time.' She paused for a moment. 'Sometimes I think we're just too similar, that's all.'

Cath narrowed her eyes. 'You don't say…'

Maggie had to laugh.

'I'm so pleased for you,' said Cath. 'I think you're doing the right thing, you know. Moving back to Glasgow. I was actually about to suggest it myself - that it might be a good time for you to move out. And there's bound to be *all sorts* of jobs up there. You can cast your net more widely.'

Maggie felt stung. As Australian Pete padded up to the table with their main courses, she felt her cheeks flush hot. *A good time to move out?* She'd only planned a visit back to Glasgow. Just for Christmas. For a few days at most. Not actually *moving back* there.

'Or Aberdeen,' continued Cath, when Pete had gone again. She was getting stuck into her steak now. 'You'd think it would be *full* of oil jobs.'

'You'd think so,' repeated Maggie, unsure what else to say.

Cath thought for a moment. 'And maybe you could give online dating a try. There's bound to be more fish in the sea up there. It's slim pickings around here.'

'Er, yes. You can say that again…' said Maggie, although the thought hadn't even occurred to her.

'Anyway. I hope it's not been too boring for you here in Archdale,' said Cath, with an air of finality, like she was about to wave her off then and there.

'Of course not,' said Maggie. 'Not at all.'

'There's no need to be polite,' laughed Cath. 'I mean, it was only supposed to be till the end of the summer. I bet you didn't expect to still be here at Christmas?'

'Technically I won't be…' said Maggie, forcing a smile. 'My train's booked for the twenty-fourth.' She didn't tell her it was actually a return ticket – one she now felt foolish for buying.

'Aw,' said Cath. 'Travelling back home on Christmas Eve. That'll be so nice and, well, *Christmassy*.'

'I hope so,' said Maggie, pushing the remains of her cottage pie around her plate half-heartedly. 'But look,' she went on. 'I just want to say thanks. Thanks a lot. For letting me stay at your place for this long. You're a mate.'

'No problem. No problem at all,' said Cath, sitting back in her chair, looking like a weight had been lifted off her.

A few minutes passed in silent chewing until the door opened and Cath began waving manically. Maggie looked round to see that – *Bollocks!* – Tiggy had arrived. She was wearing a bright red pinafore, with a matching Alice band in her hair. Her outfit, combined with her pigeon-toed stance, made her look like an overgrown five-year-old.

'I forgot to tell you,' said Cath, taking care to hide the evidence of the steak she'd just devoured. 'Tiggy's going to join us for a drink.'

Oh, man, thought Maggie. This is all I need!

'Have you two had your *little chat*, then?' droned Tiggy, giving Cath a knowing look. 'Let's move through to the bar area, shall we? It's *marginally* nicer in there.'

'Sure,' said Cath, jumping up. 'I'll just pay the bill first.'

'No way,' said Maggie, picking up the slip of paper. 'Allow me to get it. As a thank you.'

'No. I insist,' said Cath, grabbing it out of her hand and heading for the bar.

'OK then,' said Maggie, giving up the fight. 'I'll be with you in a minute. I just need to go and, er, use the facilities.'

Maggie virtually ran there, grateful for the chance to compose herself. Pressing her head against the cool tiles next to the mirror, she didn't even notice the gravy stain on the front of her white shirt.

So *that's* why Cath had been so nervy this evening: she'd basically brought her here to ask her to move out. And Tiggy knew all about it. How humiliating not to have picked up on any of this! There must have been some signs that she'd outstayed her welcome. How could she have missed them?

Well then. She would take the hint. She would leave straightaway – tomorrow, ideally – not even wait till the twenty-fourth. But something was stopping her. She felt stuck. Immobilised. Like a fly in a web.

Cath was quite right. She *had* found it boring round here. It wasn't Archdale's fault. It was a perfectly nice place in its own way – just the wrong place for her. But no matter how bad things were for her here, they'd be worse in Glasgow.

It wasn't that she had a problem with the city itself. It was a great place: cosmopolitan, friendly and fun. But she had nobody there. She was only eighteen when she'd left to go to university in London. And, brim-full of enthusiasm for her new adventures, she'd lost touch with everyone from her old comprehensive, so there were no old pals she could just pick up and reconnect with. Only Joyce. Who had a busy life of her own. And who would soon suss out just how low her daughter had sunk.

And so Cath was also quite wrong. Going back wouldn't feel 'nice and Christmassy' at all. Not in the slightest.

Carols at The Farmer's

A long fortnight later, it was the night before Maggie's departure and she found herself back at The Farmer's for the last time. A slightly tipsy Father Christmas was weaving his way towards her through the knots of people thronging the pub, followed by a line of small children. 'Mince pie, Maggie?' he offered, with a theatrical bow that nearly made him drop his tray.

She would normally have declined as she couldn't abide the things, having been scarred for life by Joyce's homemade versions. But she could see that Santa was actually Tiggy's husband Phil – or, rather, she could smell his expensive aftershave – and so she took one to be polite. She could discreetly stick it in the bin once he'd moved on to his next victim.

Maggie hadn't wanted to come out this evening – had wanted a quiet night in before the journey home tomorrow – but Cath had forced her into it. She'd assured her that 'Carols at the Farmer's', held every year on the twenty-third of December, was not to be missed. It was the centrepiece of the festive season in the village and Archdale Silver Band would be providing the musical backdrop – gusty renditions of 'Silent Night', 'Good King Wenceslas' and all the other classics.

Maggie had doubted whether anything could make a dent in the desolate winter months, could tempt the locals out of their cosy cottages to come and prop up the bar. But there was a real buzz in the pub tonight; it was the busiest she'd seen it since the night of the quiz, and Australian Pete was struggling to keep up with demand. Half the customers seemed to be senior citizens, though – Mrs Winterson and her cronies from the café, still giving Maggie dirty looks – and the other half were members of Cath's family, now arrived in Archdale for their Christmas visit.

Cath's eldest son Richard was here, having just flown in from the States with his American girlfriend, Katy. Willowy, long-haired and preppy, she seemed to be just as good-natured as Richard. Maggie had worked with a lot of Americans over the years and had never met one she didn't like. Yes, it was easy to mock them for their 'have-a-nice-day' fake sincerity, but there was something about their cheerful politeness that she secretly admired. She also felt a certain sympathy for Katy: Philadelphia to Archdale was quite the gear change!

Cath's twins, David and Alison, had driven up from London this afternoon and were still bickering over a wrong turning that had added twenty whole minutes to their four-hour journey.

Cath's parents too had just completed the long drive from their home in Dorset and Maggie was genuinely pleased to see them again – a feeling which seemed to be mutual. The last time she'd seen them had been at Cath's wedding to Simon in the spring of 1996 – a hastily-arranged affair as Cath was already up the duff with Richard. Her parents had put on a hugely tasteful reception in a marquee in their back garden, never once seeming less than thrilled at the 'accelerated' pace of events (although Maggie knew for a fact that they weren't). Worse still, Simon had just landed a new job up north and was taking their daughter even further away from them – out of London and halfway up the country to a village in Derbyshire.

Now in their seventies, Cath's parents were still a classy couple. Dressed in the favoured uniform of wealthy country folk – expensive jeans, cashmere sweaters and waxed jackets – they were doing their best to turn a blind eye to their younger granddaughter's attempts to score some mulled wine, despite being underage. Maggie wondered why Lauren was even bothering – warm Muddy Duck tasted no better than it did at room temperature – but she still found herself downing it anyway.

There weren't many things that Maggie would miss about Archdale, but Lauren was definitely one of them. They'd had a proper giggle decorating the Christmas tree at Higher House last week, when Cath had claimed she was too busy to join in. It had been quite emotional for Maggie: putting up the tinsel for a Christmas that she wouldn't be around to see. And doing it with Lauren had transported her to a parallel universe in which she was doing the same thing with her own daughter. Only for a moment, though, before she pushed the idea down and out of her mind. Those sorts of thoughts weren't very helpful and there was no point in thinking them. None whatsoever.

Maggie wondered about Pippa, Cath's sister. Maggie had asked Cath whether she would be coming for Christmas too, but apparently Pippa had decided to have it at home with her own little family this year. Maggie had got the distinct impression that this was a sore point with Cath and so she hadn't pressed it.

From what Maggie could see, the only other one missing was Simon. What an idiot he was, to be missing out on these special moments with his family – and all because he couldn't keep it in his trousers! He'd be sitting there all alone in his one-bedroom flat in Leeds – although, given his recent exploits, he might not actually *be* alone, of course.

In fact, he wasn't due to arrive at Cath's until tomorrow afternoon because – big and important and indispensable as he was – he was 'needed at the office'. Maggie would be long gone by then: she'd have checked out of the spare room hours before he arrived to take her place. The two of them would pass like ships in the night and Maggie couldn't have been more relieved.

Cath, aglow with maternal pride and the heat from the open fire, was herding her flock towards the biggest table in the corner. As they all took their places, Maggie insisted she was happy just to perch on the little wooden stool at the end: they were all clearly keen to catch up on each other's news and she had no wish to get in the way.

When the Silver Band stopped for a break to get its breath back, Cath seized the opportunity to say a few words, tapping the side of her glass with a teaspoon. 'Listen up, everyone,' she announced in a high voice. 'I'd just like to propose a small toast.'

'Oh God, Mother,' said Lauren, slinking down in her seat, conscious that most of the rest of the pub was gawping at them now. 'Do you have to?'

'Yes, Lauren, I do!' said Cath, indignantly, shooting her a look.

'Go for it, Mum,' said Richard. 'Don't listen to her,' he said, digging his baby sister in the ribs.

'Yes. Well,' said Cath, trying to regain her thread. 'I'd just like to start by saying how nice it is to see you all in the same room. For once.'

'Here's to all being in the same room!' toasted Richard, raising his glass, and everyone else followed suit.

Maggie scratched at the back of her head and looked away, feeling a bit like a cuckoo in Cath's nest.

'And also,' continued Cath, over the chat and laughter. 'I'd very much like to welcome Katy to Archdale.' She smiled over at Richard's girlfriend. 'Katy, I hope you enjoy your first English Christmas!'

'To Katy. And an English Christmas!' echoed Richard.

Katy blushed the colour of her mulled wine. 'Thank you so much for having me to stay at your home, Mrs Bridges,' she replied. 'I'm sure I'll have the most wonderful time.'

'You're very welcome,' said Cath, blushing back. 'And please feel free to call me Cath.'

The slight awkwardness Maggie had been feeling turned to genuine discomfort. She felt like an intruder in a private, family moment where she didn't belong. Would it be rude to excuse herself and disappear to the loo? But Cath was off again.

'And finally. Last but not least…' said Cath. 'I'd like to raise a toast to Maggie.'

What? Maggie squirmed in her stool as they all turned to look at her. What on earth was Cath thinking? The mulled wine had clearly taken its toll.

'Maggie's been staying in Archdale for a while,' burbled Cath, 'but sadly she's leaving us tomorrow morning to go back to Scotland.'

'Awww,' chorused the table as one.

'And so I'd just like to wish her *bon voyage* and all the best!'

Christ, thought Maggie, wishing the tattered pub carpet would rise up and swallow her whole. 'Thanks everyone,' she said, weakly, holding up her glass to acknowledge their good wishes. 'And a very merry Christmas to all of you, too!'

Good, thank God that's over, she thought, until she spotted Tiggy over Cath's shoulder, mincing over to their table. Her so-called fashion choices were dubious at the best of times, but she'd really outdone herself tonight: she appeared to be dressed up as a sexy elf, although the word 'sexy' was doing a lot of heavy lifting in this case. Even so, the male half of the table's eyes were bulging out of their heads, as Tiggy bent over to rummage in her giant Christmas stocking.

'This is for you, Maggie,' she announced in her nasal croak, struggling to pull something out of it.

Although it was wrapped, Maggie could tell that the item was booze of some description. She opened it anyway to find that she was right: it was a bottle of lethal-looking Caribbean rum, the sort of thing you'd find at the back of a drinks cabinet, next door to the ouzo and the raki. This would end up going the same way as the mince pie…

'You shouldn't have,' said Maggie, truthfully.

'Oh, it's nothing,' beamed Tiggy. 'Just a little something to see you on your way. A Christmas-present-cum-leaving-present, if you like. I thought it would be right up your street.'

What a cow! thought Maggie, getting to her feet. Now really *would* be a good time to go to the loo, as giving one of Santa's little helpers a slap wouldn't be a great look.

Threading her way through the crowd of revellers to the bathroom, she felt a hand on her shoulder. Alarmed, she swung round to see Rob, who had left his favourite spot at the bar in order to follow her.

'Is that right, then?' he asked, nodding over in Cath's direction. 'You're off tomorrow? Back to Scotland?'

'Yep,' said Maggie. He seemed quite sad about it. 'I'm on the eleven o'clock train, from Buxton.'

'I could give you a lift to the station,' he offered.

'That's really kind of you,' said Maggie. 'But I've already got a lift. Cath's dropping me off.'

'It's no problem,' he insisted. 'I'm going over that way anyway. I need to pick up some fence posts.'

'Oh, right.' She hesitated for a moment. It was a tempting offer. Cath would have enough on her plate tomorrow, prepping Christmas dinner for nine people the following day. She could do without having to drive her to Buxton as well.

'OK,' said Maggie, eventually. 'Thanks. That would be great.'

'No bother,' said Rob. 'I'll pick you up at ten. Actually, make that quarter-to-ten to be on the safe side. I'll give you my number in case you need it.'

'Perfect, thanks,' said Maggie.

And as the two of them stood there swapping numbers, while the band started up a jaunty version of 'Last Christmas', Maggie realised that Rob was something else she would miss about Archdale.

It's Beginning to Look a Lot Like Christmas...

Maggie had set her alarm for eight, but was awake long before it went off. It was the cold that had woken her up: the heating hadn't come on yet and she could actually see her breath in front of her face.

Higher House was as silent as the grave, despite all the rooms being full. She reached across for her phone. It was only five to six and there was no need to get up yet. The clothes she'd be wearing for the journey were all set, hanging there on the back of the chair, and her wheelie case was standing to attention, already packed.

She thought about Rob and felt genuinely touched by his offer of a lift. Village life might have proved too claustrophobic, gossipy and dull for her tastes, but it did have its advantages: she couldn't have imagined any of her old city neighbours going out of their way to help her like this. And it wasn't like she'd be able to pay him back, given she'd never see him again.

Maggie wrapped her duvet – and the extra blanket – around herself like a mummy. She'd got used to using Jazz as a bed-warmer over the last few months but, now that the rest of the family had come home, the dog had moved back into Lauren's room, which she was sharing with her big sister, Alison.

It would be even colder than this in Scotland – in every sense of the word. It had been nearly six months since she'd seen Joyce face to face and things were bound to be slightly frosty to begin with. The flat was small, but she'd have it to herself most of the time, while Joyce was out carousing with her pensioner pals. It might get a bit lonely. But there was no use worrying about that now. She was packed and ready to go, no turning back…

A familiar metal clunk echoed up the stairs from the kitchen: the sound of the back door being unbolted. Followed by the sound of voices. Voices that sounded rather formal and strained. She held her breath and listened some more. One of them was definitely Cath's.

She needed to go downstairs and investigate – check that nothing was wrong. And so she forced herself up out of bed, throwing on the old dressing gown Cath had lent her, lest the sight of her unshaved legs give Cath's father an attack of the vapours.

It wouldn't even be light yet, but she opened the curtains anyway and looked out.

Bloody hell! The garden was covered in its own extra blanket. Of snow.

Maggie ran downstairs in her bare feet. Her only thought was whether the trains would still be running. Cath was bound to know. Or the National Rail website.

Peering round the kitchen door, she recognised the back of the head sitting opposite Cath: the close-shaved style to hide the fact he was going bald, the silver spectacles curled round the back of his ears. *Fuck! It's Simon. He's early.*

She considered turning tail and just tip-toeing back upstairs, but he had sensed her presence and there was no backing out now.

He stood up and came towards her, arms open to give her a hug. 'Ah, Maggie. Long time no see.'

'Hi Simon,' said Maggie, wincing over his shoulder at Cath. 'Really good to see you.'

'There's some coffee in the pot,' said Cath, in the high-pitched voice that signified she was nervous.

'You're early,' said Maggie to Simon. 'I thought you weren't coming till this afternoon?'

'Well,' Simon replied. 'I had no choice. I knew the snow was coming and that I'd have to try and beat it over the Pennines.'

Beat it over the Pennines?! Smug and pompous as ever, thought Maggie, forcing a smile. 'Good for you. I've got to brave it later on. I'm getting the train back to Scotland.'

Simon gave a mirthless laugh. 'I very much doubt it,' he said.

'Really?' said Maggie. She looked at Cath for support. 'Won't the trains be running?'

Simon carried on before Cath had a chance to speak. 'The trains are probably fine. It's the roads in the valley that'll be the problem. Not to mention up on the tops. Have you seen the size of those flakes? They're coming down thick and fast. It's set to last all day.'

Unless she was mistaken, he looked positively chuffed to be the bearer of this bad news.

'I can't believe it,' whined Cath, shaking her head at Maggie, unable to hide her exasperation with the situation. 'Last winter was really mild.'

Maggie sighed deeply, pulled out a chair and sat down. *Bloody snow.* It was bad enough being stuck here – but to be stuck here with Simon the Insufferable? That truly *was* 'cruel and unusual punishment'. And also, how long would the snow hang around for? It could be days before it disappeared.

Her despair was interrupted by her phone vibrating in her dressing gown pocket. She pulled it out and looked. *Rob!* Ringing to say her lift was off.

Cath and Simon watched her as she answered it, straining to listen.

'Hi Rob,' said Maggie, downbeat.

'*It's beginning to look a lot like Christmas…*' Rob sang tunelessly down the phone.

'Haha, very good,' she laughed, although she wasn't feeling it. 'Thanks for ringing to cancel, but there was really no need.'

'What you on about, you daft mare?' he said, teasing her. '*Cancel*? I'm just confirming we're still on. In case you were worried.'

'But…' said Maggie. 'The snow…'

'Not a problem,' said Rob. 'I've put the snow tyres on the Land Rover. They'll get us to Buxton.'

'Nice one,' she beamed, as Simon's face dropped. 'I'll see you later.'

* * *

The ancient Land Rover bounced its way up out of the valley – up Winnats Pass, the narrow gap between the peaks at the western end. The landscape was unrecognisable now that all the greens and greys had been replaced by a uniform layer of white. Unexpectedly, the snow had outlined all manner of curves and dips that Maggie had never noticed before, and she found herself wondering where the 'woolly ladies' were now and how they were coping with the freezing temperatures.

If anyone would know the answer to this, it would be Rob – and she'd just opened her mouth to quiz him about it – when he pulled over and stopped by the side of the road. From the look on his face, she knew this wasn't good.

'We won't be able to get any further,' he said, indicating the brow of the hill. And Maggie sat right up in her seat, to see two stationary cars blocking the way at the top.

'It looks like they've been abandoned,' sighed Rob. 'Bloody idiots in tinny little cars.' Just because the Land Rover had been able to plough its way through the snow didn't mean that every other vehicle on the road would be able to manage. 'Probably grockles,' said Rob, shaking his head.

'*Grockles*?' repeated Maggie.

'Tourists.'

'Right.'

Rob began the slow process of turning the vehicle around and they were soon creeping back down the hill, back where they'd come from.

Bugger, thought Maggie. Now she'd have to go back to Cath's with her tail between her legs. Where Cath would be pretending not to be pissed off with her and Simon the Smug would be utterly unbearable with his told-you-so's.

The Most Wonderful Time of the Year?

Cath's kids were long past the age of getting up at sparrow's crack on Christmas morning, but her parents were a different matter. Maggie had been dozing away on the couch right up until some cutlery clanged to the kitchen floor, followed by the noise of the taps thundering into life.

'Sorry,' whispered Cath's mum through the hatch into the lounge, as Maggie pulled the covers up over her head, wishing she was invisible.

When Rob had dropped her back from the abortive trip to the station yesterday, the words that came out of Cath's mouth were full of sympathy and understanding, but her face had told a different story. And, although Maggie had only been gone half an hour, Simon had wasted no time usurping her in the spare room: he'd already changed the sheets and placed his pyjamas, neatly folded, in the centre of the pillow – like a flag planted at the South Pole. He'd then taken great pleasure in informing her that she'd have to sleep on the couch. If she'd felt like an outsider the other night at the carols in the pub – like a squatter in Cath's clan – this was on a whole new level.

By contrast, the rest of Cath's family had been kindness itself, assuring her there was more than enough food and drink to go round – which had only made her feel *more* awkward if anything. David had even offered to trade places with her and sleep on the sofa instead, but Maggie had been firm in her refusal: the lad was only up from London for a couple of days and she had no intention of turfing him out of his childhood bedroom! Plus she wouldn't be hanging around much longer herself: as soon as the snow was gone, she'd be gone too.

* * *

It wasn't *just* the mince pies and the twee, cloying adverts on the telly. Maggie had another problem with Christmas. An ideological one. Why did it always fall to the women to put all the effort in – cooking the dinner, writing the cards, buying the presents and doing all the clearing up afterwards? While the men just had to pour the sherry, carve the turkey and feign gratitude for gifts of pants and socks. Having said that, sometimes the women were their own worst enemy – biting their tongue, refusing all offers of help, generally turning the whole thing into a festival of female martyrdom.

She had a feeling that Cath would go right over the top with the celebrations today, so had decided to keep her head down and make herself as scarce as possible. With this in mind, she'd already taken Jazz out for a snowy tramp through the fields – and peeled a mountain of veg – before Cath had even got up.

When Cath eventually did emerge from her room – hair perfectly straightened, face fully made up – Maggie could tell she was determined to do whatever it took to put on a perfect Christmas. Nothing – not her bitterness towards Simon, nor her annoyance at Maggie's continued presence – would get in her way.

Cath's first act had been to order Richard to lay a fire, which had been extremely successful and was now blazing away, far more effective than the temperamental central heating.

Next, Cath had put on 'It's the Most Wonderful Time of the Year', the opening song of her specially-created Christmas Day playlist. And, ever since then, she'd been floating round the place in her best dressing gown, lighting expensive candles and forcing glasses of Bucks Fizz on anyone who entered her orbit.

Maggie had politely refused every time: Christmas Day could be a long slog, emotions could run high, and drinking on an empty stomach didn't seem like the wisest course of action. No matter how civilised things started off, it didn't take much for the day to descend, *Eastenders*-style, into threats of divorce and/or death before the Queen had even started her speech. Or, at least, that's what she could remember from her earliest Christmases: when her mother and father were still persevering under the same roof and one of their seasonal traditions had been the annual Christmas Day screaming match, once he'd been at the whisky.

Maggie wasn't expecting anything like that today, but there was still fertile enough ground for a family row. If Cath's parents had never really been that fond of Simon ever since he'd knocked her up out of wedlock, then his recent 'dalliance' with a woman from work had done little to improve their opinion of him. Meanwhile, Lauren had previously made her views on her father crystal clear and Maggie couldn't imagine that her older brothers and sisters felt any different about him.

A minor flare-up had occurred around twelve noon when Cath and Simon had disagreed about the roast potatoes. Once they'd been parboiled, Simon had insisted they had to be coated in semolina. *Semolina?!* Maggie wasn't sure what semolina had to do with roast potatoes – she'd thought it was a pudding – but it must have been important as Cath was dead against it and the debate had got pretty heated.

Cath and Simon were citing Delia Smith and Nigella Lawson to support their respective positions, like expert witnesses in a court of law – Cath brandishing her recipe book, Simon retaliating with his iPad. Maggie worried that Cath might go up like a firework but, in the interests of household harmony, she'd ended up giving way: the potatoes would indeed be coated in semolina.

Whatever the rights and wrongs of the situation, Nigella's fluffy orbs had tasted very nice indeed. In fact, the whole meal had been as delicious as it had been convivial: all ten of them sitting around Cath's bounteous table in the 'proper' dining room, with Jazz curled up underneath.

And as the appreciative youngsters cleared the table afterwards (led by Katy and her lovely American manners), Maggie took on the job of washing up. Consistent with her policy of keeping a low profile, this suited her absolutely fine – until Cath's dad told Simon to 'be a gent' and go and give her a hand.

Maggie was scouring away at the roasting tins as Simon dried off the pots and pans on the draining board.

'Where shall I stick this?' he asked, waving a dried-off cheese grater in front of her.

'Don't tempt me,' said Maggie, with a dirty laugh.

Simon laughed too.

'You know, it's funny,' she said.

'What is?' he asked. 'The thought of me being buggered with a cheese grater?'

Maggie laughed heartily: it wasn't very often that Simon attempted self-deprecating humour and she felt that she ought to encourage it.

'I expect, as Cath's friend, you think it's no more than I deserve,' said Simon.

'Nah,' said Maggie. 'I just meant that it's funny you having to ask me where things belong. In your own house.'

Simon nodded wistfully. 'I guess the kitchen was never really my domain.'

'Ah,' she said, not looking at him. 'But it would appear that you're now an expert on roast potatoes?'

'Are you cross-examining me?' he asked, holding his hands up, and she couldn't tell if he was amused or annoyed.

The last dish now washed and dried, Maggie was just wiping down the surfaces when Lauren poked her head through the hatch from the lounge.

'Maggie!' she called. 'We're going to have a game of charades. Will you be in my team?'

* * *

The charades had been a right laugh. Their team had won, of course, but that was hardly the point. Knackered now, Maggie sank down further into the comfy armchair by the flickering fire, nursing a large glass of red. Everyone else had ditched their party hats by now, but her own was still perched on her head.

When she came round to top up Maggie's drink, Cath's mask of congeniality slipped for the briefest of moments. 'You know all that *coating* crap?' Cath muttered, *sotto voce*. 'He must have learned that from *her*.' Then she waved her phone under Maggie's nose. 'I'm just about to put some happy family photos on Facebook. That'll show her... The semolina slut!'

Maggie couldn't believe she was still friends with the 'other woman' on Facebook, but thought it best not to stir the pot. 'What lovely photos,' she'd said instead, and left it at that. The peace may have been fragile, but peace there was – as if someone had called a truce all round, like that football match in the trenches of the Great War. Even Lauren was being civil to her dad. And Cath's parents were being positively warm towards him. They were obviously people-pleasers as well, she thought. Which made a lot of sense when you came to think of it: that must be where Cath got it from. But then Simon was on his best behaviour, too. Maybe it was all down to the calming influence of Katy, the newcomer – an unwitting UN peace-keeping mission in the form of one young woman? Whatever it was, no *Eastenders*-esque drama had materialised.

And now they were all exchanging presents. Cath liked to do this bit after dinner, when all the work was done and everyone was relaxed. But this was Maggie's cue to feel uncomfortable again.

After the ordeal of the failed expedition to Sheffield, she hadn't been able to face another shopping trip and had decided that doing it online was the way forward instead. She'd ordered some walking boots for herself and some Christmas gifts for Cath and Lauren – nothing much, just a hamper of nice toiletries that she knew they liked, as a thank you for having her to stay. But of course – Sod's Law – her walking boots had arrived OK, but the toiletries had gone AWOL from a warehouse off the M1 and were still out there apparently, somewhere in the vicinity of Leicester.

Maggie was mortally embarrassed about this – it made her seem ungrateful and tight – but no one else was remotely bothered. David had just gifted his brother, Richard, a pogo stick and Cath was more worried about her six-foot son's head bouncing off the light fittings, asking how on earth he was supposed to get it back to America.

Their laughter was contagious and Maggie couldn't help but join in. Today had been really lovely. One of her best Christmases in years. Even doing the washing up with Simon had been quite amusing.

Yes, this is what Christmas was all about: family. Which she didn't really have. Her phone call to her mother this morning had been the beginning and end of it. Joyce would never say anything, of course, but she must often have felt the absence of grandchildren on Christmas Day, opening their presents and generally running riot. *Oh, well,* thought Maggie. *What could she do about it?* Not much.

She knocked back another mouthful of wine. Where was her phone, anyway? Which used to be surgically attached to her ear, but which never rang these days. It was just an alarm clock now – and usually not even that.

She eventually found it in the kitchen and was surprised to see she'd had a text. Joyce maybe? Nah. One of those annoying spam marketing things, more likely.

It was Rob!

Lunch tomorrow at mine? 12.30? Turkey leftovers!

Maggie felt a buzz of excitement. It was only a text, but it felt like a lifeline.

Deep and Crisp and Even

Rob had offered to come down and fetch her in the Land Rover, but Maggie had insisted on walking up to the farm instead. After all the feasting of Christmas Day, she was ready for some fresh air and exercise.

The snow had stopped falling by now, but it was nearly a foot deep in places and there was no sign of a thaw. Boxing Day was always a quiet one, but today it was preternaturally so: the snow had silenced the birds and the traffic alike and all the sheep had been taken inside. As she crunched up the lane to Rob's place, she was grateful for her new walking boots: at least her feet were warm and dry, even if she couldn't feel her face.

Up ahead, the chimney of the farmhouse was smoking away – a good sign. She was just so relieved to be out from under Cath's feet – to actually have somewhere to go – that it hadn't occurred to her to feel nervous. But now, as she approached the door and knocked, she had butterflies in her stomach.

She heard the door being unbolted and was wondering whether to shake his hand, kiss him on the cheek, or do neither, when it creaked open. Except that it wasn't Rob behind it. It was a woman – late sixties or so – wearing an old-fashioned housecoat and a grim expression. Rob's mother? Of course. He'd mentioned that he lived with his parents.

'You must be Maggie,' said the woman, without an ounce of warmth.

'I am,' said Maggie. 'I've come to see Rob. We're supposed to be having lunch…?'

The woman looked her up and down. 'Our Robert's had to go down to the barn. One of the ewes is—'

'Look. No worries,' said Maggie, taking a step back. 'We can always rearrange for another day. When it's more convenient.'

'I think that's probably best,' said the woman. 'I'll tell him you came.'

'Thanks,' said Maggie, already retracing her steps in the snow. Having so looked forward to lunch out, she was suddenly grateful to be off the hook.

Starting back down the hill, she heard a whistle and turned to see someone battling up the snowy field towards her, frantically waving. Even with his hood up and half a dozen layers on, she could tell it was Rob.

'Maggie,' he was calling. 'Where are you going?'

She stood and waited until he had caught up with her.

'Aren't you going to stop for some lunch?' he asked, out of breath.

'I was. But, er, your mum said you'd been called away so maybe it would be better to do it another time?'

'No, don't worry, it's fine, I've finished now,' he insisted. 'And Mum's made a turkey pie.'

White meat in a pie? *Really?* Things were getting worse by the minute. Maggie opened her mouth but nothing came out. What excuse could she make? He already knew she was stuck here and didn't exactly have other commitments.

'I just thought you might want a break from the Higher House crowd,' said Rob. 'A bit of a change of scene.'

He was right. She *had* wanted a change of scene – although lunch in the company of his sour-faced mother wasn't quite what she'd had in mind.

But she couldn't go straight back to Cath's with her tail between her legs again. Not for the second time in three days.

'OK,' she said, in a thin voice. 'Sounds good.'

* * *

It wasn't as if she'd wanted the moon on a stick or anything. Just a turkey sarnie and a few fancy crisps. A chat and laugh with Rob over a couple of glasses of wine. In a comfy chair. In front of a roaring fire ideally.

But it wasn't panning out that way. The bottle of wine she'd brought with her, zipped up inside her cagoule, was still sitting there on the sideboard mocking her: no one had shown the least bit of interest in opening it, preferring to stick to water. And the dining room itself was gloomy and austere – very much in need of modernisation. Much like the parents themselves.

The dad was slightly more cordial than the mother, but only slightly. They were only a couple of hundred miles apart but, in many ways, Derbyshire was the polar opposite of Glasgow. Her home city was like a huge, overgrown village where it was impossible to go to the supermarket without coming away with the full details of the cashier's life story along with your weekly shop. Derbyshire folk, on the other hand, didn't like to waste words. And Rob's parents were no exception.

Maggie was trying to come up with some conversation – and failing. What she knew about farming and agriculture would have fitted easily on the back of a postage stamp. She couldn't even bear to listen to *The Archers*, for goodness' sake. Yes, she was a fan of Radio 4 – mainly for the politics and the pontificating about the arts and stuff – but as soon as that bloody theme tune came on, the radio went off. Maybe she was doing them a disservice, but Rob's parents didn't seem the sort who were big into the arts. And politics was probably best avoided as a matter of principle.

The clanking and scraping of cutlery on china was doing her head in. She'd always suffered from misophonia, even before she'd known the word for it: the sound of people eating had always gone right through her – made her blood run cold for some reason – and now it was cranked up to the max, *argh*, as she desperately cast around for something, anything, to say. But Rob beat her to it.

'Maggie's Scottish,' he announced, somewhat superfluously, as they'd already heard her speak.

'So I can hear,' said the mother, and carried on spooning pie into her miserable mouth.

'Which bit?' asked the dad, after a while.

'All of me!' said Maggie, and immediately wished she hadn't, when only Rob laughed at her joke. She cleared her throat and carried on. 'Glasgow, actually.'

'Ugh,' grunted the dad. 'For or against?'

'I beg your pardon?' said Maggie, stabbing at a lump of meat through the watery gravy.

'Scottish independence. For or against?'

'Well,' said Maggie, sensing a potential landmine. 'I can see pluses and minuses on both sides but, ultimately, yes I'm in favour of it.'

'But you're living in England?' said the mother, without looking up.

'Well. I've lived all over the place,' said Maggie. 'In fact, I've just come back after nine years in Hong Kong.'

'Maggie's looking for a new job,' said Rob, trying to steer the conversation back to safer ground.

'What line of work are you in?' asked the dad.

'I'm a lawyer,' said Maggie, taking a sip of water.

'Hmm,' said his dad. 'There's not much call for lawyers round here. Not much crime at all. Apart from the occasional quad bike getting nicked.'

'That's, erm, good,' said Maggie. She had no desire to get into how criminal law wasn't her area. 'So then,' she continued. 'How long have you lived in Archdale?'

'A hundred and fifty years,' replied the dad. 'Give or take.'

'That's how long the farm's been in the family,' Rob clarified. 'Mum's family.'

'Wow. A long time!' said Maggie, stating the obvious. Cath had warned her about this sort of thing when she'd first arrived here: that you weren't really, truly accepted in Archdale until you had ten generations buried in the graveyard. Cath herself had been here over twenty years now and was still very much classed as an 'incomer'. That's why she was always doing her simpering best to suck up to everyone. To fit in. Even Tiggy was still regarded as something of an interloper, apparently, and she had been born here.

'And it'll remain in the family a few hundred more,' said his mother, decisively.

She seemed pretty confident about that and Maggie wondered if the business with the loan company was all sorted out now? She was about to ask the question when she caught the panicked expression on Rob's face, imploring her not to say anything.

Maggie took the hint, reaching for her water instead. She felt drained all of a sudden, like she'd been unplugged at the mains. She needed to get away.

'That was delicious,' she said to Rob's mother. 'Thank you very much. And I don't want to be rude and rush off, but I'd better be going. Give myself time to walk back down before it gets dark.'

Rob's mother had gone to fetch her cagoule before she'd finished her sentence. Rob walked her to the door and out down the path. 'Look, I'm sorry about all that,' he said. 'They're alright really. They can just be a bit, y'know, *stiff* sometimes.'

'No, I'm sorry,' said Maggie. 'Sorry if I nearly said the wrong thing. About the farm. I thought—'

'My parents don't know anything about it,' he said, bluntly.

'You're kidding?' said Maggie, shocked. 'I know you were trying to keep it quiet, but…'

'Well, they know about the loan. They had to countersign the documents and stuff. But I've been the one handling the repayments.'

'So they don't know the farm's at risk?'

Rob stopped and hit his forehead hard with the heel of his palm. 'Oh God. I can't believe how stupid I've been, getting us tied up in this thing.'

Stupid? Or desperate? 'I'm sure you were only doing it for the best,' said Maggie.

But he wasn't listening. 'You heard what she said. That farm's been in my mother's family donkey's years. And I've lost it.' He snapped his fingers. 'Just like that.'

Maggie felt for him. 'You're under so much pressure. Maybe you need to talk to someone,' she suggested, gently.

'I've spoken to Jim about it.'

'Well… No… What I meant was… Maybe you should try speaking to a counsellor or something?'

'A counsellor?' he repeated, like she'd suggested he fly to the moon. 'What would I say? That I'm a dickhead and I've fucked everything right up? Sorry,' he added, embarrassed by his language.

'No. You swear away. I'd be swearing like a fucking trooper if I was in your shoes,' Maggie said, making him smile.

The smile vanished again. 'Nah. I sometimes think it would be best if I just took a shotgun down to the barn and…' he trailed off, with a weary laugh. 'I believe it's the farmer's preferred method, after all?'

'Don't you think you'd better start by telling your mum and dad?' said Maggie, resisting the temptation to say any more. She'd be leaving here soon, this wasn't her problem to solve and, anyway, God knew she had enough issues of her own.

'Look,' said Rob, collecting himself. 'It's brass monkeys out here. Let me drop you back down at Cath's. It's no trouble. Honestly.'

'No thanks,' said Maggie, firmly. 'I'm fine. The walk'll do me good.' She didn't want to arrive back at Cath's too soon, after all – didn't want her asking any questions.

She said goodbye to Rob and trudged back off down the snowy lane, waving behind her. When she was out of sight, she stopped for a moment to take a breath. The icy air filled her lungs, flooding her with relief.

'Should Old Acquaintance Be Forgot…?'

'There you go!' said Cath, handing her another steaming mug of Lemsip at arm's length. 'I won't get too close,' she said, plonking herself down in the furthest chair from Maggie. 'I don't want to start the new year by catching your lurgy.'

'Cheers,' rasped Maggie from her horizontal position on the couch.

This was it… Hogmanay! The last day of the old year. The Scots had basically invented it, but Maggie had never been a huge fan of New Year's Eve: a night of enforced merriment when all the amateur drinkers filled the pubs to bursting point. And this particular New Year's Eve was definitely in contention for the worst one ever; her and Cath sitting there watching Michael Bublé on the telly, crooning away on a freezing stage by the River Thames. What had poor old London town done to deserve this?

And to make matters worse, she'd been laid low by a real bugger of a head cold, complete with pounding eyeballs, streaming nose and a throat like the bottom of Joyce's budgie's cage – the result of the germs passed on from all that air-kissing, hugging and hand-shaking over the festive period.

The snow had obligingly disappeared just in time for Cath's family to catch their various planes, trains and automobiles back to where they'd come from. Richard, Katy and the twins had clearly been champing at the bit to get away and ring in the New Year with their new friends in their new home towns. Her parents too had been keen to get back down south for a second Christmas dinner with Cath's sister, Pippa, and her family. With Simon back in Leeds again, that just left Lauren – and Maggie back in the spare room. The house felt decidedly empty and Cath had spent most of the last few days cleaning it.

Rob had texted Maggie to say he was going down to The Farmer's for the New Year fancy dress party, and ask if she wanted to come. But she was glad her 'illness' gave her an excuse to avoid it: after the awkwardness of Boxing Day, she was in no particular rush to see him again so soon. And Cath hadn't made the party sound that appealing in any case. A fairly recent tradition by Archdale standards, it mainly attracted the younger age group – and she wouldn't have fancied being vommed on by a bunch of overwrought teenagers. Needless to say, Lauren had been keen to get down there to meet up with Dan and her other friends, dressed in the leftover costumes from her *Zombie Grease* school show.

According to Cath, Tiggy and Phil usually hosted a *soirée* on New Year's Eve for the grown-ups, but this year they'd fancied a change and decided to go to Edinburgh for the Hogmanay fireworks instead. They were having an *amazing* time – if their constant stream of loved-up selfies on Facebook was anything to go by – but Maggie couldn't understand why anyone would want to go to Edinburgh at this time of year, when it was crowded, expensive and bitterly cold. Mind you, as a Glaswegian, she couldn't really understand why anyone would want to go to Edinburgh full stop. It was just a castle on a hill, for goodness' sake, and the natives were as miserable as sin. So miserable that the government had had to invent the Edinburgh Festival just to get them to cheer up a bit after the war. Not that it had worked.

Maggie sneezed violently and Cath passed her the box of tissues from the coffee table without saying a word. She blew her nose, which was red raw by now, matching the shade of the tartan throw. Her forehead was sweating like a frying mushroom, but she couldn't seem to get warm in her bones. The fact that the boiler was now on its last legs wasn't helping matters. She'd asked Cath about getting a plumber in, but the suggestion had been given short shrift. There was no point repairing it, Cath had said, as the whole central heating system really needed replacing and Simon couldn't afford the expense just at the moment. So, for the time being, they just had to bloody well freeze. *Roll on the hot flushes*, thought Maggie, bitterly. *Something else to look forward to.*

She glanced at the clock above the fireplace. Still only half eleven. It had been a long day and night, feeling as rough as this…

'Right,' announced Cath, getting to her feet. 'I'm off to bed.'

'But it's not even midnight,' Maggie croaked.

'I'm not really bothered,' said Cath. 'It's been a horrid year and I don't expect the new one to be any better. I'd rather just go up and read my book. Goodnight and Happy New Year when it comes.'

As Cath stomped wearily up the stairs, Jazz took her cue to jump up next to Maggie on the couch, who was grateful for the warm body beside her.

The TV revellers were gearing up for the midnight countdown in front of Big Ben and Maggie's woozy thoughts went back to new years past in London with Andy. They'd always set off to some bar or party with such high hopes, but it was invariably an anti-climax. Everywhere was crowded, expensive and it was always impossible to find a taxi home – they'd usually end up walking miles to get back to their little flat in Earl's Court – but it hadn't seemed to matter. They'd always find something to laugh at. After a few years, they'd got wise to it all and decided that staying home was the best policy. And so that's what they'd done, stayed in, just the two of them, making plans and schemes for the year, and years, to come. Making plans for a family of their own.

And they'd come so close. So very close. But there was nothing left of their family now. Nothing left of Andy. Nothing left of herself hardly, which made it hard to see the actual point of her life. Of her existence.

She wished she could lose herself in a book like Cath, but she'd found she wasn't able to concentrate like she used to. She didn't even have the strength to flick through one of Cath's glossy magazines, full of women doing their damnedest to 'have it all'. The generation of women juggling families, careers, waxing appointments, you name it. *Well, what if you had nothing to juggle?* What if your career had come to a full stop? What if you had no job even, let alone a career? No husband, no children and no prospect of having any. Staring down the barrel of the menopause. What if no one would miss you if you weren't here?

She thought about what Rob had said on Boxing Day... the thing about 'going down to the barn with a shotgun'. *Maybe he had the right idea?* She could always do away with herself. Apart from the fact that she'd probably fuck it up and end up as a vegetable – a burden on the state.

What about pills? How many paracetamol could she cobble together from her own bedside drawer and Cath's bathroom cabinet? Not enough, probably.

Or she could just get mortally drunk and jump off a cliff into the sea. That would do it. Where was the nearest sea to here? Bridlington maybe? Did it have cliffs? What about Flamborough Head? That *definitely* had cliffs. How would she get there, though? She didn't even have the energy for the journey.

And there was no way she could do that to Joyce.

But she didn't really want to kill herself. She just didn't want to be alive anymore. *There was a difference.*

Self-pity was for losers – such an unattractive quality, she'd always thought – but she didn't even feel sorry for herself. This was a different thing altogether. Just a flat feeling of *nothing*.

BONG! The first chime of Big Ben rang out and she automatically drank a toast to herself with the last bitter mouthful from the mug. The crowd on the TV linked arms and launched into the old familiar song that was part of her DNA – '*Should old acquaintance be forgot...*' – and she felt a boiling tear roll down her cheek, followed by another one.

Maggie rubbed them away with her balled up, snotty tissue. She couldn't remember the last time she'd cried and she wasn't about to start now.

* * *

Sunday - January sixth, mouthed Maggie, running her finger down the calendar in the kitchen. Where had the first five days of the year gone? 'Epiphany,' it said in the box, in tiny red letters. What was that, again? Something to do with the three wise men, she vaguely recalled. Twelfth Night – when you were supposed to take down your decorations. Or was that yesterday? She could never remember. Either way, Cath had got rid of the tree and everything days ago.

Tipping her coffee dregs down the sink, Maggie peered out the window – you couldn't even *see* the tops today for the grey-white mist. Tomorrow, Monday, the rest of the world would return to normal after the Christmas standstill. Tomorrow would be the *real* start of the new year. Cath would be back working in the café and Lauren would be back at school. And it would be a big year for Lauren with her A-levels lurking on the horizon this summer.

Once again, she envied Lauren the adventures to come: starting university, making friends, travelling the world – that sense of possibility stretching out into the endless future, writing the story of your own life, while at the same time cramming as many new experiences as possible into one day. These days, weirdly, Maggie found that a couple of minor tasks could expand to fill a whole morning.

Like *this* morning, which was nearly over and all she'd done was wash her clothes, hang them on the lifeless radiators and take Jazz for a wander up the lane. With nothing else she *had* to do, it was a struggle to do anything at all; her motivation, her get-up-and-go, had completely deserted her.

But she did have something else she had to do, which she'd been meaning to do ever since the snow had gone. She needed to re-book her train to Glasgow and then she had to call Joyce and let her know when to expect her. She would sort it this afternoon when she got back from her driving lesson. Talking of which...

She looked out the window again, but there was still no sign of Val. Oh, well. She didn't even know why she was persevering with these driving lessons anyway. What was the point? She'd be back living in a city again soon. Once she got around to booking her ticket. Yep. She would definitely book it later. This evening. After the lesson with Val. Definitely. Or she could just leave it till the morning. What difference would another day make?

The Hair of the Dog

Still trembling, Maggie got out of the car and waved Val off. The lesson had been another nerve-shredder and she'd had to ask Val if they could stop at The Farmer's on the way home, so she could buy some wine to take back to Cath's. She really needed a drink and hadn't been all that surprised when Val bought a bottle for herself too.

The cosy glow in the kitchen window told her someone was already home. As she pushed open the back door, straight into the strains of James Blunt – 'strains' being the word – she knew it must be Cath.

The worktop was covered in flour and Cath was slicing into a cooking apple. Very forcefully. And she didn't turn round, though she must have heard her come in.

'Hiya,' said Maggie, as upbeat as she could manage, clanking her carrier bag of booze on to the table top. 'Everything alright?'

'Fine,' said Cath, not missing a beat with the knife.

Maggie could tell that things were far from fine. 'You look like you could do with a drink as well,' she offered, taking a bottle from the bag. 'Glass of red?'

'I don't think so,' said Cath, witheringly, to the chopping board. 'It's three in the afternoon, for goodness' sake.'

Maggie went to the dresser and reached for one of Cath's posh balloon glasses. There used to be half a dozen of them, but there were only three left on the shelf now. She could remember dropping one on the tiles – and another had cracked when she'd put it in the dishwasher – but what had happened to the other one? They might look very nice, but they were so impractical. The glass was just too thin.

Pouring herself a large one, she pulled out a chair and sat down. She went to take her jacket off, then stopped herself. 'Bloody hell. It's Baltic in here. Is the heating on?'

'It's finally given up the ghost…' muttered Cath.

'Oh. Hasn't Simon got his act together yet?' Maggie thought for a minute. 'How will we manage without any heating? Any hot water?'

Cath swung round to face her, the knife still in her floury hand. She swallowed hard before speaking. 'Perhaps you ought to find alternative accommodation if this place isn't to your liking?'

'OK. OK,' said Maggie. 'Sorry I spoke!' She held her hands up in mock surrender, but soon realised this was a mistake.

'Honest to God, I'm heartily sick of all this,' said Cath, her colour rising.

'Sick of what?'

'Sick of you. And your attitude. The dog up on the sofas and beds all the time – *She's up there on your bed as we speak!* – and dog hair bloody everywhere. Your fringe clippings in the bathroom sink. The whole place looking like a Swiss laundry. Your pants hanging from every banister and radiator in the house. Your laptop and all your other crap cluttering up every available surface…'

'Wow,' said Maggie. She couldn't remember ever seeing Cath properly lose her rag before. 'I didn't know you felt like—'

'I haven't seen you for the best part of a decade and yet you turn up at my house out of the blue, eating all my food, boozing every night like you're still a student, barely lifting a finger. You need to bloody grow up.'

'Listen, Cath…' pleaded Maggie.

'No, *you* listen, for once,' Cath growled. 'I'm sick to death of being everyone's skivvy. Everyone's whipping boy. If it's not you, it's bloody Simon. He's doing what he's done for years, strutting around the place doing exactly what he wants, going where he likes, pleasing himself, while I've been bringing up his kids and making him separate high-carb packed lunches for all his bloody cycle races, triathlons and God knows what else. And I'm sick of this village as well. Sick of running a shitty café for bugger all money. Sick of making apple-flaming-turnovers for shitty bake sales. Not to mention all the years of running a taxi service – driving all and sundry to various clubs and hobbies all over the bloody place.' She paused for a quick breath. 'I've got a degree, remember! I can speak four fucking languages, for fuck's sake. I could have gone anywhere. Done anything. I can't believe I gave up my bloody career for this… Gave up my life for it… And now Simon's fucking business is on the skids and—'

'On the skids?' interrupted Maggie, taking a gulp of wine. 'I thought you said it was just struggling a bit?'

'More than a bit,' said Cath. 'The government's changing some tax rule or other and that's apparently pulled the rug out from under his main area of work. All the partners, including him, have just had to put a cash injection into the firm to try and see it through the next few months.'

'God,' said Maggie to herself. 'An accountant with cashflow problems? The irony…'

But Cath's blood was up again. 'Everything's just a joke to you, isn't it?' she spat. 'Well, this is serious. He's paying out fifteen hundred pounds for that flat in Leeds every month, while I can't afford a new boiler and all the bloody window frames in this house are basically rotting away. Shame we can't all have rich husbands like Tiggy, eh?'

Tiggy? thought Maggie. What's *she* got to do with it?

'And now I can't afford Lauren's next round of school fees, let alone pay for a car for her, even an old banger. And all you can do, Maggie – *literally, all you can do* – is make snide remarks.'

'Woah!' objected Maggie. 'I'm sorry. I had no idea things were that bad…'

'Oh, give it a rest, will you? Of course you didn't realise because you're all wrapped up in yourself and your own problems.'

'How much is a new boiler, then?' asked Maggie, trying to calm her down.

Cath gave an irritated shrug. 'I dunno. Simon's always taken care of that sort of thing.'

'Roughly speaking.'

'Why? A couple of thousand… Something like that…'

'I can give you it,' Maggie offered. 'And Lauren's fees. She's only got a couple of terms left, hasn't she?'

'The unpaid fees… it's seven thousand and something!'

'Not a problem,' said Maggie. 'You can pay me back. One day.'

'You what?'

'When Simon's situation sorts itself out. No rush.'

'You mean… You've got, what, nearly ten grand you can give me? Just like that?' She snapped her fingers.

'Yes,' said Maggie. 'I've got a few quid in the bank…'

'So,' said Cath. 'Let me get this straight. I've been letting you sponge off me rent-free for months because I thought you were strapped for cash. But you could easily have gone and got a place of your own?'

'I've *tried* to give you some money,' said Maggie. 'Several times. And you've always refused to take it.' *This was all she could think of to say.* Yes, she could easily have afforded to rent a place – could've afforded to go on a world cruise for six months – but she hadn't wanted to. It was Cath's company and friendship she'd wanted. But she couldn't admit it.

'Was it all just a load of lies?' Cath was raging.

'All what?' asked Maggie, mystified.

'All that stuff about you rejecting your boss's advances. Him replacing you with a younger model. That you got "no pay-off, no nothing"…'

'That was all true,' said Maggie, fiddling with the stem of her glass. She wondered whether she should confide the rest of the story to Cath. It might do her good to tell someone what had really happened, might stop it buzzing away at the back of her head like a persistent fly. She decided to go for it.

'It just wasn't the whole truth,' she confessed, but Cath only glared at her, daring her to continue.

'He did take his revenge by promoting someone younger over my head,' Maggie went on. 'But it wasn't a woman – it was a younger *man*. That was even more of a smack in the face.' She took another glug of her wine. 'It's all such a boys' club, Cath, you wouldn't believe it… And so I resigned in the heat of the moment. Told him where to stick his job.' She swallowed. 'But, as I said, I've still got a few quid saved up.'

'You *resigned*?' said Cath, taking it in. 'So you weren't actually fired, then?'

'Believe me, I regret it now,' Maggie, with a heavy sigh. 'Hardly a minute goes by when I don't—'

'So you basically lied to me?'

Maggie shifted in her seat. 'None of it was *technically* a lie.'

'Right, that's it, I've had enough,' said Cath, wiping her hands on a dish towel. 'Why are you still here anyway? You were meant to be gone weeks ago. I don't know why you're still hanging around, frankly.' She threw down the towel. 'I think you should leave tomorrow.'

'Don't worry,' said Maggie, standing up unsteadily. The wine was well into her bloodstream by now, on its way to her brain. 'I'll go tonight.'

She grabbed her laptop and snapped the lid shut. A beeping sound filled the silence and it took her a few seconds to realise it was her phone ringing out, for the first time in ages. A Glasgow number.

Accepting the call, she didn't recognise the voice immediately. But it turned out to be Muriel, her mother's next door neighbour, who was shouting down the line as if trying to bridge the distance to Derbyshire. Muriel didn't mince her words and got straight to the point: she was very sorry to have to tell her that Joyce had died of a massive heart attack. At the bingo.

Maggie slumped back down and stared at the phone that was now silent. Through the whooshing in her ears, she was vaguely aware of Cath's voice saying something behind her, like she was speaking underwater. *I'm so sorry, Maggie. You can stay as long as you need. If there's anything I can do…*

Within seconds, Maggie was upstairs, going from room to room, collecting her still-damp clothes from the radiators, folding them as she went. *Focus on the practicalities*, she told herself. It was Sunday. Would there be a train to Glasgow tonight? Yes, probably. There was bound to be one from Manchester. How would she get to Manchester? Just phone a taxi from somewhere, anywhere, and sod the expense. And where would she stay tonight? Muriel would likely have a key for Joyce's flat…

There was one thing she was sure of: she knew how to organise a funeral.

Dear Maggie

Higher House
Archdale
Derbyshire

30th January 2019

Dear Maggie,

I've tried calling and emailing a few times, but I haven't managed to reach you. So I'm sending this letter to your mum's address in Glasgow, hoping that it reaches you OK.

I'm so very sorry about Joyce. I know what she meant to you. I can only imagine how you must be feeling and I hope you're managing to find a way through.

I'm even more sorry for the way I've behaved towards you over the last few months – and the way we've parted on bad terms like this. I wasn't really annoyed about the money thing at all and I'm not really sure what came over me.

Not that I want to make excuses or anything, but the last year has been utterly soul-destroying. I've always tried my best to be the perfect wife. The perfect mother. Trying to please everyone. Never rocking the boat. But now I'm asking myself – what good has it done me?

Now my three eldest are all away doing their own thing – and Lauren will follow them in a few months if things go to plan. I should have been looking forward to taking my foot off the gas a bit, spending some quality time with Simon, just the two of us. But he ruined all that with his cheating.

I feel as if I've got no one in my corner. After everything that Simon did to rupture the family, what I really wanted was for my dad to knock Simon's bloody block off – or threaten to knock his block off at least – but my parents are just so bloody reasonable!

Even my own sister doesn't want to know. I've hardly heard from her since all this drama went down. I think she's worried that divorce might be contagious and that her perfect little life down south would be infected if she had anything to do with me.

My so-called friends have been no better. I've reached the conclusion Tiggy's not quite as good a mate as I thought. I first realised it on that Crete trip. She was a bit of a nightmare, to be honest – talking about herself all the time, being rude to the locals, you name it. God, how I wished I'd gone with you to Dublin instead. But, in the interests of harmony, I just put up with it (story of my life!).

And now Lauren's told me that Tiggy's daughter, Freya, has been bullying her and that she's been bunking off school to avoid her. I'm still not sure what's behind it all, but I suspect it might be something to do with a boy – probably Dan. Anyway, I've tried to raise it with Tiggy, but she's just washed her hands of the whole thing and refuses to believe that her darling daughter could possibly be a little shit.

I'm not even angry, Maggie, just disappointed and empty – and I can't pretend that everything's alright anymore. I'm humiliated and heart-broken at what my life's become – compared to what I'd hoped it would be when I first started out, when you and I first knew each other. You being here reminded me of that – made me feel the failure all the more acutely – and, I'm ashamed to say, I took it out on you. Because you were the nearest. And I shouldn't have done that.

And I'm worried about you, Maggie. You've had a rotten time of it as well (the way your boss treated you was outrageous – I'm absolutely fuming on your behalf!) and I'm worried that you might be depressed or something. I'd give anything to see the old Maggie back again – the bolshie, idealistic one I used to know at uni (maybe without the binge-drinking bit! Sorry. I'm rambling now…).

You do know that you're welcome to come back and stay in Archdale any time? I mean it. Even though I'm sure you'd rather – What is it you always say? – 'cough up both lungs' than come back here. And, do you know what, I can't say I blame you. I'd run a mile from here myself if I could.

I miss you.

Much love,
Cath x

P.S. Lauren's furious with me for 'falling out' with you. She nagged me to get on and write this letter, in fact. Then she mumbled something like, 'Could we just go back to arguing about margarine?', but I've no idea what that was about…

Part 2

The Second Coming

Cath glanced at the clock above the coffee machine: it was only half past three, but it had been dark for hours. In fact, it had never really got light today.

She was folding the napkins, setting up the tables for the morning, the usual routine. Although she wasn't really sure why she was bothering – the café would doubtless be dead again tomorrow. Even her most diehard regulars couldn't be relied on to turn out in the depths of a February that was even more dreary than usual.

She dried her hands, took off her apron and shook her hair loose. Turning the sign on the door from 'OPEN' to 'CLOSED', she felt a twist of dread in her stomach at the thought of going home and pulling shut the curtains.

The prospect of pizza with Lauren in front of the telly tonight had been the only thing keeping her going, but Lauren had just texted to say she'd been invited to Dan's for tea instead – and the thought of pizza-for-one wasn't all that appealing.

Switching off the radio, she could hear a low rumbling outside. Thunder in the distance, maybe. Although she'd checked the forecast earlier and it hadn't said anything about a storm.

The sound of a car engine pulling away, followed by a rat-tat-tat on the glass of the door, gave her a frisson of déjà vu.

The figure standing there was rugged up against the elements in the standard winter wear for round here: a long, dark puffa coat and sturdy walking boots. *It couldn't be, could it?*

It was.

'Maggie?!' she exclaimed. 'Come in. Come in.' She opened the door wide. 'It's bitter out there.'

'Are you sure?' said Maggie, pulling back her hood and peeking inside to see if anyone else was there. 'I'm not still barred from the last time, am I?' she joked.

'Don't be silly,' said Cath. 'Come and take a seat and I'll make us a brew.'

Maggie followed her inside, trailing a wheelie case behind her – nearly twice the size of the one she'd brought the last time. Its wheels on the cobbles had clearly been the source of the mysterious rumbling.

Cath threw her arms around her, hugging her tight. She was frankly amazed to see Maggie back in Archdale – *Why hadn't she rung to tell her she was coming?* – but her questions could wait for now. It was enough just to see her again and know that she was alright. Having received no reply to her letter, she'd been starting to worry.

'You smell nice,' said Maggie, returning the hug. 'I take it the boiler's sorted and the hot water's back on?'

'Hmm. Yeah,' said Cath, ushering her into a seat. 'I ended up borrowing the money…'

'You borrowed it?'

'From The Bank of Mum and Dad. Can you believe it? At my age.'

Maggie shook herself out of her big coat. 'It's an ugly looking thing, but it's very cosy,' she said, throwing it over a chair. 'I reckoned I'd need it.'

'It's really great to see you again,' said Cath over her shoulder, as she coaxed the coffee machine into giving up its inky brown liquid.

'It's only been a few weeks…' said Maggie.

'I know, but still.'

'I'm like a bad penny, eh?' said Maggie, fiddling with a teaspoon. 'Or a dog returning to its own vomit.'

'Not at all,' said Cath, bringing over two frothy mugs and sitting down next to her. She looked more closely at Maggie. 'Your hair looks nice. Sort of softer.'

'Yeah, well,' said Maggie, running her hand through it. 'Probably because I went to the hairdresser instead of cutting it myself. I wanted to look smart for the funeral.'

Cath put her hand on top of Maggie's. Maggie looked weary, as if tears might not be far from the surface. 'How did it go?' Cath asked, gently.

'It went well,' said Maggie. 'But I'd rather talk about other things, if that's OK?'

'Sure. Understood,' said Cath, giving her hand a squeeze.

'How's everything around here?' Maggie asked her.

'Fine. Everything's fine.'

'How's Rob? Is he alright?'

'Rob?' echoed Cath, interested that she'd singled him out for special mention. 'Same as ever, I think.'

'Good.' Maggie sounded strangely relieved.

'Anyway, it's good for me that you're back,' said Cath. 'I need some help with *this* place, actually.'

'Really?' said Maggie, looking around. 'You don't seem exactly run off your feet…'

'Well, no,' said Cath. 'But I've still got to stay open. And Neil's gone hiking in the south of Spain for three months, so I'm on my own. You could try out that loyalty card idea you were talking about…'

Maggie didn't look very keen. 'Thanks for the offer,' she said. 'But, after the last time, I think it's better if I just leave you to it.

And besides,' she took a careful sip of her coffee, 'I'm working for the competition now. I wouldn't want there to be a conflict of interest.'

'*The competition*?' asked Cath, wrinkling her nose.

Maggie nodded. 'I was fed up in Glasgow. Bored of not working. Of not having a purpose. And so I phoned Australian Pete to see if he was still looking for some help at the pub.'

'*The pub*?' snorted Cath. '*The Farmer's Arms*?' Was she hearing things? This had to be a wind-up. 'But you loathe The Farmer's Arms.'

'*Loathe*'s a bit strong,' said Maggie. 'I mean, it's not my favourite pub in the world or anything, but it's got its advantages.'

'Like what?'

'Well,' said Maggie, thinking hard. 'It's nice and warm when the log fire's going...'

'And I thought you hated Australian Pete?'

'Don't be daft,' said Maggie, taking another sip. 'I don't hate him, as such. I just find him intensely irritating.'

'Fair enough,' said Cath, doubtfully. 'It's just... I thought you'd have more pride than to take a job pulling pints...'

'It's my "pride",' – Maggie made the inverted commas in the air – 'that's making me want to do something worthwhile with my time.'

'Pulling pints is worthwhile...?'

Maggie folded her arms and grinned at her. 'Tell me. What's the difference between serving beer and serving cups of tea in a café like you? Don't be such a terrible snob...'

'Hmm. I suppose I'll get used to the idea,' shrugged Cath. 'Anyway, I'm rattling around that big house up there on my own. It's a bit miserable if I'm honest – even *with* a functioning boiler.

It'll be nice to have you back. You can have Richard's bedroom if you like. It's a lot bigger than the spare room and I'm sure he wouldn't mind.'

'Thanks again,' said Maggie. 'But I won't have to.'

Cath looked up from stirring her froth.

'I'm moving into the pub,' Maggie continued. 'Into one of the B&B rooms upstairs.'

It was Cath's turn to grin now. 'You're joking, right?'

'Nope,' said Maggie, solemnly. 'When I rang Pete about the job, we got talking. He actually asked me if I could manage the place for him.'

Cath was sure she was hearing things now. 'He asked if you could *manage the place* for him?'

'Only for a couple of weeks,' said Maggie, draining her mug. 'Well, closer to a month, actually. His brother's getting married back in Australia – Wagga Wagga or somewhere – the arse end of nowhere, basically – and he wants to go back home for the wedding.'

'But... hang on... unless I've missed something... you haven't actually managed a pub before?'

'How hard can it be?' declared Maggie. 'I think he just wants someone with half a brain who can keep an eye on that young barman who works for him – and the girls in the tearoom, who seem to change on a weekly basis.'

'Oh well,' said Cath, not sure what else to say.

'And so, you see, I won't *just* be pulling pints,' said Maggie.

'No,' agreed Cath, clearing away their mugs and rinsing them in the sink. She looked at the clock again. 'D'you fancy going round there now?' she suggested. 'To the pub, I mean. I could do with a drink.'

'I'd rather not, if it's OK,' said Maggie. 'I'll be spending all my time there soon enough. I'll just pop round to see Pete and drop off my suitcase. Back in ten minutes.'

'Fair enough,' said Cath, watching her zip up her coat.

'And then it'd be nice to go and see Lauren. If she's at home?'

'OK. She's off to Dan's later, but I'm sure you'll catch her before she goes.'

'And Jazz, of course.'

'Let me see… Jazz?' said Cath, pretending to think about it. 'I don't *think* she's got any plans for the evening…'

Maggie chuckled and headed back out into the gloom, turning left in the direction of The Farmer's.

Cath stood and stared after her. So it wasn't a wind-up after all.

'You're A Lang Time Deid'

Back at Higher House, Jazz had given Maggie a euphoric welcome and her heart had been well and truly warmed. Now, as they sat down to their pizzas, the aroma of cheese and pepperoni was filling the kitchen, making the dog salivate. Maggie was dying to break a bit off and give it to her, but she didn't dare.

'She's waiting for the crusts,' said Cath. 'It's OK. You can give her them. Lauren always does.'

'Oh well,' said Maggie. 'Since this is technically Lauren's pizza, it would be rude not to!' And she dropped a long, cheesy crescent into Jazz's mouth.

'It was good to see Lauren just now,' Maggie went on. 'Good to see her looking at bit cheerier about life. No thanks to that Freya. Or bloody Tiggy for that matter.'

'Ah. You got my letter, then?' said Cath.

'God, yes, your letter,' said Maggie, sitting up and leaning in. 'I was going to say about that, I had absolutely no idea that this "Freya" girl was Tiggy's daughter. When Lauren mentioned a while back that she was giving her grief—'

'Hang on,' interrupted Cath. 'Lauren told you about it?'

'Yep,' Maggie admitted. 'When you were away in Crete.'

'Really?' said Cath, exasperated. 'Why didn't she tell *me*?'

'I expect she didn't want to worry you,' said Maggie, treading carefully. 'You've had a lot on your plate. And also... I guess it was all a bit awkward, what with Tiggy being a friend of yours?'

'Some friend,' huffed Cath. 'When I brought it up with her, she couldn't bring herself to believe that her precious little princess could also be a nasty little bully.'

Maggie screwed up her face. 'I'd believe literally anything of Tiggy's spawn.'

'You're awful!' Cath gasped, although Maggie could see she was trying not to laugh.

'Well, it's true,' Maggie continued. 'She's probably a chip off the old block, the poor girl. It's not her fault.'

'At least her father took it seriously.'

'Phil got involved?'

'Yep,' said Cath. 'He wasn't happy at all. Had a very stern word with her, apparently. Laid down a few ground rules.'

'Well, good for him,' said Maggie. 'I'm glad to hear it.'

'He seems to get it that he's actually her parent. Rather than trying to be her best mate.' Cath patted the sides of her mouth with her napkin. 'Anyway,' she said. 'That's enough of all that. Tell me, how was the funeral?'

'It was nice, actually,' said Maggie. 'Really nice. The rain pissed it down, of course, but that's Glasgow for you.'

'Funerals should always be rainy and miserable,' said Cath. 'That should be the law. It doesn't feel right otherwise.'

'True.' Maggie nodded.

'And did you, y'know, get everything sorted out…?'

'Yeah,' said Maggie, chomping into another slice of pizza. 'I had to speak to the council about giving back her flat, obviously. Other than that,' she sighed, 'it's not like she had a lot. A couple of bank accounts. Some furniture. Mainly sentimental stuff. All the postcards I'd sent her from my travels over the years… I've put it all in storage with my things from Hong Kong.'

'I really feel for you. It must be so awful. And all such a shock as well…'

'Yeah,' said Maggie. 'I really thought she'd go on for ever…' She tossed Jazz another crust. 'I won't lie. I'm gutted. And even more gutted that I put off seeing her for six months. What on earth was I thinking?'

'Don't be too harsh on yourself,' said Cath. 'You've had a really hard time lately. You need to practise some self-care.'

'*Self-care?*' asked Maggie, squinting at her. 'That's a new one.'

'Not really,' said Cath. 'It just means you need to be a little bit kinder to yourself.'

'Go on, say it!' said Maggie. 'I'm waiting…'

'Say what?' asked Cath, confused.

'Isn't this the bit where you suggest I take a mindfulness class with Tiggy?'

'Ugh, no!' said Cath. 'I was actually going to suggest that I run you a nice bath.'

Maggie laughed. 'Nah, you're alright,' she said. 'I'd better get back down to the pub and unpack and stuff. Show Australian Pete that I mean business.'

'Alright,' said Cath, reaching across the table for Maggie's empty plate.

'No,' said Maggie, grabbing it back from her. 'I'll wash up before I go. I'm not having you doing everything.'

'Cheers,' said Cath, sitting back in her seat. 'I won't stop you.' She hesitated as Maggie got on with soaping the plates. 'I meant what I said in the letter, by the way. I'm sorry for how I behaved towards you. As I said, I'm not really sure what came over me.'

'Oh, I dunno. Maybe it should come over you more often,' said Maggie over her shoulder. 'Maybe it's a good thing. You're far too nice to people – and I include myself in that.'

Cath blushed and looked at the floor. 'Tell me,' she said, after a moment. 'Why have you come back to Archdale?'

Maggie carried on rinsing, wondering how best to reply.

'Oh, don't get me wrong,' Cath continued, hastily. 'I said you were welcome back any time and I meant it. But I never thought you'd actually *come* back.'

'I missed Jazz,' said Maggie. And it was true: she'd missed the simple, uncomplicated affection, as well as the excuse to get out of the house for a walk every day.

'Oh, come on,' said Cath.

'Well,' said Maggie, turning to her. 'As you know, I'm Scottish, and we're known for being, let's say, careful with money.'

'Ye-es?' said Cath.

'And, well, do you remember that return ticket I bought before Christmas…? I didn't want to let it go to waste.'

'Come off it,' said Cath, throwing her rolled up napkin at her. 'You're not getting out of it that easily.'

'Well,' said Maggie, stopping her scrubbing of the oven dishes momentarily. 'That's a very good question.'

'I'm all ears,' said Cath.

'You know, it's funny,' said Maggie. 'But Joyce dying has been such a wake-up call.' She paused. '*You're a lang time deid.* That's what she used to say.'

'Pardon me?' said Cath.

'*You're a long time dead,*' Maggie translated. 'Life is short – even when it's quite long, like Joyce's. And you've got to make the best of things.'

'It's a cliché, but it's so true.'

'Joyce always did that,' said Maggie. 'Made the best of things. When my dad abandoned us and she was left with me, just the two of us.' She wrung out the dishcloth, twisting it tightly, staring at her reflection in the dark of the window. 'I always wanted to protect her, you know? I never wanted to show weakness in front of her or cause her any worry.'

'I can understand that,' said Cath. 'A bit like Lauren with me.'

'And then, with all this losing-my-job business, I really felt that I'd let the side down. Storming out of the office like that. Like a damn fool, I brought it on myself.'

'You didn't let the side down,' said Cath. 'You're human, Maggie. Yes, even you! You made a mistake. It happens.'

'That's the thing,' said Maggie. 'Everyone at the funeral kept telling me how proud Joyce had been of me and what I'd achieved. How she never stopped talking about me.' She couldn't risk turning round to look at Cath. She could feel a treacherous prickle behind her eyes and knew that any sympathy would only turn it to tears. *Better to keep talking.* 'And so I've decided to try and live up to her opinion of me. I've been focused in on myself for far too long. And I need to do something about it.'

'That sounds really positive,' said Cath. 'As long as you're careful and take it slowly. Baby steps and all that.'

'I'd convinced myself I had nothing in my life, but that's not true. I'm still young – sort of. I've got my health, touch wood. And I've got other things…'

Cath coughed theatrically. 'Like, the *very best friend* a girl could ask for?'

'Indeed!' said Maggie and laughed. 'You know, if I'm honest, I think I've been wallowing a bit. I need to buck up. *To keep buggering on.* That's what Joyce would say.' She balanced the last of the dishes on the draining board and picked up a towel to start drying. 'I need to broaden out my job search a bit – into other areas of the law, not just oil and gas. And I'm also going to try and do something useful with myself in the meantime.'

'Yeah. I get that now,' said Cath. 'That's why you've taken the job in the pub.'

'And something else as well,' said Maggie. 'I'm going to go round to Rob's and look over that loan stuff for him. See if I can help in any way.'

'Ah. Rob. I see,' said Cath, raising an eyebrow.

'See what?' asked Maggie. 'What are you implying?'

'Well, it's just… I've noticed that you two seem to, er, get on very well.'

'What? Piss off!' laughed Maggie, flicking Cath with the dish towel. 'That's not why I'm doing it. I just don't like the idea of him – of *anyone* – being shafted like that.'

'Hmm,' said Cath. 'And his rugged good looks have got nothing to do with it, I suppose?'

'Oh? D'you think he's good-looking?' asked Maggie, pretending the thought had never occurred to her. 'I suppose he is. Although I don't normally go in for that whole farmer thing and, anyway, I've never been one for mixing business with pleasure or anything like that.'

'Erm. Would you like to remind me how you met Andy? Or did I imagine that?'

'Oh, come on. Rob's about as different from Andy as it's possible to get,' said Maggie, keen to gloss over this technicality. 'So. As I was saying, I start my first shift at the pub tomorrow evening, so I'm going to arrange to go up to the farm and see Rob in the afternoon. But hang on a minute, here we are again, talking about me. What about you? What about *your* self-care, missus?'

'Oh, I'm fine,' said Cath, breezily.

'You see! You're doing it again,' said Maggie, sitting down opposite her. 'I'm not sure that you actually *are* fine. All that stuff you said in your letter…'

'Well, I'm a bit happier now that Lauren's happier.'

'And what about Simon? I thought things were a bit better on that front? You seemed to be getting on OK at Christmas?'

'Well… We've been fighting a lot about money. I earn hardly anything from the café – it's just a nominal wage – but it's years since I had a proper job. Nobody would want me and I probably couldn't do anything else anyway.'

'That's not true,' said Maggie, although she wasn't sure she believed it herself, if her own recent experience was anything to go by.

'I need to take a leaf out of your book and find something meaningful to do with my time,' said Cath. 'Something to fill the void when Lauren leaves home.'

'Maybe I can start helping instead of hindering,' said Maggie. 'Everything you said before was right. I've been so selfish. I've had my head so far up my arse, it didn't even occur to me how *you* were feeling.' Cath tried to protest, but she carried on. 'It's time I gave *you* a bit of support. I need you to know that – what was the phrase you used in your letter? – *I'm in your corner.*' Maggie stuck her fingers down her throat. 'Sorry. That was a bit barfsome.'

'And also faintly terrifying,' laughed Cath. She looked at her watch. 'Bloody hell, it's quarter to ten. We've been droning on for hours.'

'Australian Pete'll be starting to think I've had second thoughts.'

'Come on, then,' said Cath, grabbing her car keys from the counter. 'I'll give you a lift down to your new digs.'

'I don't suppose I can put it off any longer,' said Maggie, rolling her eyes, putting on a show of reluctance.

But she was knackered now and secretly relieved to be going. She was very good at talking and she'd said a lot of stuff tonight, all very noble, all of it true. But she still couldn't come straight out and say it to Cath: that, in the few weeks since Joyce's funeral, she'd felt more alone than she'd ever felt in her life. That the main reason she'd come back to Archdale was that she didn't really have anywhere else to go.

Deep and Meaningful

Maggie's room above the pub was as poky as anything, but it did have its own en suite bathroom. Just as well as she wouldn't have relished sharing a toilet with Australian Pete till he left on his travels.

To say it wasn't the cleanest room in the world was an understatement, though. The skirting boards were sprinkled with a liberal dusting of spider carcasses – big ones at that – but creepy crawlies didn't really bother her anymore. In the Far East, she'd got used to the cockroaches running amok in the summer – sometimes over the buttons of her speaker-phone while she was on a conference call.

Pete had left two towels on the bed for her, which she held up to the light. Maggie had to laugh: the material was so thin you could have 'spit peas through them', as Joyce would have put it.

She pulled back the duvet to inspect the bed and a reassuring wave of washing powder smell hit her nose. There was only one pillow, but it too passed the sniff test, which was the main thing. The place needed a woman's touch really – although she probably wasn't the one to provide it. A proper woman, someone like Cath, would have the place ship-shape in no time.

She flopped down on to the bed and looked up at the stripy wallpaper. *God!* It was curling away from the damp patch in the corner of the ceiling like it was trying to escape.

She'd already turned down the scalding radiator, but the room was still uncomfortably hot. And she wasn't sure if she was imagining it, but the smell of several centuries of stale beer seemed to hang in the air, so that she could almost taste it. She'd tried opening the window a bit, but had to close it again as the plangent chime of the church bell every fifteen minutes would only keep her up all night.

Not to worry. It was February after all. Much better to be too warm than too cold.

She switched off the bedside lamp and focused her attention on the round paper light shade in the centre of the ceiling... imagined it was the ceiling fan in her bedroom in Hong Kong... The one she used to dream was a helicopter's blades, like Martin Sheen in *Apocalypse Now*, drunk in his hotel room in Saigon...

She closed her eyes and pictured billowing silks in burnt orange and hot pink... dark-haired, loose-limbed young women flying through the streets on roaring scooters... a gin and tonic in a tall glass on the roof of the Rex Hotel in the shade of the early evening.

She was sound asleep before the next muffled chime

* * *

The following day, she set off up to the farm to see Rob as promised: they'd arranged to meet there at twelve-thirty, the time he stopped for his lunch break every day.

She'd felt quite bullish when she was texting him earlier but, with every step she took, her resolve was turning to trepidation. She hadn't seen him for weeks – not since Boxing Day, when they hadn't exactly parted on great terms.

The rain, which had been grim and swirling overnight, was just a fine mist now. And, compared to her stifling room at the pub, the air was like a cool glass of water. Just the right temperature for walking up a hill. But it wasn't as much fun without Jazz for company. Maybe she could ask to borrow her for a few days if Cath and Lauren didn't mind? She'd have to run it past Pete, but he would be off soon in any case.

Australian Pete wasn't too bad really. When Cath dropped her off at the pub last night, he'd already lugged her suitcase up to her room for her. And then she'd expected him to lord it over her this morning – to patronise her as he was 'showing her the ropes' in the pub – but he'd been surprisingly OK. With a sense of humour as dry as the deserts of his native land.

The poor guy seemed to be exhausted more than anything: worn out and desperate for a holiday. He'd told her that he hadn't actually had a proper break in the three years since he'd taken over the pub. And, from what he was saying this morning, he hadn't had a particularly easy time of it since he'd arrived in Archdale.

He'd already given her most of his life story, it felt like. He'd grown up in a mining town in New South Wales and then, when he was ten, they'd come on holiday to Derbyshire, tracing their family tree. For reasons Maggie couldn't fathom, the young Pete had fallen in love with the Peak District: the lush, green landscape had been a novelty compared to the bone-dry earth of his part of the world. And, eventually, his boyhood love of the place had evolved into the grown-up dream of running his own pub there one day – maybe even starting his own little brewery.

However, as is the way with these things, the reality was a lot tougher than he'd imagined. For one thing, The Farmer's Arms wasn't his own pub: it was owned by one of the big pub chains, which apparently put the rent up every time he managed to increase the meagre profits. Which in itself wasn't easy. As she'd seen for herself, business was dead in the winter months – and wasn't exactly buzzing in the summer either.

Maggie reached the gates of the farmyard ten minutes early, just as Rob's mother was pegging out some washing on the line, in defiance of the moisture in the air. As Maggie struggled to unbolt them, she could see the woman watching her through the gaps in the damp sheets.

'Hello again,' Maggie called over to her. 'Could you possibly help me with this?'

The woman came over and unlocked the gate. He's in the kitchen,' she said, abruptly. And that was that.

Maggie knocked on the back door and tentatively pushed it open. Rob was sitting at the kitchen table, head bent over a cardboard folder stuffed with papers. He jumped up at the sight of her, a broad grin on his face, which quickly turned solemn again. 'I was very sorry to hear about your mum,' he said.

'Ah, thanks,' she replied. 'It was a bit of a shock. Er, so...,' she pointed at the table. 'Is that the file?'

Rob nodded. He reached over and produced a single sheet of paper out of it. 'This letter arrived while you were away. Just one line. It says they'll be "putting matters in the hands of their solicitors" if I don't pay what's owed within seven days. That was two weeks ago.'

'Pretty standard,' said Maggie, running her eye over it. 'It's called a "letter before action". It's like a final demand.'

Rob sighed deeply while she sifted through the other documents in the file.

'I guess that explains the look on your mum's face?' she said, without looking up. 'I take it you've told them by now?'

'Yeah,' he confirmed. 'I told them on Boxing Day, after you'd gone. It didn't exactly come as a shock.'

'So she knows why I'm here, then?'

'Yep.'

'It's just… She looked at me like I was something unpleasant she'd stepped on in the farmyard.'

'Would you like a brew?' he offered, changing the subject.

'I'll have a coffee, please. Splash of milk, no sugar.' But she wasn't quite ready to let it go. 'Seriously, though,' she continued. 'What's her problem with me? It can't *just* be because I'm Scottish?'

Rob turned round from the kettle with an awkward smile. 'She thinks you're my, y'know… girlfriend or something.'

'*Girlfriend*?' Maggie laughed. 'I'm forty-six, for Chrissake!'

Rob said nothing.

'Girlfriend?' Maggie said again, compelled to fill the silence. 'Let me guess,' she went on, mischievously. 'They've had a good look at me and they don't think I'm farmer's wife material?' She paused. 'Well, they're right. I've never been a very practical person. Joyce – my mother – she always used to say that I "*couldn't put a nut in a monkey's mouth.*"'

Rob reached up to the shelf for the jar of own-brand instant. 'My parents want me to settle down with a nice Derbyshire lass.' He pronounced the words like they were some form of death sentence. 'They've been pushing me for an heir for years.'

'An *heir*?' repeated Maggie, shaking her head. 'Heir to *what*, exactly? The family debts? It's not like there's going to be anything left to inherit.' The words were out before she could stop them. Rob's face fell and she cursed her mouth for running away with her. Then it dawned on her what he was getting at.

'Wait! I get it,' she said, doing that thing of lashing out to hide her hurt. 'My breeding years are behind me? I'll never have a child? Is that it?'

Rob bridled uncomfortably and she could tell she'd hit the nail on the head.

'It's alright. You can tell your mother not to worry.' She laughed again, grimly this time. 'There's no danger of me being your girlfriend.'

'Oh… OK,' he said, as Maggie sat down and pulled the loan agreement out of the file. The kettle was whistling away discordantly on the hob – and she was desperately trying to focus on the dry legal clauses in front of her – but she found that she couldn't stop talking. Like her tongue had been loosened. Like when you'd had too much to drink, only in this case she was stone cold sober.

'I *did* have a child,' she heard herself say, turning the pages. *Why was she talking about this now? For God's sake shut up, woman!* 'A baby girl. We called her Joy. After my mother. But she was very premature and she died. She would only be a couple of years younger than Lauren, Cath's daughter.'

'Listen, I'm really sorry,' said Rob, clearly mortified. 'I didn't mean to—'

'*We* had a child, I should say.' She couldn't stop herself now. 'Andy and me. My husband. And then he died as well.'

'I know,' said Rob.

'I don't really like to talk about it,' said Maggie. 'Don't want people to think I'm a saddo. God alone knows why I'm talking about it now.' She looked up at Rob for a moment. 'Hang on. *You know?*'

He nodded his head. 'I'd heard you were widowed. On the village grapevine, like.'

'Of course you did!' she said, sitting back in her chair. Why *wouldn't* he know? It was literally impossible to keep anything quiet around here.

Rob poured out two mugs of coffee, handed her one and sat down next to her. 'What happened to your husband?' he asked in a soft voice. 'If you don't mind me asking?'

'Has the grapevine not told you the answer to that one as well?' she said, archly, and then felt bad about it. 'Sorry… It was ten years ago last week. He was killed in a road accident. In Uganda.'

'Uganda?'

'Yeah. He was an ophthalmologist. An eye doctor,' she clarified. 'He worked for a flying eye charity.'

'He sounds like a good bloke.'

'He was.' She smiled and took a sip of her coffee. 'He was also an annoying, mouthy Mancunian. A United fan who worshipped Alex Ferguson. He used to say that that was why he liked me so much – I'm from the same part of Glasgow as his idol.'

Rob chuckled and took a sip from his own mug. 'How did the two of you meet?'

'It was very romantic,' dead-panned Maggie. 'I was dressed up as a cavewoman for the purposes of handing over one of those massive fundraising cheques to him.'

'A cavewoman?' He chuckled.

'I know,' she said, cringing. 'The law firm I worked for in London used to do some free legal work for his charity and I was the junior lawyer assigned to it at the time. There *was* a reason for the cavewoman costume, but I can't quite remember it now.'

'So you've lived in London as well?' he said. 'Sounds like you've had an interesting life.'

'I suppose I have,' said Maggie. It was very easy to forget that sometimes.

'I feel even more boring now than I did before,' said Rob, running his hand through his hair. 'I've had no real drama in my life. Until now, that is,' he said, indicating the pile of papers in front of him.

'There must be something,' said Maggie. 'If you think hard enough.'

'Not really,' said Rob, shaking his head. 'I had a fiancée once, but she left me for another bloke and went to live in Sheffield.'

'Well,' said Maggie, kindly. 'More fool her.'

'I'm not exactly a great bet, am I?' he went on. 'A failing farmer, covered in muck, who still lives with his parents. And not even *that* for much longer.'

Maggie picked up the folder of documents and waved it in front of him. 'Let's not be too defeatist, shall we?'

'Is there *anything* we can do?' he said, and she could hear the weariness in his voice. 'Any way I can get out of this?'

'Maybe not,' said Maggie, truthfully. 'Even though it's unfair and the interest rate is a joke, that doesn't mean it won't stand up legally.'

His neck seemed to sink down into his broad shoulders.

'But I've got an idea,' she said. The cogs of her brain were clanking round, back to first year contract law at university. 'It might be a bit of a long shot, I'm not sure…'

'Go on.' Rob looked at her pleadingly, not even trying to hide his desperation.

'Well. You could argue that they've effectively mis-sold you the loan. That they only got you to sign it by saying they would find you a cheaper one at the end of twelve months. A longer-term loan at a better interest rate. Which they haven't done.'

'And?' said Rob, his brows knitted.

'Misrepresentation!' said Maggie, triumphantly.

'Miss *what*?'

'Misrepresentation,' she said again. 'They induced you to enter into the contract by misrepresenting the facts,' said Maggie. 'Which is the polite, legal way of saying that they basically lied to you. Listen', she said. 'I've googled this company and they've basically been doing the same thing to farmers all over the country.'

'And you think that this – this *misrepresentation* thing – might work?'

'I really don't know, to be honest. But I know a man who might,' she said, gathering up the documents from the table. 'Do you mind if I take these away with me?'

'Sure. No problem,' said Rob.

'It's just… I need to go back down to the pub now. I'm working later.'

'You're working? At the pub?'

'Yeah. Didn't I say? I'm covering for Australian Pete while he's away. He's off to Australia on Wednesday.'

Maggie chuckled at his surprised expression as she made for the door, the folder tucked under her arm. 'I'm sure I'll see you down there some time…?'

'For sure,' he said, his grin back again. 'Definitely!'

Maggie Phones a Friend

On her way back down to the village, Maggie pulled her phone out of her coat pocket. There was no time like the present and she hoped that Giles's number was still in it. It had been a few years since they'd last spoken – three, maybe four? – but he'd definitely be the one to help her, if anyone could.

Their paths had gone in quite different directions since they'd left university. While Maggie had entered the murky world of international commerce, Giles had become a barrister specialising in civil litigation. He'd quickly established himself as a rising star before the Chancery Division of the High Court in London, not to mention being the first black advocate to be admitted to his prestigious chambers. He also owed her a few favours after all the cases she had pushed his way over the years, when cross-border financial transactions had gone sour and become cross-border financial disputes.

Maggie scrolled down and dialled his number, which was picked up within three rings. No change there: he'd always been an efficient goody-two-shoes.

'Maggie Macbeth!' he announced, his clear, plummy tones ringing out down the line. 'To what do I owe this pleasure?'

Wow. His accent was even grander than when they'd first met at uni, when he was box-fresh from his Kenyan boarding school.

'Hi, mate,' she said. 'Good to hear you're still posher than the Queen Mother.'

'How the devil *are* you, Begbie?' he replied, teasing her back. Begbie had always been his affectionate nickname for her, after the Glaswegian psycho in *Trainspotting*. At least, she assumed it was affectionate.

'Never mind that,' said Maggie. 'I need to pick your brain.'

'Pick away,' Giles drawled. 'Pick away.' And, as Maggie told him all about Archdale and Rob and the details of Rob's predicament, she could almost hear him frowning down the phone.

'Can't they sort it out amicably?' he asked. 'Come to some agreement? Out of court? The letter might just be a warning. They might not actually want to follow through.'

'Nah,' said Maggie. 'They will. This loan company, they're bastards, basically. No other word for it.'

'I see. I see.'

Maggie floated her idea for Rob's defence but, as she'd suspected, the issues were far from clear-cut.

'Hmm. Misrepresentation can be a hard one to prove,' said Giles. 'It depends so much on the particular facts and circumstances. I wouldn't get his hopes up too much at this stage.'

'The guy's desperate,' said Maggie. 'Even if it's only a punt, so be it. I think we've got to give it a go.'

'Understood,' said Giles. 'Look. Call me again if they serve him with formal legal proceedings.'

'I think it's more a case of *when*, to be honest.'

'Well, when they do – under the rules of procedure – he'll have twenty-eight days to lodge the basics of his defence.'

'Four weeks?' said Maggie. 'Well. That'll certainly focus the mind.'

'It's enough,' said Giles. 'And, in the meantime, I'll have a bit of a think.'

'OK, mate. I appreciate it.'

'Listen, I'm terribly sorry, Begbie, but I'm afraid I've got to run. I'm flat out in the middle of a big trial at the moment.'

'No problem,' said Maggie. 'What's the trial? Anything juicy?' But the line had already gone dead.

She stood and stared enviously at the silent phone, nostalgic for the days when she too used to be busy and important.

Flying Solo

A few days later, Maggie was standing behind the bar of The Farmer's Arms, her back to the till. She'd waved Australian Pete off a couple of days ago with her firm instructions to have a good time – and her equally firm assurances that everything would be totally fine in his absence.

And so far, it *had* been fine. A bit *too* fine. Boring, in fact.

With the start of March, the weather had improved slightly, but the pub was still deader than the ten-generation-skeletons in the church graveyard. Even now, at six o'clock on a Friday evening, not a single customer had crossed the threshold. Was there some sort of 'happening' in the village that she hadn't been told about – some Scout jamboree or bizarre pagan festival she'd been excluded from? Or maybe Phil and Tiggy were hosting one of their legendary *soirées* she'd heard so much about.

She wasn't too bothered in any case. Pete hadn't had much time to induct her into the mysteries of the pub trade and a few quiet evenings like this would give her a chance to learn the ropes at her own pace. A chance to get over her fear of venturing back down to the gloomy cellar to change a barrel – and spraying herself top-to-toe in beer in the process, like she'd done the first time she tried it.

It would also give her time to do some research into whether Rob actually had a viable legal case or not. In the bad old days, you would have to do this by going to a proper library and digging out tome after tome of dusty law reports. But things had come a long way since then and she'd be able to read most of the relevant case law online. She was bound to find some ammunition in there somewhere.

The door of the pub swung open and Maggie turned to greet the new arrival with her best customer-service smile. 'Oh. It's you,' she said, her face returning to normal. 'I thought it was a punter!'

'I *am* a punter,' said Cath, indignantly, taking up a stool at the bar. 'I thought I'd better turn up and give you something to do.' She looked around the empty room. 'Where is everyone?'

'No idea. I assumed there must be something on in the village...?'

'Not as far as I know,' said Cath. She pointed at the wall behind Maggie. 'I can't believe all those horse brasses are still up. I thought you'd have got rid of them by now?'

'I've not had time,' Maggie lied. 'There's been so much to do, ordering the beer and all that. Not to mention the crisps.'

'Hmm,' said Cath, sceptically. 'It sounds about as busy as the café.'

'Guess what, though, I've ditched the Muddy Duck,' said Maggie. 'I've ordered some new house wine that's actually drinkable. A Pinot Grigio and a nice, mellow Shiraz. Australian, of course.'

'Hallelujah!' said Cath, clapping her hands.

'And some fancy new types of gin.'

'Gin...?' said Cath, sceptical again.

'Gin's big news at the moment – in the real world. At least it was, the last time I checked.'

'If you say so.'

'In fact, would you like to try some?' Maggie offered, reaching for a bottle. 'I've got one here. The label describes it as "a fiery brew, with a thumping base note of pot pourri".'

'Pot pourri?' said Cath, pretending to retch. 'I think I'll have a glass of the house white instead, please.'

'Chicken!' grinned Maggie, fetching the wine from the fridge behind her.

Cath was rummaging in her purse for some cash, but Maggie waved it away. 'This one's on me.'

'Cheers,' said Cath. 'So, are you the only one working tonight?'

'Yeah,' said Maggie. 'I told Ryan he could take the night off.'

'Ryan?'

'That young barman – skinny, too much hair gel…'

'Oh, yeah,' Cath nodded. 'The slightly vacant one?'

'He's actually a trained chef as well,' said Maggie. 'And he's a nice lad. Apart from the fact that he calls me "mate".'

'Er… You call people "mate" all the time.'

'Yes, but I'm old enough to be his mother.'

Cath chuckled. 'True.'

'Well, anyway,' continued Maggie. 'He wanted to go into town. On a night out with his *actual* mates.'

Cath took a sip from her glass and licked her lips. 'This wine's a vast improvement on the Muddy Duck,' she said. 'And you seem pretty chipper.'

'You think so?'

'Yes. I do.'

'Well. What's not to be happy about?' said Maggie, leaning theatrically on the bar. 'I'm forty-six, I'm supposed to be in my prime and I'm living on my own in a grotty room above a pub. Ain't life grand?' She poured a small glass of red wine for herself and put a tenner in the till. 'Except I'm not on my own, am I? I'm sharing my living space with a spider the size of my hand, like some latter-day Robert the Bruce in his man-cave.'

Cath couldn't help but laugh at her. 'That bad, is it?'

'Yes, it is. But, just like Robert the Bruce, I'll keep on trying.'

Cath swirled the wine in her glass, thoughtful now. 'Sometimes I think it's better to be on your own,' she said. 'Family's over-rated.'

'What's the matter?' asked Maggie. 'Is it Simon?'

Cath grunted. 'Nah. It's Pippa.'

'Things still frosty between you two?'

'Yeah,' said Cath. 'I invited her to come up here and stay for the weekend – to bring the kids with her – but she clearly doesn't want to.'

'I'm sorry,' said Maggie, unsure what to say next. Maybe being an only child wasn't so bad after all?

'There's nothing to be sorry about,' Cath continued, breezily. 'So, what about Rob? Did you go round and see him?'

Yes. Yes, I did, Maggie wanted to say. *And it was a proper clusterfuck – really embarrassing. His parents hate me. They think I'm his 'girlfriend' and they're pissed off because I'm too old to 'give him an heir'. A fucking heir! And I ended up telling him all about Andy… blurting out about the baby… about Joy. And now I feel like a right tool.*

But she didn't say any of this. It was best not to dwell on it. And it was certainly best not to mention her baby. She and Cath had never really discussed it at the time and, on the very rare occasions when it had come up since then, Cath's reaction had always been weird, like she was uncomfortable talking about it.

'Yeah. I did go round,' was all she replied.

And?' said Cath. 'Did you have a look at the paperwork?'

'Yeah,' sighed Maggie. 'It's going to be an uphill climb, but I've got an idea. I gave Giles a call and he—'

'*Giles?*' said Cath.

'Yup. Giles.'

'Giles-from-uni?'

'Yes, Giles-from-uni. Posho-barrister-Giles. How many Giles's do you know, for goodness' sake? Actually, don't answer that.'

'Oh?' said Cath, flicking her hair behind her ears. 'How is he?'

'Busy,' said Maggie. 'Very busy. He's got a big trial on at the moment. But what I'm thinking is… I can do the research and stuff and – assuming that the case goes to court – Giles will be able to represent Rob and argue our side of things.'

'Cool,' said Cath. 'Sounds like a plan.'

The door opened again and a jolly-faced group of ageing hikers filed through it and up to the bar. 'Seven pints of Gnarly Old Root, please miss, when you're ready,' said the leader of the group, with just a bit too much relish.

'Coming up!' beamed Maggie, in her best hearty voice. And she turned to the pump, wondering why on earth they had to give the beer such suggestive names.

Topping up the creamy heads on the glasses of treacly brew, she glanced back down the bar towards Cath. She seemed to have a gleam behind her eyes that Maggie hadn't seen since she'd arrived in Archdale – hadn't seen for years, in fact.

That was the thing about being all wrapped up in your own problems. It was so easy to forget that other people existed – that they had their own wants and needs too. Even easier to forget that Giles and Cath had had a brief 'dalliance' in their last year at uni, long before Simple Simon had appeared on the scene.

The Great Storm

Maggie had been working at the pub for over two weeks now and this was the most knackered she'd been since she started. She closed the door of her tiny room and kicked off her shoes, grateful for some peace at last. They'd had a sizeable writing group booked in for an early dinner – the vegan, gluten-free brigade – and, boy, it had been hard work.

For a start, the catering delivery hadn't turned up this morning and she'd had to ask Cath to drive to Tesco and buy up half their 'free-from' aisle. It could have been worse: Cath had been insisting on going to Waitrose until Maggie pointed out that The Farmer's Arms's budget didn't extend that far.

On her return, Cath had offered to step in and help her by taking the orders at the tables, while Ryan manned the kitchen, preparing the food. Which was great, apart from the fact that Cath's hieroglyphics on the notepad were basically illegible. This had caused a series of mix-ups and delays, with the meals all coming out at different times, but the members of the writing group had mostly taken it with a calm good grace.

When Maggie had finally got rid of them all, the pub went back to being deathly quiet and she'd deemed it safe to hand the reins to Ryan for the evening shift while she went for a lie down.

Curled up on the bed now, she lay there in the dark, listening to the rain drumming on the roof. The crap weather was back again with a vengeance, even though Easter wasn't far away. She'd been out of the UK a long time, admittedly, but wasn't spring supposed to be kicking in by now? Even just a little bit?

She stuck her earphones in and found a repeat of *Gardeners' Question Time* on Radio 4. She wasn't remotely interested in gardening – probably because she'd never had a garden – and she didn't know a begonia from a brassica, but it was easily the most soothing programme on the airwaves. No shock jocks, no angry phone-ins, just nice, gentle people with questions on how to encourage their clematis. Unthreatening. Calming. Relaxing.

She closed her eyes and let herself be carried off on a burble of bedding plants.

After a while, the sputtering of water against the windows grew louder and the wind started swirling, as the rain became a storm. It began to pound so hard she thought the room was vibrating – until she pulled her earphones out and realised it was actually Ryan hammering on her door.

'Maggie, mate!' he was saying. 'You need to come down. It's the rain. The cellar's flooding!'

'Fuck's sake,' spat Maggie to herself. Just her flaming luck. Why did this have to happen while Pete was away? And what was she expected to do about it anyway?

Grabbing her phone, she charged downstairs after Ryan in her stocking feet, following him behind the bar to the hole in the floor where he'd pulled back the trapdoor.

Ignoring his protestations to be careful, she edged down the narrow stone staircase, four steps into the musty blackness, groping for the light cord, which was halfway down the stairs. *What was the point in that?*

She pulled it and waited an age for her eyes to adjust, but the dim light of the energy-saving bulb made bugger all difference.

She carried on regardless and her foot soon landed, ankle-deep in the freezing water.

Pulling her phone out of her back pocket, she pressed a button until the light came on and held it up to survey the situation. She needed to try and save whatever stock she could – pass as much as possible up the stairs to Ryan… But the low ceiling meant she had to bend almost double as she waded across to grab hold of a box of cheese and onion.

Striding back over to the staircase, she could feel the water level inching up like the panic rising inside her.

'What we gonna do, Maggie?' Ryan was calling down the stairs.

Good question. What *was* she going to do? Only one thing came to mind. She'd have to phone Rob. *Assuming she had a signal.*

Maggie climbed the first few steps again, dialling his number, gripping the phone tight. Dropping it in the water would be the last thing she needed.

It was ringing out. *Hallelujah!* But he wasn't picking up. *Fuck.* What now?

She killed the call, pushed the box of crisps up through the hole, and listened. 'Ryan?' she called.

No answer. No sign of him. *Where had he gone?*

The sound of the cold dripping water was making her want to wee, but she descended the steps again to see what else she could salvage.

'Maggie!' Ryan was back at the top of the steps. 'Rob's on the landline. Says he got a missed call from you. I've told him we're flooded out.'

She turned and headed for the stairs again, back up to the light, her best black trousers soaked and sticking to her legs.

Ryan passed her the handset, but it wasn't good news.

'Listen, Maggie. I can't help you,' said Rob. 'The wind's ripped half the roof off the barn. It's full of ewes about to lamb. I need to stay here and try and sort it.'

'Oh, bollocks!' said Maggie. 'I don't know what else to—'

'Listen to me,' Rob interrupted. 'You need to ring Jim.'

'Jim?'

'Yeah. My mate, Jim. He can get the fire brigade lads to come out.'

'Fire brigade? Right…'

'Alright? I've got to go.'

'No! Wait there a sec! I haven't got Jim's number.'

Rob recited the number and she tried to memorise it, repeating it over and over in her head.

She was breathing heavily now as she dialled it. *Don't just go to voicemail. Please answer it. Please…*

Suddenly a click on the line. 'Jim. Jim? Is that you?'

'It is… Who's this?'

'Maggie. Scottish Maggie. From the pub. The Farmer's Arms. Rob gave me your number… Rob Elliott.'

'Oh. Right. You OK?'

'Not really. The pub cellar's flooding. Rob told me to call you.' For the second time in minutes, she felt utterly pathetic.

'OK,' said Jim. 'I'll call it into the station as a shout – get the lads on to it. We'll get it pumped out.'

'Wait. Is this an appropriate use of the fire service?' she asked, suddenly unsure. 'It's not really an emergency – I mean, it's not life or death – is it? I'm sure Pete's probably got insurance or something.'

'You what?' said Jim. 'The Farmer's Arms is my local. Emergencies don't come much bigger than this!'

And then he laughed and Maggie found herself laughing too, mainly from relief, as he told her to sit tight and wait.

Within a few minutes, she and Ryan could hear the determined *nee-naw* of the fire engine speeding towards them through the filthy night.

A bunch of blokes in bulky hi-vis jackets and safety helmets – half a dozen of them in total – turned up with Jim. As they filed past Maggie, one of them lifted his visor and raised a sardonic eyebrow at her. She recognised him as Les the butcher, whom she'd somehow managed to avoid since the issue with the traffic cone that first day.

'I assume it's OK to park the fire engine outside?' Les asked, pointedly, and then chuckled.

'No problem at all. Trust me!' she said, before disappearing in search of a kettle and some mugs. A cuppa was the least she could offer them, coming out from their warm houses on a night like this.

When she returned, she could hear their good-natured banter floating up through the trapdoor as they pumped the water away. Maggie smiled and forgot about her freezing cold feet for a moment.

It's true what they say, she reflected. In this life, it's all about *who* you know…

A Blast from the Past

'Haven't you got a home to go to?' Maggie quipped, setting a foaming pint of bitter on the bar in front of Rob. This was the fourth time he'd been in to the pub in the three days since the flood. With the possible exception of Cath, he'd easily been her best customer during her tenure at The Farmer's. Not that she was complaining: she was always pleased to see him.

'I'm meeting Jim,' Rob explained. 'It's my birthday,' he added, as an afterthought.

'Is it?' said Maggie. 'Happy birthday!' Although, from the look on his face, 'happy' hardly seemed the word. 'Why didn't you tell me?' she asked, wiping down the bar. 'I'd have got you a card. You can have that drink on the house, by the way. And Jim can have one too when he gets here.' She winked at him. 'As long as you don't tell Australian Pete…'

'Cheers,' he said. 'Are you having one yourself?'

'Hmm. To be honest, I've found that drinking and working behind a bar don't really mix. But I'll make an exception in your case and have a glass of wine with you. I can't have you drinking on your own, can I?' She poured herself a glass of red. 'So, how old are you then?'

'Forty-two,' he mumbled in reply.

'Ah,' said Maggie, dramatically. 'The big four-two. I remember it well. It's not that bad, actually – better than the alternative at any rate.'

'Eh?' said Rob. 'What alternative?'

'Well, er, y'know…' she made a cut-throat gesture, 'not reaching forty-two.'

'Hmm, I suppose so.'

Maggie took a sip of her drink and leaned in towards him. 'Did you get many pressies, then?'

'I got this,' he said, producing a thick, brown envelope from the back pocket of his jeans and slapping it down on the bar.

Maggie didn't have to ask what it was.

'It says I've got to sign a form and send it back to the court,' said Rob. 'And then, basically, I've got four weeks to file what my defence is going to be… That's the end of April. Not much time.'

'Rubbish!' said Maggie, trying her best to be upbeat. 'It's plenty of time. I like deadlines anyway. They're just so, well, *bracing*.'

Rob sighed. 'I can't even remember what the defence *is*, to be honest.'

'We'll need to get our arse in gear,' said Maggie, her thoughts racing. 'I'll need to let Giles know.'

'Giles?' said Rob, looking up.

'My barrister mate. He's gonna help us out. He owes me one.'

'That's good of him.'

'Yeah.' She grinned. 'He's not such a bad egg, I suppose.'

She went to rinse out some glasses, as the door opened and Rob turned round in his stool. 'You've got a customer,' he muttered to Maggie, keen to study his beer mat suddenly.

Maggie could see why. It was Tiggy, decked out in a pair of denim dungarees, looking like she was on her way to a Bananarama reunion. *Tiggy*. Imagine going through life being called that. Such a mean, spiky little name. Maggie hadn't actually set eyes on her since coming back to Archdale, but she knew this day would eventually come. She tugged at her apron self-consciously, as Tiggy approached the bar.

'Ah,' said Tiggy in her characteristic croak. 'I'd heard you were back in town.'

'Indeed I am,' said Maggie, evenly.

'Working as a barmaid?' Tiggy smirked. 'Bit of a comedown for a lawyer, isn't it?'

Maggie was stung by the remark, but she didn't show it.

'Mind you, you're not really a proper lawyer, are you?' Tiggy continued, angling for a reaction. 'I've heard this is the only bar you've ever been called to.'

'Excuse me, ladies and gentlemen,' announced Maggie, looking around the pub at the sprinkling of other customers. 'Did everyone hear that loud clang just then? That was another one of Tiggy's "jokes". Going down like a lead balloon as usual.'

Rob was trying hard to stifle a laugh and Maggie almost felt guilty: taking the piss out of Tiggy was far too easy.

'Anyway. You don't need to worry,' Maggie went on. 'Pete'll be back before you know it.' Which she was relieved about; she'd been enjoying her stint playing at being a pub landlady, but funnily enough, with Tiggy's arrival, the end couldn't come soon enough.

'Probably just as well,' said Tiggy, eyeing Maggie's glass of wine. 'Before you drink all the profits.'

'Now then,' said Maggie, rising above her jibe. 'What can I get you? We've got some new house wine?'

'Ugh. No thanks. I'll just have a gin and tonic.'

Maggie handed her the gin menu.

'Wow,' said Tiggy. 'Flavoured gins? How tacky. I'll just have a Tanqueray and tonic, thank you very much. I like to keep it classic.'

'Fine.' Maggie was glad to be able turn her back on her, towards the optics.

'I'm meeting Eve,' said Tiggy, in a tone full of meaning, clearly intended for Rob's benefit. 'She's split from Steve, you know.'

Eve and Steve? Maggie parroted under her breath. *Ridiculous.*

'Really?' Rob asked Tiggy, showing unexpected interest.

'Yup,' replied Tiggy with an air of triumph. 'She's moving back to Archdale. Just as soon as she finds a suitable property.'

Maggie froze. She guessed that they were talking about the ex-fiancée Rob had told her about – the one who left him – and the rest of their conversation seemed to confirm this. She eventually turned back round with Tiggy's drink, placing it in front of her.

'Oh, that's far too much ice,' Tiggy whined.

'Fine,' said Maggie, grabbing back the glass to try and scoop some out.

'Oh, it's OK. Just leave it,' said Tiggy, snatching it back. 'Just remember for the next time.' Then she pointed her bony finger at the official-looking envelope on the bar in front of Rob. 'I assume that's not good news?'

'No. It isn't,' Rob admitted, and told her the latest developments.

Maggie was surprised at his frankness. So much for trying to keep things quiet.

'What an awful business,' said Tiggy to Rob, shaking her head. 'Best of luck with it all, though. I hope you're standing up to them.'

'I am,' said Rob. 'Maggie's helping me with it.'

'Oh? That's great,' said Tiggy, looking at Maggie. 'She's got the time to devote to it.'

'I've got no more time than anyone else,' said Maggie. 'Just the statutory twenty-four hours in a day.'

'No, well, what I meant was… It's not like you've got any *family* commitments or anything.'

'True, I don't,' said Maggie, simply. It didn't really matter what hurtful barbs Tiggy came out with. Nothing she said could make her feel any worse about herself than she already did.

As Tiggy went to pull up a stool, Rob grimaced. 'Poor Phil,' he said to Maggie, in a whisper that was a bit too loud. 'Having to be married to *her*. She's always been a bit of a nightmare.'

Maggie just nodded and kept busy until an icy draught told her another customer had walked in. She glanced up to see a petite blonde dressed from head to toe in designer labels. Probably in her early thirties, she was sporting a deep tan that she certainly hadn't got in Archdale and her waist-length hair looked like it had been ironed flat.

'Eve!' Tiggy jumped up to greet her and Eve came over and kissed her on both cheeks. Then Eve approached the bar, sidling up close to Rob like a cat.

'I *thought* you might be here on your birthday,' she said. 'Let me buy you a drink. A double Glenfiddich? I assume that's still your favourite?'

Rob just nodded, drained his pint and Maggie realised that he was quite drunk. He must have had something to drink before he left the house? She hadn't really noticed until now – it must have hit him all at once.

'A double Glenfiddich,' Eve repeated at Maggie behind the bar, brusquely, like she was used to telling people what to do.

Against her better judgement, Maggie did what she was asked and placed the double whisky in front of him. He downed it in one and slammed it back down on to the bar, harder than he'd meant to.

'Guess what,' Eve turned to Tiggy. 'I've managed to find a place in the village.'

Tiggy clapped her hands together. 'Where? How wonderful! That was quick.'

'I know! I found out that Rose Cottage is up for rent. It's absolutely perfect for me. Nice and cosy with a lovely secluded garden at the back. It'll be ideal for barbecues in the summer.' She turned to Rob and leaned her head against his shoulder. 'I don't suppose you'd be able to help me move in, would you, Rob? It's not for a few weeks yet. I need to give notice on my current place…'

'Yeah, sure, that's fine,' slurred Rob. 'Just let me know when you need me. No problem…'

It was then that Jim turned up, hurrying through the door. 'Sorry I'm late,' he said. 'I just had to—' He stopped. 'Oh, hi Eve. You're back, are you?'

Rob stood up unsteadily to hug him. 'There's a free pint for you in the pump, Jim. *Shhhhh* though,' he giggled, putting his finger over his mouth. 'Don't tell Australian Pete.'

Maggie and Jim exchanged a look.

'I think you might have had enough, birthday boy!' said Jim cheerily, grabbing him by the arm. 'I'll give you a lift up the road.'

Maggie mouthed her thanks at Jim as he propelled Rob towards the door, the thick, brown envelope stuffed in his back pocket.

Poor bugger, thought Maggie. If he was drinking too much, who could blame him with all this repossession stuff hanging over him.

No, she had to feel sorry for him. And relieved that he had a good mate like Jim to take him home from the pub – away from this Eve character. Rob didn't need that sort of hassle on top of everything else.

Procrastination

Maggie had been brushing vigorously at her teeth for two full minutes. She was looking forward to a much-needed morning off, as Ryan had agreed to hold the fort at The Famer's.

She mentally ran through her 'to do' list. The first and most important thing on the agenda was to text Giles and let him know that it was all systems go: she'd meant to contact him last night, but it had slipped her mind amid all the drama of Eve turning up.

Then she'd need to get a move on with this legal research she was meant to be doing – which, now that she'd given it some more thought, might be easier said than done. For one thing, she wouldn't be able to access all the online legal databases and resources that she used to take for granted working as part of a big company. She'd need to open an account and take out a subscription and all that malarkey before she could do anything at all.

She couldn't be arsed with any of that this morning, though. She'd really missed Jazz's furry little presence since she'd been at the pub and planned to go up to Higher House and take her out for a walk instead. The weather was a bit brighter today and she was keen to stretch her legs and try and get the beery pub pong out of her nostrils at the same time.

Cath would be down at the café this morning, but she'd be able to get in to the house with the spare back door key that lived under the orange wheelie bin. Or was it the green one? *One* of the 'seven-deadly-bins' at any rate…

Maggie had forgotten what a schlep it was, the walk up to Cath's. She filled the time by imagining her imminent trip out of Archdale – to the High Court in London for Rob's hearing. It would be a pretty low key affair, she expected, before a single judge in a back room. And it probably wouldn't take very long. But she'd still get to pass through the soaring arches of The Royal Courts of Justice on The Strand, across the mosaic marble floor, down the maze of secret corridors.

For the first time in ages, she could see the attraction of a trip to the capital: for the first time in ages, London was more than just a collection of shitty memories.

Cath could come with her and they'd have a right laugh, just like the old days. And Rob would come too, of course; it would be fun to show him around some of her old favourite haunts. They'd travel down by train to St Pancras – first class – and their first stop on arrival would be Maggie's favourite Italian coffee shop, much better than the brown-sludge-serving-tax-avoiding high street chains. She could maybe take Rob to the British Museum: he'd definitely enjoy that as he'd told her he was into his history and stuff. And then, later on, the three of them could have dinner in that new place on the South Bank she'd read about in *The Observer*, followed by cocktails at Borough Market or Butler's Wharf. At this rate, they'd struggle to fit the hearing in! But that wouldn't really matter as, thankfully, it was Giles who'd be doing the hard bit by that stage: he'd be the one doing the talking in court.

Then the guilt began to kick in. *What was she like?* Relishing the thought of a trip to London on the back of Rob's misfortune. It was a serious business, not a bloody tourist trip. Still, what was it that Joyce used to say? *'It's an ill wind that blows nobody any good.'* She might as well enjoy the ride while it lasted – take her pleasures where she could.

Maggie eventually reached Higher House to find the back door wide open and Cath sitting at the kitchen table with three lever arch files and a pile of paperwork in front of her.

Cath pushed her hair out of her eyes and looked up. 'Oh, good,' she announced. 'Just the person I wanted to see.'

'I thought you'd be at work?' said Maggie, not liking the sound of this.

'Nah, no need. Neil's down there this morning. He's back from hiking the Sierra Nevada or wherever it is he goes in the winter.' She paused for a second. 'Anyway. I was wondering… Could I ask you for some help with Wakes Week?'

'Wakes Week?' asked Maggie, suspiciously. 'What's that when it's at home?'

'It's basically the village carnival,' said Cath. 'I've foolishly agreed to be on the organising committee this year.'

'Funny name for a carnival,' scoffed Maggie. '*Wakes*?' It was so dead around here, it felt like a wake *every* week. After her reveries of London, she felt dragged back down to earth. She'd always hated compulsory enjoyment and this sounded like the worst kind. 'I only came round to take Jazz out for a walk,' she moaned.

'Great. I'll come too,' said Cath. 'I could do with a break from this.'

'Nice one.' Maggie picked up the dog's lead and Jazz came hurtling down the stairs at top speed.

'So,' said Maggie, as they turned out of the gate at the bottom of the drive. 'When is this carnival, then, and what delights can I look forward to?'

'Middle of June,' said Cath.

'That's ages away,' said Maggie.

'It comes around sooner than you think,' Cath continued. 'And there's an awful lot to do before then. There's the well dressing to organise...'

'Well dressing? What's that?'

'It's an old Derbyshire custom,' said Cath.

'I was afraid it might be...'

'It's when the villagers give thanks for the wells – the water sources. We decorate them with pictures of traditional scenes made from flower petals of all different colours. You need to see it, it's really stunning.'

'Hmm,' said Maggie, as they carried on down the lane. 'Is that it?'

'Nah, there's loads of other stuff as well. There's a scarecrow competition, family picnics and duck races. And the blokes do tug-of-war. And then there's the five-a-side football tournament...'

'Sounds thrilling...'

'It's alright. Assuming it doesn't pour with rain the whole week. Which it usually does.'

'Even better.'

'And we put up loads of bunting in the village and all the local businesses decorate their frontages – the café, the pub, the butcher's...'

'Bunting? Oh joy.'

'Really, though, it's just an excuse for everyone in the village to get out of the house and go drinking every night for a week.'

'Fair enough,' said Maggie. 'Sounds like it could be good business for the pub at least.'

'It will be!' Cath enthused. 'And I've said I'll organise an Auction of Promises at The Farmer's.'

'An Auction of *what*?'

'It's basically a charity auction. The money goes towards the maintenance of the church and stuff. People offer up something of value – their goods or services or their time – things other people might want to bid for.' Cath paused. 'We usually have a big quiz night instead but, if you – er – recall, the last one ended on a bit of a sour note. I don't think Australian Pete wanted to risk another one.'

Maggie pulled a face. 'Oh God. I was a real nightmare, wasn't I? I'm still embarrassed to think of it.'

'Oh, forget it,' said Cath. 'All water under the bridge. Now then, would you like to offer up your services for auction?'

Maggie just laughed. 'You're joking, right? What useful skills have *I* got to offer?'

Cath thought for a moment. 'Dog-walking?' she ventured. 'There's always a demand for that.'

Maggie wasn't that keen on the idea of walking other people's dogs. *What if she lost one?* 'Tell you what,' she said instead. 'How about I donate a three-course meal for four, plus wine, at The Farmer's.'

'Well, I suppose that would really be Pete donating it…' said Cath, uncertainly.

'I'll talk to him,' said Maggie. 'I'm sure he won't mind.'

'Done!' Cath stopped and stretched out her hand to shake Maggie's. 'That's great. I'll put you down on my list.'

They turned off the lane, over the stile into the fields, and Maggie let Jazz off the lead. She felt her phone buzz in her pocket. It was a text from Giles:

Got your message. How about I come up for Easter to discuss things? Be nice to see you and Cath again. I fancy a quiet weekend in the country once this trial's finished.

Sounds like a plan, Maggie texted back, suspecting that a weekend away wasn't the only thing he fancied.

'Everything OK?' asked Cath when she'd finished.

Maggie snapped her phone shut in triumph. 'That was Giles. He's coming up here at Easter. For a "council of war".'

Cath looked bemused.

'For a meeting,' Maggie clarified. 'To discuss Rob's case.'

'Really?' said Cath, smoothing a stray tendril of hair. 'Is he coming on his own?'

'If that's your way of asking whether he's still single then, yes, I think he is,' Maggie teased her. 'I get the impression our Giles is a bit too busy for *lurve*.'

'That's not what I meant at all,' insisted Cath, blushing pink. She looked at her watch. 'Well, I guess I'd better be heading back. I took this morning off so I could start getting organised for this auction and stuff. I can't spend all of it chatting to you.'

'We'll come with you,' said Maggie, calling Jazz to her. 'I need to get back as well.'

'Tiggy's next on my list,' said Cath, rolling her eyes, as they retraced their steps. 'I need to bite the bullet and give her a call – see what she can donate.'

'Ugh,' said Maggie. 'I saw her last night. She was in the pub.'

'Oh, yeah?' said Cath. 'I haven't heard from her in a while. Not since the business with Lauren and Freya…'

'Yep,' said Maggie. 'She was meeting up with that Eve. Rob's old fiancée.'

'Was she now?' said Cath, and Maggie could see that she was slightly put out.

'Are you jealous?' asked Maggie.

'No,' said Cath, unconvincingly.

Maggie put on a gossipy voice. 'So anyway... Eve's split up with her boyfriend in Sheffield and she's moving back to Archdale. Into Rose Cottage, wherever that is.'

'Really?' Cath eyes widened.

'Yup. And now it looks like she's trying to get her claws back into Rob.'

'No way!'

Maggie nodded solemnly. 'She bought him a drink in the pub last night. For his birthday.'

Cath chuckled at her. 'Is that all? Hardly getting her *claws* into him...'

'Well it wasn't just that,' said Maggie quickly. 'He was quite pissed and she was acting all flirtatious, taking advantage of him. She asked if he could help her move into her new place. A bit bloody cheeky, I thought. She seems to have a real sense of entitlement. One of those little princess types...'

Cath stopped dead and turned to face Maggie. 'You know, I think it might be *you* who's jealous?' she said, grinning away. 'You've got a thing for him, haven't you? Admit it.'

'Not at all,' huffed Maggie. 'I only feel sympathy for him. He's not exactly short of troubles at the moment.'

'Are you *sure* it's only sympathy?' pressed Cath.

'Quite sure.'

'Alright. If you say so.'

They started walking again.

'Actually, it's good to hear that Rob and Eve are back on good terms,' said Cath. 'It was a real *big love* between those two. I remember he was so cut up when she left him. I certainly don't remember any other girlfriends...'

When they arrived back at the gates of Higher House, Cath offered Maggie a lift back down to the pub.

Maggie checked the sky for clouds. 'I'm alright, actually,' she said. 'Thanks, but I'm fine to walk.'

She handed Jazz's lead back to Cath and set off down the hill again, her thoughts churning. Cath was right. She hadn't wanted to admit it but, if she was honest with herself, she *had* felt jealous. And she was mortified. Just a few short weeks ago, she'd marked the tenth anniversary of Andy's death. She knew better than anyone what a *big love* was. And if there was still something there between Rob and Eve – some embers to be rekindled – then that was completely understandable. That was their business, not hers. She needed to swallow any feelings she had for Rob and leave them both to it.

Her phone buzzed in her pocket again. Fucking hell, she thought. This had better not be Giles ringing to say he can't come at Easter after all.

She pulled it out and looked at it – *an international number*. Some news about a job, maybe? One of her old contacts? Excitement rising, she accepted the call.

'Oh, hi, Maggie. How *are* ya?' said the faint, familiar voice down the long-distance line.

'Pete?! Hi. What a surprise,' she said, trying her best to hide her disappointment. Why was he calling her? He'd be back the day after tomorrow in any case. And she couldn't wait: she was frankly desperate to move out of that cramped little room and back in with Cath. If she had to stay in Archdale till Rob's case was decided one way or the other, she'd much rather stay somewhere comfortable. 'Have you set off yet?' she asked Pete.

'Not yet. I'm still in Waggamalong. How are things at The Farmer's?' He sounded quite anxious.

'Fine. Yeah. Everything's great at this end.' The sorry tale of flood in the cellar could wait till he got back. She didn't want to worry him and it wasn't like there had been much damage in the end in any case. 'How are things with you?'

'Not great, Maggie. My mum isn't very well. She's got to go into hospital for some tests next week. I feel like I should stay with her, but I need to get back to the pub.'

'No, you don't, mate,' said Maggie. 'We're managing fine without you. It's better, in fact,' she added, mischievously. 'Everybody says so.'

'No way,' he said, laughing in spite of himself. 'I couldn't leave you in the lurch like that. It wouldn't be fair.'

'Don't talk such bollocks, Pete, will you?' she sighed. 'You should stay as long as your mum needs you.'

'You sure?'

'Quite sure,' said Maggie. 'Now get off the phone and go and change your flight.'

Back in the Saddle

A few days later, Maggie found herself doing something she hadn't done since she was twelve years old – riding a bike. The blood was already pounding in her head and the muscles in her thighs were burning, even though she'd only been going for a few minutes on the flat road along the valley bottom. This was mad! Even scarier than driving.

On top of that, an impatient vehicle of some description had been right up her backside since the last junction. *A bit close for comfort.* Whatever happened to the legal principle that 'a cyclist is allowed a wobble'? Who was it who'd said that again? Lord Chief Justice Someone-or-Other in – what was the name of that case?

She was dying to look round and flick the Vs at the driver, but didn't dare. She needed to concentrate on staying upright as she turned into the village.

Breathing heavily, she stuck out her arm and turned the corner – as the offending white van screamed straight ahead, spewing fumes, glad to be rid of her. Seeing Cath's café up ahead, she pulled over on to the pavement outside it: she would call in for a brew and a bun, to steady her nerves before opening up the pub.

Pushing inside the door, she wasn't expecting Cath's reaction.

'What's that on your head?' Cath asked, stifling a giggle.

'It's a bicycle helmet,' Maggie replied, tartly. 'Surely you must have seen one before?'

'Yep. It's just that… you don't have a bike.'

'Ah well, you see, that's where you're wrong. It's chained up outside.'

Cath went to the window to see it with her own eyes: a prehistoric sit-up-and-beg with a tatty wicker basket on the front, the kind of thing Miss Marple might have used.

'It's a gift from Rob.' Maggie blushed. 'He turned up at the pub with it as a surprise. It's his mother's old bike. He's fixed it up for me. So that I can get around the place more easily.' She paused. 'Unfortunately, he's also insisted I wear this helmet.'

'Very thoughtful of him,' said Cath, biting her lip now.

'It is,' said Maggie, defensively. 'Considering that he's really busy with the lambing and stuff.' She had to admire his dedication to the farm and the animals, especially with the future of the whole thing being up in the air. And she was touched that he'd taken the time to try and make her life a bit better, when his own was falling apart around his ears. She loosened the chinstrap and took the helmet off, aware she'd now have a terminal case of helmet hair.

This tipped Cath over the edge into outright laughter.

'What now?' snapped Maggie.

'Oh, I don't know,' said Cath, sitting down and dabbing at her eyes with her apron. 'I just never thought I'd see the day, that's all.'

'How could I refuse?' wailed Maggie. 'He'd gone to so much trouble, I'd have felt really churlish not to give it a go. And anyway, I'm quite enjoying it.'

Their raised voices had drawn Neil out from his hidey-hole in the back shop, his nose having got the better of him. He looked down at Cath disapprovingly. 'It seems I have to do everything around here,' he said, through pursed lips. 'Now, what can I get you, Maggie?'

'Thank you, Neil,' said Maggie. 'At least someone's got some professionalism around here. Could I have a coffee, please?'

'Coming up,' said Neil, clicking his heels and turning to the machine.

'Have a seat, Maggie,' said Cath, composing herself. 'Would you like a piece of homemade flapjack? To keep your strength up?'

'Hmm. OK,' said Maggie.

'Listen,' said Cath, placing the peace-offering in front of her. 'I was wondering if there's anything I can do to help you with Rob's case? Book the train tickets? Anything.'

'Sure,' said Maggie. 'We can get the tickets booked once we've got a date for the hearing.'

'It'll be great to be back in London again,' said Cath. 'Think of all the shopping.'

'Shopping?' said Maggie, screwing up her face. 'And anyway, I thought you didn't have any money?'

'I can still look, can't I?' said Cath. 'And also, I was thinking about Giles...'

'Oh, aye?' said Maggie, suggestively.

'Where is he going to stay when he comes up to Archdale?' asked Cath, ignoring her.

'I dunno.' Maggie shrugged. 'At the pub. One of the B&B rooms, I guess.'

'You can't put him up at the pub!' snorted Cath.

'Why on earth not?'

'It's... well... It's sort of beneath him.'

'Beneath him?' repeated Maggie. 'Little Lord Fauntleroy isn't exactly a stranger to pubs, from what I can remember.'

'I was thinking he could stay at mine,' offered Cath. 'I've got plenty of room.'

Now it was Neil's turn to raise an eyebrow.

'Yeah, fine,' said Maggie. 'Whatever.'

'I'd better give the place a good clean,' Cath went on. 'I'll start tonight. The house is due its spring clean anyway.'

'OK,' said Maggie. 'Don't peak too soon, though, will you? You've got a whole week until he turns up.' She finished her mug and took it to the sink. 'Thanks very much, Neil.' She saluted him. 'Right. That's me. I'm off to work.'

'Really?' said Neil. 'But it's only half past nine.'

'I know. But I need to go and get organised. The pub seems to have got a bit busier lately for some reason.'

'Why don't you try and get some more staff in?' asked Cath. 'It's a lot of work for just you and Ryan.'

'I was talking to Ryan about this the other day, actually,' said Maggie on her way out. 'I think it's quite difficult to recruit long-term staff. Nearly all the young people want to leave the village. There's nothing for them here. All his mates have had to move away to get work. Not many of them want a minimum wage job as a farm labourer or a pint-puller.' She paused. 'And then, if they do stay, they've got no chance of being able to afford their own home or anything.'

'I guess so,' said Cath, following her to the door. 'I've never really thought of it like that. I suppose my lot are quite lucky. They've got... opportunities.'

'True enough,' said Maggie. 'True enough.' And she strapped the helmet back on top of her head, straddled the bike and wobbled off down the pavement.

Council of War

It was the Saturday of the Easter weekend and Cath had been up and down like a meerkat all morning, waiting for Giles to arrive.

He was supposed to have been leaving work early and driving up from London yesterday evening – Good Friday – but something had cropped up at the last minute. This had taken Maggie straight back to all those times in the past when she'd had to cancel her own plans because of work – dinner plans, theatre plans, weekend plans – and she couldn't really say she envied him that aspect of his life. She was glad she didn't need to do that sort of thing anymore, not that she ever had 'plans' these days anyway.

But all was well. Giles had rung at eight o'clock this morning to say he was just setting off and that, factoring in the necessary time for a pit stop on the motorway, he'd be with them by midday.

'Sit down, will you?' Maggie implored, as Cath bobbed back to the kitchen window for the third time in as many minutes. 'You're making me nervous.'

She'd been going to suggest that Cath try and distract herself by making some sandwiches for lunch, but then she'd spotted six types of homemade salad taking up most of the fridge, covered in cling film, awaiting their big moment. Cath must have cleared Waitrose of its entire stock of edamame, pomegranate and couscous in one of her commando raids, and mere sandwiches would have been surplus to requirements.

An unexpected noise made them both jump – a familiar sound and yet one that was nearly extinct: the rhythmic, shrill whine of the landline ringing out in the hallway, filling the house. Cath turned to Maggie in alarm.

'It might be Lauren,' suggested Maggie. 'Lost her phone or something? Or maybe Simon's been crushed to a pulp on his bike?'

Cath frowned and disappeared to answer it, missing the crunch of big tyres coming to a halt outside the back door.

'He's here!' called Maggie, from the window.

Cath rushed back to the kitchen. 'It was one of those bloody nuisance calls,' she was chuntering under her breath. 'Disturbing people on a Saturday morning.' She looked outside. 'Oh. You mean Rob,' she said, disappointed.

'I'm not late, am I?' said Rob, sticking his head round the door.

'No. No. Not at all,' said Cath, remembering her manners.

'I had to feed the cade lambs,' he explained.

'*Cade lambs*?' Maggie had never heard the term.

'Orphans, basically. When the mothers die, we have to bottle feed them. What time is Giles—?' But the rest of what he had to say was drowned out by a spluttering roar as loud as the fighter jets that sometimes thundered down the valley on training manoeuvres.

The three of them went to the window to see a rangy, leather-clad figure blasting up the driveway on a Harley Davidson. Screeching to a stop, the effect was ruined when the rider lost control of the front wheel on the loose chippings and the bike fell on to its side, trapping him underneath.

Rob rushed straight outside to lift the bike off him, with Cath close behind. Finally upright again, the guy pulled off his helmet to confirm what Maggie suspected: that yes, indeed, the mysterious leather-man was Giles.

'Oh my God. Giles! It's you!' cried Cath, clucking around him. 'Are you hurt?'

'I'm fine, I'm fine,' he said in his smooth, posh voice. 'Only my pride.'

'Enjoying your mid-life crisis, are you?' said Maggie, happy to mock him now she was sure he was OK.

'I've only had it two days,' he grinned.

'We can tell,' said Maggie, folding her arms.

'Oh, no,' said Cath, patting the paintwork. 'And now it's all scuffed.'

'Not to worry.' Giles took the bike and parked it alongside Maggie's old push bike. Then he double air-kissed Maggie and Cath in turn, before Maggie introduced him properly to Rob. Watching the two men share a firm handshake, it was almost comical – Giles's soft, well-moisturised hand in Rob's rough, manly one.

The pleasantries over, Giles turned to Maggie. 'I'm bound to say, Begbie, I never thought I'd see the day when you'd be living somewhere like Archdale.'

'I'm not *living in bloody Archdale*, mate,' she said, indignantly. 'I'm—'

'Hang on,' Cath challenged her. 'What's so bad about Archdale?'

'Erm…' Maggie was aware of Rob's eyes on her, waiting for her response. 'Nothing,' she said, quickly. 'Nothing at all. It's a perfectly nice place. It really is.' She paused. 'But this is just a temporary hiatus, a blip, before I find another job and move on to pastures new.'

'Well, I certainly got an interesting reaction from the villagers,' said Giles, unzipping his leathers to reveal a salmon pink shirt tucked into designer jeans.

'You stopped off in the village?' asked Cath.

'Yah. I was trying to buy a bottle of wine, actually. Didn't want to arrive empty-handed,' he explained. 'But the pub wasn't open yet and the garage is only, quite literally, a garage. No shop or anything.'

'Don't worry. I've got plenty of wine,' said Cath, waving away his concerns.

'Thanks,' said Giles. 'I got some strange looks actually. I'm not sure any of them had seen a black man before…'

'They were probably just looking at that ludicrous bike,' said Maggie. 'It'll go down in the Archdale annals, you know. They'll talk for years about the day a tall, dark stranger rode into town on his iron horse…'

'Well then,' said Giles, rubbing his hands together. 'Shall we make a start on the, er, business in hand? Might as well get it out of the way?'

'Sure,' agreed Maggie. 'I've got the file of documents here.' She pushed it across the table towards him.

'I'll just go and fetch the court summons,' said Rob. 'I've left it out in the motor.'

'Not just yet,' said Cath, reaching out her hand to stop him. She smiled indulgently at them all as she opened the fridge. 'First, we'll sit down and have some lunch.'

Maggie let out a deep breath. She hadn't really been looking forward to the legal bit and had been keen to get it over and done with as soon as possible. She should really have read through the file in detail before now, but she hadn't. Between running the pub and starting her driving lessons again and helping Cath with the Wakes stuff, she hadn't had time to do her homework. And that wasn't like her. Not like her at all.

* * *

'Thanks, Cath. That was a gorgeous spread. So tasty,' said Giles, and Rob nodded vigorously in agreement.

'You're very welcome,' beamed Cath, as she cleared away the plates.

Then Rob went and fetched the court papers and Giles pulled them out of their brown envelope, spreading them out in front of him like a deck of cards.

From across the kitchen table, Maggie was craning her neck to read them for the first time. Upside down at that.

The first page started in the customary fashion. In bold type in capital letters: **IN THE COUNTY COURT OF SHEFFIELD...**

Really? *The County Court of Sheffield.* So not the High Court. Not London.

Maggie's heart beat faster. Her trip down to The Big Smoke was disappearing over the horizon. But then, this made total sense. The case meant everything to Rob, but it wasn't big or complex enough to trouble the High Court. Of course not. Obvious now.

Then she was gripped by another thought. A scarier one. She hoped it hadn't occurred to Giles as well.

She began babbling nervously – about the loan company and how awful they were and the bare-faced lies they'd told Rob – but Giles was already waving that first page in front of her face. He broke into a broad grin. 'It looks like you won't be needing my services after all,' he chuckled.

'Really?' said Maggie, knowing full well what he was getting at.

He pointed at the first line. 'It's in the County Court.'

Cath and Rob exchanged a look, trying to follow what was going on.

'And you won't have that far to go,' continued Giles, gleefully. 'Seeing as it's in Sheffield.'

'What?' Now it was Cath's turn to be disappointed. 'No trip to London? No shopping?'

Giles turned to Rob. 'You see, you won't need a barrister to represent you after all… Maggie will be able to do it all by herself.'

Bollocks. Maggie grabbed the document off him and read it again. *Shit. There it was. In black and white. Why hadn't she read the thing properly when Rob had shown it to her?*

'But I've only ever appeared in court once,' she started to say. 'And it was as the accuse—'

But Cath was giving her a death stare that said, *Shut up immediately.* And fair enough. She didn't really want Rob knowing about her run-in with the criminal branch of the law.

Rob's hand was on her arm now. 'Is that OK with you, Maggie?' he asked. 'You'll be really good at it. I know you will.'

'Ah well… OK… yes,' said Maggie, her mouth dry as anything. 'I'll give it a go.' What else *could* she say? His faith in her was touching and she couldn't very well let him down. Not at this stage.

'OK. Good. That's settled,' said Giles, business-like again. He turned to Rob. 'Now. Maggie's already told me the gist of the case, Rob, but if you could just talk me through all the facts and circumstances as they happened, we can look at our options for the defence.'

* * *

'Right. Thank goodness that's done,' said Cath, jumping up from the table well over an hour later. 'Let's all have a nice glass of bubbles to celebrate, shall we?'

And as she fetched her best flutes for the fizz, Rob thanked Giles for his help.

'Don't thank me,' said Giles. 'Thank Maggie. She'll be the one doing all the work.'

'Yeah,' said Rob, smiling over at her. 'She's a star.'

Maggie smiled back, but she was squirming inside. Giles seemed to be enjoying this just a bit too much and no one had ever called her a 'star' before. *It was bloody unbearable.*

Cath filled four glasses and Giles raised his up with a theatrical flourish. 'I'd like to wish you all the best with your case, Rob – and here's to Maggie setting Sheffield County Court alight with the flaming sword of justice!'

'Jesus, Giles, pack it in, will you?' pleaded Maggie. Like most barristers, he was a frustrated actor – and very hard to shut up once he got going. 'Let's talk about something else…'

Soon, they'd finished one bottle and were on to the second. The mountain of salad and artisan bread they'd had for lunch wasn't great for soaking up the booze and the noise levels crept up and up as the bubbles went to their heads.

Only Maggie heard the knocking on the window. She went to open the back door and Simon stepped inside, a vision in red and black Lycra. He didn't look best pleased about the impromptu piss-up taking place in his old kitchen. Or his estranged wife sitting a bit too close to a handsome bloke he didn't know.

'Sorry to interrupt,' he said, like he wasn't sorry at all. 'I've just come over to give the new bike a bit of a workout on the hills.'

'New bike?' said Cath. 'How much did that cost?'

But Simon ignored the comment and pressed on. 'I thought I'd take the opportunity to pop in and discuss the repairs to the house, etc. But I can see that you're, erm, busy.'

Giles stood up and went to shake his hand as Simon covered the front of his cycling shorts instinctively. Giles, by contrast, was completely unruffled. 'You must be Simon,' he purred, getting even posher. 'I'm Giles. Very pleased to meet you.'

Simon looked painfully awkward, but not as awkward as Cath. 'Perhaps I could give you a call on Monday, Simon?' she said, tightly. 'Now's probably not the best time.'

'No— No— I can see that,' stuttered Simon. 'Monday it is, then.'

Maggie felt a bit sorry for him and walked him back out to his bike. The feelings of pity soon vanished, though.

'*Giles?*' hissed Simon. 'Is he the one from uni she always used to witter on about? *Giles this, Giles that.* What's *he* doing here?'

'He's come up from London for the weekend. He's giving Rob some legal advice on his—'

'The weekend? He'd better not be staying at my house…'

Maggie said nothing.

'He bloody is, isn't he?' said Simon, interpreting her silence exactly right. 'Where's he sleeping?'

'How should I know?' said Maggie. 'I'm staying down at The Farmer's at the moment. I'm covering for Australian Pete while he's away…'

Simon's face was fast approaching the scarlet of his skin-tight cycling top. 'What's going on, Maggie? Am I to understand that a strange man is staying under the same roof as my wife? Unchaperoned?'

'*Unchaperoned?*' echoed Maggie. 'What century are you living in, mate?'

'It's not on, Maggie. It's not on at all,' he muttered darkly, as he bounced off down the stone chippings on his bike.

As she watched his bony arse sail off into the distance, one of Joyce's favourite phrases sprang to mind: '*What's sauce for the goose is sauce for the gander…*' Yeah. It was alright for Simon to have an affair, but it was a different story when the boot was on the other foot. Not that Cath was having an affair, of course. Just a harmless bit of flirting with an old friend. And why the hell not?

She was sure Cath would be utterly mortified by Simon showing up like this – she'd always hated a 'scene' – but, when Maggie went back inside, she was surprised to find that Cath had recovered admirably. 'Guys,' she was saying. 'We need to give some thought to dinner…'

'I couldn't eat another thing at the moment,' protested Giles, and Rob agreed, although Maggie suspected he was probably starving again by now and just being polite. 'Maybe we could grab a snack later?' Giles suggested.

'Hmm,' said Cath. 'It's just as well I've got a nice leg of lamb for Easter lunch tomorrow.'

'You can count me out,' said Maggie, shaking her head. 'I don't eat lamb.'

'Really?' said Rob.

'Since when?' asked Cath.

'Yeah,' said Giles. 'All those doner kebabs you've put away over the years,' he said, patting his non-existent belly. 'Were they just figments of my imagination?'

'Well I won't be having any more,' said Maggie. She'd got used to the idea of the sheep as her friends now and the thought of eating one of them made her feel quite sick. Almost as sick as the thought of appearing in the County Court. 'And anyway,' she changed the subject. 'You've all got to go down to the pub now, because I'm working this evening. And I suggest that we set off now, while Cath's still capable of driving.'

'You're working?' asked Giles, confused. '*Tonight?*'

'Yep. I'm working at the pub in the village.'

'You're working at that pub?' he repeated, trying not to laugh and failing miserably. 'Let me get this straight. Not only have you washed up in Nowheresville, Derbyshire – but you're also working in a *pub*?'

'Oh, piss off, will you?' said Maggie, standing up and herding the three of them towards the door.

Later on that evening, from her vantage point behind the bar, she couldn't help noticing that Cath was setting quite a pace on the drinking front – although Giles and Rob weren't far behind. The 'pre-loading' back at the house had been a bit of a tactical error, she reflected, half-expecting them to order a round of Jägerbombs at any moment.

Rob was the first of them to see sense. He came over to tell Maggie goodnight, that he was off to start the long walk home as he had to be up early in the morning. And then he thanked Giles yet again.

Giles, three sheets to the wind, was responding to Rob with drunken bravado, making Maggie feel uneasy. Giles had been 'playing the big man' all day – playing to the gallery of Cath and Rob – equally adoring in their different ways. But, amid the warmth and conviviality of this afternoon, was it possible Giles had been a bit *over*-confident? Filling in the court forms with an outline of their defence, sealing up the envelope and gaily dropping it into the red post box outside the church – had he given Rob false hope about their chances of success? Maggie couldn't help worrying that he might have done.

It was nearly closing time when Cath rang Lauren, to ask her to come down in the car and give her and Giles a lift home. 'There's got to be *some* benefits to having grown up kids, right?'

she said, squinting at the phone, trying to work out which button to press.

'You do realise that your car's in the car park?' said Maggie, wearily. 'You drove us down here in it. Remember?'

'Oh God.' Cath giggled. 'So I did!'

'Why don't we walk home, Cath?' suggested Giles, slurring his words. 'It's not that far, really. And have you seen the moon? It looks stunning out there... like mother-of-pearl on blue velvet...'

'Sure. Let's do that,' Cath responded, throwing her arms around his waist for support.

Maggie watched them pin-balling out of the door, with an overwhelming sense of déjà vu. It could easily have been 1992 again – chucking-out time in the bar of the student union.

She winced to herself. *Mother-of-pearl on blue velvet? Seriously?* She just hoped Cath knew what she was doing.

Return of the Prophet

A couple of weeks passed and Maggie was really settling into the rhythm of pub life. They'd had a coach-load of fifty Welsh pensioners in for lunch and she was surveying the full extent of the debris from her stool at the bar: clearing all this away would be like the clear-up after Glastonbury.

She was feeling quite proud of herself for getting The Farmer's on to the tourist map in her own small way, which she'd done by ringing around the tour companies that did trips to the Peak District and promoting the pub as a pit-stop for rest and refreshments. The baby boomer market was very lucrative, after all, and the cost of a free lunch for the bus driver and tour guide was a small price to pay.

She'd known that she and Ryan would need some extra help in the kitchen, however, and so she'd made arrangements to draft in Neil to help them, having requested he be released from his duties at the café. Despite his reservations about disloyalty to Cath, Neil was obviously delighted to have been asked. And he was a very efficient worker, Maggie had to admit. More importantly, he had the grey-hair-factor that commanded respect when dealing with his fellow senior citizens, who could otherwise be a bit spiky.

Maggie had only just seen off the last of them, but the door had opened again now and a massive rucksack was edging through it as the newcomer struggled with the rest of their luggage. They'd better only want a drink, she thought, as there was barely a morsel of food left in the entire place.

She went to hold open the door. 'Pete!' she exclaimed, surprised to see it was him – even more surprised to see him sporting a prophet's beard. Was he a hipster now or what?

'You're early,' she said. She hadn't expected him back till later this afternoon, once the chaos of lunchtime had been restored to order.

'Jim came and picked me up from the airport,' Pete explained. 'Saved me having to get a taxi.' He eyed up all the tables littered with their dirty plates, smeared napkins and half-squeezed condiment sachets. 'Plague of locusts, was it?'

'Something like that,' said Maggie, laughing.

'Shhh,' he said, putting his finger to his lips, listening intently. 'What's that?'

'What's what?' said Maggie.

'That music. If you can call it that.'

'It's The Smiths, of course.'

Pete screwed up his face. 'What was wrong with *my* music?'

'Look, Pete. I like INXS as much as the next woman – they had some really good songs, don't get me wrong – but not all day, every day, on repeat.'

Before Pete could protest, Neil emerged from the kitchen, apron still pristine, to collect some plates. 'Hi Pete. Good trip, was it? Sorry, I'm a bit busy, can't linger.' And he disappeared back where he came from.

Pete gave Maggie a quizzical look. 'What's *he* doing here?'

'I roped him in to help me and Ryan. We've been really busy.'

'I can see that,' said Pete. 'Here,' he said, shaking his jacket off. 'I'll give you a hand to clean up.'

'Nah, you're alright,' said Maggie, gathering some dirty glasses. 'It won't take long for us to sort the place out. And anyway, you look knackered. You should go and get some kip.'

'You look a bit bleary-eyed yourself,' said Pete. 'You hungover?'

'I wish!' said Maggie. 'It's probably just hayfever. My eyes have been streaming all morning. Spring's a bugger.' She dumped some more glasses on to the bar. 'How's your mum doing, by the way?'

'Ah, the old girl's alright,' said Pete. 'She's had to have an op, but she's bearing up OK. My little brother's looking after her. Now that he's back from honeymoon.'

'Ah. That's good news,' said Maggie.

'How have things been here?' he asked. 'You seem to have it all under control.'

'It's been fine,' said Maggie. 'If you don't count the flood.'

'Oh yeah,' said Pete, rubbing his eyes. 'Jim said something about that.'

'There's nothing to worry about. I'll tell you all about it once you've had a sleep and a chance to unpack. Let's just say we need to review the lighting situation in the cellar. Those stairs are a bloody death trap.'

'And how's things going with the case?' asked Pete.

'The case?'

'Rob's case. The court case. Jim's told me all about it. That you'll be doing your Rumpole of the Bailey bit and all that.'

Oh God, she thought. He's only just touched down from the other side of the planet and he knows all about it already. The whole bloody village will know by now. *No pressure!*

'Hey, what's that?' Pete asked, changing the subject, pointing at a bottle on the shelf behind her.

'Ah, well now,' said Maggie. 'I took the liberty of ordering some new house wine. The Muddy Duck, it was, er…' How to describe it without using the phrase 'gut-rot'? 'It could be quite, er, acidic.'

'Hmm,' said Pete, turning the bottle over in his hands. 'How much does this stuff cost?'

'It's *a wee* bit more expensive, but it's been very popular,' said Maggie. 'And it's Australian. Oh, yeah, and I need to update you on some of the other changes I've made.'

'Other changes?' said Pete. 'Sounds ominous.'

'And also, I've donated a meal for four plus wine to Cath,' she continued. 'She's organising an Auction of Promises. For the end of Wakes Week.'

'Really?' he whined. 'But I'm already providing the venue for that. And the buffet. Isn't that enough? I'm not made of money, you know.'

'Aw. You won't say no to the fragrant Cath, will you?' said Maggie, knowingly.

'Nah,' he grinned. 'I don't suppose I will. When is it, anyway?'

'Not till the twenty-first of June. Loads of time. Right!' said Maggie. 'Let me give you a hand upstairs with your stuff. Before you collapse on me.'

On the way through the hallway, they passed Maggie's own luggage sitting in the corner of the swirly red carpet.

'That's mine,' Maggie informed him. 'Now that you're back, I'm moving back in with Cath.'

His face fell at this. 'You'll still be able to do a few shifts, though, won't you?' he said, a note of panic in his voice. 'I could use the help, to be honest. I'm a bit stretched.'

'Sure,' said Maggie. 'No bother at all.'

She could easily cycle down here on her bike now that the weather was a bit better and working at the pub a while longer would help take her mind off the case. But it couldn't go on *too* long; she couldn't risk bar work becoming her full-time 'career'.

* * *

Cath was waiting by the back door as the pink Micra pulled up outside Higher House and Val and Maggie got out. Val opened the boot and Maggie hauled her wheelie case out across the flattened seats, followed by her bike. The little car was like a Tardis.

'Would you both like a brew?' called Cath. 'I've just put the kettle on. And I've made a batch of cherry scones.'

'Thanks. I'd kill for a cherry scone,' replied Val, matter-of-factly. 'But they're on the banned list at Slimming World and, anyway, I've got to go home and check on Mum. It's been a few hours.'

'Another time,' said Cath.

'Definitely,' said Val, cheerfully. She turned to Maggie. 'I'll see you later, then. Is seven o'clock OK?'

'Sounds good,' said Maggie, waving her off and following Cath inside. They hadn't really had a chance to catch up properly since Giles's visit last weekend. Lunch on Easter Sunday had been a bit of a stilted affair and Giles had seemed keen to get back to London straight after it, citing work reasons. Maggie was unsure whether to bring the subject up or not, but eventually decided to go for it.

'So what happened between you and Gorgeous Giles, then?' she asked. 'You both looked pretty cosy from where I was standing? Toddling off from the pub together, arm in arm... Although I wasn't sure if you were actually holding each other up. You were both pissed as newts.'

'Thanks, Maggie.' Cath blushed richly. 'Subtle as a battering ram, as usual.'

'Oh, come on,' said Maggie. 'You'd ask the same thing if it was me. Not that I'd be daft enough to get embroiled with Giles, mind you.'

'I'm not *embroiled* with him,' said Cath, taking an indignant bite of her scone. 'In fact, I've not heard a word from him since he left here,' she mumbled through the crumbs.

'Well. He always seems so busy with work,' said Maggie, diplomatically.

'Hmm,' said Cath. 'I reckon it's bad manners. Not texting someone or anything,' Cath shifted in her seat, 'After you've snogged them.'

'Oh, aye. Are you sure that's all it was?' Maggie asked, side-eyeing her.

Cath flushed crimson.

'Oh God! You slept with him, didn't you?' said Maggie.

'I can barely remember it, to be honest,' admitted Cath, her head in her hands. She groaned through her fingers. 'I feel like I'm nineteen again – and not in a good way.'

'Fucking hell, Cath! What were you thinking?'

'That's just it, I wasn't,' she said, throwing the tea-cosy at Maggie. 'And keep your voice down, will you? Lauren's upstairs revising. She's got her A-levels in a few weeks. It's all a bit... *fraught.*'

'Why?' whispered Maggie. 'She's a bright girl. She'll sail through them.'

'I know,' said Cath, wearily. 'But you know what it's like.'

'Sure,' said Maggie. Although she didn't really know what it was like. Passing exams was one thing she'd never had to worry about. Something she'd always been very good at. Maybe the only thing.

'Anyway, thanks again for letting me move back in,' she said. 'And for letting me have Richard's room. I really appreciate it.'

'Not a problem,' said Cath. 'As I said, it'll be nice to have a bit of adult company.'

Maggie waited a moment, took a mouthful of tea and steeled herself. 'I want to pay you rent, though. At the market rate.'

'Look, Maggie, there's no need to—'

Maggie raised her hand to stop her. 'No, Cath. I insist. I don't want you accusing me of taking advantage again. I want to pay my way. And I'm quite sure you could use the cash.'

'Well, OK then,' said Cath. 'If you're sure.'

'Quite sure,' said Maggie, getting up to clear away the tea things.

'So,' said Cath, sitting back in her chair. 'I take it you've got another driving lesson this evening?'

'And how, pray tell, have you worked that one out, Sherlock?'

'Well,' said Cath, leaning in. 'When she dropped you off earlier, I distinctly heard Val say she would see you at seven o'clock.'

'Ah, well. I'm afraid to tell you that you've jumped to an erroneous conclusion.'

'Really?' said Cath. 'How so?'

'I am indeed seeing Val later, but not for a driving lesson.'

'No?' said Cath.

'No. She's invited me round to her place for a meal. Although I'm a bit worried now that she's mentioned Slimming World. It doesn't bode well for the size of the portions.'

'Oh well,' sniffed Cath. 'I guess she owes you one. You've paid her enough in driving lessons.'

'Ouch,' said Maggie. 'Bit bitchy! Can I get you a saucer of milk?'

'Sorry,' said Cath, holding her hands up.

'I think she wants to talk,' said Maggie, putting the mugs in the dishwasher.

'From what I know of Val, she's very good at talking.'

'She's alright,' said Maggie. 'I get the feeling she might be quite lonely. I don't think she's ever been married or anything

– and she's run off her feet looking after her elderly mum. She's got an older brother, but he sounds a selfish git.'

'Doesn't she live in one of those new houses on the edge of Backdale? How are you planning on getting there? Want a lift?'

'Thanks, but no,' said Maggie, firmly. 'I'm gonna try and cycle over there. It's a lovely evening and I need to try out my new lights.'

'You're going to cycle?' Cath looked dubious. 'Isn't it a bit far?'

'It's a bit further than I'm used to,' said Maggie. 'But I'll give it a go.'

The Elephant in the Room

Maggie was awakened by the bright May sunshine, forcing itself through the gap in the blinds. It looked like her morning off would be a nice one. *Result!* She grabbed her phone from the bedside table to check the time. Only half six – plenty of time to take Jazz out on a decent yomp.

Standing in the shower under the steaming jets, she had an unfamiliar feeling in her stomach. The anxious churning that had become the norm over the last few years seemed to have been swapped for a feeling of, well, stillness. She felt 'centred' somehow – almost calm.

The last few weeks since she'd moved back into Cath's had been pretty stress-free. Enjoyable, in fact. Cycling down to the pub to help Pete when he needed her. Having a laugh with Rob and the other customers – both the locals and tourists alike. And on the evenings when she wasn't working, it was very pleasant hanging out with Cath: chatting over supper at the kitchen table, devouring box-sets of their favourite shows or sitting reading in the conservatory like two old dears, taking advantage of the lighter nights.

Maggie got out of the shower, wrapped herself in one of Cath's huge, fluffy bath towels and went to get dressed.

'Someone's in a good mood,' said Cath, emerging from her room on to the landing, and Maggie realised that she'd actually been whistling. Whistling Ed Sheeran. O*h, God!* she thought. *This is how it starts.*

She skipped down the stairs, planning out her day in her head. She'd have a coffee first, obviously. Maybe two. Then she'd take Jazz out, come back, give Jazz her breakfast. Strip the beds after that. Give the bathroom a good clean. Hoover the downstairs – possibly the upstairs too, if she had time. Then she'd make something easy for lunch that Cath and Lauren could have as well. Some soup, perhaps. A few batches that she could freeze. Her culinary skills hadn't improved much in the last few months, but she'd discovered there was a singular satisfaction to be found in blitzing up all the leftover vegetables in Cath's blender. Yes, soup was easy, healthy and you couldn't really go wrong.

Cath came drifting into the kitchen as she was putting on Jazz's lead. She handed Maggie's phone to her. 'Here,' she said. 'You left this upstairs. I think you've got a text.'

Maggie took it. It was Rob:

Letter from the court this morning. Hearing set for the 21st June. Six weeks!!!

Bollocks, thought Maggie, her gut turning over. *Shit just got real.* She dropped the dog's lead and sat down.

'Whatever's the matter?' asked Cath.

Maggie let out a sigh. 'It's from Rob. The court date's been set.'

'When for?'

'Friday the twenty-first of June.'

'That's the Friday of Wakes Week,' said Cath straightaway. 'Same day as the Auction of Promises.'

'Really?' grunted Maggie. 'That'll be a fun day…' She looked down at Jazz's little face, all worried that the walk wasn't going to happen after all.

'Come on, girl,' said Maggie, grabbing hold of the lead again. 'Let's go and clear our heads.'

* * *

Her chores completed, Maggie was chilling in the lounge till it was time to ride down to the pub for the afternoon shift.

She was patiently waiting for *The World at One* to start on Radio 4. She'd become addicted to American politics, hooked on hearing the latest instalment of the Trump soap opera, wondering how long they'd take to impeach him. The drama was better than any box-set.

A set of angry footsteps stomping down the stairs and into the kitchen told her that Lauren had emerged from her pit and was looking for some lunch. And the sound of the fridge door opening was like the Bat-Signal to Jazz, who'd already scampered through to see what scraps she could score.

'Piss off, you daft dog,' she heard Lauren grumble, which Maggie interpreted as not a good sign. However stressed or annoyed Lauren got, she always had infinite patience for her rescue hound.

But the imminent arrival of the dreaded A-levels meant that Lauren's nerves were on a hair trigger these days. And, though she meant well, Cath wasn't exactly helping matters – always sniping at her about her slovenly appearance, her sullen face or something else.

Lauren was intent on studying Psychology at university. Apart from her natural interest in the subject, she was convinced it was a growth area for the future. In her own words, it would be 'fertile ground for a long career, given the number of fucked up people in the world – especially if my own family's anything to go by'. Maggie hadn't really approved of her swearing like that, but she couldn't fault the girl's logic.

Lauren needed two As and a B to get on to the degree course at Bristol. This was her first choice, in defiance of her mother, who wanted her to apply to Sheffield or Manchester – somewhere closer to home. Cath's second choice would have been for her to study in London – close to her older brother and sister – but, like many youngest children, Lauren was keen to shake off her role as the 'baby of the family' and to forge her own path. And you couldn't really blame her.

Maggie swung her legs off the sofa to go and have a word with her, bracing herself for a chilly reception.

And a chilly reception was what she got. Lauren looked dreadful. Still in her pyjamas, with hair that looked like it hadn't been washed for a month, her general demeanour reminded Maggie of herself only a few short months ago.

'Want me to make you a sandwich or something?' Maggie offered. 'Or there's some of my homemade soup in the fridge.'

'Nah. It's OK,' mumbled Lauren, staring at the floor, where Jazz was still sitting, ever hopeful. 'I'm not that hungry. I just needed a break, before my head explodes.'

'How's it all going?' ventured Maggie.

'It's not,' sighed Lauren. 'God. I can't wait for this all to be over.'

Maggie said nothing, just left a space for her to fill if she wanted to.

Lauren looked up and smiled at her: she'd sussed what Maggie was up to. 'I've been so worried about Maths and Biology that I've spent all my time on those two,' she said. 'And now I'm really not ready for English Lit and that's the first exam and…' She shook her head helplessly. 'I've really mugged myself off.'

Maggie wasn't sure what this meant, but she guessed it wasn't good. She decided to try a different tack. 'What books have you been studying for English? Anything interesting?'

'Oh. Y'know. The usual old crap,' Lauren ran her hand through her hair, until she hit a tangle.

'Like what?'

'Ugh. *Of Mice and Men*, *To Kill a Mockingbird*, the usual.'

Maggie brightened. '*To Kill a Mockingbird* is one of my favourites. It's a great book.'

'I wouldn't know. I was bunking off English when they covered it. Trying to avoid Freya…'

'In fact, it's one of the main reasons I went into the law,' Maggie continued, lost in thought. 'Talk about misguided! There was me thinking that the law was all about fairness and justice – and then I ended up working for a bloody oil company. Satan himself, basically. How does that even happen?'

Lauren giggled in spite of herself.

'You see,' said Maggie, encouraged by this. 'What you've got to remember about *To Kill a Mockingbird* is that, although it's got so many layers to it, it's basically a story about a girl and her dad.'

'Maybe that's why I don't like it,' huffed Lauren. 'I can't identify. My dad's such a git.'

'Not as much of a git as mine was,' Maggie began.

'How come?' asked Lauren, sensing a story.

'Never mind,' said Maggie. 'Tell me. When's the exam?'

'Three weeks today,' Lauren replied, in a small voice. 'It's the first one.'

'Ach,' said Maggie. 'That's plenty of time. Now. You've just got to take a deep breath and prioritise those tasks which are the most important.'

'Yep.' Lauren nodded. 'I'm going to spend the next couple of days drawing up a revision timetable.'

'Will you be colour-coding it, using loads of marker pens and Post-its? That sort of thing?'

'Yep,' said Lauren again. 'Why?'

Maggie screwed up her face. 'If I can give you one piece of advice – and I think I'm qualified to give it, as I've sat more exams than most people have had hot dinners – I would say don't bother spending hours on a revision timetable.'

'Really?' said Lauren. 'But I thought you said I needed a plan?'

'I suppose I did. But your plan should be to get stuck in and get on with re-reading the books and reacquainting yourself with the characters and the themes. And then you should try tackling some past exam questions, so that you're match fit. Don't be putting it off, messing around with coloured pens.' Maggie couldn't believe she was actually saying this, given her own world-class levels of procrastination when it came to the research for this court case. She'd been doing her absolute best to avoid it: there wasn't a vegetable in the house that she hadn't liquidised and she'd even considered cleaning the oven the other day.

Lauren was biting her lip, bless her. She looked so pale and worried about everything and Maggie wanted nothing more than to put her arm round her shoulder and tell her everything was going to be alright. But she decided against it as Lauren would no doubt think it pretty lame.

'And don't you be sitting up in your room stewing,' Maggie said instead. 'You come and see me if you get stuck, OK?' She grinned at her. 'I'm always available for advice and assistance.'

'Cheers, Maggie,' said Lauren, her stomach growling now. 'I think I might be ready for some lunch now.'

'Good,' said Maggie. 'Now you go back upstairs. And I'm bringing you up some of my soup whether you like it or not. Sweet potato and spinach! Whoever could resist?'

'OK.' Lauren was smiling again as she headed for the stairs.

'Oh, and Lauren,' Maggie called after her. 'In *To Kill a Mockingbird*, if you ask me, Atticus misses a bit of a trick during the trial. There's a point he should have spotted, that could've made all the difference.'

'What's that?' asked Lauren, intrigued.

'I'll tell you tomorrow,' grinned Maggie. 'Once you're up to speed.'

'OK,' said Lauren, and disappeared up to her room.

Maggie shook her head and went to fetch her latest batch of soup from the fridge.

'You'd have been a good mum, you know,' said Cath, leaning against the back door, arms folded.

Maggie jumped and the fridge door slammed shut on her. 'Jeez!' Maggie looked round. 'Where did *you* spring from? You nearly gave me a heart attack. I thought you were down at the café?'

'I decided to close early,' said Cath. 'You *would* though.'

Maggie froze. 'Would *what?*' she said, trying to put off for a little bit longer the conversation they'd never really had.

'Would have made a good mum.'

'You reckon?' said Maggie. It was something she'd done her best to avoid thinking about over the years – a thread she'd taken the specific decision not to pull. 'Maybe so, but not at the nappy stage,' she said, briskly. 'Maybe later on. When they can actually talk and stuff.'

'*You're* allowed to talk, you know, Maggie. About Joy. About *your* baby.'

Maggie turned to face her. 'Look, Cath. I know you mean well, but I don't really want people feeling sorry for me or anything like that. I don't want it to become my *identity*, to be defined by it. God knows the "widow" label is bad enough.' She paused for a second. 'And, to be perfectly honest with you, you've never seemed particularly keen to talk about it either. Like you were embarrassed or something.'

'Embarrassed?' said Cath, gently. 'Is that what you think?'

Maggie nodded. 'I thought you might be embarrassed *for* me.'

Cath looked down at her feet. 'I *have* wanted to talk to you. Many times. But I suppose – if anything – I felt guilty.'

'Guilty?' asked Maggie. 'How come?'

'Oh, I don't know. Guilty for having four healthy children. Lauren was only just two, remember. I thought that if I talked about it, it'd be like rubbing it in or something.'

'You actually thought that?' said Maggie. 'Well that's just daft.'

'D'you think?'

'I do, I'm afraid,' said Maggie, going back to rummaging in the fridge. 'I just didn't think it would be my one and only chance. To be a mum. I thought it would happen again. Thought we had plenty of time. I was only thirty-six when Andy…' She trailed off, unwilling to go there again.

'It's not *necessarily* your only chance,' said Cath, softly.

'Oh, come off it, will you?' scoffed Maggie. 'Are you having a laugh? Not at my age.'

'There's more than one way to be a mum, you know.'

'I know. I know,' said Maggie, finding the Tupperware container she'd been searching for. 'Right. Have you had your lunch already or can I interest you in some of my soup?'

'I'd love some,' said Cath, unzipping her jacket and taking a seat.

'Really?' said Maggie, surprised. 'Are you sure?'

Homework

Maggie tightened her grip on the handlebars, stood up on the pedals and dug in for the steepest part of the climb back up to Cath's. She'd struggled with this gradient the first few times she'd attempted it, but thought she must be getting fitter as it seemed to be getting easier and her lungs and thighs no longer burned like buggery.

She was even starting to enjoy it a bit, now that the effort wasn't overwhelming – especially on an evening like this one when the petrichor was filling her nostrils. 'Petrichor' was her new favourite word, and she'd decided to try and crow-bar it into conversation wherever possible from now on. It meant 'the pleasant smell that comes with the first rain after a period of warm, dry weather' and it was especially appropriate this evening as there had been a light shower while she'd been at work.

Pete had said she might as well leave early tonight as the pub was pretty quiet, and she'd quickly taken him up on his offer. Rob's text this morning about the date for the court hearing had brought her up short – had made it all a bit too real – and she needed to pull her finger out. Pronto. She needed to do her research and figure out what her main argument was going to be. It couldn't be put off any longer. She had to take on board the advice she'd given to Lauren. Just like riding a bike again, the best way of doing it was just to get on and do it – to face it head on. And that meant tonight.

'You're home early,' called Cath, from the conservatory. 'Are you hungry? I made a chicken tartiflette earlier and there's some garlic ciabatta in the fridge.'

'Thanks, but I'm alright,' replied Maggie, not sure what a 'tartiflette' was. She was thirsty more than hungry and, anyway, stopping to eat would only be a distraction. She'd just grab a quick drink of water at the sink. That was *one* good point about living round here: the stuff that came out of the reservoirs was so much tastier than what came out of the tap in the city. Here, there was no need to drink water out of plastic bottles that were slowly but surely choking the planet. Taking a final gulp, she headed straight upstairs to her room.

Sitting down at Richard's old desk, she fired up her laptop and avidly read all the links Giles had emailed her. There were more than thirty law reports to wade through, similar cases with different lenders over the years. There were even some from Australia and New Zealand (he'd been very thorough, she'd give him that). But the deeper she delved into them, the less they seemed to help. In each case, although the terms of the loan were undoubtedly harsh and unfair, that wasn't enough in law to overturn it. Rob had been fully aware of the terms at the outset, but had still willingly signed up to them. No one had twisted his arm, after all.

Maggie would need to show that this AP Finance lot had used dirty tricks to get him to sign the thing. That they'd falsely promised to find him a better deal after twelve months – at an affordable interest rate – when they had zero intention of doing any such thing.

The problem was that they had been smart – very smart. Rob had told her that they'd only given him these assurances on the phone. None of this was written down anywhere. It would be his word against theirs. Nigh on impossible to establish. This was probably the reason why none of the company's other victims appeared to have taken their case to court: they'd probably been advised not to bother.

Maggie wasn't looking forward to breaking this news to Rob. She rubbed her eyes, which were stinging now, and turned to look at herself in the wardrobe mirror. She was still wearing her cycle helmet and she looked ridiculous. She *was* ridiculous. Why had she got herself involved in this whole sorry business? When Jim had first told her about Rob's predicament at the quiz all those months ago, she'd politely told him that she couldn't help. Why hadn't she stuck to her guns? Suggested he go and talk to the Citizens Advice Bureau? Or that he try and get Legal Aid? Not that he'd have succeeded, as that kind of thing had all been cut to the bone these days. Ugh. What a mess!

Tiggy was right. She wasn't a 'proper' lawyer – at least, not the right sort of lawyer for the job in hand. Not like Giles, who was always brim-full of confidence in his own position. *Maybe she didn't have it in her?*

But it was too late now. She'd allowed herself to get sucked in and now she had to go through with it.

And what would happen when she failed? Which she probably would. She would feel personally responsible and bloody awful and the whole thing would be awkward beyond belief. Although at least she wouldn't have to hang around and witness the heart-breaking aftermath – watching Rob and his parents being pitchforked off their land, lugging all their belongings in a series of battered trunks, like something out of a Thomas Hardy novel.

She got up and yanked her wheelie case out from under the bed. Unzipping it, she pulled out her black business suit – the only thing she hadn't bothered to hang in the wardrobe when she'd moved back in. She'd brought it with her in case she needed it to wear to any interviews that might crop up – a vain hope, she now realised. It had turned out to be redundant, much like herself.

Yep, this wretched case would most probably be her very last act as a member of the legal profession. What would she do when it was finished? She still couldn't see where her next job – her next proper job – was coming from.

She hung the suit in the wardrobe and reflected how far she'd fallen in her career in such a short space of time. Years to build it up, demolished in minutes – seconds really – because of her own stupid fault. She should just have swallowed her pride and her anger and stayed where she was, working for that slimy creep Dalton. She could always have asked for a transfer within the company – it was a global corporation after all. She could have moved to the other side of the world – to the US or Canada. Or else she could just have stuck it out for a month or two while she found another, similar job with another company. Everyone knew it was much easier to find a new position when you already had a job to begin with – much harder when you were already unemployed, already on the 'outside'. And now she'd been – *how many?* – she counted on her fingers, eleven months, nearly a year, out of the game. No one would want to employ her again. Her career was basically over. She shook her head in disbelief. For a supposedly clever person, she had been *a right fucking idiot.*

A tentative knock on the bedroom door interrupted her thoughts. It was Cath, in her dressing gown, clutching a cup and saucer. 'I've brought you a camomile tea,' she said, setting it on the bedside table. 'I thought it might help you to sleep.'

'Ah, thanks.' Maggie looked at her watch, unable to believe it was a quarter to midnight. She felt shattered all of a sudden and slumped down on to the bed.

'Is there anything else I can do?' said Cath, watching her from the door. 'You seem a bit, not yourself?'

'I'm fine,' Maggie lied. 'Still, er, just a bit disappointed that we won't get our trip to London for the hearing.'

Cath spluttered. '*I'm* not! That would mean having to see bloody Giles again.'

'Sorry.' Maggie grinned up her. 'I'd forgotten about that.' *Had blanked it out, more like.* 'Anyway,' she said. 'Tell me. What've you got on the agenda tomorrow?'

'Nothing very exciting,' said Cath. 'Just loads to do for Wakes Week.'

'I hear you, sister,' said Maggie. 'I've stupidly consented to make a scarecrow for Australian Pete. To go up on the wall outside the pub.'

'For the competition?' said Cath, amused. 'Good for you!'

Maggie shrugged. 'I've got no idea what I'm doing. I'm thinking of modelling it on myself,' she said, pulling at her hair.

'Oh, shush, will you?' said Cath. 'Stop doing yourself down.' Then she yawned. 'I'm going to turn in now. Night night. I'll see you in the morning.'

'Night, night,' said Maggie, pulling the duvet over herself.

On her way out the door, Cath hesitated and turned back. 'I've just got one question…'

'Go for it, Columbo,' said Maggie, her eyes already closed.

'Right… So… After Rob's court hearing, how long will we have to wait for the verdict?'

'Verdict?' Maggie sat bolt upright again, cleared her throat imperiously and turned to face her. 'You're using incorrect terminology there, Cath. You see, you only get a *verdict* in a *criminal* case where there's a *jury*.' She paused for effect. 'In a civil case, you get a *judgment*. From a *judge!*'

'OK. OK,' huffed Cath. 'When do we get the *judgment* then? A few weeks later, I guess?'

'Afraid not,' said Maggie. 'It's the County Court. We'll find out on the day itself.'

'Really?' said Cath. 'Fu-uck.'

Well Dressing

June snuck up on them with surprising stealth and, before they knew it, it was Wakes Week. It was very early days – only the Monday morning – but all worries about the weather had so far come to nothing and the five-day forecast was looking bright.

Maggie was enjoying the warmth of the sun on her bare arms, striding out on the road from Higher House down to the village, her little rucksack on her back. Archdale was positively sparkling in the distance, as its criss-crossed bunting fluttered daintily in the breeze.

Crossing the cobbles in front of the church, she followed the path through the freshly-manicured churchyard, savouring the scent of the cut grass. Her eye was drawn to the ancient grave stones with their cursive script, to the old Derbyshire names that were now familiar to her from the war memorial and all the other old signs in the village: Eyre, Ollerenshaw and Elliott, Rob's own family name. She passed the wives buried with their husbands, the children buried with their mothers and carried on to the church hall beyond – the place that used to be the schoolhouse in days gone by and which now performed various other village functions.

This week it was the venue for the creation of the mysterious 'well dressing' Cath had told her about. And, as Maggie wasn't working at the pub till tonight, she'd offered to go and help out with it, even though she wasn't exactly sure what it would entail. Not that she had 'offered' as such, Cath had basically guilt-tripped her into it.

Just because this well dressing was a custom from the olden days, it didn't necessarily mean it was any good. Loads of things were customary in the olden days – cod-pieces, child labour, burning 'witches' at the stake – and most of them were best left there. That's what Joyce always used to say while watching the *Antiques Roadshow*, and Maggie had always agreed with her.

She turned the solid metal door handle of the church hall, but to no avail – it wasn't even open yet. She looked down at her watch. Fifteen minutes to kill. What to do?

She decided to circle back on herself, back into the dappled light of the churchyard – noticing for the first time the gargoyles along the parapet, all engaged in unspeakable activities.

She wandered on, around the walls of the church itself, until she felt the urge to stop for a moment – to reach out and touch the rough limestone of the solid, time-worn walls. Carrying on towards the sturdy south door, her fingertips still grazing the stone, she came across a sign and an arrow pointing: 'Saint Peter's Church. Open for Wakes Week – Display of Church Treasures.'

Following the arrow, around along the path to the main door of the church, she pushed inside into the musty cool. And as her eyes adjusted to the low light, she saw that she was alone. She tiptoed around, feeling the stillness, reading the embroidered banners with their crosses in the shape of sheaves of wheat and the old familiar symbol of the crossed keys. Then she sat down on one of the simple wooden pews and looked up at the stained-glass window – very old but simple and striking, show-casing the free-falling dust motes in its violet spotlight.

Maggie couldn't believe she'd never ventured in here before. On her various overseas travels, she'd always made a point of visiting all the different churches and temples along the route – many of which weren't a patch on this one, frankly. Sure, they might have been grander and more celebrated, but they were usually crowded and rarely had this sense of peace.

Floating back round to the church hall, her mind on higher things, she found the door wedged open now, with a scribbled note pinned to it:

Well dressing in progress. Visitors welcome.

The heady aroma of the petals made her nose fizz as soon she stepped inside, where a huge wooden frame in the shape of an arch was balanced on a few small tables that had been pushed together to make one large one.

Neil was bustling around the edge of the room, very much in his element, quite clearly in charge. And old Mrs Winterson was beavering away in the corner, flanked on each side by several of her henchwomen. The old lady barely looked up from her work and didn't say a thing to Maggie. It was hard to tell whether she was annoyed by her presence or just being your typical Derbyshire woman-of-few-words…

Neil, on the other hand, was delighted by Maggie's arrival. He launched into an explanation of the well dressing tradition for her sole benefit, with no detail left out: 'Well dressing is an ancient summer custom in which the villagers come together to decorate the wells, springs and other water sources with designs created from flower petals – giving thanks for the continued blessing of clean water. The custom is most closely associated with the Peak District of Derbyshire and Staffordshire and…'

As he warmed to his theme, Maggie wondered just how long his speech was going to last.

'Large wooden frames like this one,' he explained, pointing at the arch, 'are constructed and covered with puddled clay, and mixed with water and salt. A design is sketched on a large piece of paper and this is traced on to the clay. The picture is then filled in with natural material – predominantly flower petals and mosses, but also beans, seeds and small cones…'

Ugh. On and on he droned, like one of her old law professors, and Maggie feared it would never end. Even so, she couldn't quite bring herself to interrupt his obvious enjoyment.

'The theme of the well dressing is often, but not exclusively, religious,' he continued. 'Like the Madonna and Child. Or sometimes – like this one – Our Lord giving one of his sermons…'

Maggie walked to the end of the table to get a better look at the picture, but it was hard to get a proper sense of it while it was lying flat.

'Sometimes the theme is a topical one, which people seem to like.' Neil was still going. 'We even had Wayne Rooney one year, for the World Cup. But, me personally, I prefer the more traditional themes.'

You would, mate, thought Maggie. *You would.*

'Now,' he said at last, pressing his fingertips together. 'Do you have any questions?'

Relieved that the lecture seemed to be over, Maggie didn't want to risk setting him off again, but she did, in fact, have a question.

'Yes I do, actually,' she said. 'Where's the well?'

'I beg your pardon?' Neil looked confused.

'The well. The well that's being decorated? Where is it?'

'Oh, that? That's long gone,' said Neil, dismissively. 'We erect the well dressing outside the front of the church. It's purely symbolic these days.'

'Oh. Right,' said Maggie. 'You know, it all seems a bit like Morris dancing to me. Another English custom no Scottish person could hope to understand in a million years.'

'Ah, well,' said Neil, with a twinkle. 'It's very interesting you should say that… The origins of Morris dancing are somewhat obscure, I'm afraid, but it's thought to be based on a pagan tradition that was brought here by the Romans. Or possibly even your lot – the Celts!'

'Touché!' said Maggie, as Neil handed her a basket of big, blue petals, hydrangeas apparently, and set her to work on filling in the background of the well dressing scene. She guessed that it must be the sky. As a novice, he doubtless didn't trust her with anything more challenging at this stage. And rightly so.

Within half an hour, Maggie's neck was killing her from all the craning over and she was seriously questioning her own sanity. It was a lovely sunny day outside and, here she was, sitting in a dusty church hall, smeared in wet clay, bored out of her mind.

The twelve chimes of the church bell eventually sounded next door – matched by the rumbling of stomachs echoing around the hall – and Maggie offered to hold the fort while the rest of them went to Cath's café for an early lunch. She couldn't stand by and allow a mass collapse of pensioners with low blood sugar, after all. Plus, nice enough bloke that he was, it would be a relief to have a break from Neil's wittering for a while. She was feeling a bit peckish herself, but the apple and banana in her rucksack would be enough to keep her going until teatime.

Sitting alone at last, peacefully pressing the silky petals into the clay, she soon found her rhythm. Clearing her mind of all her worries – all thoughts about the court hearing at the end of the week – she simply focused on the job in hand. One petal at a time. No more, no less.

The only interruption was when a school trip of thirty ten-year-olds from Lancashire turned up – shooed through the door by two beleaguered teachers, keen for a break from tramping round the countryside in the heat of the day.

Feeling obliged to explain what on earth she was doing, Maggie found herself spouting the same old spiel Neil had given her this morning, with some added jokes and some new bits she'd made up for interest value.

Rather surprisingly, her shtick seemed to go down pretty well: the kids seemed keen to get involved and do some 'petalling' for themselves and so she exploited their labour to the max while she took a tea-break.

When Neil and the women came back from lunch in due course, they were amazed at the progress that had been made. The thing was basically finished. 'Great!' Neil enthused. 'We'll be home in time for *Countdown*.'

Then he disappeared outside to make a phone call and, within a few minutes, Rob, Jim and Les the butcher turned up. Rob gave Maggie the thumbs up and the three men then eased the frame out of the door of the hall and on to his flat-bed truck. He drove it fifty yards to a spacious spot in front of the church and then they hoisted it up outside the gates.

Maggie could see the image much more clearly now than when it was lying on the table. She had to admit it looked amazing: Jesus standing there, his arm outstretched, talking to his disciples – with the over-arching words: 'Love each other as I have loved you.'

She'd never been remotely religious, not even slightly, but she couldn't help feeling strangely moved. She found herself thinking about all the villagers down the years – down the centuries – coming together to do this same thing, at this time, in this same place. Quite unexpectedly, she felt tears pricking her eyes.

Wakes Week

It had been a very long day – with the well dressing and then her shift at the pub – and it wasn't over yet.

'She's on her way, Maggie,' called Ryan, beckoning her from the door of the pub. 'Hurry up!'

'I can't,' Maggie called back from behind the bar. 'I'm too busy. I've got to change the barrel and then—'

'You go ahead,' said Australian Pete, waving her away. 'I'll cover for you.'

'Really? OK. If you're sure,' she said, drying her hands on her apron.

Maggie rushed outside into the balmy evening. The *'she'* that Ryan was referring to was Mrs Winterson, whose seniority in the village gave her the dubious honour of judging the scarecrow competition. And there was still no sign of the old lady, although everyone else and their dog seemed to be there, congregating on the corner. They were all awaiting the unveiling of the scarecrow Maggie had made – which Ryan had stuck up on to the side of the pub and covered with a manky dust sheet he'd found in the cellar.

Cath came straight over to Maggie. 'I was just saying to Neil, you've all done a sterling job with the well dressing.'

'You think?' said Maggie, pleased.

'Everyone says so. It looks great. I'm very impressed.'

'Don't tell anyone, but I quite enjoyed it,' Maggie whispered behind her hand. 'I found it very – what's the word? – *therapeutic.*'

Their conversation was interrupted by Rob, Jim and Les the butcher returning from the tug-of-war, which had just finished. Maggie assumed that their team (Farmers and Firemen) must have lost as the three of them looked quite deflated. By contrast, Tiggy's husband, Phil – sporting a trilby and a winner's smile – looked very pleased with himself, even though Rob was ribbing him about being a bit of a cheat.

'Tut-tut, Phil,' said Maggie, joining in the teasing. 'You'll be getting yourself a bad reputation…'

'Just keep your nose out, will you, Maggie?' Phil replied, more sharply than necessary.

'Alright, alright,' said Maggie. 'Keep your hat on!' It was quite funny seeing him ruffled as she'd never seen him lose his good humour before.

Normal service was soon resumed, though: the smile was firmly back on his face by the time Tiggy came waltzing up to them like the Queen of Sheba, propelling Mrs Winterson by the elbow. An expectant hush descended as they came to a stop below Maggie's scarecrow and waited.

When Ryan gave her the nod, Maggie whipped off the dust sheet to reveal her handiwork – and total silence from the crowd made her regret her artistic choices for a moment. Maybe 'Boris-Johnson-on-a-zip-wire' hadn't been such a good idea after all…

Cath looked embarrassed, Ryan looked confused (he clearly had no idea who it was meant to be), but Rob and Jim were laughing heartily, which she was pleased about.

'I know,' said Maggie, to Mrs Winterson. 'Not very convincing, is it? It's far too smartly turned out.'

Mrs Winterson's face remained flinty. She'd obviously decided to say nothing – that discretion was the better part of valour

– but Tiggy couldn't help wading in. 'It's not really supposed to be a political thing, Maggie,' she bitched. 'It's just meant to be a bit of fun. A bit of a laugh.'

'Oh, come on!' said Maggie. 'The guy's a joke. And anyway, what about Jim? He's got Donald Trump strung up outside the garage!'

This provoked a few giggles among the crowd, but Tiggy turned away and guided Mrs Winterson on to their next stop.

Rob, Jim and the others drifted around the corner to the car park, to snap up the last available table. Australian Pete had just acquired some new red umbrellas for the picnic benches and, without a smidgen of irony, was now referring to the car park as the 'beer garden'. But the umbrellas were certainly coming in handy this week, to shade the drinkers from the sun's rays.

Maggie headed back inside the pub to give Australian Pete some help. The place was properly heaving for a Monday – and just getting busier.

'Can I have a word?' asked Pete, when she was back behind the bar and the rush had died down a bit.

'Sure,' she said, fully expecting a bollocking about the scarecrow thing. He hadn't actually said a word about it so far, which wasn't like him at all.

'I've got some news,' he continued.

'Oh, God. What is it? Is it your mum?'

'Nah. Nothing like that.' He broke into a grin. 'We're celebrating.'

'Celebrating? How come?'

'I've been doing the accounts this week. The profits are up for the last quarter. *Well* up on last year.'

Maggie clapped him on the shoulder. 'That's great,' she said. 'Well done.'

'I know. It's amazing.' He grinned. 'Especially when you take into account all the freebies you keep giving away…'

'Er, hang on,' she spluttered in mock indignation. 'I reckon it's all down to my canny planning and business development. It's obviously been working.'

'You know what? I think you might be right,' admitted Pete. 'Now then. Can I get you a drink? I think you've earned it.'

* * *

Maggie ran her finger down the Wakes Week timetable Cath had given her earlier in the week. It was now Wednesday, which meant it was the 'Duck Race' this evening, followed by the 'Pet Show'. It was a punishing schedule and no mistake…

The Duck Race would be happening down in Rob's lower field and he'd called her this morning to ask if she wanted to join him there. A warm evening was forecast and he'd suggested they take a picnic – or, rather, that he would bring one for them to share. All she had to do was bring herself.

Maggie had said yes straightaway. She couldn't remember the last time she'd been asked on a picnic by a man. By anyone! It was probably that first summer she'd spent with Andy: he'd asked her out to Regent's Park after work on one of those close August evenings when the heat in London had been building all summer and it had been such a relief to escape the traffic and the fumes and the sound of 'Dancing In The Moonlight' by Toploader blaring from every bar and car stereo. Not that Rob was 'asking her out', of course. Although he hadn't said he'd invited anyone else. She kind of hoped that he hadn't: it would be nice just to spend a bit of time with him on their own, relaxing down by the river.

When five o'clock came round, Maggie packed her rucksack with Cath's tartan throw and a few extra goodies from the fridge. Setting off down to the lower field with Jazz on the lead, her thoughts turned to Eve, Rob's ex. She'd have moved back to Archdale by now and Maggie wondered if Rob had helped her with the move like he'd promised. He hadn't mentioned anything about it, but then why would he? He wasn't obliged to tell her his every move. It was weird that she hadn't seen Eve around, though, in the pub or anywhere else. Maybe she wasn't a pub kind of girl; she looked more of a fancy wine bar type. Or maybe she was busy tarting up her new cottage. Or hanging out with Tiggy…

As Maggie followed the curve of the river Arch, on past the silvery stone bridge, the distinct aroma of charred meat grew ever stronger, spurring Jazz to follow it. And when the field in question opened up in front of her, any hope of a cosy picnic for two receded from view. There were over a hundred people in attendance, spread out on a rainbow of rugs and deckchairs, most of whom seemed to be burning beef burgers over disposable barbecues.

Where had all these people been during the winter, she wondered. Sweet little kids on their dads' shoulders, being fussed over by their mums; Lauren and a gang of teenagers sipping garish fruit ciders from the bottle; and the older generation as well, who'd come prepared with tents, wind-cheaters and all manner of other contraptions that had proved to be unnecessary. And there were dogs. Loads of them. Black Labradors and Cocker Spaniels mostly. Proper pedigree dogs with kennel club names. Sheep dogs. Gun dogs. Working dogs-with-jobs. Not former-rubbish-dump-residents like Jazz. Not that Jazz seemed unduly bothered.

Rob flagged Maggie down by standing up and whistling through the haze of thick, grey smoke. He'd already laid out a rug for them to sit on, together with some paper plates and red napkins.

He sat himself down on the rug and, from a coolbox, he produced a tasty-looking platter of antipasti, chicken satay and some mini pork pies. This was followed by a chilled bottle of Pinot Grigio and some proper glasses. *Heaven!*

'I've got some strawberries for afters,' he grinned up at her.

'I'm impressed,' she said, settling down on the rug beside him.

She lay back on her elbows as Rob poured the wine. Closing her eyes, she felt the warmth of the earth seep up into her bones and listened to the clumps of clover alive with bees and other buzzing things…

'We're so lucky to live in a place like this,' murmured Rob and, for the first time, Maggie agreed.

She lifted her head and squinted down the field to the riverbank. She hadn't really paid the river much attention before – normally just hurried past with Jazz in the rain – but there was something special in its soothing burble on a day like this. 'It's gorgeous here,' she said. 'Today.' And it was.

'You know,' said Rob, shielding his eyes from the glare. 'I think this is the first sunny Wakes Week we've had in years. Normally it's a quagmire down here. Or else we've had to call off the race altogether. Health and safety!'

Maggie chuckled at this and Rob dropped the bombshell that the duck race wouldn't actually involve any running or, indeed, any ducks: there would just be a bunch of plastic numbered balls released into the river. Maggie was slightly disappointed, although it was probably just as well, she wouldn't have to worry about Jazz trying to catch any birds.

After a while, Cath and Neil came over to join them and spread out another blanket to sit on. Cath had brought some leftover muffins from the café and Neil was hugging a huge, pink Thermos flask. As they settled themselves down and got comfortable, Maggie could see two old duffers staggering in their direction, intent on talking to Cath.

But it wasn't Cath they wanted at all – they actually wanted to speak to Maggie for some reason – and so she got to her feet out of politeness.

'Ay up,' said the older of the two men. 'Are you the Scottish one?' The temperature might have been eighty degrees in the shade, but he was still wearing a battered, green Barbour jacket that looked like a family heirloom.

Maggie nodded, unsure what was coming next. The pair of them looked like they'd been drinking most of the day and the smell of Gnarly Old Root was over-powering.

'Thought so,' he said, putting his arm around her shoulder, struggling to make himself heard over the swell of shouts and cheers that accompanied the 'ducks' being released. 'You *look* proper Scottish.'

What on earth does *that* mean, Maggie thought, but his mate was chiming in now. 'It's this Friday, isn't it?' he asked. 'The day after tomorrow.'

'It's scandalous, that's what it is,' said the first one.

Maggie had twigged by now what they were on about. *The hearing. Oh, God. She was the talk of the village.*

'Well, best of luck,' said the first bloke. 'We might not be here next year.'

'Oh. Don't be so morbid,' said Maggie. 'You're not *that* old, either of you.'

They laughed. Matching gravelly laughs. 'Nah, love. You've got the wrong end o't stick. We might not be in *this field* next year is what we meant. God knows who the new owners might be, who this mortgage company might sell it to. They mightn't let us have the Duck Race here.'

Maggie noticed that Rob had gone very quiet. And as the two old guys wandered off, she lay back down on the grass next to him and closed her eyes again, her worries about Friday soaring to the surface. The early evening sun was shining red through her eyelids, piercing her brain, which was throbbing now. But she hadn't had much of the wine, not nearly enough for a headache. Maybe she just needed some sleep.

She imagined she could hear the swishing of a snake through the grass, slow and sinister. *Were there snakes in these parts? Surely not. Puff adders perhaps. Were they still a thing...?*

Something blocked out the light and warmth of the sun. A dry, croaky voice came next, 'Oh hi, Catherine, there you are. I've been looking for you *everywhere*.'

Cath leapt up and Maggie knew who it was without opening her eyes. But she had to look anyway, if only to see what ridiculous outfit Tiggy was wearing. She wasn't disappointed. It was a tie-dye seventies sundress, big floppy hat and wraparound shades. Like Margo Leadbetter from *The Good Life*, only more annoying.

'I'm hosting an "at-home" tomorrow night,' Tiggy declared, clocking Maggie and Rob on the rug together. 'A sort of impromptu girls' night in – while the men are playing in the five-a-side footy tournament. I'm laying on some drinks and nibbles...'

Mother of God, thought Maggie. *Yet another social event!* And why was it that the men were called 'men' and yet the women were only 'girls'?

'Oh... Thanks,' Cath replied.

'Yah, Phil's refereeing,' said Tiggy. 'I'd only be home alone otherwise. Six-thirty for seven. Don't be late now.'

'Er, great,' Cath stuttered. 'Count us in.'

Us? Maggie shivered.

'Great. Oh, and another thing,' said Tiggy, raising a bony finger.

What now? thought Maggie.

'We're going to have a bit of a "Buskers' Night" on Friday evening. In the pub – right after the Auction of Promises. It's to mark the end of Wakes Week. Anyone who wants to can bring their musical instruments along and everyone else can join in with the singing.'

'A little sing-song? How nice,' said Maggie, from her spot on the grass.

Tiggy looked down at her. 'Not a sing-song as such. More of a, y'know, *jam session*.'

'Ah,' said Maggie. 'A jam session indeed? Will you be getting your tambourine out?'

Tiggy pursed her lips. 'Yes, actually. I will be.'

'Oh, good,' dead-panned Maggie, although her attention was now drawn to something else – a mass exodus of spaniels, Labradors and all the other dogs from the field. She looked at her watch. 'Right. It's nearly half seven. I've got to run.' She jumped up and grabbed Jazz's lead.

'Run where?' asked Cath.

'It's the Pet Show. It starts in ten minutes.'

Tiggy smirked her usual smirk. 'You're entering Jazz? What category? *Best Mutt?*'

'Waggiest Tail,' said Maggie. 'Look at her. She's clearly got the waggiest tail here. Her whole body wags. It'll be a travesty if she doesn't win.' She turned to Rob and smiled. 'Thanks so much for the picnic,' she said. 'It was really lovely.' And then she was off.

The judges of the Pet Show evidently agreed with her. That night Maggie fell asleep with a smile on her face – thinking of Jazz downstairs in her basket, sporting her first-place rosette.

She slept right through till the morning.

The Girls' Night In

The following evening, Maggie was pacing up and down her bedroom, one hand on her hip, clutching her notes with the other. 'And therefore, Your Honour, in conclusion, I would argue that—'

She wasn't aware of the doorknob turning or Cath sticking her head inside.

'Maggie…?' said Cath, tentatively.

Maggie gasped and sat down on the bed. *How embarrassing to be caught like this, practising in front of the mirror…*

'I wondered what you were doing up here?' Cath continued. 'It sounded like a baby elephant was stomping around the place. Is everything alright?'

Maggie let out a massive sigh. 'I'm just worried. Worried I'm going to let Rob down and then he'll lose the farm and I'll look a twat in front of the whole bloody village.' She took a breath. 'Apart from that, I'm totally fine!'

Cath sat down on the bed beside her. 'You shouldn't look at it like that. You've told Rob about your misgivings – that things probably won't go his way – but he thinks it's worth a try anyway. He knows you're doing your best and he's grateful for your help and everyone knows that.'

Maggie just grunted.

'Now,' said Cath, not giving up. 'What was it you said to Lauren, again? "Get stuck in and get on with it?" Whatever it was, it seems to have worked – she's beavering away like anything *and* she actually looks half-way human again.' She nudged Maggie in the ribs. 'You need to take a leaf out of your own book. And also, you need to get changed – we're leaving for Tiggy's in half an hour.'

'Oh, God!' Maggie rolled away from her and curled up into a ball. 'The *girls' night in*. Do I have to...?'

Cath pouted. 'You said you'd come with me!'

'I said no such thing,' said Maggie, turning back to her. 'Tiggy's a monster... And I don't know why you even *want* to go. Why didn't you just say no?'

'I *don't* want to go. But you saw the way she collared me. I didn't have any choice in the matter.'

Maggie shook her head. 'Still not learned your lesson?' she muttered. 'I thought you were done with all that people-pleasing stuff?'

'I just didn't want to be seen as a party pooper. Not during Wakes Week...'

Maggie's eyes threatened to roll out of her head. 'And I don't know why she invited *me* – she plainly can't stand me.'

'Oh, it's always the more the merrier as far as she's concerned,' said Cath. 'It's all about being seen to be popular.'

'Listen,' said Maggie. 'I really don't think I've got the energy for another social event. This week's done me in. I'm totally knackered and I could really use a night in. I need to save my energy for court tomorrow.'

'C'mon... It'll take your mind off things,' said Cath. 'And Val will be there. You like Val...'

'I suppose,' said Maggie. An evening spent sitting on her own, getting more and more nervous, was even less appealing than a night round at Tiggy's. 'As long as we're not too late back, though. It's an early start in the morning and I'd like to at least *try* and get some sleep.'

'Great!' said Cath, and disappeared out of the room before she had a chance to change her mind.

Maggie got to her feet again, back in front of the mirror. She took a deep breath and started again: 'And so, Your Honour, in conclusion I would argue that—' *Hold on a minute.* Was it 'Your Honour' or 'Your Worship' in the County Court…? She quickly googled it to check and was disappointed to discover it was just a simple 'Sir'.

Then, closing the laptop, she went to the wardrobe to find something to wear tonight. Jeans and a T-shirt. Both black, to suit her mood.

* * *

The fancy French doors of Tiggy's converted mill were open when they arrived and Cath and Maggie carried on inside, straight into the open-plan kitchen-diner.

The place was all mood-lighting and exposed brick – and all the women were perched on high leather stools along a huge central island. Tiggy was holding court at the head of things, resplendent in a royal blue, all-in-one cat-suit with a white trim. Val was there too. And so was Eve. She was wearing a tight, white dress that showed off her tan and seemed to be eyeballing Maggie with particular interest.

The air was thick with perfume as assorted department store fragrances battled for supremacy – with each other and with Tiggy's scented candles – filling Maggie's nose and making her want to sneeze.

'Oh, welcome both,' said Tiggy, breezing up to greet them, clutching the stem of her expensive wine glass. 'I wasn't sure if you'd make it, Maggie. I thought you might have stayed home to do your "revision" for tomorrow? Now, then. What can I get you to drink?'

'I'd like a lime and soda, please,' said Maggie. 'As you say, it's a big day tomorrow and I'd like to have a clear head.'

'Same for me, please,' said Cath. 'I'm driving.'

'Oh,' said Tiggy, disappointed. 'That's a shame. I've got a lovely Chablis in the wine fridge.' She paused a moment. 'People make the mistake of drinking white wine far too cold. This keeps it at a perfect nine degrees.' She raised her glass at them. 'It's delicious.'

'Can I have a top-up?' Eve called from her stool. 'I'm staying over tonight in Tiggy's guest suite,' she announced to the group, 'so I can have as much as I like.'

'No problem, babe,' said Tiggy, positively beaming at this description of her spare room.

Babe? Really? Was Tiggy trying to regain her lost youth or what? Maggie looked around the room. There didn't seem to be much in the way of food. Just a few dishes of canapés dotted here and there. Cath had been right. Wakes Week was basically an excuse for midweek drinking: a chance to get out of the house for a night on the booze – away from spouses, kids, ageing parents and all the rest of it.

'Essential supplies coming through!' boomed a male voice, barrelling through the open doors. It was Phil, lugging a crate of chilled prosecco. 'I can't have you girls going without your "lady petrol" now, can I?' he said, with a wink. 'I hope you all appreciate it – I'm making myself late for my refereeing duties at the five-a-side.'

'Oh, thanks Phil,' they all cooed in unison. All except Maggie.

Phil popped open a bottle and there were dainty squeals as the foam sprayed everywhere. He grabbed a crystal flute from the sideboard. 'C'mon, Maggie. You'll have a glass, won't you?'

'No thanks, I'm fine,' said Maggie. She couldn't understand why everyone seemed to love the stuff: it was far too sweet and the mimsy term 'lady petrol' made her hate it even more.

'I'm sure a little one won't do any harm,' he said, fixing Maggie with his charming grin. 'Go on. Half a glass…'

'No thanks, mate. Seriously.' He was only being generous but, by God, the pressure to drink alcohol these days was huge. It made her feel sorry for teetotallers.

'OK. Suit yourself,' said Phil, a bit put out.

'I'll have one, darling,' said Tiggy, holding out her glass to him.

'Ah. I'm sorry, love,' he said, pointing at his Rolex. 'Would you mind sorting yourself out? I need to get going now.'

A low level 'Awww' went around the room at the thought of his departure.

'I'll just put the other bottles in the wine fridge,' he said. 'It keeps the wine at nine degrees exactly, you know.'

'You don't say?' said Maggie, sarcastically, and Cath dug her in the ribs.

'Bless him,' said Val to Tiggy after he had gone. 'Your Phil. He's so lovely.'

'I know,' said Tiggy, the personification of smug. 'I'm a very lucky girl.'

'Talking of which,' said Eve. 'When are you two off to your place in Barbados?'

'Next week,' replied Tiggy. 'I can't wait. 'We're going to spend a couple of weeks island-hopping.'

'I'm *sooo* jealous,' said Val. 'It'll be Torquay again for Mum and me this year. Barbados sounds idyllic.'

It was hard to disagree – the thought of clear seas, white sand and palm fronds swaying in the breeze. But, nice as it was, Maggie couldn't understand why Tiggy and Phil wanted to go on holiday to the same place all the time. They obviously had a few quid to spend and it was a big world out there. Why not see a bit more of it?

'And that's not all,' continued Tiggy, adding some drops of a lethal-looking dark syrup to her glass, which was turning the prosecco purple. 'He's taking me on a spa day tomorrow, to prepare ourselves. A few treatments and a bit of a chill-out...'

Tiggy took a swig and turned to Eve. 'Anyway Eve, I meant to say that your eyebrows are looking *a-maz-ing* at the moment. Where did you get them done?'

'Aw thanks, babe,' said Eve, smoothing them down.

Maggie had to look away while Eve answered the question: the eyebrows looked like two slugs had crawled halfway down her forehead and died.

'They make you look so young!' trilled Tiggy. 'But then you *are* so young. Compared to the rest of us.' She looked at Maggie pointedly.

Bloody hell, thought Maggie. *Was that a dig?*

'And did you get your manicure done in the same place, Eve?' Tiggy wittered on. 'They've made a terrific job of it. I like the way your nails are all different shades of the same colour.'

Eve held up her hands so everyone could see, as Maggie looked down at her own unloved nails. She couldn't remember ever having them done professionally. *Was that bad...?*

'What do you think of *my* new nails?' said Val, thrusting her chubby hand in front of Tiggy. 'From the new neon range.'

Tiggy laughed at her. 'I've never seen *that* colour before,' she said. 'And I'll likely never see it again.'

Everyone else laughed and Val visibly deflated.

'I quite like it,' Maggie lied. Tiggy was right. The varnish was actually the colour of bile, but she felt sorry for Val and felt duty bound to stick up for her pal. 'It's, er, different.'

Cath, who hadn't said much at all so far, cleared her throat. 'So,' she said. 'Are you all coming along to the Auction of Promises tomorrow night?'

'Definitely,' said Tiggy, as most of the room nodded. 'Not forgetting the Buskers' Night afterwards.'

'Not forgetting that, of course,' said Cath, tightly. She seemed riled at Tiggy for trying to piggy-back on to her pet project.

'What are you offering for auction?' Tiggy asked, turning to Maggie.

'Nothing, really,' Maggie admitted, swirling her lime and soda around her glass. 'Australian Pete's offering dinner for four at the pub. But no. I don't think any of my skills would be that useful around here.'

'Oh, I'm not so sure about that,' slurred Tiggy, and Maggie realised she was quite pissed. More than quite. 'A free divorce maybe?' Tiggy continued, aiming the comment at Cath, who looked totally mortified.

Tiggy leaned in towards Eve. 'Maggie's a lawyer, you know.'

'You said,' said Eve. She turned to Maggie. 'I thought you worked at The Farmer's?'

'She does,' Tiggy sniggered, before Maggie had a chance to explain herself. 'But in her spare time she's helping Rob with his case against that mortgage company. She seems to spend a *lot* of her time with him.'

Eve bristled. 'Well, if he loses, it might work out for the best.' She laughed inanely. 'He can always move in with me!'

What an airhead, thought Maggie. She wasn't serious, was she?

'You know, it's been really great *connecting* with him again,' Eve went on. 'I was even thinking we could get back together.'

She was so matter-of-fact – like Rob had no say in the matter – and Maggie couldn't bear to listen to any more of it. 'So, what do you do for living?' she asked Eve, changing the subject.

'I'm a fitness instructor,' Eve announced proudly, running her hands over her hips. 'A personal trainer.'

You fucking *would* be, thought Maggie. 'Oh, that's nice,' she said instead. 'I assume *you're* donating your services to the auction? I'm sure they'll be very popular.'

'Nah,' said Eve. 'I'm carrying an injury at the moment, unfortunately. My gluteus medius is playing up.'

'Oh dear,' said Maggie. 'A sore arse, basically? What a nightmare.'

Eve glared at her. 'It's more my hip,' she said, tartly.

'And I'm offering a mindfulness course,' said Tiggy, filling the awkward silence. 'And Phil's auctioning his business skills – two hours of advice to whoever needs it.'

'I'm donating as well,' Val chipped in. 'A package of six driving lessons.'

'Maybe I should bid for those!' said Maggie, making Val smile.

'Oh, have you not passed your test yet?' asked Tiggy, so that everyone could hear. She picked up the bottle of prosecco and tried to pour it into Maggie's glass, until Maggie put her hand over it. 'Don't be fooled by this show of abstemiousness, ladies,' Tiggy said. She was really slurring now. 'Our Maggie here can drink quite a lot when she puts her mind to it. A little bird told me that she's only ever appeared in court once. And that was as the accused!'

What the…? How the hell did she know about that? And what did it really matter? Suddenly tired, with twelve pairs of eyes on her, Maggie stood up and threw her bag over her shoulder. 'You know, I think I'd better be off now,' she said. 'I've got an early start in the morning.' She gave the nod to Cath, but Cath wasn't budging. She was just sitting there on her stool, staring straight at Tiggy, like something had snapped in her brain.

'You know what?' said Cath in a controlled voice, addressing Tiggy direct. 'You can be a real bitch sometimes. A thoroughly nasty piece of work. And you know what else?' She slammed her glass on the counter in front of her. 'You can shove your fancy candles up your arse. *And* your wine fridge! Like Maggie said, we're going now. Goodnight.'

Embarrassed silence followed. No one else moved a muscle, apart from Val, who followed Cath and Maggie out into the garden. 'Just ignore Tiggy,' she whispered to Maggie. 'Look, I just wanted to say best of luck for tomorrow.' She stood on tiptoe and kissed her on the cheek. 'I'll be thinking of you. Sending you positive vibes…'

Cath was still trembling on the drive home. 'You were right, you know,' she was ranting. 'Tiggy *is* a monster. She's not a true friend. Not in the slightest. Just wants to be the "Queen Bee", the centre of the universe, holding court like that, loving the sound of her own scratchy voice. She's been against you from the very start. She felt threatened when you came back into my life – so worried that she wasn't my best-est friend anymore. How fucking childish can you get?!'

Maggie nodded and made the right noises, but she was in no mood to give Tiggy any more airtime – in no mood for triumphant 'Told-You-So's'. Even though she *had* told Cath so. Many times.

No. She needed to focus on tomorrow. On the job in hand.

D-Day Dawns

This felt weird – wearing a business suit again for the first time in ages. Weird and restrictive. Not as weird and restrictive as having to wear these tights, though. How had she put up with this for all those years? It felt like they were trying to strangle the tops of her thighs.

She realised she'd forgotten something and went to the wardrobe to get it – the thing Giles had sent her in the post last week. She'd been pathetically excited to receive a parcel, but disappointed to open it to find a plain, black court gown, together with a note:

You'll be needing this, Begbie. Best of luck!

Maggie held it up in front of herself. Well-worn and shapeless, she guessed he'd found it lying around his chambers in London – probably on the floor, judging by the state of it. She slipped her arms into the wide sleeves, pulled it on and drew herself up to her full five feet ten inches. Even so, it was far too big for her – and what was that on the shoulder? A frizzy, ginger hair by the looks of things – one of Jazz's. How on earth had *that* got there? She tweezed it away and wondered if she should knock on Cath's door.

Cath had offered to drive her and Rob into town for the hearing – had insisted on it, insisted on supporting them in the public gallery too – and Maggie was very grateful. But she was getting a bit agitated now. They were going to have to leave very soon to be sure of getting into Sheffield on time and there had been no sign of Cath downstairs at breakfast with Lauren. Not that Maggie had had the stomach for any breakfast – not at the best of times and certainly not today.

She went to the window and scanned the driveway below. There was no sign of Rob either, come to that, and he was supposed to be here by now. She would drop him a text. Right after she'd had a wee – her fourth that morning.

Heading to the bathroom, she bumped into Cath on her way out of it. 'Wow,' said Maggie, looking her up and down. *Was this Cath's idea of a joke?* If so, her timing wasn't the best. Normally the epitome of good taste in her neutral greys and beiges, Cath had picked today of all days to don a violet bandage dress that was more suited to an eighties-themed disco than a court of law. The elasticated material was clinging to every curve, thrusting her boobs forward, impossible to ignore. Nude peep-toe heels completed the look.

'What on earth are you wearing?' Maggie stuttered, unable to help herself.

Cath's face fell. 'What are *you* wearing, more like? You look like a refugee from Hogwarts.'

'Thanks very much,' huffed Maggie, pulling off the robe and stuffing it into her black leather briefcase – an old one of Simon's that Cath had lent her.

Cath turned back to the bathroom mirror and gave a half-twirl. 'Don't you like it? I'm wearing it to the auction tonight. I ordered it online.' She stroked the stretchy material. 'I just fancied a different look, you know? I'm fed up of dressing like I'm invisible. Just blending in with the background.'

'Ah, I see,' said Maggie, relieved. 'You're wearing it *tonight*? Well, you'd better hurry up and get changed. We need to leave in ten.'

'Well, no. I thought I'd wear it today as well. I need to get down to The Farmer's early tonight and I might not have time to get changed later.'

'Jesus, Cath,' said Maggie, alarmed. 'The hearing won't take *that* long? I hope.'

'Look. I'm wearing it and that's that,' said Cath, firmly. 'If nothing else, if things are going badly, it'll help distract the judge.'

'What? So you're still intending on coming into the building, are you?'

'Yes.'

'Actually *inside* the courtroom?'

'Sure I am,' said Cath. 'You said I could sit in the public benches, didn't you?'

Maggie rolled her eyes. Is this what Cath was going to be like from now on? The 'new' Cath? She wasn't sure she could cope.

'Oh God! Don't be so stuffy,' said Cath.

Maggie looked at her watch. It was too late for her to change now in any case – the wheels of justice waited for no man. Or woman. 'You *are* wearing a coat, though, right?' said Maggie.

'A jacket,' said Cath. 'A bolero jacket. It's far too warm for a coat.' And Maggie was grateful for the small mercy.

They were interrupted by the doorbell ringing and it was Rob, thank God.

And as they set off in the people carrier, Maggie let out a long breath. She was relieved that it was just the three of them going to court today. Quite a few of the villagers had wanted to come with them, apparently, and Cath had had a hard time persuading them not to. *Just as well really – talk about off-putting!* If the judgment didn't go their way, that was one thing. But failing in front of them all? That didn't bear thinking about.

From her berth in the passenger seat, she darted a look in the mirror, checking out Rob in the back. His hair was still damp from the shower and he was radiating the fresh smell of soap and clean skin. Unlike Cath, he was perfectly attired for the occasion in a sober, navy suit. He looked surprisingly good in a shirt and tie, she thought, but why should that be surprising? He had the broad shoulders and lean build to carry it off, after all.

'What's all this?' said Cath, squinting ahead as they approached the centre of Archdale.

'What's *what*?' said Maggie, looking out the window.

It was a crowd of people on the pavement. And some sheets billowing out in the breeze – banners of some sort. Right outside Cath's Community Café.

'It looks like a protest or something,' said Cath. 'I knew I shouldn't have discontinued the cherry Bakewells. It didn't go down at all well when I told them.'

'What's going on?' asked Rob, peering out the back, equally bewildered. 'And what's Jim doing there? Why isn't he at the garage?'

As they drew nearer, half the village seemed to be there, shouting stuff – not words of protest, but of encouragement – including Neil, Australian Pete, Ryan and the girls from the tearoom... Les the butcher was there too. And standing next to Jim, completely dwarfed by him, was Val. And Val's elderly mum in her wheelchair in front of them.

'Good Luck, Maggie!' proclaimed one of the homemade banners. 'Stick It To 'Em!' said another. It was being held aloft by the two old boys who'd approached Maggie at the Duck Race, who didn't appear to have sobered up even now.

Eve, sporting full hair and make-up, had elbowed her way to the front and was blowing a kiss at them, her focus firmly on

Rob. And on the sidelines, Mrs Winterson was hovering, not saying a word – obviously just here for the entertainment value and to get the gossip.

'Bloody hell,' said Cath, coming to a stop in front of them all.

Maggie wound down her window and a big cheer went up. She managed to catch Val's eye. 'What are you all doing?' she mouthed to her. 'Why didn't you warn me?'

'We wanted it to be a surprise,' Val replied.

'Great. Thanks,' said Maggie, forcing a smile and giving them all the thumbs up, but wanting nothing more than to slide down in the seat and hide. From the expression on Rob's face, she guessed he wanted to do the same.

Maggie tapped at the clock on the dashboard – a signal for Cath to get going again – and then closed up her window.

Soon they were cruising along the valley bottom and Maggie was back with her thoughts. There had been no sign of Rob's parents in the throng, she'd noticed. Although, in Rob's absence, they'd probably had to stay home and do whatever needed doing on the farm. Fiddling while Rome burned in other words.

And there was no sign of Tiggy either. Not that Maggie would've expected her to be there. Tiggy was never terribly keen on anything where she wouldn't be the centre of attention. But why was she even thinking about Tiggy? She didn't want to think about Tiggy. Had better things to do, literally, than think about Tiggy and her shitty little digs at her last night. That stuff about being the 'accused'… But Cath was even worse than Tiggy – for telling her all about it. How else could she have found out?

Maggie hissed across at Cath, under her breath, so that Rob couldn't hear. 'Anyway. Why did you have to go and tell Tiggy about my, y'know, *trouble with the police?*'

'I'm sorry,' Cath hissed back, flustered. 'It must have slipped out ages ago. I was probably boasting about all the great nights out we had when we were younger. I didn't think you two would ever meet each other!'

'Oh, right,' said Maggie. 'You thought it would be funny to tell her all about *the-hilarious-night-out-when-Maggie-got-arrested? Such fun.*' She drew Cath a look. 'It wasn't actually that hilarious from my point of view, I can assure you.'

'I can't believe she even remembered it. I told you – she's just jealous. Of our history.'

'Hmm,' said Maggie, as the engine began to struggle on the climb out of the valley. 'And that bloody "Scottish Widow" thing. What was that all about? She called me that the first time she met me.'

'That was nothing to do with me,' said Cath, pressing hard on the gas. 'She made up that nickname all by herself.'

'You surprise me,' said Maggie. 'That's actually quite witty. For her.'

Maggie checked on Rob in the mirror again. He'd only gone and fallen asleep and no wonder. He'd told her that he hadn't been sleeping at nights. And putting a brave face on things was bloody exhausting – she honestly didn't know how he'd managed it. But the strain was definitely showing now. He needed to know his fate one way or the other, so he could move on with his life. But what kind of life would he be moving on to?

Passing the looming presence of Stanage Edge on their left, they soon reached the tops. Maggie couldn't believe it: the landscape up here was so different from down below, all sepia moors dotted with patches of yellow gorse. It was still quite early, but there was a heat haze already and a vibe that was almost lunar.

'Anyway,' said Cath, cheerily, as they gained speed along the straight road. 'I just wanted to say that – whatever happens – all this has been great.'

'Shhh. Keep your voice down.' Maggie put her finger over her mouth, nodding towards the back seat. 'Let's wait and see what the result is first.'

'I've realised I want more of it,' whispered Cath.

'More of what?' grumbled Maggie.

'More excitement. More… feeling useful again.'

'*Useful*? You didn't even have to book the tickets to London in the end.'

'Yes. Well,' said Cath, wounded. 'Even just making the tea. Providing moral support…'

'Yeah, you liked seeing Giles again, more like.'

'Maggie!'

'Sorry. Ignore me. That was out of order,' said Maggie. 'I'm just babbling. I'm a bit nervous, OK?' She cast Cath a sideways look. 'Listen, thanks for driving us here today and for everything else that you've done. And anyway,' she continued, forcing herself to be a bit more upbeat. 'I'm looking forward to seeing Sheffield. It's not London, but it'll be nice to see somewhere new…'

Twenty minutes later, they'd left the moors behind and were chugging down the tree-lined avenues of suburbia – on to Ecclesall Road with its coffee shops, bars and restaurants. Maggie had read that this was one of the most popular areas of the city and she could easily see why. The place was bustling with students and workers and arty types – much more happening than she'd anticipated.

But the traffic was bloody awful. 'We're going to be fucking late at this rate,' she moaned, when they hadn't moved for ten minutes. 'This is the worst tailback I've ever seen.'

'Really?' said Cath, sarcastically. 'Worse than London? Worse than Hong Kong? I don't think so.'

They kept up the bickering until they were mobile again, crawling into the town centre, where the next problem would be finding somewhere to park. Maggie rubbed at her jaw – she'd been clenching it on and off for so long it was painful. *Come on, come on…*

The only space to be found was in a multi-storey car park, half a mile from where they needed to be – and Cath swore blind she knew the way to the court on foot. But following her lead was a mistake, and they had to resort to the map that Maggie had printed off the night before just in case.

When they finally arrived at court, they were sweaty and flustered – not poised and serene and majestic, as Maggie had hoped. Although the County Court itself wasn't very majestic either. It was a modern, squat, generic building – as far from The Royal Courts of Justice as it was possible to get. And in front of the main doors, all the smokers, the debt collectors and the soon-to-be-divorcés were all clustering. Standing apart from them, on his own, was a soon-to-be-divorcé that Maggie recognised. Simon.

Simon acknowledged Maggie and Rob, before settling his eyes on Cath's cleavage.

'What are you doing here?' Cath asked him, pleasantly surprised.

'I thought I'd pop down from Leeds on the train,' said Simon. 'To show my support. From what you've said, I know this is important to you.'

Cath smiled at him. 'Thanks.'

'Is it just the three of you?' he asked, looking around. 'No Giles? I thought he was involved in this.'

'No,' said Cath, colouring up. 'Maggie's handling it by herself.'

Simon turned to Maggie and shook her hand surprisingly firmly. 'Good luck, Maggie.'

'Cheers, Simon. I appreciate it,' she said. Although she appreciated it on Cath's behalf even more, as she could see his presence meant a lot to her.

'Right, then!' said Maggie. She took a deep breath. 'Let's get this over with.' And she led the way inside.

Trial by Ordeal

'It's a bit low rent, isn't it?' whispered Cath, as they entered the fusty waiting room. 'I'd expected the "wheels of justice" to be slightly more impressive…'

And she was right. The inside of the building was much like the outside – all very bland and uninspiring – purely functional. Other than the coat of arms on the wall, there was no sense of history, no stained glass or marble statues. And the underlying whiff of bleach wasn't helping: coupled with the heat from the boiling radiators, it was making Maggie feel sick. Why were they up full blast in the middle of flaming June? The sweat had already soaked right through her white shirt, she didn't dare take her jacket off – and she'd be even hotter when she pulled that bloody robe on.

Maggie stopped to read the case-list that was pinned to the notice board. *Bugger!* Theirs was scheduled as the last of the day. Next, she scanned the other occupants of the waiting room – all the other worried-looking punters and the other lawyers – and wondered which of the latter was going to be representing the mortgage company.

So far, she noticed, no one had actually gone into or come out of the courtroom – maybe the judge was held up in the traffic as well, maybe they hadn't even started yet. And so she took a seat next to Rob, blew her fringe out of her eyes and waited.

Rob was just sitting there, hands clasped, staring between his knees at the floor. Further along the row, Cath, who had already removed her jacket and heels, was making a forceful point in Simon's ear that Maggie couldn't really hear.

After a while, the court usher shuffled in: a round man in equally round glasses and a too-tight suit, who was mopping his brow with a huge white handkerchief. He apologised profusely for the delay and called the first case, prompting Maggie to delve into her briefcase, to go over her notes one last time.

For two hours they sat there, the four of them in a line, watching all the other cases being called. And for Maggie, who just wanted to get the bloody thing over and done with, it was an exquisite form of torture.

The usher appeared again to call the next case. 'Not long to go now,' he assured Maggie in passing. 'We've got a *very* full caseload today. Not ideal on a Friday. Hopefully we won't have to carry you over until Monday.'

'*Monday?*' spluttered Maggie. There was no way she would survive until Monday and, looking at Rob's anguished face, she wasn't sure that he would either.

'I'm only joking,' said the usher, patting her arm. 'As I said, not long to go now…'

'Cheers.' Maggie smiled weakly. But the wait would be too long for Simon, who had to make his apologies and head off, back to Leeds for a meeting.

Lucky him! Maggie wished to God that she could just follow him out the door, but she couldn't and, as the grumbling of her stomach grew louder, she wished instead that she'd had something to eat this morning.

'Here,' said Cath, producing a banana from her handbag.

'Thanks, Mum!' said Maggie, gladly accepting it. The thing was brown by now – ripening fast in the heat of the waiting room – but she still devoured it in three bites.

Not that it made much difference. She was starting to sag now, as what was left of her adrenaline drained away, but *hold on* – the usher was back again. Surely it was their turn now? All the other cases had been called.

The usher came up to Maggie and bowed down to talk to her. 'Hello again. Just to say, I'd go out and get some lunch if I were you. You won't be on till this afternoon.'

'Really?' Maggie groaned, watching Cath stuff her feet back into her shoes.

They headed towards the door, although Rob seemed too fed up to follow them.

'You too, love,' said the usher, kindly, cupping Rob's elbow.

'*Love?*' said Maggie to Cath. 'Did I hear that right?'

Cath smiled at her confusion. 'Oh, didn't you know? It's completely normal in Sheffield for grown men to call each other "love".'

'Weird,' said Maggie, shaking her head. But there was something quite sweet about it too.

* * *

The three of them nipped around the corner to a greasy spoon café but, when it came down to it, no one had much of an appetite. Maggie, keen to get back in case they missed their slot, ordered the quickest thing on the menu: soup and a roll. A mistake, as the piping hot broth only made her sweat even more.

When they arrived back in the waiting room, there was only one other person in attendance – an ancient 'gentleman barrister' with a grey comb-over and a face like a Dickens character. He didn't acknowledge them or even look up. He was wearing a white, wing-tipped collar and a lustrous black gown – much swisher than her own, which was now full of creases from being crammed inside the briefcase. Even from this distance, she could see that his robe was made of silk, which meant that he was a QC – Queen's Counsel – well used to appearing in the highest courts in the land. Did that give him some kind of inside information, she wondered? How had *he* managed to avoid sitting here all morning with the rest of them, wilting in the heat? *And where was his client?* There didn't seem to be any sign of anyone from AP Finance. Not that it was compulsory for a client to attend court in these circumstances, but even so…

Eventually, the usher emerged again to indicate that the time had come. He pointed Cath in the direction of the public gallery and led Maggie and Rob – along with 'Sir Basil Smallbone QC' – into the courtroom. *Basil Smallbone?! Bloody hell. It wasn't just his face that was Dickensian.*

Installed behind the bench up at the front, waiting for them, was the judge – who wasn't at all what Maggie was expecting. She was a woman, for a start – attractive, not that much older than Maggie, dressed in a black zip-up robe, with plain blue bands on the collar. And there was no wig covering her chic, blonde pixie cut. Her watchful eyes had come to rest on Cath, seemingly startled by her purple dress and the static electricity it was generating on contact with the plastic seats. Maggie shrugged inwardly: so much for Cath's strategy of impressing the judge.

The usher showed Maggie to her seat at the front, and Rob to the seat just behind her. Then he poured Maggie a glass of water. He gave her an encouraging smile and she could just tell he felt sorry for her. And why not. She felt sorry for herself. And now her phone was pinging in her pocket. *What now?*

It was a text. From Cath. Some inspirational-quote-bollocks she'd clearly got from a fortune cookie – or most probably from

Facebook: '*A woman is like a tea bag: you can't tell how strong she is until you put her in hot water.*' Ugh. Oh well. If nothing else, it was a useful reminder to switch off her phone.

Silence then descended and the judge nodded at Maggie's opposite number, Sir Basil, who rose to his feet. 'Madam. This is a very simple case and I do not propose to bring any witnesses,' he declared in his clipped, entitled tones, twisting the silk of his robe between his skeletal fingers. 'It hinges on a very straightforward question of law that shouldn't take up too much more of your time this fine afternoon.'

Maggie hated his smarmy guts already, even if he *was* a hundred years old.

'I've got as much time as it takes, Mr Smallbone,' said the judge briskly, her Yorkshire accent like a breath of fresh air in the claustrophobia of the room.

'It's "*Sir*", actually,' he corrected her. '*Sir* Basil…'

Sir, actually, parroted Maggie, under her breath. *Meh.*

'As I said,' continued the judge, ignoring him. 'I've got as much time as it takes. Now then,' she went on, unzipping her gown. 'I'd like to suggest that we dispense with these heavy robes in this heat. I don't know about you, but I can't suffer it a minute longer.'

Well said, love! thought Maggie, her own gown already off before the judge had finished her sentence.

'Ah. Very well,' garbled Sir Basil, clearly gutted at having to ditch his silk.

He disrobed to reveal a three-piece chalk-stripe suit underneath and Maggie had to give him his due: despite the broiling heat, there wasn't a bead of sweat on his face, which retained the pallor of the undead.

After a delicate cough, he got on with setting out the facts of the case, the facts that Maggie had been through in her head a hundred times. The signing of the loan agreement, the lending of the money to Rob, the missed instalment payments… 'And now,' he went on, 'the seeking of an order for repossession of the mortgaged property – the property known as Ash Tree Farm – which is the matter before the court today.'

'Objection!' Maggie leapt out of her seat, her arm in the air. 'The name of the farm in question – the mortgaged property – is actually *Elliott's Farm*. Although I'm sure my learned friend's client will soon be instructing him to repossess this Ash Tree Farm as well. They seem to be making a bit of a habit of it – fleecing farmers up and down the land!'

The judge turned wearily to Maggie. 'I think you've been watching too many US dramas, Ms Macbeth. In case you didn't know, we don't stand up and shout "Objection!" Not in this country.'

'My apologies, Madam,' said Maggie, sitting down again. She *did* actually know it. That it wasn't the done thing. But she'd done it anyway to get the point across. She'd wanted to make the judge aware of the situation: aware that Sir Basil's precious client was shafting people left, right and centre.

Once Sir Basil had finished his spiel, the judge thanked him. 'Now,' she said, turning her attention to Maggie. 'Ms Macbeth. If we could hear from you now.'

Right. Here goes. Maggie got to her feet as her stomach fizzed up like an Alka-Seltzer and her right leg started shaking uncontrollably. *Bollocks! How could it let her down like this?* She gripped the lectern in front of her to steady herself, glad that the judge couldn't see it behind the desk. Although Rob probably could.

She took one last look round at him, sitting there behind her, pale and drained of life. *God, look at him!* The injustice of the whole damn thing rose up inside her like a burning wave, flooding her body, cancelling out her nerves.

'Thank you, Madam,' said Maggie, nodding towards the bench. 'As you are aware from the papers previously lodged with this court, the basis of our defence is as follows...' She listened to her own voice ringing out. *At least that wasn't shaking.* And although her notes were right there in front of her, she found that she didn't really need them. Looking down the list of bullet points she'd prepared earlier, she knew what issues she had to cover: the Punitive Interest Rate, Misrepresentation by AP Finance, Inducement to sign the contract, Asking for the loan agreement to be 'set aside', to be cancelled. And as she worked her way through them, unlikely as it seemed, she found herself rather enjoying it.

Then, winding up her submission, she put her notes aside and leaned forward on the lectern for dramatic effect.

'So much for the legal arguments,' she announced solemnly. 'However. In deciding this case, I would urge you to remember that – at the heart of it – we have a very human story. The story of a decent family being stripped of their land – of their livelihood, their very future – by what is, essentially, a glorified payday lender!'

She glared at Sir Basil and sat back down, like a rapper doing a mic drop. And there was definitely a muffled 'Yesss!' from Cath at the back – in contrast to Rob, who just sat there behind Maggie in silence.

Sir Basil rose again to speak. 'If I may...' he snivelled. 'My, ahem, learned friend's *legal* argument seems to rest on the notion that her client was induced to enter into the loan agreement by a promise of a cheaper financial arrangement after a year – an arrangement which failed to materialise.' He paused. 'However – and it is this point which is the key to the case – it was only my client's intention to use its *reasonable efforts* to procure such finance *in good faith*. This was never intended to be a guarantee and – quite simply – that is the reason why nothing was put down in writing to this effect. Or, to put it another way…' For this bit he saved his most oily expression, 'It was only my client's intention to *try and help*.'

Aye, right! thought Maggie. But she wasn't in the least surprised: it was the comeback she'd been expecting all along.

The judge thanked both parties, advised that there would be an adjournment while she made her decision and they all filed out of the courtroom in silence. Yet another wait…

* * *

Back in the waiting room, the clock on the wall ticked round ominously. The only other sound was Sir Basil braying into his mobile phone out in the corridor:

'Yes, I'll be back in London in time for dinner, darling. Easily. No, this won't take long at all. You should see who they've put up against me. Some woman by the name of "Macbeth". Oh, very funny, darling. Yes, it'll certainly be a *tragedy* for her client. Oh, no, she's not a QC. Not even a barrister by the looks of her. Her courtroom etiquette is quite appalling.'

But his conversation was quickly cut short by the usher coming out again, summoning them all back in. Maggie looked at the clock again: it had barely been ten minutes and she suspected this wasn't a good sign.

When everyone had settled down, the judge cleared her throat to speak: 'Now then. This is my last case of a long week and I intend to get straight to the point.'

She turned to address Sir Basil. 'I have to say that I'm inclined to agree with Ms Macbeth. From what I can gather, your client has conducted its business in a highly questionable manner, to say the least. It appears to have taken advantage of a desperate man willing to clutch at any available straw – to borrow at any cost – in order to save the farm that has provided his family with their living for generations. In fact, I would go further and say that, in my considered opinion, your client's behaviour has been morally reprehensible.'

She turned her gaze on Maggie now. 'Morally reprehensible, but insufficient in law to justify the remedy sought here today by the Defendant. Accordingly, therefore, I have no option but to find in favour of the Claimant.'

'Is that us?' Rob whispered hopefully from behind her, and Maggie shook her head gravely.

The judge carried on: 'And now, of course, we have to turn to the issue of costs.'

Christ! thought Maggie. Just when you thought things couldn't get any worse. A sizeable chunk of the winning party's legal bills and other costs would need to be paid by the loser – by Rob.

She looked across at Sir Basil, just in time to see a smirk cracking his granite face; the smirk of a man anticipating his fees hitting his bank account.

The Long Road Home

Maggie slumped against the window of the passenger seat as they inched their way out of Sheffield through the rush-hour traffic. Not that she was bothered this time: the journey home could take as long as it liked. She was in no hurry to get back to Archdale. *Ever.*

Back in the courtroom, stoic to the last, Rob had thanked her for trying her best. Hell, he had even thanked the judge for her time – and Maggie had been impressed by his dignity in adversity.

Which was all very admirable and all that, but what was he going to do now? Apart from go out and get royally drunk? *As long as that's all he did...* She remembered again that conversation they'd had on Boxing Day, the two of them knee-deep in the snow outside his house. The one about the shotgun. That was just a joke, wasn't it? He wouldn't do anything stupid, would he? He had plenty of friends and family and stuff, but she'd still have to keep an eye on him.

Rob hadn't said a word since they'd got back in the car – probably wondering how he was going to break the news to his mum and dad – and neither had Maggie.

'Anyway,' said Cath, the first one brave enough to break the silence. 'The judge definitely preferred you to that other old fossil.'

'So what?' said Maggie, glumly staring out the window. 'It's the law. It's not a popularity contest, you know.'

'And you called it exactly right… what you said ages ago… before it got to court. You always said it was a bit of a long shot.'

'Hmm,' said Maggie. She knew Cath was only trying to cheer her up. But – for once – being right was giving her no pleasure at all. None whatsoever.

Cath reached down into her bag for her phone and passed it across to her. 'Here. This'll give you a laugh. Tiggy's put one of those vom-inducing posts on Facebook. It's a photo of her and Phil on their spa day in matching dressing gowns. *Relaxing before their Barbados trip.*'

'Ugh,' said Maggie, handing it back to her. 'I thought she said she likes to keep out of the sun? Why does she go to the bloody Caribbean all the time in that case? Why not have a holiday home in, I dunno, Scotland if you don't like the sun? Somewhere there's no chance of seeing it?'

'Because she wants to show off?' Cath sniffed. 'The same reason she does anything.'

They were back on Ecclesall Road now, with the sun low in the pinky-blue sky. Maggie gazed longingly at the string of smart pubs and bars, closed her eyes, imagined condensation on a glass of chilled white. 'I could do with a drink,' she said, hoping Cath would take the hint and stop for a bit.

'We can't, I'm afraid,' said Cath, firmly. 'We've got to get back for the auction. At least, *I* do.'

'Oh, man,' said Maggie, rubbing her eyes. 'I'd forgotten about the Auction-of-Fucking-Promises.'

Cath shot her a look. 'Alright, alright. There's no need to swear.'

Maggie shook her head. 'No, seriously. I can't face it, Cath. The whole of Archdale will be there – gawping at us – wanting to know the gory details.'

Rob leaned forward from the back seat. 'That might be a good thing,' he said, flatly. 'I think I'd rather tell everyone at once. Get it over and done with.'

'Hmm. I suppose,' said Maggie over her shoulder. Although this meant she had to go to the bloody thing as well now: she couldn't very well leave him to face them all on his own.

The traffic was easing now as they crossed the border from South Yorkshire back into Derbyshire – across the moors again, to where the peaks stretched out before them like a watercolour. Then, zig-zagging down through the sharp bends, they passed the breath-taking drop of the Surprise View, above the fields and the trees and the waving wildflowers.

Before long, they were pulling into Archdale again, turning right at the church. In front of it, the clay and the petals of the well dressing had been blanched by the Wakes Week heatwave, but it retained a beauty of sorts, like an old photograph.

'You know, it's nearly a year since I first arrived here,' Maggie said aloud, as they turned into the car park of The Farmer's, its red umbrellas in full bloom. 'Tonight can be my leaving drinks...'

Cath brought the car to a halt and the three of them got out. 'I need to go and help Pete set up,' she said, preoccupied with thoughts of her auction. 'There's quite a bit to do,' she wittered, tottering off as fast as her slingbacks would allow.

Maggie turned to face Rob. 'Shall we do this, then?' she said, cocking her head towards the door of the pub.

Rob nodded and Maggie slipped her arm through his, leading the way. But then her phone started ringing.

'It's Giles,' she sighed. 'He'll want to know how we've got on. Do you mind if I take it?'

'Sure. No problem,' said Rob. 'I'll wait with you.'

She pressed the button to answer it. 'Hiya, Giles. I suppose you'll be wanting an update?'

'Do I take it that the news isn't good?' asked Giles.

'No,' said Maggie. 'It isn't.'

'Ah. I'm very sorry to hear that. And very sorry for Rob. Please pass my sympathies on to him.'

'I will do, mate. Will do. I'm with him now.'

'It was always going to be a difficult one,' said Giles.

'Yep.' Maggie sighed. 'I suppose it was. Listen, Giles. I appreciate you calling, but I need to go now. We've not told his parents yet...'

'Yes, of course,' said Giles. 'But very quickly, there was another reason for my call...'

'What is it?' asked Maggie, not liking the sound of this. What did he want? It better not be anything to do with Cath. He wasn't exactly her favourite person at the moment.

'Well,' said Giles, getting to the point. 'Do you remember my mate Nick?'

'Nick?' Maggie racked her brain. 'Nick who?'

'Nick Barnes. The CEO of Spark Oil.'

'Oh yeah,' she said. 'I met him a couple of years ago. On the negotiations for that Indonesian joint venture. I was on the other side...'

'Yes, well, he remembers you too. He thought you were really good.'

'Oh. Thanks,' said Maggie. 'He was a nice guy.'

'Well, this is the thing. He's looking to appoint a Head of Legal.'

'Really?' said Maggie, a plume of excitement expanding inside her. *Did this mean what she thought it meant?* Instinctively, she found herself wandering away, out of Rob's earshot.

Taking the hint, Rob pointed to the pub, signalling he would see her inside.

'I'll only be a minute,' she mouthed to him, cupping her hand over the phone.

'The job's basically yours if you want it,' continued Giles, matter-of-fact.

What? Her eyes were on Rob, his hands in his suit pockets, kicking a loose stone in the direction of the pub door. He looked so forlorn.

'Giles,' Maggie whispered. 'Is this a wind-up?' It had been a long day and her head was thumping. 'It had better not be…'

'Of course not,' said Giles. 'Why would I—?'

'Spark Oil?' she interrupted, focusing back on the facts. 'Based in their London office, I assume?'

'No, actually,' said Giles. 'It's—' but his words were cut off as the line went dead.

'Fucking hell!' she shouted at the useless phone. The reception in this place was as crap as ever. *What should she do?* Should she ring him back or wait for him to ring her again? The latter was probably the etiquette, but there was no way she could— *Oh wait, it was ringing again.* She pressed the button hard. 'Yep? You were saying…?'

'Yeah. That's the thing, the job's actually in—'

Not again. More hissing on the line. Utterly infuriating. 'Where? Where is it?' *Please don't cut off again…*

'Singapore,' said Giles, the line suddenly clear. 'The job's in Singapore.'

'Oh,' said Maggie. 'Right.'

'You'll be OK with that, won't you? You love it over there.' He paused a second. 'Maggie? Are you still there?'

'Yes. Yes, I am,' she said, although her mind wasn't. It was six thousand miles away. At least.

'Well, look. You don't have to say anything straightaway. You've got a few days to think about it. But don't take too long. He's keen to fill the post quickly.'

Maggie watched Rob as he kicked the stone to the gutter and headed into the pub.

'Of course,' said Maggie to Giles, businesslike again. 'Completely understandable. Could you send me Nick's number and I'll give him a call on Monday?'

The phone went silent again and she stood there staring at it. *Wow!* She'd basically just been offered her dream job – or as close to it as she was likely to get at this age.

She raised her eyes skyward and closed them. After all the hopelessness of the last twelve months, here was the chance to get herself back on track. She couldn't quite believe it.

A Dog with Two Dicks

Maggie pushed open the door, into the thick, heavy air of The Farmer's Arms. Australian Pete had had the windows open all week, but it hadn't made a whit of difference.

Most of the seats were already taken, she saw, as she looked for Rob. There he was in his usual spot, of course: the stool at the end of the bar, sitting between Jim and Les the butcher, a double whisky in front of him. Australian Pete and Ryan were leaning in from the other side of the bar and, from the looks on all their faces, he'd already told them the worst. Maggie felt awful all over again, like she'd let them all down.

And there were Rob's parents, sitting at the table in the corner. *Christ!* His dad looked shell-shocked and his poor mother was a faint trace of her usual self, her eyes red and sunken. Maggie had to look away: the woman might have been a total shit to her, but it was impossible not to feel sorry for her.

Maggie shook off her jacket, hung it on a peg and went and joined the lads.

'Want a drink?' asked Jim, putting a friendly arm around her shoulder. 'I reckon you deserve one.'

'Cheers, Jim,' said Maggie. 'Could I have a lime and soda, please?' The desire for alcohol had deserted her somewhere along the line – probably because her tongue was stuck to the roof of her mouth and her stomach had been turning over since the call from Giles. Maybe it was guilt – guilt for having a future when Rob's had been taken away from him? But he *did* have options.

It wasn't too late for him to train as a teacher – wasn't that what he said he'd really wanted to be? She'd just been reading something in the paper about it. How the profession was keen to recruit older people from different walks of life, people with different experience. But that was a discussion for another day. And he still had his mates, who were doing their best to rally round him. 'Don't worry,' Australian Pete was saying over and over, as Les nodded. 'We'll sort something out. We wouldn't see you out on the street, would we, lads?' Hmm, and neither would Eve, Maggie thought: she'd be waiting there, ready in the wings, poised to make her move.

The only other talking point seemed to be Cath's outfit, which was drawing glances from all sides – admiring or startled, depending on the glancer. Lauren, who'd just turned up with Dan, was definitely in the latter camp. 'God, Mum! What have you got on?' had been her first words before she was even through the door.

Cath had just ignored her. She was too busy flapping around, trying to conjure up some atmosphere, concerned that her precious Auction of Promises was going to be a wash-out. Australian Pete had left Rob's side now and was trying his best to help Cath salvage the evening. Good to his word, he'd laid on a free buffet and he'd really pushed the boat out this time: in place of the usual sausage rolls and peanuts, there were hot pork sandwiches and homemade chips – this despite the fact it was still sweltering outside. The pub's increased profits had clearly gone to Pete's head and Maggie hoped for his sake that this act of reckless extravagance wasn't going to wipe them out again.

To take her mind off her churning thoughts, she followed Cath to the 'stage' – a raised platform with a microphone – to ask if there was anything she could do to help. But before she could offer, Tiggy materialised: shiny-faced from the spa, wearing a souped-up peasant smock, clutching the leather handles of a brimming straw basket. The dreaded tambourine was poking out the top of it, ready for the 'buskers' session later.

Tiggy kissed Cath on both cheeks, all sugary sweetness. 'I just wanted to say, best of luck tonight, Catherine. I'm sure it'll be great.' Then she drifted off to bore someone else, while Cath frowned after her.

'I didn't think she'd even be talking to me,' said Cath to Maggie, under her breath. 'I thought I'd be *persona non grata* after what I said to her last night.'

'Nah,' said Maggie, shaking her head. 'She's just a bully. And that's what happens if you stand up to a bully. They back down.' She paused. 'Anyway, I notice she didn't even ask about Rob. The self-centred mare.'

'Hold on! Wait a second,' Cath called after Tiggy. 'Is Phil here? I could do with talking him through his auctioneering duties. We don't want any hitches.'

Tiggy floated back over to them. 'Don't worry. He's outside. He had to make a phone call.'

'Hey ladies!' Australian Pete arrived to join the three of them, his arms stretched out, eyes shining. He beckoned them to come closer. 'Wait till you hear this… I've actually organised a surprise "special guest" to come and be the auctioneer.' He paused for effect. '*And* to lead the jam session afterwards.'

'What? Who?' said Cath, visibly irritated at this last-minute change to her careful plans.

'Aw, you'll love it, Cathy,' said Pete. 'He's all the way from sunny Manchester.' He turned to Tiggy. 'Someone *you* know very well.'

'Who?' asked Tiggy, irritated too.

'Merlin Crocker!' said Pete, triumphantly.

Merlin Crocker? thought Maggie. *The lead singer of Tiggy's old band?* Oh, God. Tiggy would be so thrilled to be back in the spotlight with him. Thrilled to be singing their one crappy hit together later on. But, actually, Tiggy didn't seem that thrilled at all. She looked mightily pissed off. Had she and Merlin had a falling-out or something? Whatever it was, Australian Pete was oblivious.

Maggie's nose got the better of her. 'Do you two not get on?' she asked Tiggy straight out. 'You and Merlin?'

'Oh, I haven't seen him for years,' said Tiggy, waving the question away, regaining her composure. 'Musical differences, you know?' And she wandered off.

Maggie rolled her eyes at Cath.

'Merlin should be here in ten minutes,' Pete continued, eagerly. 'I told him seven o'clock sharp...'

The pub was really filling up by this stage. Val and her mum were here – even her useless brother was in tow. Eve had showed up as well and had made a beeline for Rob's parents – as if they weren't suffering enough. Neil had also arrived, bringing with him Mrs Winterson and her coterie of companions: the senior ladies of the village had been allocated the few remaining seats in front of the stage, making it standing-room only. Even Simon had slipped in at the back of the room, his second surprise appearance of the day. He'd sure covered a lot of miles today and Maggie had to hand it to him: he was pulling out all the stops to get back in Cath's good books. Either that or he must really like hot pork sandwiches.

Maggie glanced at her watch. Another half an hour had slipped by, Merlin Crocker was now officially late and Cath wasn't taking it well. When Rob came up to ask her if he could say a few words on the microphone, she looked like it might tip her over the edge, but she couldn't really say no.

Rob stepped up on to the stage and took the mic with both hands to stop them from shaking. *Oh, my*, said Maggie to herself, willing him to keep it together. *This was going to be so hard.*

'I'll keep this mercifully short,' said Rob, nodding over at Cath. 'As most of you probably know by now, we – er – didn't get the result we wanted today.'

A sympathetic murmur rippled through the room and, again, Maggie had to admire his stoicism – the way he could talk about this disaster for his family like he was a football manager discussing a one-nil defeat to Barnsley.

Rob continued: 'But I couldn't let tonight pass without thanking all of you for the help and support you've given me and my parents over the last few months.' There were more supportive noises, but he swallowed hard and kept going: 'And there's one person I'd like to thank especially…'

Oh God, thought Maggie. *He wouldn't, would he?*

'… and that's Maggie.'

He just did. She couldn't help but blush scarlet and stare at the floor as a rousing round of cheers and applause ricocheted off the walls. Risking a quick look up, she was amazed to see that Rob's parents had joined in too. Which was something at least.

'Thanks for everything, Maggie,' Rob said again. She could feel his eyes on her. 'I honestly don't think I could have got through these last few months without you. I've said it before and I'll say it again, you're a star… But, er, look, I'd better hand the microphone back to Cath now and let her get on with things…'

The crowd clapped Maggie again and Rob stepped down from the stage, where Eve was waiting. Eve threw her arms around him, burying her head in his chest, then followed him back round to his friends at the bar. Watching them, Maggie felt a pang of sorrow on her own behalf this time – for the loss of what might have been, between her and Rob, if things had been different. As it was, she was always going to lose out to a personal trainer more than ten years her junior…

As the last few claps died away, Tiggy's croaky voice piped up from the other side of the room, dripping with condescension. 'Yes, don't worry, Maggie. You tried your best. It's nothing to be ashamed of.'

Nothing to be ashamed of? thought Maggie. *What the…?* But all heads had turned to look at Mrs Winterson, who had grabbed hold of her walking stick and was struggling to get to her feet with Neil's help.

Oh no, thought Maggie. Not another speech! Not more faint praise and mimsy platitudes! This was like death-by-a-thousand-cuts.

The old lady started to speak, her voice ringing like a clear, tinkly bell through the still, stuffy air. 'That's quite enough from you,' she said, turning four square towards Tiggy. '"Nothing to be ashamed of" my arse! This Maggie woman's only been in Archdale ten minutes and she's done more for the village than your family's done in a hundred years.'

Maggie's eyes widened, as stunned as the rest of the room by this outburst. No one quite knew how to react, least of all Tiggy.

The silence was broken by the door swinging open and a surge of hysterical laughter that came from the newcomers: a middle-aged bloke flanked by two nubile young women in vest tops and denim shorts. They could easily have been his daughters, but they weren't, Maggie guessed, from the way they were draped all over him.

The guy began strutting around the pub like he owned the place, introducing himself to people at random, shaking hands with them like he was on a red carpet. No doubt every carpet was a red carpet to Merlin Crocker. Ageing rocker he may have been, but it had to be said he was ageing pretty well. He was still whippet-thin, still with the same collar-length hair, still in the same crushed velvet suit despite the sultry conditions.

Merlin spotted Tiggy and bowled straight up to her. 'Hello stranger,' he drawled, his voice a curious mix of Mick Jagger and Liam Gallagher, and bloody loud too. 'It's been a long time. Good to see you again, Ann-TIG-oh-nee.'

Antigone? thought Maggie. That's her name? Ann-TIG-oh-nee. So *that's* what 'Tiggy' is short for – the kind of naff, pretentious name she would've expected.

Merlin was trying to hug Tiggy, but she didn't seem too keen to hug him back. Yes, there was definitely some tension there and Maggie was relishing Tiggy's discomfort. Sorry, *Antigone's* discomfort!

'Oh, man,' Merlin honked at Tiggy. 'I've just seen that bell-end, Derek Nobbs, outside. I can't believe you're still with him! He's out there on his phone looking well-chuffed with himself. He's like a dog with two dicks.' He snorted with laughter and his two companions joined in, which was just as well as no one else seemed to know what he was on about.

Then the door opened again and Phil came strolling in.

'Oi! *Nobbsy!*' called Merlin, toasting him with a bottle of beer, and taking a swig. 'How long has it been?'

Not nearly long enough, judging by the look on Phil's face. It hadn't really been a day for laughing, but Maggie had to admit this was pretty funny – like a French farce or something. All it needed was someone's trousers to fall down, and there was still time for that.

Maggie pretended to fish in her bag for something, anything, just to hide the grin on her face. *Derek Nobbs? That was Phil's real name?* Hilarious. No wonder he'd changed it. She replayed the name in her head. *What the actual...? Antigone? Wait a minute.* Her recall wasn't quite what it used to be, but something was stirring at the back of her brain, a memory from months ago...

She put down her glass and tapped Merlin on the shoulder. 'Excuse me, mate.'

'Wassat, darling?' he said, laying on the charm.

'Did you just call him Derek Nobbs?' Maggie asked, pointing towards Phil. 'Is that his real name?'

'Yeah, man,' giggled Merlin, like it was the funniest thing in the world. 'Lame, ain't it?'

Maggie opened her mouth and closed it again. *Nah.* It couldn't be. Just a coincidence, surely. She should really check her facts first. Not plunge straight in and make a tit of herself...

Cath had caught her eye, aware that something was up. Her expression was saying, 'Be careful', but Maggie pressed on anyway. 'Hey, Phil,' she called over to him. 'I've got a question for you, if you don't mind. Tell me, have you ever heard of a company called AP Finance?'

Phil just shrugged. 'I don't think so.'

'Or *Antigone* Property Finance, to give it it's full name?'

A flicker of something crossed his face. *What, though?* And then he laughed at her, spreading his arms wide, looking to the room for support. 'What's this all about, Maggie? Have you gone mad? I feel like I'm being cross-examined or something.'

Maybe she *was* going mad. Why was she doing this – getting involved, causing a scene? She'd be leaving soon and none of this would be her problem anymore. Or maybe that was all the more reason to do it? If she was wrong, she'd soon be gone in any case. It wouldn't matter. She might as well go for it.

'This company...' she went on, pacing now. 'This AP Finance... it's only got the one director – a "Mr D Nobbs" – and it happens to be registered in the Regis Islands – a tax haven that's a short hop from Barbados, where you conveniently happen to have a holiday home.' She was half-petrified, half loving this – glad of the practice run she'd had in court this afternoon.

The sweat ran down inside her shirt as she came to a sudden stop, her hand on her hip. 'Yes, ladies and gentlemen, this delightful outfit has not only tricked *Rob's* family out of their land, it's been doing the same thing to loads of other farmers up and down the whole country.' The shock in the room was tangible – even Merlin was agog. 'And your man, here – your friendly-neighbourhood-Phil – he's the brains, or should I say the grasping mitts, behind it.'

Tuts and gasps filled the pub and someone shouted, 'Shameful!' But Phil just stood there, clenching and unclenching his fists, as his legendary bonhomie deserted him.

'You've done what?' said Tiggy, elbowing her way through the crowd towards him. If she had known about any of this, she was doing a great job of hiding it...

'Darling,' Phil gabbled, clearly rattled. 'None of this is down to me personally. My employees and advisers – they do it all. They effectively run the business for me. I knew nothing about Rob's situation. Nothing at all.'

'You seriously expect me to believe that?' growled Tiggy. 'You control every aspect of our lives with an iron grip. I can't even stack the dishwasher without you butting in every five seconds, telling me how to do it.' She was reaching into her basket now. 'You're a lying piece of shit,' she cried, as she pulled the tambourine out of her bag and launched it at his head, forcing him to duck. 'I can't believe you've been doing this at all, let alone shitting on your own bloody doorstep. On *our* bloody doorstep.' She indicated Rob. 'On our friends and neighbours.'

Maggie bit her lip. *Fucking hell! This was most un-Tiggy-like language.*

'Don't be cross, dear,' Phil whined.

But Tiggy hadn't finished with him. 'You're a fucking cold-hearted sociopath. And I'll tell you this,' she said, retrieving her tambourine from the corner where it landed. 'You'd better rip up that bloody court order or else!'

'Or else what?'

'Or else I'll divorce you and take you to the fucking cleaners. That's what.'

'I'm afraid that won't be possible, my sweet,' sneered Phil, quite menacing now. 'Remember the pre-nup you signed when we got married?'

Maggie jumped in on Tiggy's side. She cleared her throat and found her voice again. 'You do realise, *Derek*, that pre-nuptial agreements aren't necessarily binding in all circumstances – for example, when you've been hiding assets from your spouse in Caribbean tax havens? Just as a random example.'

Tiggy turned to her with a look bordering on love – *quite scary, really* – and the fight appeared to go out of Phil. 'Hold on. Hold on,' he was pleading now. 'There's no need to go into all that. I'll do whatever you want, Tiggy.'

'Good!' said Tiggy. 'You're not leaving this pub until you've reassured Rob that he won't be losing his home.' She threw her arms wide. 'In front of all these witnesses.'

Phil nodded. 'Of course,' he mumbled.

'C'mon, Phil. Speak up,' said Tiggy. 'You're not usually this shy.'

Phil turned to Rob. 'You won't, mate. I give you my word.'

'More to the point,' said Tiggy to Rob. 'I give you mine.' And with that, she marched towards the door and Phil followed behind, like a neutered dog coming to heel.

When the door had shut behind them, a massive cheer went up – the biggest of the night. Then chairs were scraped back, drinks were ordered and people were crowding around Rob's parents, who looked to be on the verge of tears. Maggie could understand it: she felt pretty emotional herself.

She scanned the room, looking for Cath to go and talk to. But she was sitting at a table with Simon and Lauren, the three of them deep in animated conversation, and Maggie didn't want to intrude.

A hand on her shoulder made her turn round. It was Rob, who seemed to have shaken off Eve for the moment. 'That was amazing,' he said to her. 'Knowing all that stuff… And being able to come out with it under pressure like that.'

A warm glow spread through Maggie – or maybe it was just a hot flush. 'It wasn't *that* amazing,' she said, modestly. 'And I'll tell you one thing I *don't* know – and that's how to unravel a court order. I guess I'll need to find out. Sharpish.'

'That can wait until Monday,' said Rob, gently. 'Now. I don't know about you, but my head's spinning with all this. Please. Let me buy you a drink. What would you like?'

She tugged at the collar of her shirt. 'What I'd really like is some fresh air.'

'I know how you feel,' he smiled. 'I'll come with you.'

Outside in the car park, the moon hung huge above them in the sky – a thin, pale disc like a communion wafer. They came to a stop under one of Pete's umbrellas and Maggie noticed for the first time that she and Rob were the same height.

'My parents and me,' he said, turning to her. 'We'll never be able to thank you enough.'

'Don't be daft,' said Maggie, softly. 'You've helped me a lot as well. More than you know.'

'Listen,' he said. 'I'm not great at this sort of thing. But just then... when I said you were amazing... I meant it.' And he took her face in his hands and kissed her. Just like that.

The Morning After the Night Before

It was a bright Saturday morning and the church clock was striking five past eight.

Up at Higher House, the air in the garden was deliciously cool, thanks to the heavy, cleansing showers overnight. Maggie breathed in the aroma of honeysuckle – pleased she could finally put a name to the sweet, heady scent.

She was kneeling over her bike, trying to remove one of the tyres with a fork from the cutlery drawer. On one side of her, the radio was blaring away and, on the other, Jazz's ginger form was stretched out on the flagstones, snoring, her rosette still stuck to her collar.

There was a knock on the kitchen window: it was Cath, who had surfaced at last. 'Want another coffee?' she mouthed through the glass, and Maggie nodded eagerly.

When she emerged a few minutes later with the tray, her wet hair piled loosely on her head, Maggie was relieved to see that she was back in her old gear: a flowing, taupe kaftan that sounded awful when you put the words together like that, but which suited her much more than that bruise-coloured bandage from yesterday.

Maggie breathed in again. 'You know, I love the smell of petrichor in the morning,' she said, reaching up to take a mug.

'The smell of *what*?' asked Cath, settling down on the bench. 'Never mind.'

Cath nodded at the radio. 'Could you turn that down a bit? Simon's still asleep upstairs.'

'Oh, sure,' said Maggie, leaning over to switch it off. 'I've just been listening to a fascinating programme. Did you know that the Peak District is actually Scottish?'

Cath frowned at her. 'What are you on about now?'

'Well. According to this programme, there were all these volcanic eruptions in Scotland millions of years ago. And the magma sort of, like, spilled over into England and formed all the peaks.'

'Is that so?' She pointed at the stains on Maggie's stripy T-shirt. 'Look at you – you're covered in oil. What exactly are you trying to do? And that's one of my good forks!'

'Oh. Sorry.' Maggie pushed her fringe out of her eyes. 'I'm just fixing this puncture – attempting to, at any rate.'

'Well, could you please try and fix it with something else?' said Cath. 'And also, I've got another request.'

'What's that?'

'Can we please have a day out shopping one day soon? It'd be nice to see you in something other than stripes and jeans for a change.'

Maggie looked down at her grimy top. 'I'd love to. I'm sure I could branch out into polka-dots or something. And it'd be nice to go back to Sheffield and see the place properly. I wasn't in the mood to appreciate it yesterday. For obvious reasons…'

'God. What a day it was!' said Cath. 'Day *and* night, I should say. I don't know about you, but I'm wrung out from all the drama.'

'Me too,' chuckled Maggie, as the tyre finally came away in her hand. 'When Tiggy threw that tambourine at his head, it was like she was chucking a frisbee. And did you see Mrs W? She was loving it.'

Cath giggled. 'I know. She actually came up to me afterwards to say – and I quote – "Thank you ever so much, dear. That was a lot more fun than the usual rubbish entertainment served up in this village".'

'Is that what she said? Really?' Maggie was impressed. 'She's a game old bird, I'll give her that… And that Merlin Crocker was alright as well – once you got talking to him.' She paused. 'Have you, y'know, *heard anything* this morning?'

'From Tiggy you mean? Yep. I texted her to check she was alright. She says she's fine.'

'Well,' said Maggie, looking up from her task. 'Fair play to her – she didn't just side with her loathsome husband.'

'No. She didn't,' agreed Cath. 'God, she was raging, wasn't she?'

'It can't have been easy for her,' said Maggie. 'It took some balls.'

'Are you sure you're feeling OK?' asked Cath. 'You're not sick or anything?'

'No. Why?'

'I just never thought I'd see the day when you'd say something positive about Tiggy.' Cath grinned. 'And when she called him a *fucking cold-hearted sociopath…*'

'Hmm,' said Maggie. 'It takes one to know one, I guess.' She thought for a moment. 'Nah, I've got a lot of sympathy for her, actually. She's probably his biggest victim. Poor cow.'

'That's very magnanimous of you,' said Cath, raising an eyebrow. 'Given how she's behaved towards you.'

'Shit. My knees are killing me,' said Maggie, crawling over to take a seat on the bench beside her. 'You know… If I'm totally honest, I'd probably have to admit that I've not always been perfect either.'

'You don't say…?' Cath took a sip from her mug. 'It's staggering that Phil managed to keep everything from her. The bloody company was even named after her!' She sighed. 'It just shows you, their relationship wasn't quite as perfect as I originally thought. No wonder she needs to meditate so much.'

'Well,' said Maggie, sagely. 'If things seem too good to be true, they usually are. What did I tell you? Don't believe everything you see on Facebook.'

'True enough,' said Cath. 'I'm not sure how many *real* friends she's got, come to think of it. I'll need to keep an eye on her.'

'She's very lucky to have you,' Maggie reflected. 'Anyway, it was a pity the auction got shelved after all the effort you put into it. What are you going to do? Reschedule it for another day, I suppose?'

'Yeah,' said Cath. 'Pete suggested the August bank holiday. It's a shame, though – you'll be long gone by then. Living it up in Singapore… I couldn't believe it when you told me last night. Amazing news!'

'Well, actually…'

'And also, I've decided, I'm just going to be the auctioneer myself next time. I'm not letting some bloke steal the spotlight after I've done all the hard work.'

'Quite right, too,' said Maggie, leaning back and gazing out over the garden. 'You know, I can't quite believe I've been here a year…'

'I know!' said Cath. 'It's really flown. You must be itching to get cracking again. It sounds like a fantastic opportunity.' She leaned back too. 'I'll really miss you, you know. You'd better promise to come back and visit.'

'Yeah,' said Maggie. 'That's the thing. I need to give Giles's mate a call and let him know, but I've been doing some thinking overnight. Most of the night, in fact.' She hesitated. 'I've decided I'm not going to take this Singapore job.'

'You're not?' said Cath in disbelief. 'But—'

'I'm done with oil and gas, Cath. It's what they call a "sunset industry".'

'A what?'

'It's dying on its arse, basically. It's not the future.'

'I guess so.' Cath shrugged. 'They say it's all about renewables now. Whatever *they* are...'

'Yup,' said Maggie, draining her mug. 'To be honest, it was all very prestigious and all that – and I'll always love Hong Kong – but I just didn't find the work itself very meaningful. D'you know what I mean?'

'Don't tell me,' said Cath, sarcastically. 'You preferred the romance of the Sheffield County Court?'

'Well,' said Maggie, choosing her words carefully. 'In a way I did. I mean, OK, technically speaking, I might have lost the case but I still relished the fight. Giving it a good go and all that.'

'I could see that,' said Cath.

'It was actually a conversation I had with Lauren – it reminded me why I went into the law in the first place. And it's made me want to take on some legal work that actually means something to me. To go freelance.'

'Sounds good,' said Cath. 'Whereabouts are you going to base yourself? I suppose you could do it anywhere. Within reason.'

'I was thinking of basing myself here...'

'Here?' said Cath. Her voice had gone up an octave. 'In Archdale?'

'Why not?' said Maggie. 'It's such a *beautiful* part of the world, after all.' And she cackled in disbelief at the words that had come out of her mouth.

'Shhh!' Cath put her finger to her lips, glancing up at the open bedroom window.

'I might even set up my own firm,' Maggie whispered. 'In due course.'

'Wow!' said Cath. 'How do you even *do* that?'

'Baby steps, baby steps. And it looks like Australian Pete will be my first client. Wait till you hear this: now the profits are up at The Farmer's, the cheeky fuckers at that pub chain are trying to up his rent to some extortionate sum. It's scandalous! I'm going to help him negotiate the new lease.'

'Well, good for you.' Cath paused. 'You know, I've been doing some thinking as well. About what I'm going to do with myself.' She swirled the dregs in her mug. 'I think I fancy going into teaching – I've heard about this fast track scheme for older people who're already graduates.'

Maggie side-eyed her. 'Not you as well? Are they putting something in the water around here?'

'What do you mean?' asked Cath, confused.

'Nothing,' said Maggie. 'I think it's a great idea. Especially with Lauren off to Bristol soon.'

Cath shivered. 'Don't remind me. But that's assuming she gets in.'

'She'll do it,' said Maggie. 'She seems quietly pleased with how the exams went. And Bristol's not that far.'

'It's far enough. Anyway, I was thinking I could teach French. Or Spanish. Maybe both?'

'You're very marketable,' said Maggie, encouragingly.

'Well, it'll help with the household finances if nothing else – another wage coming in.'

'True. How *is* Simon's business?' asked Maggie.

'Hmm. Well, the firm's not quite out of the woods yet, but he's cautiously optimistic.'

'Nice one. Fingers crossed in that case. Please just tell him not to take out a high-interest bridging loan for any reason, will you?'

Cath shook her head vigorously. 'I can honestly say I don't think *any* of us round here will be doing that any time soon. Not after what poor Rob's been through. Talking of whom…' She gave Maggie a knowing smile.

'What?' said Maggie, as innocently as she could manage. 'What *about* him?'

'Oh, come on.' Cath nudged her. 'It's obvious.'

'Is it?' Maggie felt herself flush.

'I saw the two of you, outside the pub last night.' Cath made a smooch-smooch sound with her lips.

'Really?'

'Yup,' said Cath, smug now. 'I was peering out the window into the car park. But c'mon… there's always been a bit of a *frisson* between you two.'

Maggie knew she was busted. 'You know, it's a bit weird. He's the first guy I've kissed since Andy.'

'Seriously?'

Maggie nodded.

'That says a lot.'

'It does.' Maggie smiled. 'He's thoughtful and kind and he's *practical*. He makes me laugh – his gallows humour in the face of adversity. And he's got nice friends. You can tell a lot about someone by their friends.'

'What does that say about me, eh?' said Cath, nudging her harder this time.

'Haha. Very funny.' Maggie pondered a moment. 'I think Joyce would have liked him…'

'He's a lovely guy,' agreed Cath. 'You make a lovely couple.'

'OK. OK,' said Maggie, pulling a face. 'You're overdoing it now.'

'You do!' Cath insisted. 'So,' she asked. 'Are you moving in with him?'

'Moving in? You're joking,' scoffed Maggie. 'I've only *kissed* him, for goodness' sake. It's a bit early for that sort of thing.' She paused.

'No. I think we'll just see each other for a bit. See what happens... And I've got a few ideas for generating some extra income for the farm. But that's as far as it goes for now. And anyway, I wouldn't want to live in a draughty old farmhouse with his mum and dad...'

'What will you do, then?' asked Cath. 'You're not moving back into the pub, I assume?'

'Er, no. I wasn't planning to,' said Maggie. She turned to face Cath. 'I was actually wondering if I could maybe, er, y'know... stay here... If that's alright?'

'Hmm, now,' said Cath. 'Where have I heard that before?' She smoothed the cotton of her kaftan over her knees. 'That might be a little bit awkward as me and Simon, well, we're thinking of giving our marriage another go.'

'Are you? Really?' said Maggie. Although she wasn't all that surprised, the way things had been going. 'That's great.'

'Well,' said Cath. 'We'll see how it goes. We're not rushing things. And anyway, he's got to give notice on his flat in Leeds. As you said yourself, baby steps...'

'I assume he's done plenty of grovelling?' said Maggie. 'You haven't let him off the hook too easily?'

'I can assure you that his grovelling has been nothing short of *profuse*.'

'Glad to hear it.'

'I dunno. It was, y'know, the er...' Cath lowered her voice, 'the *situation* with Giles that made me realise things aren't always so cut and dried, made me realise it was Simon I wanted. We've built a life together. A family... But I've told him I'm not taking any of his shit anymore – on *any* front.'

'Oh, that reminds me!' said Maggie. 'I actually spoke to Giles about the, er, *situation*.'

'Fucking hell, Maggie,' hissed Cath, looking up at the window again. 'You didn't.'

'I did. It was a couple of weeks ago, when I was on the phone to him about the case. I forgot to tell you.'

'You spoke to him about it? Without telling me?'

Maggie shifted in her seat. 'I didn't want to stand back and watch you two falling out. You've been friends for years... Anyhow, he told me that he backed off because he'd got the impression that there was unfinished business between you and Simon and that you still had feelings for him.'

'Well,' said Cath, briskly. 'His *impression* was correct. And Simon's a bloody saint compared to *perfect* Phil.'

'You can say that again,' said Maggie. It was her turn to lower her voice now. 'Simon might be a selfish git, but he's not a thoroughgoing shit like Phil.' She paused a moment. 'Although in a way you've got to admire him.'

'Admire Phil?' said Cath. 'What on earth for?'

'Managing to keep all his dodgy dealings a secret – it's bloody impossible to keep *anything* quiet around here.'

'True,' Cath nodded, ruefully. 'Very true.'

'But he couldn't keep them secret from me,' said Maggie, with pride. 'Of all the villages in all the world, I had to walk into *his*. Or something like that...'

Their laughter was interrupted by Simon calling down to them from the window above. 'Morning!' he announced, peering out over the ledge. 'I'm going to make some brekkie. Can I interest anyone in a full English?'

'Yes, please,' they called back, as Jazz woke up and scampered off to the kitchen.

The two of them sat in silence, enjoying the sun on their faces.

'I'm really chuffed for you and Simon,' said Maggie after a while. 'That you're working things out.'

'Aw. Thanks,' said Cath. 'That means a lot.'

'And, don't worry,' said Maggie. 'I'll move out as soon as he moves back in.'

Cath shot her a look.

'Honest!'

Acknowledgements

I'd like to thank Heather and the terrific team at RedDoor Press for all they've done in helping bring the book to fruition.

Friendship is at the heart of this book and I'd like to thank my friends, old and new, for being there for me during the process.

I'm grateful to Derbyshire itself for inspiring me and to Lesley for introducing me to it in the first place. As Maggie might (now) say: 'It's such a beautiful part of the world...'

Thanks also:

To Natalie, for the moral support and for helping me keep a 'foothold' in London!

To Rachel, for the wonderful photos.

To Beverley and the friends I've made through her writing groups in Sheffield, for the stimulation, the encouragement and the laughs.

To Jane, for her various kindnesses: a testament to the benefits of Twitter.

To my dogs, Archie and Jazz, for all the walks on which the book was written in my head. Jazz is the only 'real' character in the book and Archie gave his name to the fictional village of 'Archdale'.

To my family in Scotland, Derbyshire and everywhere else.

And finally to Jim, who is the best.

About the Author

A native of Glasgow, Stacey Murray was an international commercial lawyer for many years – in the City of London and in Hong Kong. In 2005, she changed career to become an independent film producer. Her first film, *A Boy Called Dad*, was acquired by the BBC and nominated for the Michael Powell Award for Best British Film at the Edinburgh International Film Festival. She lives in hope – literally, in the village of Hope in the Derbyshire Peak District – with her husband and two rescue dogs. She tweets @TheStacemeister.

Find out more about RedDoor
Press and sign up to our
newsletter to hear about our
latest releases, author events,
exciting **competitions**
and more at

reddoorpress.co.uk

YOU CAN ALSO FOLLOW US:

 @RedDoorBooks

 Facebook.com/RedDoorPress

 @RedDoorBooks